W9-BUV-115

Can't Stand
the Heat

Daisy Jones
1507 S. Curtiss Dr.
Urbana, IL 61802

Also by Shelly Ellis

THE PLAYER & THE GAME

Published by Dafina Books

Can't Stand the Heat

SHELLY ELLIS

KENSINGTON BOOKS
http://www.kensingtonbooks.com

DAFINA BOOKS are published by

Kensington Publishing Corp.
119 West 40th Street
New York, NY 10018

Copyright © 2013 by Shelly Ellis

All rights reserved. No part of this book may be reproduced in any form or by any means without the prior written consent of the Publisher, excepting brief quotes used in reviews.

If you purchased this book without a cover, you should be aware that this book is stolen property. It was reported as "unsold and destroyed" to the Publisher and neither the Author nor the Publisher has received any payment for this "stripped book."

All Kensington Titles, Imprints and Distributed Lines are available at special quantity discounts for bulk purchases for sales promotions, premiums, fund-raising, and educational or institutional use.

Special book excerpts or customized printings can also be created to fit specific needs. For details, write or phone the office of the Kensington special sales manager: Kensington Publishing Corp., 119 West 40th Street, New York, NY 10018, attn: Special Sales Department, Phone: 1-800-221-2647.

Dafina and the Dafina logo Reg. U.S. Pat. & TM Off.

ISBN-13: 978-0-7582-9091-5
ISBN-10: 0-7582-9091-8
First Kensington Trade Edition: May 2013
First Kensington Mass Market Edition: April 2014

eISBN-13: 978-0-7582-9092-2
eISBN-10: 0-7582-9092-6
Kensington Electronic Edition: April 2014

10 9 8 7 6 5 4 3 2 1

Printed in the United States of America

To the little one in my tummy, I'm proud of all of my work, but you are—by far—my greatest creation. I look forward to seeing the mark you make on your little part of the world.

Acknowledgments

I've had people ask me what's the hardest part about writing. *Coming up with story ideas? Sitting down at your desk and toiling over plot lines, dialogue, and descriptions? Just getting the damn thing done?* I always say, "Unfortunately, no. Those are all the easy parts." The hard part is getting your book off your computer screen and on bookshelves—as I'm sure many aspiring novelists can attest to. My own journey from computer screen to bookstore was a trying though rewarding one, and there were many people who helped me along the way.

First and foremost, I would like to thank my husband, Andrew. He's a no-nonsense guy with a big heart who is always there for me with a shoulder to cry on, an ear to listen when I need to lament, and he is always there with a hug and a kiss for all of my successes. Thank you for being there. You're a wonderful partner, a great friend and I'm happy to travel on this journey with you at my side. I'm a lucky woman.

Next, I want to say thanks to my mom and dad—first cheerleaders. Mom, thanks for talking me into submitting to my first writer's contest and telling me my work was just as good as the books you read at the library. Dad, thanks for haranguing me at the kitchen table when I was 7 years old for not writing longer sentences for my homework assignments. After all, a writer has to start somewhere.

A special thanks to Mercedes Fernandez, my wonderful editor at Kensington. Not too many unagented authors can say they were plucked out of the slush pile and rewarded with a book series contract. I say it all the time—I feel like I won the lotto! Thank you for discovering my work, being a champion for the Gibbons girls and their craziness, and for your support, encouragement, and feedback. Also, thanks to the rest of the Kensington team (Editor Selena James, Publicist Adeola Saul and the sales and marketing team) for all your hard work. I am honored to work with you.

I would also like to thank the editors I've worked with in the past: Glenda Howard, Deborah Johnson Schumaker and Sidney Rickman. (Sidney, I wish I could carry editors like you in my pocket! My writing would definitely be a lot cleaner.)

I'm new to Kensington and still a babe in the book industry, but some authors have been very welcoming and encouraging and helped me shake some of my anxiety. Thanks to Cydney Rax, Cheris Hodges and Phyllis Bourne for your kind words over the Web.

I would also like to say thanks to the Washington Romance Writers. And to go way, way back . . . thanks to all my English and Journalism teachers who convinced me that I was meant to be a writer, as opposed to a civil engineer or a computer scientist. Though the other fields definitely came with better pay, this one has been a lot more gratifying (and I suck at math).

Thanks to the book blogs, book clubs, and review sites that have shown their support for my work in the past: OOSA Online Book Club, Urban Reviews Online, Eye on Romance, Shades of Romance, Night Owl Reviews, etc. An author's career can be made by word of mouth, so I definitely appreciate your words in particular.

And finally, thanks to the many family and friends that I didn't name individually because that would probably require a book in itself. (And I'd definitely get myself into trouble if I named some of you but not all of you.) Much love and many thanks!

Prologue

"Lauren? Lauren!"

Lauren Gibbons had been staring blankly at her reflection in her oval vanity mirror, seeing her face glaze over into a brown blur as she became lost in thought. At her boyfriend James's angry barking, her image and the room suddenly came rushing back into focus.

"Huh?" Lauren murmured. "What?"

James sighed. "Did you hear anything I said?"

She glanced at the hairbrush she held over her head. She had forgotten it was there.

"I'm sorry, baby. I was . . . distracted." She smiled apologetically. "I was brushing my hair."

"So you can't do both at once?" James strode out of his walk-in closet, unbuttoning his shirt cuffs. "Too challenging for you?"

She slowly set the brush on the vanity dresser top and watched cautiously in the mirror as he paced around their four-poster bed.

He had plenty of room to pace—easily. Their bedroom was massive, with vaulted ceilings and enough square footage for eight California king-size beds. It was filled wall to wall with imposing mahogany furniture and decorated with artificially aged gold candelabras, sconces, and knickknacks. James said the decor made him feel like royalty, but Lauren had always had a very different take on the room. Like James, their bedroom made her feel crowded at all sides despite the expanse. She felt downright claustrophobic.

She watched James in the mirror's reflection. James flexed his fingers anxiously and frowned, making his wrinkles even more pronounced. He seemed in a particularly bad mood tonight . . . agitated, perhaps, but it didn't take much to set him off these days. His quick temper was one of the many reasons she wanted to leave him. In fact, only seconds ago she had been wrangling over when she would finally do just *that,* before he rudely yanked her from those thoughts.

"I need to know what you plan to wear. I want to see it."

Lauren turned slightly on the upholstered bench to face him. "Wear to what?"

"What do you mean, 'wear to what'? I swear, if you were more focused on what's going on around you than on primping and preening in front of that goddamn mirror, I wouldn't have to keep repeating myself!"

She flinched. There it was: the feeling of the walls pressing in, of the furniture getting closer and closer, bearing down on her. Lauren closed her eyes and took a deep breath. She opened her eyes again.

"I just didn't hear you, James," she began quietly, trying to placate him. "Calm down, baby. It's not that big of a deal. Just—"

"I was talking about the cocktail party on Thursday—a very important cocktail party, I might add. So don't tell me it's not that big of a deal! I expect very important clients to be there and I want to see what you're wearing. I don't want anything tasteless or too revealing."

Tasteless or too revealing? Funny, those same ensembles were what drew him to her in the first place. Back then, he had liked when she was sexy and alluring. Now, whenever they went out together, he acted as if she should wear a nun's habit or a burqa.

"You want to inspect my clothes?" She stood, shrugged out of her satin robe, and tossed it over the vanity bench. "James, give me some credit. I've been dressing myself since I was seven years old. I know what's appropriate and what isn't. I swear that I'll wear something nice. OK?"

"And I can only imagine what your interpretation of 'nice' is. No, I want to see the dress. If it isn't right, I need time to look through that football field of a closet of yours to find something suitable. I want you to show it to me tomorrow. No later. Understood?"

Lauren clenched her fists at her sides. She was getting tired of this, of James ordering her around and acting as if he *owned* her. She had tried to ignore it at first. She certainly had enough incentive to swallow down her frustrations: the fifteen-thousand-dollar-a-month allowance, the Bentley parked in the driveway, and the sparkling trinkets he surprised her with on a weekly basis. But she couldn't keep quiet for long. She had reached her breaking point a few weeks ago and told him that she was tired of him giving her orders, and he had laughed at her. He had actually *laughed* at her. It had taken all her willpower not to walk out on him that very minute.

"Then I'm not going," she said.

He took off his shirt and tossed it on their bed. "What?"

"I said I'm not going to the party!"

She pushed back her shoulders. At her full height—five-foot-one-half-inch—she wasn't a very imposing figure. But all the same, she wanted him to know that she meant business, that she meant what she said.

"If you feel you have to approve of what I wear before you're willing to bring me in front of your precious law partners and clients, then . . . then . . . damn it, I'll stay home!"

He narrowed his eyes at her. His stare was glacial, meant to freeze all the willpower out of her. But she was too hot with anger to be intimidated by him tonight.

"Lauren, don't issue me ultimatums. You're not in a position to. Just be a good little girl and do as I say." He raised his eyebrows. "All right?"

"You treat me like a child and it's getting old!" She threw up her hands. "In fact, it's past getting old! It's damn near ancient!"

Lauren's heart thudded in her chest. They had been together for two years, and half of that time she had made excuses for him and excuses to stay, but she finally had to admit it: Their relationship had to end. It was time to tender her resignation. She had fulfilled her role as James's arm candy, his young plaything, and he as her sugar daddy.

James gazed at her, looking both irritated and dumbfounded. "Lauren, I don't know what the hell has gotten into you, but if you don't—"

"If I don't *what?* If I don't what, James?" She blew an angry gust of air through her nose and crossed her arms over her chest. "Look, I'm through listening to you! I'm tired of putting up with all your bullshit! I'm done!"

"You're done? So you're done with me *and* my money? You're done with all those clothes in your closet? You're done with the trips to St. Bart's and Paris?" He chuckled. "I know you, Lauren. I know you better than you know yourself, sweetheart. There's no way you're done with me."

And he's so sure of himself. He's so sure I won't walk away from him.

But she would prove him wrong.

"Go to hell, James."

Lauren then turned and walked toward the bedroom door, intending to march to one of the guest rooms. There was no way she was sharing a bed with him tonight. In the morning, when she had a clearer head, she would pack her things and make plans about what to do next. She could move in with her mother or one of her sisters. She still had a few culinary classes to complete, but maybe she could get a job as a cook somewhere. She was talented. Why not? Maybe she could finally pursue *her* dreams for once.

Lauren could feel the sense of claustrophobia waning. She felt freer, lighter with each step she took.

But that feeling abruptly ended when James grabbed the back of her nightgown, pulling the silk fabric tight across her chest, catching her by surprise. She heard one of the seams rip just as he seized a hunk of her hair. The pain radiated from her roots to seemingly every nerve ending in her body. Her hands instantly flew to her scalp and she winced and screamed.

She shrieked and kicked as he hauled her back through the bedroom door, making her lose her slippers during the struggle. Her feet left winding twin tracks in the plush carpet as he dragged her across the room.

James pulled her to her feet and she clawed at his hands and face, leaving a bloody trail along his cheeks and neck, but he made no attempt to fight her off. At six foot two, he practically towered over her and he outweighed her by almost one hundred pounds. He easily had the advantage. It was a fight she couldn't win.

She had no time to prepare or brace herself when he backhanded her across the face. It felt like he had taken a two-by-four and walloped it across her cheek. He slapped her again with the same force and she lost her balance. She grabbed for her vanity, clutching for its side to keep from tumbling to the floor. But both she and the vanity went crashing to the carpet. Perfume bottles, makeup compacts, hairbrushes, nail polishes, and combs went flying everywhere. The air suddenly filled with the acrid, sickening smell of several power-ful scents released at once.

Lauren rolled onto her stomach and tried to crawl away from him. He was blocking the path to the door, so she tried to seek the safety of a corner near one of the bureaus, but he caught her by the ankle and dragged her back. Suddenly, James was crouched over her, slapping her, punching her, and shouting as he did it. His shouts were just as loud as her screams.

He was mostly incoherent, but any soul who was close enough to hear could get the gist of what he was yelling: She had no right to walk out on him. He was James Henry Sayers! *No one* walked out on him, especially a well-paid hooker like her.

Lauren fought at first, but she grew weaker with each punch. When she couldn't fight anymore, she crouched into a fetal position, waiting for the blows to end or for her to lose consciousness—whatever came first.

Then suddenly, the phone rang. As if someone had waved a magic wand, the deluge of violence abruptly ended. James glanced over his shoulder at the open bedroom door.

"I was . . . I was expecting this call," he said with an eerie calm through huffs of breath. He sat back on his shins, licking his lips. "I have to . . . I have to take this."

Her hands were still shielding her face, but between her fingers she watched as James slowly rose to his feet. He gazed down at her one last time, wiping the sweat from his brow.

"I wish you wouldn't talk so much trash, Lauren. I hate it when you mouth off to me. I deserve more respect than that."

He turned to head to the doorway, tiredly dragging his feet as he walked.

"Go in the bathroom and clean yourself up. Then clean this place up, will you?"

He rubbed his sore knuckles and shut the door behind him.

Through the bedroom wall, Lauren heard James pick up the phone in his office. She lowered her hands and pushed herself to her elbows, then to a sitting position. Tears spilled onto her cheeks. She was trembling so much that her teeth chattered.

James had hit her. No, he had *beat* her. It was as if some switch had clicked on inside of him, and for the first time she had seen what was seething beneath his sarcasm, beneath his belittling. He was psychotic. He was a monster. She had to get out of here.

Lauren could still hear him talking on the phone in the other room.

Though her body was riddled with pain, though she could barely see through her burning red eyes, she rose to her feet. She limped toward the bedroom door and, after some hesitation, cracked it open, peering into the hallway. She could hear James more clearly now. He was laughing. Who would have guessed he had been beating up his girlfriend only minutes earlier?

The office door was ajar, but luckily the stairs were in the opposite direction at the end of the hall. If she was going to get out of this house, she had to do it now.

Lauren took a few steadying breaths, feeling her stomach tighten, feeling her muscles jitter. She was in pain, but she hoped adrenaline would carry her the rest of the way. On the third breath, she bolted—too terrified to look back.

Chapter 1

*(Unwritten) Rule No. 1 of the Gibbons
Family Handbook:*
*A woman must embody grace, sex, and glamour
at all times. She is the image of perfection in the
eyes of all men around her.*

Not feeling very graceful, sexy, or glamorous at this
early hour of the morning, Lauren was in no mood to
follow the family rules today. Respectfully, the old
family handbook could just go to hell right now.

Damn, it's hot, she thought after she slammed her
car door shut with her hip and made a mad dash across
the nearly empty parking lot. Rivulets of sweat
streamed between her breasts and down her back in the
scorching Virginia sun, causing her T-shirt to cling to
her like a second skin, making her silently curse her
car's busted AC. Her curvy bottom shimmied as she
ran in her khaki shorts.

As sous chef of Le Bayou Bleu, Lauren tried to be
one of the first to arrive at the kitchen for prep work for
the lunch and dinner service, but she was running a little late today.

"Hey, Lauren!" Malik called out with a smile.

The willowy line cook leaned against the soot-covered brick wall near the doorway. His white short-sleeved shirt was unbuttoned, revealing a white tank top and a pack of cigarettes tucked inside the waistband of his jeans. He tapped his lit cigarette, spilling ashes onto the concrete.

"What's up, beautiful? You just gettin' in?" he asked.

"Don't remind me!" she shouted back with a laugh.

"¡Oye, mi amiga!" shouted Miguel, a plump fry chef who sat kitty-corner to Malik. He was hunched on a wooden crate with his squat legs spread wide. A cigarette hung limply from the side of his mouth.

"Hey, Miguel!" Lauren yelled back.

She didn't break stride as she spoke, making her way toward the heavy steel door leading to the restaurant's kitchen. She tugged the door open and stepped inside, letting it slam shut behind her. She was instantly met with the sound of clashing steel, stacking glasses, the steady churn of mixers, oven doors opening and closing, and shouting voices. To her ears, it was more melodious than a Beethoven symphony.

Lauren bypassed the kitchen and went straight to the women's locker room. She usually shared it with the waitresses and the only other female chef at the restaurant, Paula Wakeman, who was a wizard when it came to pastries. But the room was vacant today. It was dimly lit and smelled of old grease and dirty socks.

She opened her locker door and quickly retrieved a pair of jeans, her apron, and a petite-sized chef's coat. She took off her strappy sandals and traded them for a pair of sports socks and scuffed tennis shoes from the bottom of her locker. She put on her jeans and pulled back her shoulder-length hair into a ponytail, securing it with a scrunchie she had worn on her wrist. After tying a red bandanna on her head and buttoning her coat, she was ready to go. She climbed over the locker room's wooden benches with apron in hand and headed to the door. As she neared the exit, she glanced at herself in the room's only full-length mirror and paused, momentarily transfixed. She stared at her reflection.

Seven months ago, she wouldn't have been caught dead in her current ensemble. Instead, she would be wearing a tight-fitting, low-cut dress, towering high heels, and jewelry that cost more than what she could now afford with her current monthly paycheck. She wouldn't be slaving away in the kitchen of Le Bayou Bleu either, but would be one of the restaurant patrons, dining at one of the best tables in the house on her rich boyfriend, James's, tab.

What a difference seven months can make, Lauren thought.

Back then, she had been the happily "kept" woman she had always been taught to be—going to spas and shopping during the day, pleasing her man at night. That life seemed so long ago and so far away. She had been so scared back then, so worn down by James's constant browbeating that it had taken her too long to realize that . . .

Lauren shook her head, cutting off those dark thoughts.

"You can take your trip down memory lane another day," she mumbled to her reflection. She hated to wallow in the past, in self-pity. It was time to move forward. "Time to get to work."

"Mornin', guys!" she said as she rushed into the kitchen seconds later, tying her apron around her waist.

"Morning! Mornin'. *¡Buenos días!*" a few voices answered in return.

Lauren looked around the room. "Where's Phillip?" she asked no one in particular. "Anybody seen him around?"

Phillip Rochon was the executive chef of Le Bayou Bleu. The dark-skinned, jolly, loud-mouthed man was from a small town not far from New Orleans, where he had learned to cook gumbo, jambalaya, and crawfish étouffé at his grandmother's elbow more than forty years ago. He had opened restaurants in New York City, Chicago, and Washington, DC, specializing in a high-end interpretation of down-home Creole cuisine. He had decided last year to open Le Bayou Bleu in Chesterton, Virginia—Lauren's hometown.

"Has anybody seen Phillip?" Lauren repeated, louder this time, stepping farther into the kitchen.

"I think he's in the front of the house," one of the cooks murmured as he laid a series of thinly sliced potatoes onto a cookie sheet covered with wax paper.

"Out front?"

That was an odd place for Phillip to be. Usually he was elbow to elbow with the other chefs, preparing vegetables, dressings, and pasta dough that would be used later that day. He was a James Beard award winner and had led restaurants with Michelin stars, but Phillip was far from a diva. He believed true head chefs still worked the line and shared celebratory drinks with their staff after a hard day of work.

To leave these guys alone to do prep work, something has to be up, Lauren thought. She walked through the kitchen to the swinging door that led to the front of the house.

Lauren rarely got to see this half of Le Bayou Bleu.

Every time she entered it, she would marvel at how beautiful the space was. The tone of the restaurant matched the food that was served there: sophisticated but earthy, cool but classic. The two were a perfect match.

The walls were set with a rich mahogany wood paneling, and over the onyx bar was a huge chandelier dripping with crystal. Along each side wall were booths with cream-colored fabric embellished with a navy blue damask pattern. The back wall of the restaurant was lined with state-of-the-art refrigerators filled with wine bottles that had vintages dating as far back as the early 1900s. At any given time, jazz or soul music would play over the hidden speakers, giving a mellow vibe to the space despite the grandeur of the surroundings.

Unfortunately, Lauren wasn't enjoying those grand surroundings this morning. She was too concerned about Phillip. She found him sitting alone at one of the dining room tables, with a glass of red wine and a half-eaten beignet on a dinner napkin in front of him. Chairs were still stacked on the table around him.

"It's a little early for wine, isn't it?" Lauren asked with a wry smile as she walked toward him. "Is it starting off to be *that* kind of day?"

He didn't respond.

"Phillip," she said as she drew closer. "Phillip!" She patted him gently on his plump shoulder, making him jump in surprise. He quickly looked over his shoulder at her.

"Aww, *chérie*, what you doin' sneaking up on me like that? You damn near gave me a heart attack, gal!"

"Sorry, I didn't mean to scare you." She took one of the chairs off the table, setting it beside his. She sat down. "I called you a few times. Guess you didn't hear me." She scanned his face. "Hey, are you OK?"

His brow was soaked with perspiration. His eyes looked sunken and haunted. He seemed to be breathing hard through his parched lips.

"I'm . . . I'm fine," he said with some effort. He swallowed loudly and wiped his forehead with a linen napkin. "I'm just . . . I'm just feeling a little peaked this mornin'."

"You look more than a 'little peaked.' You look like you need to go to a doctor."

"Naw, *chérie*, it ain't nothin' like that. Just . . . just give me a few minutes to get myself . . . together."

She stared at him, sensing that he was vastly underplaying how bad he felt. He didn't look like he could stand up for very long, let alone spend several hours in a steaming hot kitchen.

"Why don't you go home, Phillip? We can handle the prep work. Come back for lunch service in a few hours."

"Cain't do that." He shook his head, sending his slicked-back ponytail flying. "You know how those boys are. If I ain't there to crack the whip behind them, who knows what kinda mess is gonna come out of that kitchen. Everything on those plates has my name on it."

Lauren held back a smile. She and Phillip knew that the line cooks were capable of handling prep work on their own. They didn't need anyone to supervise them, but it made Phillip feel better to believe that his presence brought order to the kitchen.

"I know, but let *me* crack the whip, OK? You're no help to anyone if you're sick. Just go home, get some rest, and come back later. We can handle it."

He gazed at her warily, looking as if he wanted to

mount another argument but couldn't work up the energy to do so. "OK, *chérie*." He slowly rose from his chair. "I'll head home." He pointed a finger down at her. "But you make those boys mind. Everything on those plates—"

"—has your name on it. I know." She nodded and smiled. "I've got it covered, chef. We won't let you down."

She watched as he walked toward the center aisle. He gave one last uneasy glance over his shoulder at her before heading to the restaurant's front door.

"Phillip! Phillip!" Nathan, Le Bayou Bleu's floor manager, shouted as he sashayed into the kitchen.

Despite his shrill cries, everyone ignored him. They were firmly in their dinner rush mode, and besides, no one was particularly fond of Nathan. He looked down on most of the restaurant staff, particularly the line cooks and dishwashers. Now that he had stepped into their domain, none of them was about to give the condescending bastard the time of day.

Nathan peered through levels of stainless-steel shelves lining the front of the kitchen. He stared at the faces that darted from counter to stove top and back again.

"Phillip! *Phiiiiiillip!*"

He suddenly narrowed his eyes at Lauren. She was cleaning the edges of a plate of risotto with the corner of a dinner napkin.

"Hey!" He snapped his fingers in her direction. "Hey!"

"My name is not 'hey,' Nathan," she replied, placing the finished plate on the top shelf. "It's Lauren. Miss

Gibbons, if you're nasty." She then gave an impish smile. "Black-eyed pea risotto with bacon ready to go!"

A food runner shoved Nathan aside, walked to the counter, and grabbed three plates, including the risotto dish.

"Watch it!" Nathan snapped.

The runner ignored him. Nathan let out a beleaguered sigh, like a king who has been forced to leave his castle and socialize with the peasants.

"Lauren, where in the hell is Phillip?"

If Lauren hadn't enjoyed tormenting Nathan so much, she would have told him Phillip wasn't there. He hadn't returned since the morning. At the start of lunch service, she had gotten a call from him saying that it looked like he was going to have to bow out for the day.

"Not gonna make it, *chérie*," he had drawled tiredly into the phone. "Gonna have to hand my baby over to you. Treat her well."

Lauren had immediately told him she could handle it, but the instant she hung up the phone, she stood in the kitchen, paralyzed with fear. She had never taken over a service by herself before. What if she screwed up? What if the service fell apart?

After all, when Phillip had hired her, he'd admitted that, of all the candidates for the job, she was the least qualified on paper. All she had was a degree from culinary school; no professional experience behind the burner. There were several other cooks who wanted to work as one of his line cooks who had better résumés than she, but Lauren wouldn't take no for an answer.

She didn't use her feminine wiles to win Phillip over. (That was an old crutch that she had given up for good when she left James.) Instead, she did her research—reading old *Food & Wine* and *Bon Appétit* articles about Phillip—and showed up at his home one day unannounced with a platter of his favorites. She put the dishes in front of him, hoping he would focus more on her plating technique than her cleavage. He was surprised by her presumptuousness but also impressed. After sampling each dish, he said he'd try her as one of his line cooks on a trial basis.

"We'll give it a few weeks, *chérie*," he had said as he shoveled another forkful of creamy shrimp and grits into his mouth, smacking his lips. "We'll see how you get along."

She had "gotten along" well, quickly falling into rhythm with the diverse, rowdy group of cooks. Despite her greenness, the others respected her and admired her natural talent.

When the first sous chef Phillip hired left two months after the restaurant opened to take a higher-profile job in New York, Phillip shocked Lauren when he told her he wanted her to fill the position until they could find a suitable replacement.

"It'll be a few weeks. Not much more than that," he had assured her. "Think you can handle it, *chérie*? Help me out in a pinch?"

But a few weeks had turned into a few months. Now it no longer seemed that Phillip was looking for a replacement. She was permanent sous chef at Le Bayou Bleu.

Phillip trusted her and had taken a chance on her. His vote of confidence meant more than anything. Tonight she vowed that she wouldn't let him down.

Lauren turned her back to Nathan, focusing her attention on one of the line cooks. "Watch the heat on those onions, Enrique!" she shouted as she walked across the kitchen. "I want them caramelized, not burned!"

"Yes, chef!" Enrique said with a nod as he removed the pan from the blue flame.

Nathan slammed his hands on the stainless-steel countertop. "Damn it, where is Phillip?"

"He's not here, Nathan," she finally answered, shouting over the kitchen din. "He didn't feel well so he went home." She pulled a ticket and started to bark orders. The kitchen's manic activity continued.

"Went home? When?"

"A while ago."

"So who's in charge of the line tonight?"

"Me." She frowned down at a plate that had been handed to her. "Way too much parsley, Tony!" She then began to address the offending parsley herself.

"You? But you're just—"

"But I'm just *what?* Phillip put me in charge. That's all you need to know," she said firmly, daring Nathan to question Phillip's judgment.

Nathan closed his eyes and took a deep calming breath. "OK. That's OK. If Phillip can't come out, then . . . then you'll just have to do it."

"Come out where?"

"Come to the front of the house to meet our VIP guest," Nathan said with a flutter of his luxurious fake eyelashes, as if she should already know the answer. "He liked his dish and he wants to meet the chef. Phillip's not here and you're in charge, so you'll have to do." He snapped his fingers again, motioning for her to follow him.

"Oh, I don't think so. It's not just Phillip. . . . Two other guys called in sick, so we're shorthanded and we're already well into the evening rush. I'm not coming off the line. Not now."

"But he's a *VIP guest!* We can't turn him down! Do you realize he's a—"

"I don't care who he is, Nathan. Short of being Jesus Christ himself, I'm not leaving the line for him. That's that. Just tell him that we're glad he liked the food but to come back another day when the head chef is around. We're too busy now."

Nathan's olive-toned face reddened.

"Now, if you'll excuse me." She turned her back to him again. "I'd like to get back to my work." She pulled another ticket. "Turtle soup, blackened redfish, jumbo crab cakes!"

Nathan was summarily dismissed. On one side of the kitchen, some of the line cooks began to snicker.

Nathan's nostrils flared. "You'll regret this, Lauren," he said menacingly, pointing at her. "You'll regret this."

He then stomped out of the kitchen, letting the door swing wildly behind him.

"You'll regret this," she mimicked in a pinched voice. She made a face and grinned.

Lauren wasn't intimidated by Nathan. She'd spent two harrowing years with James Sayers, the biggest, baddest bully in Chesterton. If she could survive James, she could definitely handle this guy.

The rest of the evening progressed at the usual back-breaking pace, but it was uneventful. By eleven o'clock, the dinner rush had ended, so they turned off the burners and packed up for the day.

Lauren flexed her feet in her tennis shoes as she leaned back against one of the counters. She languidly sipped from a glass of red wine. Her feet hurt. Her back hurt. She had a cut on her index finger and a grease burn on one of her wrists, but she had never felt so happy and exhilarated in her life. It was like this every time she ended the workday, but today she felt particularly good. For the first time, Phillip had entrusted his kitchen—his baby—to her, and she had passed the challenge with flying colors. Pride is what she felt. She had experienced it so few times in her life.

Man, I love my job, she thought with a smile.

"What are you grinning about?" their pastry chef, Paula, asked as she walked toward Lauren and swatted her with a hand towel on the leg.

"I'm grinning about the bubble bath I'm going to take later when I get home," she lied.

The plump blonde leaned back against the counter beside her. "Oh."

Lauren laughed. " 'Oh.' What do you mean, 'oh'? Were you expecting me to say something else?"

"I don't know. I just thought . . . I just thought you might be smiling about a guy, maybe."

Lauren set down her wineglass, unbuttoned the top button of her chef's coat, and crossed her arms over her chest. "I haven't met a guy in a long time who was worth smiling about."

"Not even me, *mi amor?*" one of the line cooks, Jorge, asked as he walked by the two women.

"You're an exception to the rule, Jorge!" Lauren called back.

He chuckled and waved as he opened the back door that led to an alleyway behind the restaurant. "Somebody should tell my wife that! *¡Buenas noches, bonitas!*"

"Good night, Jorge," they said in unison, before watching the steel door slam behind him.

Paula turned back to Lauren. "You're too young to have an attitude like that."

"And this from someone at the ripe old age of thirty-two?"

"Hey, I've got two years on you, missy. I'm still riper and older than you—like a fine wine. I know what I'm talking about. You're way too cynical about men and relationships for someone your age."

If you've seen what I've seen and been through what I've been through, you'd be cynical too, Lauren thought sullenly.

In her life and in her family, Lauren had witnessed and experienced enough Jerry Springer episode worthy relationships that the idea of falling in love with a man turned her off completely. But Paula hadn't grown up in Chesterton and hadn't lived in their small town long enough to know the Gibbons family history.

If she did, she'd drop the subject.

"Come on, let me set you up with someone," Paula persisted. Her words broke through the hazy bubble of Lauren's thoughts. "I know about five guys offhand who would *drool* over you."

"Thanks, Paula, but no."

"But, Lauren—"

"I said no."

Paula rolled her eyes. "I swear, you're so stubborn sometimes."

"Stubborn's my middle name."

"And I guess 'mule' is your last name?"

Lauren smiled despite herself. "*Hardy* har har."

"Hey! Excuse me!" a male voice suddenly called out from the other end of the darkened kitchen near the entrance leading to the dining area.

Lauren and Paula exchanged a look.

"Is anyone back here?" the voice asked.

They could see his head bobbing over the metal shelving in the "pick-up" area. He certainly was tall.

"Why don't people read the sign on the door? Can't they tell this is the kitchen?" Lauren whispered.

Paula giggled.

"Sir, if you're looking for the bathrooms, you'll have to go back where you came. They're at the other end of the hall. This area is for staff only," Lauren began, pushing away from the counter. She walked toward him as he rounded the corner. "You can't come—"

Her words froze on her lips as their eyes met. Her breath caught in her throat.

The man who had wandered into their kitchen had the physique of a football player, though she doubted that he was part of any defensive line. A face that nice couldn't have encountered too many contact sports.

His eyebrows, nose, and full mouth were finely sculpted yet masculine. Even his high cheekbones looked like they could have been carved out of marble, making her wonder whether, if she reached out and touched them, they would be smooth and cool to the touch. His skin was the color of nutmeg and his almond-shaped eyes were ink black, but not flat and expressionless. They seemed warm and kind as he smiled faintly. His dark, curly hair was closely cropped to his head.

"I wasn't looking for the bathroom," he said. "I was looking for the chef. I wanted to compliment him on tonight's meal."

"Oh," Lauren uttered breathlessly. "Oh, well, I know he would . . . appreciate that. So you . . . you liked the food?"

"Oh, yeah." He gave a vigorous nod and a chuckle. He then patted his rock-hard stomach. The ripples of muscles were visible even through his white dress shirt. The shirt was unbuttoned at the collar and rolled up at the sleeves, revealing the tattooed scales of the Chinese dragon that encircled his forearm. "I just decided to come here on a whim," he said. "Honestly—and please don't take offense—I wasn't expecting much from this place."

She didn't take offense. People rarely expected a lot from small-town restaurants. Soup from a can and gravy and potatoes from store-bought packets is what they usually anticipated.

"I'm glad I was wrong, though, because it was the best food I've tasted in a *long* time." He looked around the now-empty kitchen. "I tried to talk to the chef earlier, but the manager said he was busy and couldn't come out." His eyes returned to Lauren. They locked gazes again. "I guess I missed him, huh?"

So this was the VIP guest Nathan had spoken about earlier? She scanned his face more carefully. He *did* look vaguely familiar. Was he famous?

"Oh, the executive chef left hours ago," Paula suddenly piped up from behind Lauren. "But if you want to talk to the chef who was on duty tonight, you need to talk to Lauren here." She nudged Lauren's arm. "She's our sous chef."

"So you're the one I should be bowing down to?"

With his eyes on her, Lauren felt like she was under the glare of a spotlight. Suddenly, she wished she wasn't in a chef's jacket, wrinkled jeans, and scuffed tennis shoes. Suddenly, she wished she had done something to her hair today and not thrown on a red bandanna to hold her locks out of open flames and saucepans. She didn't look like an alluring woman but rather a twelve-year-old boy in search of the nearest skater park.

Lauren had felt so much pride minutes earlier and for some strange reason, it was being whittled away in this man's presence.

"Well, uh . . . well, no," she answered nervously. "No, not really."

The stranger's smile faded.

"I mean, there are lots of line cooks in here and, uh, Phillip—he's the executive chef—came up with the menu. He's great at coming up with dishes. I just make a few suggestions here and there, but it would be wrong to take credit for his brilliance. They're mostly all his ideas."

Oh, Lord! What the hell am I saying? What's gotten into me?

Lust: that was what had gotten into her, and it had come out of nowhere.

"I mean . . . we're a team, here," she continued to babble. "I can't take credit for this all by myself. We're . . . uh . . . we're a team. It's a team effort. I couldn't do it without . . . everyone's help."

The kitchen fell silent with the exception of the steady chug of the dishwashers.

"Well, my compliments to the team, then."

"We appreciate it," Paula said. "Go, team, go!"

The stranger laughed while Lauren turned to narrow her eyes at Paula. Paula grinned apologetically in return.

"Well, thank you for the wonderful dinner."

"You're welcome," Lauren said, finally regaining her calm. "Thank you for patronizing our restaurant. We hope you'll come back soon."

"Oh . . ." He gave a slow and meaningful nod. "I most certainly will."

Butterflies started to flutter in her stomach again.

Don't start, she silently told herself. *He enjoyed the food. That's all he meant.*

He stared at her for several seconds more, not saying anything. Lauren stared back. Paula coughed loudly to break the awkward silence and he smiled.

"Well, it was nice meeting you ladies." He headed back out of the kitchen. "Good night."

"Good night!" Paula called after him.

" 'Night," Lauren whispered.

The door shut behind him.

Paula grabbed Lauren's shoulders and turned her around. "Oh my God, he was *so* checking you out!"

Lauren yanked her bandanna off her head. "No, he wasn't! He was staring at me like I was an escaped mental patient. I wasn't making any sense."

"Yeah, what was all that stuff about 'team effort'?"

"Don't remind me."

"He made you nervous, didn't he? You *liked* him, didn't you?"

"I don't know him, Paula." Lauren walked across the kitchen to a door that led to the women's locker room. "I talked to him for two minutes."

"Thirty seconds is all it takes. Ever heard of love at first sight?"

"Ever heard of a *quickie divorce?* " Lauren muttered as she shoved open the wooden door. "Because that's what happens when you believe in love at first sight."

She slouched onto one of the wooden benches perched in between two rows of green metal lockers.

"I told you to stop being so cynical. It doesn't become you." Paula began to tap her fingernails on one of the lockers. She dropped her other hand to her hip. "Is it just me or did that guy look like someone I've seen before?"

Lauren nodded. She unbuttoned her chef's jacket and opened the locker directly in front of her. "No, it's not just you. I thought I recognized him from somewhere, too. I just can't place where. He must be someone important, though, if he was the VIP Nathan was raving about earlier."

Each woman tried to summon a recollection of his face.

"I know his name," Paula said. "It's right on the tip of my tongue. But I just can't think of it."

"Well, don't strain yourself. It's not like you win any money for remembering."

"He said he'd be back here to eat again. Maybe you'll find out his name and you two will have a chance to talk a lot longer than two minutes."

"I doubt it." Lauren tossed her chef's coat into her locker and retrieved her sandals. She sat down and changed out of her tennis shoes and sports socks. "Besides, I'm not interested."

"Oh, come on, Lauren! How can you *not* be interested in him? Are you *blind?* That man was beautiful! Did you see his tattoo?" She closed her eyes and groaned. "Oh, I love a man with tattoos!"

"Yes, Paula, I noticed him . . . *and* his tattoo." Lauren rose to her feet and shut her locker door. "But he just didn't do it for me," she lied. "Besides, I'm just focused on other things."

"Like what?"

"My life . . . my goals . . . *me*. I'm focusing on me.

I'm making myself better. I'm my biggest priority—in a good way."

And I've still got a lot of work to do.

Lauren climbed over the bench and waved. "See you tomorrow."

"Wait! What are you going to do if he comes back?" she called as Lauren walked toward the door.

Lauren glanced over her shoulder. "If *who* comes back?"

"The guy from ten minutes ago! Mr. Gorgeous! Who *else?*"

"Feed him, I guess," she answered nonchalantly. "Nighty-night."

Paula sighed. "Good night, Lauren."

Chapter 2

"Twenty minutes," Lauren muttered the next morning as she pulled her car to a stop in the circular, paved-stone driveway. "Keep it to twenty minutes and no longer. Tell them as soon as you get in that you can't stay long."

Lauren had just left Phillip's place. She had decided to check on him that morning, not liking the sound of his voice over the phone the day before. She found him in good spirits and looking much better than he had looked when she had last seen him. He promised that he would make it to the restaurant on time and would be raring to go.

"All I need is my apron and my spatula, *chérie!*" he had growled in his Louisiana drawl. "It only takes me one day to mend. Nothin' is gonna stop me!"

It had been hard to leave him. In Phillip's fatherlike presence she felt warm and reassured. She felt the opposite now as she sat in front of her mother's palatial home. Lauren could think of a million places she'd rather be, but Saturday brunch at Mama's was a family tradition that had lasted as long as Lauren could re-member. Yolanda Gibbons didn't mandate that all her girls attend, but Lauren knew she would be punished with cold silence if she didn't.

Lauren opened her car door with a loud, ear-piercing squeak, climbed out, and slammed the door shut with her hip. As she walked up the slate pathway leading to the manor's French doors, she passed several bushes of blooming pink and white dahlias and then her sisters' cars that were parallel parked along the curb: one black Lexus SUV, one silver BMW sedan, and one blue Mercedes-Benz convertible. The sparkling automo-biles stood out like a line of preening beauty queens while Lauren's rusted, dented 1991 Toyota Corolla sat at the end like the ugly girl in high school who would never get asked to prom.

She took a deep breath before ringing the doorbell. After a few seconds, she spotted the silhouette of one of her mother's many maids through the stained-glass window. One of the French doors slowly opened.

"Good morning, Miss Gibbons," the petite woman greeted timidly in her thick accent. She dipped her dark head and stepped aside, then gestured Lauren to step through the doorway.

Lauren nodded after wiping her feet on the doormat. She stepped into the air-conditioned foyer and smiled. "Hi, Esmeralda. How's it going?"

"Very good, ma'am. And you?"

"Eh, I could be better." She glanced around her.

The foyer was decorated in baroque style with rich mahogany and cherrywood furniture, jewel-colored upholstery, and glass vases spilling over with roses and freesias that were cut from the terraced garden in the backyard.

Lauren's mother thought the space set the right tone for whoever entered her home. She wanted it to look opulent and sophisticated.

Lauren had always found it gaudy, though. She felt the same sense of claustrophobia she had felt whenever she stepped into James's mansion a mere five miles up the road. This much opulence was overbearing.

"Are they in the dining room?" Lauren asked.

Esmeralda quickly shook her head. "No, in the sun-room today."

"Is everyone here already?"

Esmeralda gave a rueful smile and nodded.

Great, Lauren thought morosely as she glanced down at her watch. *I'm the last one, as usual.*

She was bound to hear some smack about her tardiness.

"All right, I guess I better head back there, then. Thanks."

Esmeralda nodded again and shut the front door behind her.

Lauren made her way through the foyer and then the corridor that led to the sunroom. On one side of the hallway was a row of windows that brightened the dark corridor with shafts of midday light. On the other side was a row of portraits.

Lauren glanced at the portrait of her grandmother, Althea Gibbons. While most people had photographs of their elderly grandmothers smiling demurely at church jubilees or family picnics, the last portrait painted of Althea was quite the opposite. The seventy-five-year-old woman had looked several decades younger than her age in a blue velvet catsuit that complemented her curvy figure. She had accented it with a sapphire necklace given to her by her third husband. Her pose was also far from motherly. She reclined on a white satin chaise with her gray hair falling around her shoulders, her ample cleavage on display, and her late Pomeranian, Coco, perched at her feet.

It was a saucy portrait that epitomized Althea perfectly. Even until the day she died of heart failure, the family matriarch refused to look anything but alluring and fabulous.

"You never know what man could be watching," Althea had always warned with a furtive glance around her shoulders, like men were stalking ninjas that could pop out at any moment. "That's why you make sure you *always* look your best, honey!" she would say with a wag of the finger. "Not a hair out of place. Not a frown on your face."

If Althea could see her youngest granddaughter now, with her faded, wrinkled jeans, white T-shirt, and face deeply creased with a frown, the matriarch would roll over in her grave.

"There you are!" Lauren's mother exclaimed as Lauren stepped out of the corridor into the well-lit sunroom. The backyard pool and lush gardens showed through the windows behind her, flanking her like a photograph of the Garden of Eden.

Lauren's three sisters turned in unison to stare at her. Cynthia and Dawn, the oldest two, exchanged glances when she entered. Her sister Stephanie silently chuckled and shook her head. The only one who didn't look up was her seventeen-year-old niece, Clarissa. The girl kept her dark head bowed and continued to stare down at her lap.

"I was beginning to wonder if you were going to make it at all. You seemed to be aiming for a record. *Where* have you been, chile?" her mother asked as she closed her newspaper, folded it neatly, and lowered it to the breakfast table. "We've been waitin' on you!"

"Sorry, I lost track of time," Lauren mumbled. She walked across the room and noticed that she had been the only one, as usual, to dress casual. Everyone else wore colorful sundresses in flower and paisley patterns and expensive fabrics.

When she reached her mother's chair, she leaned down and lightly kissed the older woman's cheek and inhaled, smelling the light, citrusy fragrance that her mother always wore.

"I can't stay long. I have to be at the restaurant by one o'clock."

"So you're late *and* you have to rush off?" Though her mother was smiling, irritation was clearly audible in her voice. "Do you plan to eat or should we just make you a doggie bag?"

Lauren flopped down in the chair between her mother and Stephanie, who was snickering again. She grabbed the white linen napkin neatly folded on the bread plate in front of her, shook it open, and slung it over her lap.

"Mama, I tell you every Saturday that I have to be at the restaurant in enough time to start preparing for the evening rush. I'm a sous chef. That's my *job!* What do you want me to do?"

An uncomfortable silence fell over the sunroom. Yolanda Gibbons slowly leaned back in her rattan chair.

Many people said Yolanda bore a striking resemblance to Diahann Carroll. In fact, all she needed was the sequined gown, big hair, and big shoulder pads, and she could have been Dominique Deveraux in the 1980s soap opera *Dynasty*. She even had the character's regal air and a glare that could freeze you dead in your shoes. She was directing that withering glare now at her youngest daughter, Lauren.

"Oh, I understand that you have a job, my dear." She adjusted her cream-colored sweater around her shoulders. "I *also* understand that your sisters have busy lives, too, but unlike you, they've always managed to make it here on time *every* week. Unlike you, they have never kept their mother waiting."

Lauren lowered her gaze to her lap at her mother's words. She could feel her sisters staring at her, their eyes silently conveying their judgment.

"*They* understand how important this is and would not dare disappoint me."

Lauren didn't say a word, knowing it was useless to argue. Anyone would be ill advised to engage in a battle of words with Yolanda Gibbons.

After some seconds, Yolanda's face gradually softened. Her glare disappeared.

"We're family, baby," her mother said tenderly. She placed her warm hand over Lauren's smaller one and squeezed. "And this is how we stay a family. Money comes and goes and men will *always* come and go, but no matter what, you have us. Understood?"

Lauren slowly nodded grudgingly. "Understood."

"And we're important. Our time together is important. It should be treated preciously."

Her mother squeezed her hand again and released it before sitting forward in her chair. She waved a hand. "Rosa, you may serve the coffee, honey."

Another maid immediately stepped forward with silver teapot in hand.

The light air and chatter immediately returned to the room. Cynthia passed around a basket of croissants and Stephanie began to boast about a pair of Ferragamo shoes she had bought last week. Dawn took a bite from a slice of bacon while Lauren quietly thanked Rosa as she poured her a cup of coffee. Clarissa took mousy nibbles on the end of a piece of toast, making Cynthia glance at her.

"*Stop* slouching," Cynthia said tightly before nudging her daughter's shoulder.

Clarissa instantly sat upright, smoothing the pleats in her pink dress.

"I guess we can begin now," Yolanda announced.

Of course, when she said that they could begin, she wasn't referring to just brunch itself. She was referring to that day's "agenda." After their plates were filled and their coffee cups and juice glasses were full, Yolanda signified that their meeting had commenced by tapping her teaspoon on the edge of her porcelain teacup. The loud clinking made everyone in the room fall silent.

Lauren stared down at her plate. *This* was the reason why she was always late to Saturday brunch. *This* was the part of the tradition that she loathed the most. It wasn't because she disliked her mother or her sisters—though they could be overbearing as all hell sometimes. It was because she couldn't stand to sit through this! These meetings always made her feel like she was a member of a crime syndicate.

Yolanda interlocked her fingers and grinned. "So, who would like to go first?" She scanned her eyes around the table.

"I will," Cynthia said, raising her slender hand. She waved her French manicured nails and proudly tossed her sun-kissed locks over her shoulder. She batted her hazel eyes and smiled. "I've made some progress with Henry Perkins, the director over at Landview Bank."

Yolanda leaned forward, now interested. *"Really?* Is this the one that was playing hard to get?"

"Oh, he was in the beginning, but not anymore. I had to show him a little somethin'—some leg and a little boob—but I think it did the trick."

Lauren rolled her eyes while Dawn frowned, causing a wrinkle to appear on her delicate ebony brow. "And how do you figure that?"

Unlike Cynthia, who looked similar to the actress Vanessa Williams in her younger years, Dawn looked more like the bust of Nefertiti carved out of black onyx.

Cynthia gave her sister the side eye and sucked her teeth. "Because he invited me to dinner Friday."

"A business dinner or a *real* dinner?" Yolanda asked.

"It's a business dinner, but he wants to go out for drinks alone afterward."

"Good. *Very* good! But you know the rules, Cindy." Yolanda pointed across the table at her eldest daughter. "Don't get too arrogant, baby, and don't take that he's attracted to you for granted. Just because a man is responding to you doesn't mean you hold the reins yet. Remember that, ladies." She slowly looked around the table again. "There could be a girlfriend you don't know about on the sidelines. He could think you're a woman who's there for a good time and he can just use you and move on to the next one. But if you're careful and you're *smart*, he won't know what hit him." Yolanda smiled as she raised her teacup to her lips. She blew the hot liquid inside to cool it down. "I'm telling you. If you play your cards right, he could be your next husband, Cindy. Give it a few years and get a divorce, and you could have a nice alimony nest egg. A bank director brings home more than just pocket change."

All the daughters, with the exception of Lauren, nodded in agreement.

Like Cynthia needs another ex-husband, Lauren thought. Between all the women at the table, they had more than a half-dozen ex-husbands combined. Of the sisters, only Lauren had yet to take the one-way ticket down the aisle straight to divorce court.

"And what about you, Steph?" Yolanda asked, turning her attention to her other daughter.

Like Lauren, Stephanie was a shade somewhere between Cynthia and Dawn, but unlike Lauren, she wore her hair long and flowing down her back. She was also taller than her petite younger sister.

"Whatever happened to that lawyer you met at that party in Arlington?" their mother persisted. "Any progress?"

Lauren ignored the rest of the conversation, focusing on her breakfast instead.

This was every Saturday brunch at the Gibbons home: a group of women plotting—over French toast, sausage, and eggs Benedict—how to chase men and take their money.

It was a family tradition that began with Althea. The family matriarch had grown up in a crowded sharecropper shack in North Carolina but through cunning and beauty managed to successfully snare three wealthy husbands and die a *very* rich woman. She passed on her skills to her only daughter, Yolanda, who then passed it on to her daughters. In turn, Cynthia, Dawn, Stephanie, and Lauren were expected to pass it on to their kin. (Clarissa's invite to their Saturday brunch was definitely a sign that her own "classes" had begun.)

For the Gibbons girls, men were just a means to an end. They bought you houses. They bought you cars.

They gave you children and they gave you money. But that was about it. The only thing that mattered was your family and that meant your sisters, your mother, and your children.

Lauren had never met her father, nor had any of her sisters met theirs. But their mother said it wasn't necessary to meet them.

"As long as he takes care of his financial obligations to you, what difference does it make whether you see him?" Yolanda would ask when the girls were younger and they openly wondered why they had not received so much as a birthday card or telephone call from any of their dads. *"We're* important," Yolanda would insist. "Not a man who knows absolutely nothing about you."

The belief that men were just a means to an end had been so deeply ingrained in all of them that even Lauren had fallen under its spell . . . for a while. She had started off on the same path as her sisters. Back then, she had used men and their money with only fleeting misgivings about what she was doing. She probably would be married and divorced by now and have moved on to the next man if it wasn't for James Sayers. She wasn't sure if it was her good fortune or bad luck to have ended up with the likes of him.

Chapter 3

James was twenty-two years Lauren's senior. He was one of the most powerful men in town and had an air about him that drew respect and sometimes awe from those around him. He had his own law firm whose clients included Fortune 500 companies with offices in Dulles and other parts of the technology corridor in northern Virginia. He had a sprawling estate that was bigger than the Gibbons manor, a brownstone in New York, a condo in DC, and a summer home in St. Bart's. He owned six cars that included a Ferrari and Bentley, and a yacht that he kept docked along the Chesapeake Bay. It seemed that there wasn't anything that James wanted that he couldn't buy or hadn't bought already.

When Lauren met him, he had let her know instantly that he was attracted to her, and something about him seemed so much unlike the other men she had dated. He was not only romantic but protective. She didn't have to pretend with James. He understood her and their arrangement instantly. He let her know that he *wanted* to take care of her and give her money and shelter. All she had to do was be the beautiful young woman on his arm, cook his food, and warm his bed at night. Lauren agreed to those terms and moved into his home.

It had seemed like a good arrangement . . . in the beginning. Lauren was happy to play the trophy girlfriend, and he seemed happy to be her sugar daddy. But after less than a year, things started to change.

Lauren began to notice it first in the little patronizing jokes James made about her. He began to call some of the dresses she wore "slutty" and tell her whenever she talked to his friends and business associates that she should keep her thoughts to herself. He ridiculed her for enrolling in culinary school. He said her talent was in looking beautiful and nothing else.

"Don't stretch yourself, honey," he would say before patting her lightly on the behind.

Later she often wondered if, in some ways, he had been jealous of her desire to become a chef. After all, how could she focus completely on catering to him if she pursued dreams of her own?

His protectiveness slowly took on a darker tone and Lauren began to wonder if James wanted to protect her—or control her. He started to text her constantly. When she arrived home, he wanted a rundown of what she'd done that day and whom she'd spoken to. She found out that he was monitoring her cell phone calls through their monthly phone bills. She started to hide her purse after she discovered him digging through it one day after she left it sitting on her vanity. By the end of the second year, Lauren had had enough. But by then, it was too late. The verbal abuse became physical.

The night he beat her, she bolted. She ran barefoot in her silk nightgown out the bedroom, down the hallway, and down the winding staircase of the East Wing. She found the hiding place for her purse, grabbed her car keys, and ran into the frigid November night.

It was seven months later, yet she could still remember that night perfectly: how the light flakes of snow fell around her while she puffed gusts of air with each panicked breath she took, and how the freezing gravel driveway dug needles of pain into the soles of her bare feet as she ran from his house. She didn't stop to go back inside and get a pair of shoes or a coat. She felt like she *couldn't* stop until she got far away from there.

Lauren had pulled off in her car just as James swung open the front door. He had bellowed after her while her tires screeched and sent gravel flying. She glanced over her shoulder to find him running after the car like a madman. She drove at nearly sixty miles per hour to the opened front gate.

As Lauren drove away, she had sobbed, both angry and hurt that James had done that to her. She cried even harder when she realized that she had really done it to herself. She had let him abuse and manipulate her for two years in exchange for what? *Money? Expensive cars? Trendy clothes?*

"But I didn't know any better," she had quietly lamented, feeling sorry for herself.

She had been taught to play this game and now it had come back to bite her in the ass.

"But now you *do* know better," a new part of her replied. "And you will never let this happen to you again."

Lauren's tears began to fade with the emergence of her new resolve. She would change herself. She would change her life. She wouldn't hunt men anymore for their money. She wasn't going to depend on anyone but herself for a sense of security.

As the snow continued to fall, Lauren felt lighter. She had finally shaken off the shackles of her old life. She was finally free.

"Lauren," her mother said after they made their way around the table and all the other sisters had shared stories of their recent conquests. "What about you, honey?"

Lauren shoved her scrambled eggs around her plate with her fork. "I don't have anything to share."

Her mother gave a heavy sigh, removing her dinner napkin from her lap. She placed it on the vintage chenille tablecloth. "It's been seven months now, baby. I think it's been long enough for you to get back out there again."

"I told you that this wasn't temporary, Mama. I'm done. OK, I'm done! I'm not doing it anymore!"

"Oh, Laurie, Laurie, Laurie. Don't let that man do this to you, honey! He's already moved on. I heard he's dating some twenty-year-old paralegal. Don't let him make you give up like this. You made a mistake! All right? It's that simple. What do I always tell you girls? Don't give a man too much power! It's one of the oldest rules in the family book . . . and you broke it. You handed over the reins to him and before you knew it, the buggy lost control. But we all learn from our mistakes," Yolanda said, looking around the table. "Don't we, ladies?"

Cynthia, Dawn, and Stephanie quickly nodded in agreement.

Cynthia turned and nudged Clarissa, who had been

gazing listlessly at her plate. The young girl looked up surprised and nodded distractedly.

She shouldn't be here, Lauren thought as she gazed at Clarissa's innocent face. *She shouldn't hear this nonsense!*

Yolanda smiled as she held up the newspaper that had been neatly folded near her plate. "I have a tip to help you along, Laurie, and it's a good one. He's a man I think would be perfect for you." She shook the newspaper open. "Are you *sure* you aren't interested?"

"I said 'no.' "

"Oh, hell!" Cynthia exclaimed. "If she isn't interested in him, than *I am!* Who is he, Mama?"

Dawn sucked her teeth. "What do you mean 'who is he'? I thought you said you were working on the bigwig over at Landview Bank!"

"Honey, I'm a multitasker!"

"Multitasker? Please! I swear you think you should get first dibs on everything."

"I'm the oldest! *Why shouldn't I?* "

It quickly devolved into bickering, with Cynthia and Dawn going at one another's throats. Their mother calmly raised her teaspoon and tapped it on the edge of her teacup again. At the sound of the clinking, all the sisters stopped arguing.

"No one gets first dibs on this one," their mother said firmly. "He was reserved for Lauren and she turned him down, so now it's whichever one of you makes headway with him first."

"Well, *who* is he, Mama?" Cynthia repeated impatiently.

All the sisters, with the exception of Lauren, listened eagerly.

"He's a football star," Yolanda said as she stared down at a newspaper article and sipped her tea. "Well, I guess *ex*-football star. He's newly retired. His name is Cris Weaver. The first name has a funny spelling for some reason. C-R-I-S *not* C-H-R-I-S."

"From where do I know that name?" Dawn paused. "Mama, did he play for the Dallas Cowboys?"

Yolanda nodded. "He did, but he retired last year. He's the one that bought the old Holston place. He's been renovating it for a while now." She tapped at a paragraph in the article. "It says here that in addition to being a football player, Cris made several good investments in dot.com start-ups and a music label. He was listed last year on Forbes's Most Powerful Celebrities list. Between money from his old sponsorships, his stock portfolio, and investments, he's estimated to be worth more than forty *million* dollars."

Their eyes widened collectively.

Stephanie let out a long, low whistle. "Damn, that beats James Sayers by a good twenty mil," she muttered.

Lauren's eyes instantly shot up from her plate at the mention of James's name. She glared at her sister.

Stephanie demured as she nibbled at a piece of toast. "I'm sorry, Laurie. I know James is an asshole, but it's true!" she whispered.

Lauren watched as her mother looked down at the photograph of Cris Weaver.

"Getting this one would mean you *definitely* hit the jackpot, girls," Yolanda said.

With mild interest, Lauren glanced at his picture. When she saw it, she gaped.

It couldn't be!

It was the same guy from yesterday, the one who had come into the kitchen to compliment her on the food!

"But it'll be a challenge," Yolanda continued, oblivious to Lauren's amazement. "My sources tell me that he officially moved into town about a week ago, but I heard he's elusive. He's rarely at his home and no one has seen him in any of the shops on Main Street. Good luck tracking him down."

"I've se—"

Lauren stopped herself.

Everyone at the table turned to look at her, but she quickly clamped her mouth shut.

Her mother stared at her expectantly. "You what, honey?"

Lauren was going to say that she had seen him at her restaurant only yesterday—in fact, she had even spoken to him—but something held her back from sharing her news. Lauren was sure that it wasn't possessiveness.

No, Lauren told herself. She couldn't covet a man she barely knew. Just because he made her heart pound like she was hopped-up on caffeine when she looked at him, and she had been thinking about him off and on since yesterday, didn't mean that she wanted to keep him to herself.

I said I wasn't interested in him and I meant it. I'm not interested in any man right now. I'm just . . . I'm just trying to protect him.

When her sisters got their hooks in a man, they could be brutal—especially Cynthia. He seemed like a nice guy. He didn't deserve to be chewed up and spit out.

"I was . . . I was just going to say that"—she tried

her best to think up a quick lie—"that I have no doubt one of you will probably track him down. You've got noses like bloodhounds when it comes to sniffing out a rich man."

"Just because you lost the fight in you," Cynthia muttered, "doesn't mean you can make fun of the rest of us. You gave up, but that doesn't mean all of us have to."

"Cynthia! Apologize to your sister for saying that!"

Lauren stood from the table. "Don't worry, Mama. I'll just take that as my cue to leave."

"Oh, sweetheart, don't rush off. Cynthia didn't mean that. Tell her you didn't mean it, Cynthia!"

"I'm not rushing off. I said when I arrived that I couldn't stay long. I have to get to the restaurant." She leaned down and kissed her mother's cheek. "I guess I'll see you again next weekend."

She turned, pushed her chair back to the table, and rushed out before her mother had the chance to ask again for her to stay.

Chapter 4

Stephanie Gibbons pulled to a stop in front of the scrolled wrought-iron gate, pressed the button to lower the driver's-side window of her silver BMW, and smiled at the stocky, uniformed guard who had been sitting on his stool at the gatepost. He had been idly flipping through a car magazine when she pulled up. He slowly raised his eyes from the tricked-out Land Rover on the page spread, saw Stephanie, and instantly perked up. His plump face brightened into a grin.

"Good afternoon," she said, pushing back her sunglasses to the crown of her head. "I'm Stephanie Gibbons. I'm here for the Baylor event."

"Uh, yeah . . . umm . . ." He fumbled as he rose from his stool, dropping his magazine to the glass booth's floor. "Umm . . . let me just . . . just check that here."

She watched as he reached for a clipboard on his small, cluttered desk. He quickly flipped its pages and scanned the names on the list. "You said Stephanie Gibbons?"

She nodded.

"Yeah, I got you right here." He tapped one of the pages with a ballpoint pen. "Go right ahead."

"Thanks."

A natural flirt, Stephanie gave him a saucy wink. She lowered her sunglasses back to her nose and pulled off as the gate slid open.

"Hey! Hey!" he shouted over the sound of her car's revving engine. "Wait, baby! Come back! Can I get your number?"

She slowly shook her head and laughed.

Sorry, honey, Stephanie thought.

A gated-community security guard wasn't exactly the caliber of man she was interested in. Now, Cris Weaver—*that* was a man who was definitely more her style! She'd be more than happy to hang off of his strong arm.

While her sisters were busy bickering at today's brunch at Mama's, Stephanie had managed to snag the newspaper with the article about the rich ex-NFL player. She now glanced at the article as she drove past several cookie-cutter houses with the same impressive facades and perfect lawns. The newspaper was folded in the passenger seat near her purse and a brightly colored gift bag.

Their mother was right: If any of the Gibbons girls managed to snag Weaver, that would definitely be a major coup. But competition for such a guy would be stiff. At least Lauren was dropping out of the contest, though that wasn't a surprise. She hadn't chased after anyone since her ugly breakup with James. But it looked like Cynthia wasn't backing down. She already had her boxing gloves on and was ready to come out swinging, taking out any woman who even bothered to look Weaver's way.

Stephanie pulled into a concrete driveway, turned off the engine, grabbed the newspaper, and looked down at Weaver's photograph.

Hmm, cute, she thought. But was he worth the battle?

Weaver certainly was, on paper, but Stephanie didn't know if she was up to challenging Cynthia. Their eldest sister had always ranked as Queen Bee in their family, and knowing Cynthia, that schemer was already drawing up plans to woo and win over Weaver in three months flat!

Nah, Stephanie thought, slowly shaking her head and tossing the newspaper aside. She'd let Cynthia have a go at Weaver first. Then—if her sister crashed and burned—Stephanie would give him a try. It was only fair and part of the family's rules of conduct. Cynthia couldn't argue with that.

Stephanie flipped down her visor and examined her reflection, making sure everything looked perfect.

"Not a hair out of place," Stephanie said, whispering Grandmother Althea's mantra, "not a frown on your face."

She flipped up her visor, pasted on a smile, and opened her car door.

A trail of people slowly made their way up the brick pathway to the front door of the Tudor-style home. A very pregnant Tisha Baylor stood in the doorway, greeting everyone. The instant she saw Stephanie, the pretty, dark-skinned woman smiled.

"Hey, girl!" Tisha shouted as Stephanie strode toward her in her stilettos, carrying the oversized gift bag.

"How are you?" Stephanie embraced Tisha and lightly

kissed her cheek. She handed the gift bag to her. "Just a little something!"

"Oh, thank you! You shouldn't have!"

Stephanie looked around the impressively decorated foyer. "Honey, I just love your home!"

"You should! You sold it to us!"

Stephanie tossed her hair over her shoulder and smiled. "I did, didn't I? Well, I guess that means it *is* fabulous, then!"

The girls in the Gibbons family might be avid gold diggers, but that didn't mean they didn't believe in also having a backup plan. They all had their own careers. Some even had their own businesses. Lauren was a chef, Cynthia was the director of the local historical society, Dawn was an art gallery director, and Stephanie was a real-estate agent—one of the top agents in Chesterton.

Stephanie had helped the Baylor family purchase their house less than a month ago. The couple had been looking for a larger home now that they were going to have their second child and had hired Stephanie as their agent. The Baylors hadn't been easy to please; they had very specific, high-end tastes and had nitpicked over every detail. But it took her less than four months to find and close on the sweeping three-story house in which they were now settled. Stephanie heard the baby room was already painted a tasteful pale pink in honor of the little girl they planned to have in July. Today they were holding a house blessing for their new home and had invited Stephanie, among many other guests, to the event.

Tisha grinned and ushered Stephanie inside. "Go introduce yourself to everyone! We're serving hors d'oeuvres in the living room."

Stephanie nodded and walked inside before strolling past the winding staircase.

"Try the cabernet!" Tisha called after her. "We had it shipped in especially from Napa!"

Stephanie made her way through the nicely dressed crowd, who sipped from wineglasses and shared polite conversation while mellow jazz music played in the background. This certainly wasn't a "down-home" house blessing by any estimation. If anyone got the Holy Spirit, Stephanie was sure a crowd like this would be aghast and disgusted. They'd probably faint.

Though not all partygoers were local, Stephanie spotted an assortment of the upper crust of Chesterton around the room: the business leaders, lawyers, and doctors who held the most power (and money) in their small town. Stephanie glanced inside her purse and discretely made sure her business cards were handy. She could very well find several new clients this afternoon.

She smiled at a group of men who were huddled in one of the living room corners, behind the sofa. One of the men—a tall, handsome brother with a goatee— looked up at her and smiled back.

Maybe I'll find a lot more than a client today, she thought as he tipped his wineglass to her.

Stephanie was always on the lookout for a new man—*especially* if he was a rich one.

Mr. Goatee murmured something to his friends before walking toward her, but then he stopped. His eager smile disappeared. She watched, confused, as he veered in another direction and walked off.

Well, what the hell was that about?

Stephanie didn't have any further chance to speculate on his sudden loss of interest. She felt someone grab her by the elbow. She turned in surprise to find James Sayers, of all people, grinning down at her.

"Steph! Hello, gorgeous! I didn't expect to see you here. How are you?"

Stephanie cringed. She was well aware of what James had done to Lauren. She had seen the bruises, scratches, and blood that November night. She, Dawn, and Cynthia had tended to Lauren's wounds. Lauren had even stayed with Stephanie for a few weeks before she found a place of her own.

Like Lauren, none of them had chosen to take a public stand against James. Their little sister wanted to keep quiet the story of what he had done to her. He was just too powerful in town, Lauren had argued. Stephanie respected Lauren's decision. It was her choice. But just because Stephanie didn't openly show her distaste for the man, didn't mean she had to like him or be around him. He made her skin crawl.

"Hey, James," she said flatly, pulling out of his grasp.

"I haven't seen you in quite a while, Steph." He shoved one of his hands into his pants pocket and drank from his wineglass. "It's been . . . I don't know . . . more than six months."

"Yes, it has." She looked away, pretending to be fascinated with one of the modernist paintings on the wall, hoping he would take the hint.

"You and your sisters used to visit all the time." He chuckled. "You were at my place so often, I was going to charge you rent!"

"Well, now that Lauren no longer lives with you, there's no reason to visit, now, is there?"

He finished what was left of his wine. His cordial smile disappeared. "Speaking of Lauren . . . how is your lovely sister? Doing well, I hope."

Stephanie slowly turned away from the painting and narrowed her eyes up at James.

This guy has got some huge balls, she thought angrily.

"She's fine, James. Just . . . *fine.*"

"That's good to hear. Can I speak with you privately for a second?"

James didn't give her a chance to reply. He dropped his hand to her back and steered her to one of the empty corners of the crowded room. Again, she tried to ease out of his grasp, but this time, he linked an arm around her waist. His hold tightened. Stephanie glanced nervously around her, hoping that James wouldn't do anything to her in front of all these people.

"I wonder if you could pass a message along to Lauren for me," he whispered into her ear.

"Why don't you tell her your goddamn self?" she snarled, trying to twist away from him.

He laughed again and faced her. "Oh, you know how stubborn your sister is! She hasn't been returning my phone calls or any of my messages. How could I possibly speak to her?"

Soon after Lauren had left him, James had called her endlessly, leaving so many messages on her voice mail that he filled the message box to capacity. He had sent bouquet after bouquet of flowers and expensive gifts to Yolanda's home, hoping that Lauren's mother would pass them along. Finally, after months of Lauren's silence, and after all the gifts were returned to his mansion, the calls had trickled off, then stopped completely. Lauren had assumed James had finally understood that she wasn't coming back. But judging by the way he was behaving now, that obviously wasn't the case.

"Why don't you just leave her alone? Just move on!"

"I'd love to do that, sweetheart," he said tightly, "but you see Lauren and I have a few financial entanglements that need to be taken care of before I can."

Financial entanglements?

"Tell your sister to give me a call. It's in her best interest to do so . . . in *all* your best interests," he corrected and grinned. "Tell her I have something to give her."

He then walked off, leaving Stephanie standing alone at the party, completely dumbfounded.

"All right! All right, everyone!" Tisha Baylor said, tapping on the edge of her water glass with a spoon. "Please gather around for the blessing!"

Conversation throughout the first floor gradually quieted as everyone made their way to the living room. Tisha stood next to a baby grand piano that featured several framed photographs of herself and her family on its glossy ebony ledge. Her husband, Derrick, stood next to her with his arm looped around her ample waist. Tisha beckoned the crowd forward.

"First, I would like to thank each and every one for coming today," Tisha said as she gazed around the room. "We're so honored that you would all attend our house blessing. Second, Derrick and I would like to thank our wonderful, *fabu*lous real-estate agent, Miss Stephanie Gibbons. Stephanie, please come up front and introduce yourself to everyone!"

Stephanie set aside her wineglass and excused herself through the throng of people. She proudly walked to the front of the room where Tisha and Derrick stood. She turned back around to face the crowd and smiled.

Stephanie noticed a few women in the crowd rolling their eyes heavenward or exchange a look as she waved, but she didn't care. She knew she and her sisters weren't going to have any fan clubs started in their honor among the women in Chesterton anytime soon. It was best just to ignore the other women's looks and comments.

"Stephanie got us this lovely home, and we are ever so grateful for all her hard work!"

"Thank you, Tisha!"

"Now, without further ado, we'd like the Honorable Deacon Montgomery to come forward and do the blessing," Tisha said.

Stephanie was astonished when the crowd parted and handsome Mr. Goatee from earlier stepped forward.

So he's a deacon, huh? Well, she hadn't figured on that one. *Interesting,* Stephanie thought.

Her eyes momentarily locked with his before his gaze shifted to Tisha and Derrick. He shook Derrick's hand and gave Tisha a warm hug. He then gave one final heated glance at Stephanie before closing his eyes and lowering his head.

"Let us bow our heads in prayer," his baritone voice boomed to the room of people. He then began the blessing.

Soon after the prayer, the partygoers slowly began to disperse.

Overall, it had been a good evening for Stephanie. She had handed out about half a dozen business cards and got at least one credible sales lead. As the party finally began to wind down, she made sure to say good-bye to Tisha and Derrick and to avoid running into James again when she noticed him talking to another couple. She had just stepped through the door and was walking down the brick pathway that led to the drive-way when she felt someone lightly tap her on the shoulder. She turned to find Mr. Goatee/Deacon Mont-gomery smiling at her.

Yes, he was one handsome man—and a nicely dressed one at that. Stephanie had to admit that about the men of the church: Their hearts might lie with the Lord, but they certainly didn't skimp on themselves when it came to their clothing budgets! This guy was decked out with what looked like a custom-tailored suit, gold cuff links, and a pale blue silk tie. She glanced at his shoes.

I don't believe my eyes! Are those Hermès?

Oh, yes, Deacon Montgomery was most definitely a baller! She was going to have to work her magic on this one.

"So you're a real-estate agent?" he asked.

"I most certainly am . . . and one of the best in town. Why? Are you looking to buy or sell a home, Deacon Montgomery?"

"Please. Please . . ." The smile on his pecan-colored face broadened and he extended his hand to her. "Call me Hank."

She shook his large, warm hand and grinned. "Pleased to meet you, Hank."

"Can I walk you to your car, Miss Gibbons?"

"You can call me Stephanie. And yes, you can walk me to my car. Thank you."

They strolled down the brick pathway that was bordered by white calla lilies and irises on one side and the Baylor family's pristine lawn on the other. When they reached the driveway, he loudly cleared his throat.

"You know, I *am* interested in buying a home . . . maybe even a house that wouldn't be too far from here. You see, we moved to Chesterton about a year ago—"

"We?" Stephanie asked with a frown. Was the deacon married?

"Yes." He cleared his throat again. "Me and my . . . my two Jack Russell terriers. They're like children to me."

"Oh," she said, nodding again. She breathed a sigh of relief.

Stephanie had dated married men in the past, but she preferred not to. Husbands came with a lot more drama, and angry wives could be psychotic. He would have to be one special man for her to put up with a crazy housewife.

"I've been renting a home for a while, but I think I'm finally ready to purchase something. Lay down some roots."

"Well," she said as they approached her BMW, "whenever you're ready to start your search, please keep me in mind." She dug into her purse, pulled out one of her business cards, and handed it to him.

"I'd like to start soon."

She unlocked her car door and cocked an eyebrow. "How soon are we talking about?"

Hank licked his lips and drew closer to her. He languidly let his eyes travel over her, lingering meaningfully on her breasts. Finally, he brought his gaze back level with her eyes.

"As soon as humanly possible," he whispered. "I'm a man who hates to wait."

Stephanie tilted her head. So this was how they were

going to play it? Well, she could do a few double en-
tendres, too.

"If that's the case, then I think we need to get started
right away. Let's schedule a meeting to discuss the details. I'm interested in finding out what you like . . .
what you're craving." She smirked up at him. "You
should draw up a list."

"Oh, you don't want that." He shook his head and
laughed. "You'd be surprised at what I'd write down."

"Believe me, honey . . ." She opened her car door
and tossed her purse inside. She turned back around to
face him and pushed out her chest, giving him quite the
eyeful. *"Nothing* would surprise me."

"Nothing?"

"I cater to many tastes. It's my specialty."

He shivered.

"Don't be scared, Hank. What's that old saying? You
never know until you try. Maybe I can give you everything you need."

"Everything?"

"And more." She winked. "I'm here to service you . . .
and trust me, I aim to please. I'll do it on my knees if I
have to."

He hungrily licked his lips again. Stephanie could
practically see the kinky fantasies that danced in his
head.

"How about dinner next Sunday at eight o'clock?
I'll bring my list with me."

"Sure! You can pick me up at the address on my
card."

He nodded and smiled, tucking the card into his
inner suit-jacket pocket. "I'll see you at eight o'clock."

"I look forward to it, Hank."

Stephanie watched as he walked down to the end of

the driveway and then made a right. Inside, she did a little jig.

Her sisters could battle over Cris Weaver if they wanted to. Meanwhile, she would focus on lower-hanging fruit and put her efforts into seducing the wealthy Deacon Hank Montgomery.

Chapter 5

"So explain to me why this is going to take three more weeks?" Cris Weaver asked as he crossed his arms over his broad chest and glowered down at Bill, his general contractor.

The portly man began to fidget. He adjusted his baseball cap and hoisted his jeans under his round belly. Sweat stains had formed earlier on his gray T-shirt around his belly button and under his armpits in the hot sun, but he was sweating even more now under the lavalike heat of Cris's glare. Standing there, those stains seemed to grow by another two inches.

He had a right to be scared. At that moment, Cris looked less like an annoyed homeowner who was bitching out his contractor and more like an angry Samoan warrior ready to do battle.

"Well, the custom cabinets won't arrive for another week, Mr. Weaver," Bill nearly shouted over the clamor of buzz saws and hammers. "They're late. I can't make them come any faster than they already are. We can't outline the granite countertops in your kitchen until we get the cabinets in. So we gotta wait two or three more weeks before your kitchen's done."

Cris nodded but still narrowed his dark eyes. "And why are the cabinets late? Is there a problem with the shipment?"

"No, nothin' like that. They're on time. It's just . . ." Bill nervously licked his lips.

"Just . . . *what?*"

"Well, the guy who measured the kitchen jiggered some of the numbers." Bill dropped his watery blue eyes to gaze at Cris's brown leather oxfords. It was easier to do that than to stare up at the man who towered over him by a good eight inches. "When I saw the numbers on paper later, I thought it looked funny. We had to measure it again. So we put a stop order on the first set of cabinets and ordered the cabinets again. They hadn't started building the first set yet, so it won't cost you extra. But it just messed up the time line a bit."

Cris sighed. Now he had the *real* answer for why his kitchen was delayed.

Bill looked up and shook his head. "It wasn't my fault, Mr. Weaver! I know I'm supposed to watch over these guys, but I can't be a million places at one time! This is a big property with a lot of workers and—"

"I'm not paying you to be a million places at once. I'm paying you just to make sure things run smoothly. This is the seventh time that something has been delayed because of some subcontractor's mistake. I'm paying some of these guys to do the same job twice that should have been done right the first time. All of this means more time and more money—and believe it or not, Bill, I'm not made out of Benjamins. This is *really* irritating me."

Bill lowered his eyes again and grimaced. "Sorry, Mr. Weaver. It's all just part of—"

"Oh, come on, Cris! Lay off the man!" Cris's friend Jamal suddenly shouted over the noise as he walked into the living room.

Cris turned to find Jamal, a friend he had known since college, striding toward them in a pin-striped suit with a wide grin on his dark-skinned face. "Stop busting the man's chops! Besides, what do you need a kitchen for? It ain't like you can cook anyway!"

Bill laughed at Jamal's joke, but he stopped when Cris turned back around and glared at him. The chuckle froze in his throat.

"Stop yapping and let the man do his job!" Jamal stood next to Cris. He clapped Bill on the shoulder. "Really, man, Cris is a good guy, but he's *always* like this. I think it comes from having a dad who was in the army. He's wound up tighter than a Swiss watch until you get a couple of drinks in 'im. Don't worry about it. Just do your thing."

Jamal then thumped Cris on the back. "Come on. Show me around the place. I bet a lot of stuff has changed since the last time I was here."

Jamal steered his friend toward the doorway leading out of the living room and into a long corridor. Though Cris wasn't finished with Bill, he let the conversation end. As the two men retreated, Bill wiped his sweaty brow. The contractor raised his pants again, turned around, and headed off to one of the downstairs bathrooms to supervise the tile installation.

"Jay," Cris said as they passed a group of lighting guys who were installing recessed cans, "why the hell did you tell him I'm uptight?"

"Because you are! You have been as long as I've known you."

Of course Jamal would say that. Even in college, he had always argued that Cris needed to lighten up, to break the chains of his strict upbringing and chill out sometimes. Cris always had been the studious one, going directly from football practice to the campus library to work on an essay for American Lit or crunch for a biology test. Meanwhile, Jamal would be partying at some hangout on campus or hitting on a girl at the student union cafeteria, completely oblivious to whatever test or paper was due the next day. But the polar opposites were assigned as roommates their freshmen year and, despite their differences, they quickly formed a bond and had been friends ever since.

"I'm not uptight," Cris muttered. "I'm just tired of being stuck in renovation that never seems to end. They told me they could do this place in two months . . . three months *tops*! This thing is already into its fourth month. I've been renting that place in DC so I wouldn't have to breathe sawdust while I slept and hear hammers banging all day! Half my stuff is crammed back at the town house. Hell, if I would have known it would take this long, I would have just ripped the whole house down and started from scratch!"

"The house had good bones. That's why you bought it. There was no reason to tear it down, and even if you did, that would have taken *another* year to build a new one."

"But that doesn't change the fact that—"

Jamal held up a hand and waved it gently like a symphony director, silencing his friend. "Just *chiiiiiiiiiill*, Cris. Do some meditation exercises or somethin'. They're just building it the way you want it. What's the rush? I mean, what else do you have to do? You're a retired man with plenty of time on his hands. Right? *Right?*"

"Yeah . . . but this just isn't how I envisioned spending my retirement," he mumbled sullenly as they walked farther down the corridor.

"I see you have your shrine up already," Jamal said, changing the subject. He gestured to a built-in cabinet encased in Plexiglas and filled with more than a dozen pictures of Cris with his old teammates, a football with all of their signatures, and his old football jersey.

Jamal paused in front of the built-in and Cris smiled as he glanced at the tokens of his past.

"Brings back memories every time you see it, huh?"

Cris nodded.

After fifteen and a half years in the NFL as a wide receiver and at the age of thirty-six (practically a senior citizen in football), reoccurring injuries and plain old fatigue had finally forced Cris to walk away from a game he loved so much. He had been playing football since he was seven years old. Back then, he had been an awkward half-black, half-Filipino kid who always had his nose in a book. He had decided one day to ask his father to teach him to play football so that he could make friends with the boys in his neighborhood who had treated him for months like his nerdiness was contagious. From that point on, he was hooked on football.

"You miss it?" Jamal asked, turning away from the built-in.

"In some ways . . . yeah. I miss my coaches. I miss my teammates."

"And the crowds, brothah! I remember being in those stands during the games. Those crowds were crazy!"

"Yeah, there was nothing like that roar or the nervous energy before every game. There is no high that's better than the one you get after a touchdown, Jamal. They need to sell that stuff in a bottle or in dime bags," Cris said wistfully, running his hand over the glass.

Jamal slowly shook his head. "How could you walk away from all this?"

"Easy. I *had* to," Cris said as they continued to stroll, passing a window where they could see the groundskeepers taming overgrown hedges. "My body couldn't take it anymore, Jay . . . getting tackled by some three-hundred-pound linebacker . . . and all the bruises, sprains, and broken bones. In some ways, I'm . . . I'm glad to finally get my life back. I mean, for more than a decade, I was football's bitch. It told me where to live, where to travel," he said, enumerating the list on his fingers, "what to eat, and even how much to exercise. I'm looking forward to finally planting some roots"—he slapped his firm stomach—"and getting fat while I'm doing it!"

"But what about the *girls*, Cris?"

"What about them?"

"You don't miss the groupies? Hell, even *I* looked forward to your castoffs!"

"You know groupies were never my style, Jamal," Cris said with a laugh.

While his other teammates collected jump-offs like they were Beanie Babies, Cris had always been one of the few monogamous guys on the team. But football didn't make having a serious relationship easy. Because of the pigskin, Cris had had his share of women come and go. The sole exception had been his last girlfriend, Alex—Alejandra Marisol Delgado de la Cruz, according to the business card she proudly brandished to whoever asked. He had met the former Miss Dallas and current marketing executive at an ESPY awards after-party three years ago. Of all his girlfriends, Alex had stuck around the longest.

Most of Cris's exes had hated having him disappear for more than half the year, but Alex had taken flights to games to be with him. She had always put him first. That's why he was shocked when she broke the news that she was not coming with him to Virginia.

She told him only two days after they had finished packing everything they owned in boxes and suitcases that she had too much family and too much going on in the Dallas–Ft. Worth area to just pull up stakes. If he wanted to move halfway across the country, she said, he would have to do it alone.

They would have finally had unhindered time together. She would have finally gotten his full attention, and *now* she wanted them to go their separate ways?

Cris had been disappointed and angered by the news, but he wasn't resentful anymore. Besides, his relationship with Alex had been good, but not perfect. She had a fiery temper. Also, she was beautiful and she *knew* it. Her vanity could get annoying sometimes.

"So is this the great room?" Jamal asked as they left the corridor and stepped through a doorway. Jamal looked around the cavernous space as they descended a series of steps. "Nice. Very nice, man! I'm diggin' it."

The drywall had been finished days ago, the hardwood floors were almost done, and the timber beams had been installed along the ceiling a week before, giving the room the masculine, rugged feel that Cris wanted. A massive stone hearth stood in the center of the room, giving the space the look of an old Viking hall.

Cris nodded and smiled as he gazed up at the ceiling. "Yeah, I like it, too. It turned out good, didn't it?"

Jamal nodded and nudged his shoulder. "You're making some progress, Cris! The place looks hot!" He paused. "But you haven't been cooped up in here every night that you're in town, right? Have you had a chance to look around Chesterton? Walk around Main Street?"

"Yeah, I went out to dinner yesterday. I was going to just pick up something quick, but decided to try one of the restaurants."

"Did you like the food?"

"Oh, yeah," Cris uttered distractedly as he walked over to the fireplace.

Among other things, he thought as he ran his palm over the stone.

For the first time in Cris's life he had enjoyed a meal so much that he felt compelled to praise the chef personally, and later, he was profoundly glad he had. When he'd wandered into the kitchen looking for the chef at Le Bayou Bleu, he had expected to find one of those beefy Cajun chefs you always see on the food channels. Instead, he found a tiny woman (she didn't even reach his shoulder) with a sienna-hued face, huge doelike eyes, and delicate hands that looked better fit for playing the piano or the violin than boning fish. She was certainly pretty—even in her stained chef jacket and jeans—but Cris was surprised by his reaction to her. All lingering thoughts of Alex had finally disappeared.

He had told her that he would come back to the restaurant, and he would, but not just for the food. The petite chef intrigued him. He wanted to know more about her and take it from there.

"Cris? Cris!" Jamal cupped his hands around his mouth.

"Huh?" Cris said, suddenly coming out of his daze. He stepped away from the hearth he had been leaning against, lost in thought.

"You drifted off for a second there, man. You're thinking about her, aren't you?"

Cris did a double take. *Am I that obvious?*

"You gotta let her go, man." Jamal laid a hand on his friend's shoulder. He squeezed it reassuringly. "It's messed up that Alex didn't come with you, but I guess she thought it was the best thing for her. You couldn't force her to come."

"Uh-huh. I know."

He didn't tell Jamal that Alex wasn't the girl he had on his mind right now. He had only met this Lauren woman yesterday. He didn't even know her last name. He wasn't sure whether, if he told Jamal about how intensely attracted he was to her, Jamal would say he was crazy or just going through withdrawal from being away from Alex too long.

"So the only thing you can do is get back out there. Have some fun. Meet some women."

"Oh, don't worry about me, Jay."

I intend to get back out there soon. But for now his desire was intensely focused on one woman in particular and he planned to track her down.

Chapter 6

"That'll be $68.54, Miss Gibbons," the young woman said as she turned away from the electronic screen over the cash register.

Lauren fought the urge to cringe. Even with her bonus card and coupons, her groceries still totaled almost twenty dollars more than she had budgeted. She stared at the bags now in her cart, at the plastic-wrapped boneless chicken and the head of lettuce. She thought she had bought the bare minimum.

There's no way I could have made my list any shorter!

Her electric and phone bills were both due in a few days. She would have to pay those soon and that would definitely put her checking account into overdraft again. That would be another thirty-five-dollar fee.

Lauren bit her bottom lip and dragged her debit card through the scanner. She punched in her password, half expecting the screen to suddenly flash red with the words, "Alert! Alert! Do not accept this broke-woman's money!"

"You know, you're one of ten people in town that do their grocery shopping here at ten thirty in the morning on Wednesdays." The eighteen-year-old cashier smiled as she turned back around to gather Lauren's receipt, which was loudly printing with an automated hiccupping and screeching sound. "And it's always the same people. I guess you guys like to have the store all to yourselves, huh?"

"No, it has more to do with my work schedule," Lauren said, trying her best to sound pleasant despite the knot forming in her stomach. "I work long hours both weekdays and weekends. My boss gives me at least one morning off to do my errands."

"Aww, that's nice of him!" The cashier handed Lauren her receipt. "And here I was thinking you were just trying to stay out of the long lines." The girl laughed and waved. "Have a nice day, Miss Gibbons!"

"You, too, Shana. See you next week." Lauren gave a distracted wave as she stared down at her receipt and scanned the line items. She slowly made her way to the sliding automatic doors, left the air-conditioned store, and walked into steaming heat of the nearly empty parking lot.

Maybe I should finally break down and ask to borrow money from my sisters, she thought. *I can ask for just a small amount of cash to hold me over until my next paycheck, then pay them back.*

But Lauren had decided months ago that she was no longer going to depend on a man to pay her bills and buy her things. No matter how hard it got for her, she wouldn't get another sugar daddy. Unfortunately, whatever money she borrowed from her mother or sisters more than likely came from the pocket of one of their many suitors or ex-husbands. So if she borrowed money from them, she would be breaking her rule. It would still mean dependence on some man's wallet—just vicariously through her sisters.

If I'm going to do this, I'm going to have to do it on my own.

"Even if it means I'm slowly going broke," Lauren muttered.

She sighed before shoving the receipt into the pocket of her jeans shorts. She picked up the pace and quickly steered her cart toward her Toyota Corolla, which she saw in the distance.

Lauren had parked farther away from the store on purpose. She had put on a few pounds in the past few months after giving up her gym membership to save money. She had decided she could exercise instead by climbing steps more often and walking longer distances, a health tip she had read about in a magazine.

She unlocked the trunk of her car and opened it with a loud creak that echoed throughout the parking lot. Lauren then loaded her grocery bags inside and shut the trunk. She glanced at her watch as she returned her shopping cart to one of the lot's cart corrals and estimated that she had enough time to stop at a library and drop off a few books that were dangerously close to being overdue.

"It's not like I need to pay *another* fine."

She unlocked the driver's-side door. Determined to make the best of her day, she started to whistle a tune she had heard on the radio earlier. It raised her spirits a little. She reached for the door handle.

"Hey, beautiful."

At the sound of her ex-boyfriend, James's, syrupy baritone, Lauren instantly froze. Her hand stayed suspended just above the handle. Her leather purse dangled from the crook of her arm. She closed her eyes and took a deep breath to calm her racing heart, which now seemed to be making a valid attempt to pound its way out of her rib cage like a sledgehammer pounding at a steel door.

It's OK, she told herself silently. *He caught you by surprise, but he can't hurt you . . . not anymore. You won't let him. It's OK.*

She heard he had developed the habit of popping up out of nowhere lately. Stephanie said he had surprised her at a house blessing more than a week ago to ask her to "pass along a message" to Lauren. Lauren was none too happy to hear that. It was one thing to harass her, but trying to intimidate her family was something else entirely.

After some seconds, Lauren finally regained her calm and turned to look up at James.

He was wearing a suit, so she guessed he had probably taken a short break from the law office. His facial features were barely discernable against the glare of sunlight behind him, but she could clearly see his bleached-white grin. He stood less than two feet away from her, and his shadow seemed to loom over her like the shadow cast by a towering colossus.

"Hello, James."

He chuckled. "Why so timid, baby?" His grin broadened. "I didn't scare you, did I?"

Oh, you'd just love to hear that you did scare me, you controlling bastard.

"No, James, you didn't. You just surprised me." She pretended to keep her cool as she opened her car door and tossed her purse onto the passenger seat. "How did you know I was here? Were you following me?"

He chuckled again, making her shudder. "Don't

flatter yourself. I just happened to be near here. I saw your car and came over because I had a gift for you." He reached into the inside pocket of his tan suit jacket. "I've been carrying it around all week."

"Is this what you were telling Stephanie about . . . what you had to give me?" Lauren nodded. "Yeah, she told me. She also told me how you manhandled her." She pointed her finger up at him. "I may have let you push me around for two years, James, but if I ever hear of you doing anything like that to one of my sisters again, I'll—"

"Oh, Lauren," he said, cutting her off. "Always full of bluster, aren't you? I really do look forward to giving you these."

She watched cautiously as James pulled out several envelopes.

"Bills." He extended the white stack to her. "Lots and *lots* of bills . . . all addressed to you."

She took the stack. She slowly began to rifle through it.

There *were* several bills there, all from credit card companies and department stores she didn't use or go to anymore. She scanned the totals in the stack: $5,547 here, $9,032 there. These were charges she had made months ago, back when she would make daily trips to Saks Fifth Avenue and Nordstrom before heading to the local spa and later meeting her sisters for lunch.

Lauren gave a dispirited sigh as she stared down at the pile of envelopes. These bills were a reminder of how sad and empty her life had been back then. She had traded so much—her talent, her self-respect, and her *voice*—for what? A six-thousand-dollar purse and a weekly manicure and pedicure?

The bills also reminded her how she was still shackled to her old life by backbreaking debt. After she left James, he had decided to punish her the best way he knew how: with money, or lack thereof. He refused to pay the bills he had footed for so long, and Lauren would have proudly paid them herself . . . if she could afford it. The cards had all been in Lauren's name and now she was nearly eighty thousand dollars in debt. Bill collectors called her apartment constantly. She rarely if ever answered her phone anymore.

It's my own fault, she thought as she continued to stare at the pile of envelopes with disappointment. *I shouldn't have been so careless. I shouldn't have bought things I couldn't afford to pay for myself.*

"I'm surprised they didn't know that you don't live at that address anymore," James said, interrupting her thoughts. "It's been *months* since you moved out. I'm surprised you haven't told them, Lauren."

He was needling her, taunting her just like he did in the old days. But she didn't have to take it anymore. She wasn't going to take it.

"Yeah, well, thanks for bringing these to me." She began to climb inside her car. "Now if you'll excuse me, James. I really have to—"

Lauren stopped midsentence when she felt him grab her forearm. Half of her body was inside the car. Her other foot remained on the parking lot cement.

Her eyes suddenly darted up to his face. She could see all his features now that he was no longer backlit. She could even see the brown freckles on his button nose. James still held his grin, but the smile didn't go past his pink lips. The rest of his face looked angry, *very* angry. His dark brows were furrowed and his eyes had narrowed into thin slits. Veins bulged along his brow.

She recognized this face. It was the precursor to his equivalent of a volcanic eruption.

"Why are you rushing off?" he said with a false lightness. He took a step toward her. "That's not all I had to say. Those bills aren't the only debt you owe, Lauren. Have you forgotten that you owe *me,* too?"

"James, I don't . . . I don't owe *you* anything," she said, fighting to keep her voice calm and not to tease his anger. "What you gave me when we were together were gifts. You never said I had to pay you back."

"Perhaps, but when I gave your sisters or your mother money, that wasn't a gift. Maybe you were paid"—he paused and looked her up and down—"for services rendered, but they weren't. I loaned them money out of the kindness of my heart, because they are *your* family."

James was telling the truth. During the years she had dated him, he had spent liberally on her family, even giving her mother a six-figure loan when she asked for it.

"But they all seem to have forgotten that," he continued. "Where did all the niceness go when I was no longer footing the bill? Now they're rude to me . . . abrupt. So now I want to collect. I want *all* my money back."

She shook her head. "That's not fair. You never stated those terms in the beginning. If you had, they never would have taken it."

"Fair?" He laughed. "Who gives a shit about fair, Lauren? I want my money, but"—he paused, holding up his finger—"I *am* willing to reconsider. I'm willing to forget and let bygones be bygones if . . ."

"If what?"

". . . if you come back to me."

"Why do you want me to come back, James? So you can beat me? *Humiliate me?* "

"So I got angry one night and made a mistake! You made mistakes, too! But I forgave you! I *love* you, Lauren."

"*Love me?* You don't love me! You want to *own* me, but you don't. Find yourself another human punching bag! I'm not going back to you, and I'm not paying you a goddamn dime!"

She tried to tug out of his grasp and climb into her car, but he wouldn't release her. Her heartbeat began to accelerate again as she frantically looked around the parking lot. With the exception of her car and his car, the lot was mostly deserted. If James decided to try something and she screamed, no one would hear her out here, and even if they *did* hear her, it would take them time to get to her. She was on her own.

"Let go of me!" She hoped that her voice wasn't trembling, even though she was a quivering mass inside.

He looked bored by her display of bravery.

"I said, 'Let go!' " She tried to tug her arm away, but to no avail. James's grip only tightened. She winced at the pain in her arm.

"Why do you insist on dragging this out, Lauren? What are you trying to prove? *Huh?* You know if you come back, I'll take care of all of this for you. I'll forget about what Stephanie owes me . . . what your mother owes me. I'll wipe the slate clean. No more bills, and you get your old allowance back. Come on." His voice dropped an octave. "Let daddy make it all go away."

Lauren cringed. She hated when he called himself "daddy."

"Let go of me, James!"

"You can move out of that crappy little basement apartment you rent." He glanced at her dented car. "I'll give you back the keys to my Bentley. Wouldn't you like to drive the Bentley again? Come on, Lauren, this isn't you, honey. You and I both know you weren't meant for the life of a pauper."

"If you don't let go of me, I'm going to scream my head off! Is that what you want? For someone to call the police and for all your friends back at the firm and at the country club to find out the son of a bitch you *really* are?"

He didn't respond.

"On the count of five, I will scream. Do you understand me?"

She could see his jaw tighten.

"One . . . two . . ." She nervously licked her lips. "Three . . . four . . ." She paused, waiting for his hold to slacken, but it didn't. "Five."

Lauren opened her mouth, letting out an ear-piercing screech that made him wince. But no one came. The automatic doors to the grocery store stayed closed. No one drove down the road in her direction. She started to scream again.

"Shut up! Shut up, damn it! Or I'll give you something to yell about!"

He let her go with a hard shove that sent her careening back against the car. Her shoulder slammed into the car door frame.

Lauren's scream caught in her throat. She bit back a moan and swallowed down the pain that now began to radiate across her shoulder and her upper arm. She didn't want to give James the satisfaction of knowing that he had hurt her yet again.

"You *stupid* bitch. You stupid little ungrateful bitch. I loved you. I gave you *everything,*" James said in a low, menacing voice. "Everything you ever needed. Everything you ever wanted. You didn't have to ask or raise a finger. I just *gave* it to you! And this is how you repay me? Huh? By trying to embarrass me? This is the thanks I get?"

He flexed the fingers of his right hand as if preparing to hit her. Lauren stared at the hand not in fear, but in anger.

All his talk about what he had given her. Yes, he had draped her in jewels, but he paired that with a black eye, several cuts, and enough verbal abuse that she couldn't look at her reflection in the mirror without contempt most days.

She wanted to punch *him.* She wanted to make *him* hurt. She wanted to scratch his eyes out, but he was taller than her and stronger than her and she was alone and didn't stand much of a chance of winning this fight. He had lots of power, too. James Sayers pulled a lot of weight in Chesterton. Calling the police would be a mistake. She had learned that lesson before.

Just get in the car, Lauren, she told herself silently. *He hasn't hit you, but don't push it. Just get in the car. Get far away from him.*

She wiped a stray lock of hair away from her face before climbing into her car and shutting the door behind her. She tossed her bills into the passenger seat beside her bag, winced at the pain in her shoulder as she put on her seat belt, and then put her key in the ignition. She didn't look up at James as she shifted the car into drive.

"Go ahead! Go ahead and pull off! Drive your junk heap to that closet you call an apartment and take your mountain of bills with you, because I'm done with you! You hear me? You were nothing when I met you, Lauren!"

She began to ease out of the parking space.

"You were nothing but a gold-digging whore from a long line of gold-digging whores! No brain and no talent to speak of! And what are you now without me? A short-order cook who's damn near bankrupt!" He gave a caustic laugh. "When they repossess your car and evict you, you better not come crawling back to me! Because I'll laugh in your face! You hear me, Lauren? I'll laugh in your face!"

As Lauren put more distance between her and James, his thundering voice began to fade. She drove ten blocks before she realized her hands were trembling. Not just her hands, but her entire body. She pulled over to a nearby curb and put the car in park.

Oh, how she hated him. She hated him for telling her that she was useless and stupid, and she was angry at herself for letting him make her feel like she *had* to listen.

"Hindsight's twenty-twenty, chérie," she could hear Phillip say in that easy way of his, and Phillip was right. Hindsight *is* twenty-twenty. She just wished she had had something remotely close to twenty-twenty vision when she'd first met James, before she racked up eighty thousand dollars of debt in clothes, shoes, purses, and spa treatments. She wished she would have warned her family never to accept money or gifts from

a man like him. If she had better sight back then, maybe she wouldn't be in the predicament she was in now.

She glanced at the bills on her passenger seat, willing them to disappear. But they didn't. They sat there silently mocking her naïveté. Lauren closed her eyes.

"What am I going to do? What the hell am I going to do?"

Chapter 7

"You can put the sofa over there," Cris said as he pointed to one side of the great room.

The two movers nodded before carrying the piece of leather furniture across the cherrywood floors. They did it in a less-than-graceful manner, side shuffling across the room like hermit crabs on a sandbar. They gave loud grunts and occasional curses with each step they took. When they finally put the massive sofa down, it landed with a thud.

"Damn, man, what you got in there?" one of them moaned as he wiped his forehead with the back of his hand. *"Bricks?"*

"No, cement," Cris muttered. "It keeps you from wearing out the cushions."

The young man frowned at Cris. He then looked over his shoulder at the other mover, gazing at him with an expression on his face that seemed to ask, "Have you ever heard of that?"

His companion shrugged in response.

"I'm just joking. It's a regular couch, just a heavy one. And there are two more where that came from." He jerked his thumb toward the doorway. "When you bring them in, you can put them over there, too."

The movers groaned. Their shoulders slumped as they walked back across the room and through the door before heading down the hall.

"I don't know why he hired us to move this stuff," one of them whispered when they were out of earshot. "He's big enough to do it his own damn self."

Cris stood alone in the great room. The house was finally nearing completion. The construction had ended, the painters were finishing touch-up work, and the movers had arrived two hours ago.

It had taken four months, but he was finally near the finish line.

"And it's about damn time," he mumbled.

"Mr. Weaver," someone said over his shoulder. "Where should we put these?"

Cris turned to find a young man in his twenties standing in the great room's doorway, holding up a walnut end table. Another one sat on the floor beside him.

"You can put those in the living room. It's two doors down."

The young man nodded.

Just then, Cris's cell phone began to ring in his pocket. He tugged it out and stared down at the numbers on the screen, squinting to see who was calling him. "Time to get some glasses, old man."

Cris held the screen closer to his face and read the numbers again. His eyes instantly widened. He quickly pressed the green button on the screen to answer.

"Alex?"

"Hey, Cris," she answered in a sexy, throaty voice. "How's Virginia?"

He hadn't spoken to Alex since the night she'd left his house outside of Dallas and told him she wasn't moving to the East Coast with him. Frankly, he hadn't expected to hear from her again.

"Virginia's . . . good. It's hot."

"It's hot here, too, honey." She laughed. "But a lot less hot without you."

He didn't respond.

"I guess I should come straight out and say it." She cleared her throat. "I miss you, Cris. It's been hard being here the past few months without you, *mi amor*."

He cocked an eyebrow.

"Well?" she said, after loudly huffing on the other end of the line.

"Well, what, Alex?"

"Aren't you going to say that you miss me, too?"

No, he thought. Frankly, he'd stopped missing her about a month after he'd moved out here. He had purposely pushed her to the back of his mind. But he couldn't tell her all this. There wasn't enough resentment or heartbreak left in him to be so mean, so he tried to think of a more delicate way to tell her the truth, but he couldn't. He changed the subject instead.

"How're your mom and dad doing?"

"How are my mom and dad doing?" Alex repeated with barely veiled outrage. She huffed again. "Cris, are you kidding me right now?"

"Why would I be kidding?"

"I tell you that I miss you and you ask me how my mom and dad are doing? What the hell is that?"

He was getting the full brunt of her anger now. The

old adage that said all Latin women had fiery tempers was a stereotype, but in the case of Alex, it was also the truth.

"Alex," he said calmly. "The last time I checked, you broke up with *me*. It wasn't the other way around. You haven't called me in months."

"You haven't called me either!"

"And now you call out of nowhere and tell me you miss me. What do you want me to say?"

The line fell silent. After some seconds, she sighed. "I want to come to Virginia, Cris. We should be together. I thought I wanted to stay in Dallas, but I want to be with you out there."

That made him instantly suspicious. "Why the sudden change of heart?"

"It wasn't 'sudden.' I've . . . I've been feeling this way for a while now. Besides, I told you the reason why already. *I miss you!* I want to be with you! Is that so bad?"

He shook his head. "It's not going to work, Alex."

She sucked her teeth on the other end. "Why?"

"Because . . ." Cris stopped.

. . . *I've already moved on,* he thought, but again he kept himself from saying something he believed might hurt her. He wasn't sure why he was being so considerate. She hadn't cared about hurting him that night when she dropped her bombshell and told him not only was she not leaving Dallas with him, but also they "needed to take a break for a while." Despite how crushed he knew he looked that night, she hadn't pulled any punches.

When Cris didn't finish his sentence and the pause on his end of the phone line lasted too long, Alex seized the opportunity.

"I *knew* you didn't have a good reason! You don't have a good reason because you and I both know that we should be together."

"That's not—"

"Just say the words, Cris," she cooed. "Just say the words, baby, and I'll buy a plane ticket right now and be out there tomorrow."

Why wasn't she listening? Didn't she realize that they were over? Did he really seem like that much of a pushover that all she had to do was call him, make a quick apology, whisper sweet nothings into his ear, and things would be back to the way they were before?

I don't think so, he thought indignantly.

"Cris? Cris? You didn't hang up on me, did you?"

He shoved his hand into his pocket and closed his eyes. "Let me think about it."

"What?"

"I said, 'Let me think about it.' Look, I can't say yes to something like that right now, Alex. I'm moving into my house today. I've got guys all over the place asking me questions. I can't . . . I can't make a split decision on this now."

The line went silent. He didn't have to see Alex to know that she was fuming on the other end. He had been with her long enough to know her reaction to those words, but to her credit, she held back her temper and didn't let it show even in the tone of her voice.

"OK, Cris," she said calmly. "You . . . you think about it." He could tell it was like eating glass for her to have to say that. "Give me a call when you're ready to talk."

"All right, I will."

"Bye, Cris. I love you."

"Bye, Alex," he said, purposely avoiding using the "L" word.

He hung up the phone and let out a puff of air he had been holding between his cheeks.

That phone call had been hard. He hadn't expected any visits from ghosts from his past, but one had certainly shown up today. Despite what she had done to him, part of him still missed Alex and wanted to tell her to hop on a flight to Dulles Airport. But another part of him fought that urge. He had to move forward, and letting Alex back into his life wasn't the way to do it. He had plans and he intended to follow them.

"Speaking of plans," a voice said inside his head. "Did you forget the very important thing you planned to do today?"

Cris glanced down at his wristwatch. "Oh, shit." He saw that it was seven minutes to three p.m. The movers would definitely have to pick up the pace if he wanted to have enough time to get to Le Bayou Bleu before the restaurant opened for the dinner rush.

He marched out of the great room with the intent to carry the furniture himself if it would speed this up.

Chapter 8

"Lauren," Paula called across the kitchen as Lauren stepped out of the women's locker room. "There's someone out front lookin' for you."

"Huh?" Lauren shouted over the cacophony of kitchen noise. She tied a black apron around her chef's coat and knotted the strings in the front around her waist. She then adjusted the red bandanna on her head, making sure every loose lock of hair was tucked underneath. "Who's lookin' for me?"

Paula's pink cheeks were smudged with flour. "I have no clue. They just told me to tell you when I saw you that someone's out front waiting." With deft hands, Paula quickly laid bars of chocolate in the center of the dough that would be neatly rolled into croissants. "Check at the maître d' desk."

Lauren's frown intensified. *What's this about?*

She was "raring to go," as Phillip would say—ready to fire up the burners and set her knives flying—and now her afternoon was suddenly being veered off course. The heady anticipation she always felt when she entered the kitchen was being dulled by confusion. She instantly tried to think of whom the guy out front might be, but she drew a blank.

James, maybe?

God, I hope not, she thought. The last encounter she had had with him had been ugly (she still had the bruises on her arm and shoulder to show for it) and, quite frankly, if she went another year without seeing James Sayers again, she would be ecstatic.

Was it a bill collector?

It better not be! She had heard of bill collectors calling people's jobs to harass them about some overdue bill, but she had never heard of one coming to someone's place of work. If it was a bill collector, then he was definitely in violation of the law and she would tell him so. She would also share a few choice words with him about overstepping her line of privacy.

Lauren slowly walked out of the kitchen, leaving the door swinging behind her. She hesitantly rounded the corner and walked toward the dining section, still nervous about whom she might find waiting.

The restaurant hadn't opened yet for the day, so it was mostly empty, with the exception of a few busboys who were preparing the dining tables for the evening crowd. She watched as they neatly set out bread plates, water glasses, and napkins. They painstakingly wiped wrinkles from white linen tablecloths and removed wilted leaves from the flower vases at the center of each table.

Lauren squinted to see if she recognized the tall black man in gray slacks and white button-down shirt who stood up front chatting with Nathan near the maître d' desk. As she drew closer, he turned around and she could see the profile of his handsome face more clearly. Lauren abruptly stopped in her tracks.

It was Cris Weaver; the guy from more than a week ago, the one who had wandered into the kitchen looking for Phillip.

After Cris's promise to come back to Le Bayou Bleu, Lauren had eagerly kept an eye out for him, expecting every night that the ex-football player would step through the kitchen door. But when he hadn't shown up after a week, she felt like a silly girl with a high school crush and gave up. In retrospect, he was probably just being polite when he'd said he would come back to the restaurant. And maybe he *did* come back after all, but just to eat the delicious food, not to flirt with the sous chef.

Lauren had eventually decided it was for the best to not see him again anyway. He would be a distraction she didn't need. She had too many things going on in her life to get sidetracked by falling for some man, she'd resolved.

But all those thoughts faded now as she gazed at him. She could instantly feel the attraction toward him sweep over her with a warm familiarity. Her heart rate increased and the butterflies began to flutter in her stomach. Unfortunately, the same insecurities she'd felt the day they met also came rushing back, sweeping over her. She hastily yanked the ratty red bandanna off her head and finger combed her shoulder-length hair into place with the hope of making herself more presentable. She then glanced down at her chef clothes and decided to give up trying. This wasn't exactly Dolce & Gabbana she was wearing.

Lauren resumed walking toward the front.

He finally noticed her coming toward them. Nathan

followed his gaze and turned to face her. Her knees felt like taffy when Cris smiled.

"Ah, there you are, Lauren!" Nathan said. He followed the greeting with the most fakey grin imaginable. "It seems you have quite a fan of your cooking here. Mr. Weaver asked if he could meet you. I told him you would be happy to." He turned back to face the towering man beside him. "Though, as I mentioned before, Lauren is *only* our sous chef, Mr. Weaver. If you're really interested in meeting the talent behind the operation, you need to talk to Phillip. He's her boss and our executive chef. You missed him last time." Nathan batted his eyes. "He's running a little late, but he should be here in a few minutes. If you'd like to—"

Cris shook his head. "No, this is *exactly* the person I wanted to see." He stared at Lauren openly. She felt her face flush with heat.

"Well . . ." Nathan glanced hesitantly at Cris and then Lauren and back again. "If you say so, Mr. Weaver. I guess I'll . . . leave you two . . . to . . . do"— he cleared his throat—"whatever."

Nathan turned and strode back to the dining room. He began to berate one of the busboys for placing a spotted water glass on one of the tables.

Lauren glanced up at Cris and met his eyes, but she had to break his heated gaze. It was too overwhelming. She shoved her hands into the pockets of her apron and stared at his chest instead.

"It's good to see you again," she said.

"Good to see you, too."

They then fell into an awkward silence that lasted for a good ten seconds.

"I bet they've been keeping you busy here," he ventured. "Every time I drive past this place, it's packed."

Well, if you drove past, why didn't you come in to see me, for God's sake?

"No more busy than usual." She forced a smile, still gazing at his second shirt button, still refusing to meet his eyes. "So how are you enjoying your retirement, Mr. Weaver? Life in Chesterton has to be different from Dallas, especially for a Dallas Cowboy."

"Please, call me Cris. And how did you know that I played for the Cowboys?"

"Oh, you've never lived in a small town before, have you? In a place like Chesterton, news travels at lightning speed. It also helped that they wrote an article about you in the *Chesterton Times.*"

"I didn't know that. I don't see why I'm worth an article in the paper."

"You're the biggest story since we got the new Savings and Loan on Main Street, which tells you somethin'. Things aren't very exciting around here, so whenever there's something or someone remotely new, they practically break out the high school marching band and fireworks."

He laughed and the sound of his laughter made her feel more comfortable. She finally quit staring at his shirt buttons and looked at his face.

"So how can I help you, Cris?"

Her eyes instantly focused on his generous mouth. She wondered what it would be like to kiss that mouth.

"Well . . ." He leaned back against the maître d' counter and crossed his arms over his broad chest. She wondered what it would be like to be embraced by those strong arms. "I have a proposition for you."

Lauren felt the flutter in her stomach again, but she quickly and silently told her nerves to calm down.

"OK." She mimicked his movements, crossing her

arms over her own chest. "And what proposition would that be?"

"Dinner. Sunday. Eight o'clock. Does that work for you?"

Wow! He doesn't waste any time, does he?

Normally, a dinner date would be out of the question with her schedule, but Sunday was one of the few nights of the week that Lauren had off. The restaurant was closed on Sundays. She was definitely free and could probably say yes to his invitation, but something held her back.

Maybe it was his forwardness that had caught her off guard. He was an ex-football player and handsome, after all. Maybe he was used to women responding to him quickly. But now that Lauren's gold-digging days were over, she had decided that any relationship she pursued would have to be done gradually. She wanted to get to know the guy first. Plus, she still wasn't sure if she was ready to start dating again. She still had so much emotional and financial baggage she carried around. Saying yes to a date with Cris now—no matter how much she wanted to, no matter how much she was physically attracted to him—was out of the question.

She hesitated. "Look, Cris, you seem . . . you seem like a . . . very nice guy."

He narrowed his eyes.

"I'm really flattered and I would *love* to go out with you, but now is just . . . well, it just isn't a good time for me. Honestly, I wouldn't be much of a date anyway. I'm working through a few things and . . ." Her words drifted off when he slowly shook his head and held up his hands.

"Wait. Wait. Look, Lauren, I think there's a misunderstanding here."

"There . . . there is?"

"Yeah, I think so." He nodded and gave a half smile. "I wasn't asking you out on a date."

Her stomach plummeted.

"I was asking if you could cater for a small get-together I'm having Sunday night at eight o'clock. The renovations at my house are done for the most part and I wanted to show off the place to a few friends of mine. I was hoping you could cook something for us . . . if that night works for you."

Lauren's cheeks burned. She had never felt so embarrassed in her life. She instantly wanted to disappear or dissolve into a puddle on the floor. She tried her best to recover from the mortification.

"Oh. I'm sorry. I . . . I just thought that . . . That was really stupid of me."

"No, it's OK." His smile widened. "You don't have to apologize. It was a misunderstanding. That's all."

"No, I *should* apologize," she said vehemently, wanting nothing more than to race back into the kitchen and hide in the locker room. "Please forget everything I just said. Let's start over again. Please?"

"No problem. Look, it's late notice, I know. But I want you to cater an event for me. I wouldn't expect anything elaborate; just elegant, simple food with some kick to it. Kind of like what you already do here. You get carte blanche on the menu choices. I'd like three courses. That's my only request."

She shoved her hands back into her apron pockets, unable to meet his eyes again. "You know, if you want someone to cater an event for you, Phillip would be much better at it than me. He's done it before. I've only done it when he supervised."

"I'm sure you could figure it out. I have total confidence in you."

"Look, really, I'm *not* a caterer. I don't have any of my own equipment."

"That's not a problem. I have a commercial-grade kitchen and appliances and the stove has barely been used except when I burned some baked beans." He chuckled. "Tell me what you need and I'll make it happen."

"I don't even have a crew to bring with me." She threw up her hands in exasperation. "It'll be just me and only me. I can't possibly do it by myself!"

"It's only a party of four. How much of a crew do you need for four people?"

"I'm not licensed!"

"So I'll look the other way. Besides, I don't need a framed sheet of paper to tell me that you'll wash your hands and not sneeze in the food."

She closed her eyes. "You just won't take no for an answer, will you?"

"Not if I can help it." He pushed himself away from the maître d' desk and stood at his full height. "Look, if it's an issue of money, I'll pay you plenty for your time and inconvenience. Like I said, I know it's short notice. Will fifteen hundred work?"

She opened her eyes, blinking in surprise. "You mean *dollars?*"

"Yes, dollars." He laughed. "I'm not in the habit of paying in pesos."

"Cris, it's not . . . it's not an issue of money. I told you I can't—"

"Not an issue of money, huh?" he repeated incredulously. "I see. How about two thousand, then?"

She continued to shake her head.

"Twenty-five hundred? *Three thousand?*"

Lauren held up her hands. "Please, stop throwing numbers at me. I'm telling you: *It's not the money!* What you're offering is more than enough—*way more*—but I—"

"Thirty-five hundred," he said firmly, cutting her off. He tugged a checkbook and pen out of his back pocket. He flipped the billfold open and started to scribble on one of its pages. "And not a penny more." He ripped the check from its perforated edge and held it out to her. "We're up to almost nine hundred a plate, Lauren. I'll expect some damn good food for that much money."

She stared down at the check in his hand. He was tossing an insane amount of cash at her to do only one night's worth of work and feed four people? *Why?* Was her food really that good? And like she said, she had never catered alone before. She couldn't vouch that she could produce five-star work in a kitchen she wasn't familiar with, with no line cooks supporting her, and with less than a week's notice.

"But you *do* need the money, Lauren," a voice in her head argued. "Remember that stack of bills you have hidden away at the back of your kitchen drawer? Did you forget about them?"

Lauren pursed her lips. Of course she hadn't forgotten. How *could* she?

Thirty-five hundred dollars wouldn't wipe away all her debt, but it would definitely put her in the right direction. Besides, maybe if she did this dinner and did it well, it could lead to more catering work. She doubted that other clients would be willing to pay $875 a plate, like Cris, but after a year or two, maybe she could raise enough money to whittle away at the more than eighty thousand she owed. She could finally walk away totally from her old life.

"You can do this, girl!" the little voice said. "You're a good cook. Even Phillip thinks you are! Why not get paid for it? It's not like the old days when men threw money at you because they wanted you on their arm or in their bed. Cris wants to use you for your talent, not your body! Why not do it?"

Lauren slowly reached out to him. With some final hesitation, she took the check he extended to her. "OK," she said quietly as she folded the paper and tucked it into her apron pocket. "I'll do it."

He grinned.

"But I have to tell you that you're really horrible at bargaining," she said. "I don't know how they do it in Texas, but when most people around here try to play hardball, they bring the price *down,* not up. I would have done it for fifteen hundred."

"I just know what I want, and I go after it. It doesn't matter how much it costs."

When Lauren met his eyes, her smile faded. She could have sworn she saw a fire flickering in those dark irises again. But she pushed that thought aside. She wouldn't be fooled this time. She had already embarrassed herself by assuming that he was attracted to her and was asking her out on a date. She wasn't about to make that mistake twice.

"Well, give me your number and I'll call later this week and go over a few sample menus. I'll let you choose between them."

"My number's on there." He pointed at the apron pocket that held the folded check.

"Oh." She glanced down at her apron and smiled.

"Of course it is. Well, thank you for the opportunity. I'll give you a call by Thursday." She extended her hand for a shake. "I'll try to come up with something that is the closest I can think of to an $875 plate."

"As long as it tastes good, that's all that matters to me." He then took her hand within his own.

Lauren instantly felt a charge shoot up her arm, like an electric current. Warmth surged throughout her entire body.

You're going to have to get this under control if you're going to work for him.

Lauren shook his hand, ignoring the physical reaction she had to him. "Talk to you then."

She then tried to walk away, but he didn't let go of her. His grasp lingered a few seconds longer.

"I look forward to it," he said quietly, before finally releasing her.

Lauren nodded, turned, and walked away. She made her way down the center aisle of tables and only glanced back over her shoulder when she was halfway to the kitchen. She saw that Cris was still standing toward the front of the restaurant, watching her. Lauren waved. He waved back. She then turned around again and bumped into one of the dinner tables. She cursed under her breath and continued to walk to the kitchen, this time at a faster pace.

Since she'd been thirteen years old, she had been taught to understand men: their thoughts, their desires, and the needs that drove them. But judging from how badly she was reading Cris Weaver, she must not know men as well as she thought. Because she could have sworn he was behaving as if he was attracted to her.

"Wishful thinking," she muttered to herself, pushing the kitchen door open.

Chapter 9

"So what did you tell her?" Jamal asked as he leaned over his plate. His fork hovered inches from his mouth. Fettuccine dangled precariously from its metal tongs.

"What do you mean, what did I tell her?" Cris lowered his water glass.

"What did you say when Alex said she wanted to come out here to Virginia? You didn't say yes, did you? Not after that fucked-up shit she did to you? I know I wouldn't!" He shook his head. "You can't let her walk all over you, man. If you let her back now, she knows she has the upper hand."

"You sure your name is Jamal Simmons and not Dr. Phil? Since when did you start giving love advice?"

"Since you started needing it!"

Cris laughed.

Now that Cris was settled into his new home, he had more free time on his hands. He had already wandered his property at least three times. He had spent a few days swimming laps in his private pool, shooting hoops on his court, watching television, and reading some horror fiction. Needless to say, he was bored, so bored that watching grass grow was starting to sound appealing. For a diversion, he had asked Jamal if he wanted to grab a bite to eat today. Jamal didn't hesitate before saying yes.

"I need to get out of this damn office," Jamal had complained. "You know I slept here one night a week ago? These four walls are driving me crazy, man! It's like I'm in prison with no conjugal visits!"

Cris had laughed. "Well, I can meet up with you for lunch, but you're on your own in trying to get those conjugal visits."

The two were now eating lunch at a small bistro not far from a strip of law offices on Chesterton's Main Street where Jamal worked. The conversation had started with them gossiping about this year's NFL draft. Somehow it had drifted to Cris's last phone conversation with his ex.

"I'm serious, Cris. You said no. Right?" Jamal leaned forward eagerly, dangling his necktie dangerously close to his plate of pasta. "Tell me you said no."

Cris lowered his glass back to the table. "I said I'd think about it."

" *'Think about it'?* " Jamal contemplated his answer. "Well, I guess that's better than saying yes. But to me, there's nothing to think about. She made her bed. Let her lie in it."

"I know. It's just . . . Jay? *Jay?* "

Cris shook his head in bemusement as his friend's attention was suddenly drawn to a curvy waitress. Jamal's eyes lingered on her backside as she passed their table. Her plump bottom moved brusquely back and forth as she walked across the room holding a heavy tray of veal parmesan and spaghetti with meat-balls over her head.

When she felt Jamal's heated gaze on her rear end, she turned around to look at him. He smiled and gave her a wink. She rolled her eyes and continued her purposeful strides to a nearby table of diners. Deflated, Jamal returned his focus to Cris.

And he's giving me love advice? Cris thought with amusement.

Jamal cleared his throat. "You were saying?"

"I was saying that I wasn't expecting her to call. I wasn't expecting her to say we should get back together either. She caught me off guard. The most I could say was that I'd think about it. I didn't want to do anything I would regret later."

"What's to regret? *She* left *you,* man! Don't tell me you're still stuck on that chick."

"No, I've already moved on. I told you that."

"So prove it."

"What? How do you propose I do that?"

"I've got an invite to this party in DC tomorrow night. It's one of those clubs downtown. I've been looking forward to this all damn week! I went there last year. This place was *crazy!* There's gonna be some hot mamacitas there. I'm telling you, man! It's wall to wall with beautiful women. It's like you've died and gone to heaven. I'm serious!" Jamal nodded. "So you're coming out with me? You wanna see what I'm talking about? I bet you could get in there and make me proud!"

Cris shook his head.

"Oh, come on, man! You've got to!"

"Jay, I am getting too damn old to go clubbing. I

hate the loud music and sweaty people. Besides, I can't do it anyway."

Jamal grumbled and shoveled another forkful of pasta into his mouth. "You can't do it or *won't* do it? I told you that you weren't over Alex!"

"This has nothing to do with Alex. I *can't* do it because I've . . . I've got a date."

Jamal dropped his fork back to his plate. *"What?"* Bits of fettuccine and shrimp flew from his mouth. The alfredo sauce splattered his chin. He quickly wiped his face with his white dinner napkin.

"You really need to wear a damn bib."

"You holding out on me, man?" Jamal asked, ignoring his friend's comment. "You've finally taken off the shackles? Why didn't you say anything? I'd expect at least a text message when you finally broke down and asked a woman out! So you got a date, huh?"

"Well, yeah . . . kinda."

" 'Kinda'? What do you mean, 'kinda'? Either you do or you don't!"

"She . . . doesn't know it's a date. I asked her to cater for a small party tomorrow night, an intimate dinner. She doesn't know that the party will be just me and her."

Cris didn't like to play games, but he had to make an exception in this case. He had held off for a week or so going back to Le Bayou Bleu, not wanting to seem too eager when he asked Lauren out. But by the time he'd finally decided to go back and talk to her, he was nervous with anticipation and eager to get it over with. He had planned to ask her on a date as soon as he saw her, but when he witnessed her response—how surprised and flustered she was—he knew instantly that he would have to backtrack. He had tried to avoid it, but unwittingly, he had still come on too strong. So he'd quickly made up the story about the dinner party. He figured that it would give him the chance to lay the groundwork with her more slowly next time.

"*Very* nice." Jamal slowly nodded his head. "All right, man. You handle your business. I hope it works." He started to eat again. "So she's a caterer, huh? Is her business in Chesterton?"

"She's not really a caterer; more of a chef."

"Uh-huh." Jamal sampled another forkful of his meal. Jamal certainly wasn't the prettiest of eaters. "A chef where? Do I know the place?"

Cris took another drink from his water glass. "At the Bayou Bleu on Broadleaf."

"The Bayou Bleu? Are you sure, man? Le Bayou Bleu's chef isn't a woman. I thought Phillip Rochon was the head chef over there. You gotta have the wrong place."

"No, it's the right one. She's his sous chef. Her name's Lauren."

Jamal stopped midbite. "Lauren?" His eyes widened to the size of quarters. *"Not* Lauren Gibbons. Not *that* Lauren!"

Cris frowned at the thread of alarm he detected in Jamal's voice. "Yeah, Lauren Gibbons. Why?"

Jamal's fork dropped back to his plate with a loud clatter, drawing the attention and stares of other bistro patrons. The annoyed waitress whom Jamal had smiled at earlier now glared at them.

"Oh, *no!* No, no, no!" Jamal waved his hands in front of his chest like he was waving down a speeding truck. "You can't do it, Cris! I should have warned you as soon as you moved into town! Trust me; you don't want to do this!" He pointed at Cris. "You got your cell phone on you?"

Cris glanced down at his jeans pocket. His phone was inside its denim compartment. "Yeah, of course I do. Why?"

"Good! Call her now and tell her your party is canceled. Do whatever you've got to do, just don't put yourself alone in a room with her!"

"Jay, what the hell are you talking about?"

"Lauren is a *Gibbons girl!* If you want to keep your wallet and the clothes on your back," he said as he pointed at Cris's T-shirt, "you don't want to mess with them! Don't let the nice face and tight body fool you! They've got a well-earned reputation around here. Any man with a brain in his head knows to keep at least fifty feet between him and one of those Gibbons gold diggers at all times!"

"Gibbons gold diggers? Did you come up with that all by yourself?"

"Oh, don't laugh, man! I'm telling you. If you mess with her, you're messin' with trouble. All they see in men are dollar signs. They've been like that for decades."

Jamal leaned across the table, motioning for Cris to lean forward, too. Amused, Cris appeased Jamal by meeting him halfway over the tabletop.

"I heard that a few of their ex-husbands have even met their maker under 'mysterious circumstances' while they were married to them," Jamal whispered gravely, making air quotes with his fingers. "The sheriff's office has never said that it was foul play, but nobody around town is convinced none of those girls had anything to do with it."

"And I guess you think they killed them?" Cris asked, holding back a sardonic smile.

"I can't say for sure, but . . . hey, you never know!"

Cris leaned back in his chair. "So she's going to steal my money *and* kill me. All because we went on one date?"

"It always starts with just one date, Cris! Then she invites you over for dinner. The next thing you know, she's your baby mama and you're paying her ten thousand a month. Year after year, you're giving her money. Finally, you're *broke* and you can't pay her anymore. What happens next? She gets pissed off, calls up some big dude named Tiny, and you're six feet under!"

At that, Cris broke into laughter. He held his stomach because it was beginning to ache from laughing so hard.

"It's not funny, man!"

"Yes, it is, Jay! Look, thanks for the warning. Really. But Lauren doesn't seem like a cold-blooded killer."

"I didn't say *she* was the killer! She'll get Tiny to do it!"

"And she certainly doesn't seem like a gold digger either."

Jay rolled his eyes. "Oh, what do you know, man?"

"Believe me, I know."

After all, Cris *had* been a professional football player for almost fifteen years. He had come across his share of groupies and gold diggers. Their type trolled the sidelines of every open practice. They finagled their way into the VIP sections of clubs where the players celebrated after a win. If they couldn't smooth talk their way past the velvet rope, they sometimes bribed the bouncers with money, even naked photos of themselves. He could spot them at thirty paces: They had the same perfect bodies, fake hair, overwhelming perfume, and tight clothes with a push-up bra and thong to match. They came in all shades and were of every imaginable nationality. Cris's father had warned him about them back in high school and Cris had been smart enough to keep them at a distance for all of his college football career and during his time in the NFL. Whenever he saw them, alarm bells went off in his head.

"Danger! Danger, Will Robinson!" he'd mutter whenever one of them tried to slip him their phone numbers.

But he hadn't heard those alarm bells with Lauren. She hadn't clawed at him. She hadn't seemed eager to get his attention with big boobs and a smile. She was quiet and proud, reserved and earnest. The fact that she wasn't constantly trying to win him over turned him on. She was beautiful, but more important, she was *real.*

What Jamal was saying about her sounded like nothing more than small-town gossip, in Cris's opinion. In the short time that he had lived in Chesterton, Cris had realized that it was a beautiful place, but it also had its downside. The secluded enclave seemed a bit elitist at times. In small towns, someone had to be the odd man out, and it looked like Lauren and her family had been chosen for that role. He wasn't surprised. A family of unattached, attractive women *would* make lots of people uncomfortable. They had to smear them somehow, and calling them a bunch of gold-digging black widows would certainly do the trick.

Jamal opened his mouth in protest, but Cris quickly shook his head.

"I can't speak for all of the Gibbons girls," he conceded before Jamal had the chance to argue, "but Lauren *specifically* does not come off like a gold digger to me. She knows who I am, Jamal. If she's really that concerned about what's in my wallet, I wouldn't have had to trick her to get her to go on a date with me. I had to do a lot of fast talking to get her to agree to cater my party! Wouldn't she have come on to me *first* if she was trying to get my money?"

"What can I say? She's got crazy skills."

Cris realized that he wasn't going to win this argument.

"They're the Jedi Knights of gold digging, Cris! Can't you see that? Lauren knows how to use reverse psychology to make you think *you* were the one who asked her out, but really she was after you all along." Jamal tapped his forehead with his index finger. "I had to go to law school to learn how to win people over, but she's been learning this stuff her whole damn life! That's how they work! They mess with your *head,* man!"

Cris slowly rose from the table. "There isn't much in your head to mess with. Look, I've gotta get going. I've—"

"Cris, if you don't believe me, talk to her last boyfriend, then. His name's James Sayers. He's always seemed like a good guy to me, and he's well respected around here. One of his law offices is on Main Street. Ask him what he thinks about Lauren."

"Yeah, that sounds like a perfect idea. I'm going to ask her ex-boyfriend if she's a gold digger. I'm sure he'll be totally honest and unbiased. Why didn't I think of that myself?"

"Why not? You're not even gonna try?" Jamal exclaimed with disbelief. "You mean you're still going to go out with her after everything I told you?"

"Rumors are not facts, Jay. All you have are a bunch of rumors about her. I'm not going to cancel a date over that." He slapped two crisp twenty-dollar bills on the table. "That should cover our lunch."

"I'm warning you, man," Jamal called after him as Cris made his way through the restaurant. "That way lays suffering and pain! Get out while you still can!"

Cris laughed as he continued to slowly shake his head.

Chapter 10

"*Mmmm,*" Hank said, licking his lips as he slowly let his gaze trail over Stephanie. "You look good enough to eat."

One of the "Jedi Knights of gold digging" stood in her doorway, giving Hank her best sultry pose, flexing her Jedi skills. For tonight's date, Stephanie had worn a skintight black halter dress with a plunging neckline and an open back. Her long hair was swept up, showing off the diamond and opal pendant necklace and chandelier earrings.

"Why, thank you, Hank." She patted his shoulder and smiled as she stepped through the door. "If you play your cards right at dinner tonight, maybe you'll get to have me for dessert."

His eyes widened. She shut her front door behind her, locked it, and walked toward his car, which was parked at the curb, leaving Hank gaping and panting as he watched her.

Forty-five minutes later, they walked arm in arm into one of the best restaurants in the city. It was a supper club nestled on K Street, where Washington, DC's movers and shakers liked to play and talk business. Stephanie was impressed. A place like this usually had a long waiting list. How had Hank managed to get them a table?

I guess he's just got it like that, Stephanie thought as they strode toward the maître d' desk, excusing themselves through the throng of people who huddled near the door waiting anxiously for a table to come open.

Thank God she had decided to focus on Hank instead of Cris Weaver. Her sisters were still trying desperately to track down the ex-NFL player, just like about half of the other single women in Chesterton. Meanwhile, Stephanie was about to enjoy a five-star meal with the handsome deacon.

"I have a seven o'clock reservation for two," he said to the blond gentleman who stood at the lacquered desk. "The last name is Montgomery."

The maître d' glanced at the electronic screen in front of him, scanned a few names, and smiled. "Yes, we have you right here, Mr. Montgomery." He handed two leather-bound menus to a tall, thin woman who stood beside him.

The hostess tilted her head and grinned. "Please follow me."

They were escorted across the dining room to one of the booths toward the back.

Not one of the best tables in the house, but far from the worst, Stephanie thought. They could be stuck near the kitchens.

The din in the restaurant was pretty loud. The conversations, laughter, and clinking of utensils and glasses created a steady wall of sound. Every table was filled with people. Even the bar was crowded.

Hank stepped aside to let Stephanie slide into the semi-circular booth first. He climbed in beside her. The woman handed them their menus.

"A waiter will be with you shortly," she said, before turning around and leaving them alone.

"I'm going to have a hard time focusing on food with you looking as good as you do," he said, huddling close to Stephanie.

Stephanie removed her linen napkin from her plate and draped it over her lap. "And *I'm* going to have a hard time concentrating with you smelling as good as you do. I love your cologne."

"Thanks."

Their waiter arrived soon after, bringing sparkling water and taking their dinner and wine orders. Over their meal, Stephanie learned a little bit more about the deacon. Not only was he a deacon at one of the biggest churches in the county, but he also owned several retail businesses: a few based in Georgia and one he had just started in Virginia. He still owned a residential property in Georgia.

"I left it furnished just in case I decide to rent it out. It'll mean buying all new things for whatever place I decide to buy in Chesterton. Unfortunately, everything I own is still back at the house in Sugarloaf," he said between bites of his scallops.

"Everything except the dogs," she corrected, making him frown.

"What dogs?"

She lowered her fork and smiled. "Your two Jack Russell terriers. . . . *remember?*"

"Oh!" He laughed. "Yeah, I took them with me. Those little guys couldn't be left behind."

Finally, the conversation made it around to Hank's "wish list."

"So," he said, pushing his plate aside. He opened his suit jacket and pulled out a folded white sheet of paper from one of his pockets. "I made a list of what I'm looking for . . . like you asked."

Stephanie finished chewing the last of her snapper and wiped her mouth with her napkin. "Hand it over. Let me see."

He gave an impish smile and handed her the sheet.

She unfolded it and scanned the itemized list.

"Five bedrooms," she read aloud, "an in-home theater . . . pool . . . four-car garage . . ." She looked up at him and smiled. "All of that's doable as long as you're willing to spend a pretty penny to get it, honey." She continued reading. "Fireplace . . . spanking me until I come . . ."

Her voice trailed off. She raised her eyebrows, trying her best to mask her shock as she continued to read the rest of Hank's list. Oh, the deacon was one dirty bunny! She had never read a list that included so many four-letter words; mentions of lube, leather, and whips; and references to positions she was sure would require both of them to see a chiropractor afterward.

When she was done, she handed the sheet of paper back to him.

"So do you think you can get me everything I asked for?"

The impish smile hadn't left his face.

Stephanie raised her wineglass to her lips and languidly sipped, to buy herself some time before she answered him.

Frankly, she didn't know if she could be quite kinky enough to fulfill *all* the deacon's fantasies, but she could bluff and act her way through most of it . . . well, maybe half of it. Maybe she'd get lucky and he'd just forget the rest.

"Have you been to the doctor lately, Hank?"

"No. Why?"

"Because you might wanna get a checkup to see that you're healthy. Wouldn't want you to drop dead during the night I'm about to give you."

He grinned. "Is that so? So my list didn't scare you?"

She lowered her glass back to the table and turned toward him, meeting his gaze. "Do I look scared?"

"Some women are a little intimidated by my . . . my tastes. You know?"

Is it the request that she put you in a dog collar and give you a ball gag, or is it the reference to the orgyfest that sends them running, Hank?

"You're the one who should be intimidated. You might not be able to keep up with *me.*"

"Oh, is that so?"

"Yes, it is."

She then leaned toward him and kissed him. When she did, he practically leaped at her.

Hank was all tongue and all hands. She had heard of strong kissers, but this man practically sucked the breath out of her! When she felt his hand climb underneath the hem of her dress, she knew she had to put on the brakes . . . *fast!* Kinky deacon was about to get them thrown out of the restaurant.

Stephanie wrenched her mouth away and pushed against his chest.

"I like my men eager, Hank, but save some for later. OK?" she said, breathing hard.

He looked at her hungrily, then slowly nodded.

On that note, Stephanie decided this would be a perfect time for a bathroom break. She would give Hank a chance to simmer in his manly juices. Leaving a man wanting more would only build further anticipation.

"I have to powder my nose, sweetheart. I'll be right back." She smiled and scooted across the other side of the leather seat and out of the booth.

"I'll be waiting."

She rose from the table, adjusted the hem of her dress, and made sure to put a little shimmy in her walk as she crossed the restaurant and headed to the ladies' room. Even with how hot under the collar Hank already seemed to be, she wanted to give him a view that would further raise his temperature.

Stephanie used the bathroom and checked her makeup and hair one final time in the mirror before tucking her clutch underneath her arm and walking back into the restaurant. As she neared their table, a familiar baritone voice boomed behind her.

"Stephanie! What a coincidence! What are you doing here in the city?"

You've gotta be kidding me, she thought with exasperation.

She slowly turned on her heel to find James gazing down at her. This man was starting to become a real pain in the ass! She had run into him more in the past couple weeks than she had in a whole year. If she didn't know any better, she would have sworn that he was running into her on purpose, but even he couldn't be *that* crazy.

"I was just having dinner with some business associates when I saw you." He strolled toward her and pointed across the room at a table where several men sat. Of course, it was one of the best tables in the house. "Are you enjoying dinner here, too? Got tired of sampling the overpriced fare at your sister's restaurant?"

Stephanie took a slow breath and pasted on a polite smile. "I'm sorry, but I'm busy right now, James. I don't have time for chitchat."

"Ah." He laughed and nodded. "I get that response a lot lately from the women in your family. But see, you *are* going to make the time to talk to me."

She crossed her arms over her chest. "And why is that?"

"Because," he said, leaning toward her. "I hold all the cards, Stephanie."

She squinted, having absolutely no clue what he was talking about. Why did James insist on talking like a James Bond villain?

"Cards? What cards?"

"I'm talking about money that you owe me . . . that *all* of you owe me. Your sister didn't tell you about our little conversation?"

Stephanie didn't answer. She was too stunned to respond.

He sighed. "I guess not. Well, I explained to her that I haven't forgotten the money that I gave to you, your mother, and your other sisters. And frankly, my goodwill and patience have run out. I want my money back."

Oh, hell, no! Is this asshole trying to shake me down in the middle of a five-star restaurant?

"I didn't know you were keeping receipts all that time, James."

"I didn't need to." He tapped his forehead. "The totals are all in here."

She rolled her eyes. "Well, why don't you just save the suspense and spit out the total like the cash machine that you are. I'll write you a check, we can both go back to our tables, and you can leave me the hell alone."

His smile withered.

"Name your price."

"Fine. Nine thousand dollars."

She gaped. *"Nine thousand dollars?* Are you joking?"

When on earth did she borrow nine thousand dollars from James? Was he counting every time he bought her a drink . . . every time she turned on a light or flushed a toilet in his home?

"That's just crazy! I'm not paying that!"

"Well, that's your prerogative. We could always settle it in a courtroom. If you'd rather pay a lawyer that amount, only to lose in the long run, that's up to you."

Now he was threatening to sue her? *What the hell?*

Nine thousand dollars meant nothing to James. It was the proverbial drop in the bucket compared to how much wealth he had. Hell, he could spend that much in a weekend! But it meant a lot more to her bank account, and he knew it.

You petty son of a bitch.

Yes, it was petty, but she wasn't sure if she wanted to tangle with him in the courtroom. The judge might not see things her way, especially since James was golf buddies with half of the district and circuit court judges in the county. He was right. If he did go through with his threat to sue her, she'd probably lose. Then she'd be short not only nine thousand dollars but another few thousand in legal fees.

Inwardly, Stephanie fumed, but she wouldn't give

James the satisfaction of seeing her go off in public. She wouldn't make a scene, even if she yearned to scream a full-on opera. Instead, she would play it cool and casual.

Stephanie walked toward the restaurant bar and politely tapped the shoulder of one of the men who was sitting hunched on the stools, nursing a Scotch.

"Excuse me, sir. Could I just squeeze in and use a spot on the counter for a second."

He raised his gaze from his glass. At first the man looked irritated at being disturbed, like he was going to say "no." But when he turned and saw her standing behind him, he looked up and down and smiled. "Sure, go right ahead."

Stephanie opened her purse and pulled out her checkbook and a gilded pen. Her stomach turned. Her hand shook as she wrote out the amount. She couldn't see him, but she could almost feel James smiling arrogantly behind her. It took all her willpower not to turn and hurl the checkbook at his fat head.

A few seconds later, Stephanie signed and handed him the check. "I want something from you in writing, a note confirming that all my debts to you are settled."

"Sure, I can do that . . . as soon as the check clears. This will clear, won't it?" he asked smugly, gazing down at her check. "I don't have to worry about it bouncing?"

That was it. She wasn't going to swallow down her anger anymore.

"Go to hell, James," she snapped. "And make sure this is the last time you contact me about what I *supposedly* owe you . . . the *last* goddamn time! I don't want to hear from you. I don't want to just happen to run into you again. If you continue to harass me, I'll—"

"You'll what?" he challenged, lifting his chin. He snickered. "Call the cops? Have me thrown in jail?"

She grinned. "No, I'll just let it slip to the biggest gossips in Chesterton that little problem that you have." She glanced down at his crotch. "You know . . . that limp dick you've got . . . that *little itty bitty* problem you have keeping it up," she said, holding thumb and forefinger together to emphasize just how small he was.

James's smile disappeared. His face instantly flushed bright red.

"Not all men can take a little blue pill. I heard you had a bad allergic reaction to it. Kind of put a damper on your sex life, huh? And Lauren said the times you *did* manage to get it up, you guys were usually done in five minutes flat." She laughed. "Way to show a lady a good time, James!"

"You cunt," he muttered between clenched teeth. He looked beyond furious. "You fucking bitch. I should—"

"I'll *also* share other choice details about you that Lauren told me, details I'm sure you'd be pretty embarrassed for everyone else in town to hear."

A vein bulged along his temple.

"That's right, James. I've got a few cards of my own. So stay away from me. Stay the hell away from my sister. Leave me and my goddamn family alone. OK?"

Stephanie could tell by the expression on his face that if they weren't in a busy restaurant, if they were alone, he would hurt her. He'd probably come close to killing her. But James would never show his rage in public. He was all about the image. That's why she knew her threat to share his embarrassing little secrets would keep him in check.

"You have a nice night now," she said airily.

She then walked around him and back toward her table. She didn't look back.

Hank gazed at her. He had probably been watching the whole conversation unfold.

She scooted onto the leather seat beside him.

"Now, where were we?" she whispered with a smile, linking her arm through his and leaning toward him.

He didn't return her smile, but remained tight-lipped instead. "Who was that?"

"No one. He's just . . . just an acquaintance." She lightly kissed Hank's lips. "Don't worry about it, baby. Now back to that list of yours. Instead of doing everything on it, would you settle for maybe ten line items?"

She watched in dismay as he tugged his arm out of her grasp.

"OK, how about fifteen?"

"I saw him talking to you at the Baylors the other day, too," Hank said, bringing the topic back to James. "Is he an ex or something?"

She sighed and finished the rest of the wine that was left in her glass. "No, my sister's ex . . . and an annoying one at that." She placed her hand on his leg and rubbed the inside of his thigh. "But that doesn't mean he has to ruin *our* fun, does it?"

Hank removed her hand and loudly cleared his throat. "I think we should . . . we should cut our date short tonight."

"But why? *Because of James?* I told you that he's my sister's ex. Not mine! Believe me! He won't bother—"

"No. No, I . . . I got a call while you were in the

ladies' room. Something's . . . come up. I need to take
care of it."

"Something's come up? You mean something's
wrong? Do you need to—"

"Nothing's wrong. It's nothing serious. I should just
take care of it, which is why I have to leave earlier than
I planned."

"Oh," she said, now deflated.

Hank waved down their waiter who passed their
table. "Can we have the check, please?"

Stephanie slumped back against the booth's cushion
and sighed. James had obviously scared Hank off. So
now she was not only short nine thousand dollars, but
she had also lost the interest of sexy Deacon Montgomery.

Damn, she thought. And she already had her leather
bondage outfit planned out.

Hank pulled in front of her house less than half an
hour later, making amazing time on the Beltway and
Dulles toll roads. He had to break the speed limit and
zip between cars to get back to her place so fast. He
claimed that whatever he had to get to wasn't an emergency, but he certainly wasn't acting like it.

She hoped, as he walked her to the door, that maybe
she could salvage the date with a good-bye kiss—
something to remind him of the hot and steamy potential they had shown earlier. The right kiss could make
him come back for more. Maybe they could try for another date next week.

When they mounted the last step on her concrete
walkway, she turned to him and smiled.

"Well . . ." she said.

"Well . . ." he echoed.

She walked toward him and toyed with one of his

suit lapels. "I had a nice time tonight. I'm sorry you have to leave so early." She gave an exaggerated pout.

"I am, too, but . . . duty calls."

She slowly linked her arms around his neck and leaned toward him, preparing to plant on his lips the sultriest, wettest kiss she could muster. But suddenly he darted his mouth in the other direction, avoiding her lips. He kissed her cheek with a light, almost brotherly peck. She blinked in surprise.

"Gotta go," he said, before abruptly tugging her arms from around him, turning on his heel, and racing back to his car.

She stood in front of her door dumbfounded as she watched him pull off less than a minute later.

"Damn it," she muttered, stomping her foot in frustration.

Chapter 11

"Should I . . . should I start plating the entrées?" Lauren asked. She turned from the stove, wiped her hands on a dishcloth, and faced her first new client, the ex-Dallas Cowboy/millionaire Cris Weaver.

He had been standing about ten feet behind her for the past hour and a half, observing her while she cooked. He said he wanted it to be part of the evening: Lauren doing her kitchen voodoo while everyone else at the party watched her work, like they were watching a show.

Whatever, she had thought flippantly on the phone as he made his request. *You're the one writing the check, sweetheart. Short of me wearing a thong bikini while I'm cooking, I'm game for just about anything at this point.*

Her casual attitude disappeared, though, when she realized *he* would be staring at her the whole time she cooked. Knowing his dark eyes were on her had been unnerving, but miraculously she had managed to not burn herself or set his kitchen on fire.

"Or I can hold off serving the entrées for a bit . . . until your guests arrive. The meat shouldn't dry out if you want to wait." She shrugged her shoulders. "It's up to you."

Cris propped his elbow against the kitchen island's granite countertop, shifted on his leather stool, and took a sip of red wine. "No, you can go ahead if it's done. I have no idea when they'll get here. I might as well start without them." He grinned. "The food smells too good not to eat."

He certainly was in good spirits for a man who was throwing a party and not one guest had shown up.

If it was me, I'd be pissed, Lauren thought as she glanced at the two porcelain platters covered with appetizers. Most of them—dates wrapped in applewood bacon and stuffed with blue cheese, deviled eggs filled with crabmeat ravigote, and white pork boudin balls—still sat untouched. It looked like the price of his dinner was quickly escalating from $875 a plate to $3,500 a plate with every minute that guests didn't arrive. She felt bad for the guy.

Lauren pursed her lips. "All right. Well, I guess you can go ahead and sit at your dinner table. I'll bring the food to you in about two minutes."

"You're serving me, too?"

Lauren opened his oven to reveal a bubbling pan filled with pork chops. The room suddenly filled with the food's intoxicating aroma. "Sure, why not? You're paying a lot of money for this." She used both ends of the dish towel to tug the pan out of the oven without burning her hands. She set it on the stove top. "I may as well give you the full service, right?"

"*Really?* And what does the 'full service' include exactly?"

At those words, the hairs started to prick on the back of her neck. A delicious thrill went down her spine.

She looked over her shoulder at him. She could have sworn he was flirting again. She thought she heard laughter in his voice, but she pushed that thought aside when she saw that he was gazing at her innocently.

Stop projecting, Lauren. He's not attracted to you.

"Plating, serving, wine refill, and cleanup," she said flatly in response. "At least, that's what I would call full service."

"I see. Well, I guess I'll wait for my full service in the dining room."

He stood from his stool, taking his glass of red wine with him. Lauren watched as he walked out of the kitchen and rounded a corner.

This is really strange, she thought as she placed a dinner plate on the countertop beside the oven.

Cris must be the mellowest guy in the world. He didn't seem at all phased at the idea of eating a dinner for a housewarming party by himself. She hadn't even seen him check his cell phone or voice mail to see if people had called to say they would be late.

I guess he's used to it, she thought with a shrug as she grabbed some tongs and began to arrange pork chops on the plate. *If I were him, though, I'd get a new set of friends.*

Minutes later, Lauren carried an entrée into Cris's dining room. It was a massive space, but he had turned down the overhead lights and lit candles in candelabras at both ends of the table, filling the dining room with a soft orange glow that made it feel smaller, more intimate. With the white tablecloth, candles, and crystal stemware, she would even venture to call the space romantic, but Cris looked rather lonely sitting at the head of the table all by himself.

"Here's your dinner." She placed the plate in front of him. She glanced at his now-empty wineglass. "Would you like more wine?"

He smiled. "Yes, please."

Lauren leaned forward and reached for a bottle of merlot. She slowly poured the wine into his glass, feeling his gaze on her as she did it. He was making her nervous again. Her hands began to tremble and the palms grew moist. The neck of the bottle bobbed in her shaking hands, spilling wine over the side of the glass and onto the tablecloth.

Her cheeks flushed with heat. "God, I'm so sorry."

"It's OK. It'll wash out. That's what bleach was invented for."

She looked around the empty table. "I'm really sorry about your guests. I hope they're all OK."

"They're just missing out on an incredible dinner." After taking a sip from his glass, Cris leaned down to smell his dish. He shook open a napkin and tossed it over his lap.

"Mmm, smells good." He licked his lips. "What did you say this was again?"

"Well, these are herb-brined pork chops." She proudly pointed down at the dish. "It's served with a sweet pea and corn succotash and baked fingerling potato compote."

"That sounds like a mouthful."

"And hopefully it tastes like a mouthful." She smiled before turning to walk out of the dining room. "Please, enjoy," she said over her shoulder.

"Uh, Lauren?"

She stopped halfway down the dining room table and turned back around to face him. "Yes?"

"I really don't think my other guests are going to make it here tonight. There's a lot of good food that's going to be left over from this and I can't eat all of it by myself. I'd hate for this to go to waste. Would you like to join me?"

He looked up at her with that kind face and pleading eyes and she knew it would be nearly impossible to say no to him.

She hesitated while furrowing her brows. "Are . . . are you sure?"

His smile widened. "Of course, I'm sure. Make yourself a plate and pull up a chair." To illustrate his point, he pulled out the chair closest to him and patted the upholstered cushion. "You're my guest tonight."

Lauren laughed until tears almost ran down her cheeks as she finished the last of the raspberry chocolate mousse in her soufflé cup.

She hadn't expected to find herself laughing when they started eating dinner. Their meal began awkwardly, with her so nervous she could barely chew her food. But by the time they started eating dessert, she was completely at ease.

She sat next to Cris with one leg tucked underneath her bottom. The buttons of her chef jacket were open, revealing the white tank top she wore underneath.

"So Mark's screaming at the top of his lungs and he's standing on top of the bench and damn near climbing on top of the lockers trying to get away from this gerbil, right," Cris said, continuing his story. "I'm standing there with my mouth open because I had no idea he was going to lose it like that. I mean, it's some fan's pet gerbil. It wasn't like it was a cougar or a bear or somethin'."

Lauren held her stomach and continued to laugh as she shook her head. "There is no way he was *that* scared!"

"I swear that's exactly what he did." Cris was laughing himself. "The only way we could get him down was to take the gerbil out of the locker room. And even then it took him a good twenty minutes to calm down. I mean, he's a big dude: six foot five, three hundred twenty pounds. He has half of the quarterbacks in the NFL shaking in their shoes when they see him comin' for them on the field, but put a gerbil in front of him and he's not so big and bad anymore." Cris shook his head. "We never let him live that one down. He kept finding stuffed toy gerbils in his locker for the next two seasons."

Lauren giggled. Her laughter began to slowly taper off as Cris resumed eating his mousse.

"This is some good stuff," he said with a mouthful of dessert as he pointed down at his cup with his spoon.

"Glad you like it." She tilted her head. "Cris, can I ask you something?"

He looked up from his cup and nodded. "Of course."

"Is there any reason why you spell Cris without an 'h'?"

He gave a knowing smile, as if he had heard this question before.

"I mean, if you don't mind me asking. I know as a people we can get pretty creative with our name spellings. I was just wondering about yours."

"Well, Cris is short for Crisanto. A lot of guys have

that name back in the Philippines where my mom's from. I just shortened it."

"Why?"

"Never liked it much," he said with a casual shrug. "Besides, when you're growing up in a neighborhood with guys named Tyrone and Hakeem, Crisanto stands out for all the wrong reasons. You know? I thought Cris sounded better . . . cooler."

"Crisanto," she repeated softly, letting the word slide off her tongue. She then gave a thoughtful nod. "I think it's nice. I like it. It sounds very exotic."

"It just sounds better when *you* say it."

Their eyes met again and Lauren felt the temperature rise in the echoing dining room. A thought suddenly popped into her head that he looked like he was going to kiss her and she badly wanted him to do it. But she pushed the thought aside as more nonsense. Lauren broke their mutual gaze and slowly rose from her dining room chair.

"I should get started on the cleanup. It's getting late."

He immediately stood from his chair, too, and dropped his dinner napkin on the table. "Lauren, you don't have to worry about that. I can—"

"No, no," she argued, gathering plates, soufflé cups, and cutlery. "Remember, it's full service. It's the least I can do." He followed her as she walked out of the dining room, laden with dirty dishes. "You paid me thirty-five hundred dollars and I ended up eating some of the food I cooked. At this point, I probably owe *you* money."

At that, an expression she was sure she was mistaking for guilt momentarily crossed his face. "Look, Lauren, I—"

"I insist, Cris." They stepped into the kitchen. She put the plates, forks, knives, and spoons in his sink. "It's not that big of a deal. I can have this place cleaned up in less than an hour. You'll see. It'll be like I wasn't even here." She then reached for one of the platters of now-cold appetizers, preparing to dump the remaining food into a nearby trash bin.

"Lauren." He suddenly grabbed her wrist, stopping her.

Her eyes leaped to his face in surprise. His touch sent chills through her. She swallowed loudly.

"Yes, Cris," she squeaked.

"I . . . have a . . . confession to make."

Uh-oh, she thought. *This doesn't sound good.*

"I probably shouldn't tell you this. I'm probably blowing it now, but it's my rule not to play games and tonight, I broke it."

He let go of her wrist.

"No one . . ." He paused. "No one came tonight because I . . . I didn't invite anyone."

"You didn't invite anyone? But . . . but I thought you said you were throwing a party." She looked around her with confusion. "Then what was all the food for?"

He looked away from her. The expression of guilt returned to his face. "Well, when I tried to ask you out to dinner, you started to say no, so I had to come up with something quick that could still get you here but something that wasn't a *date*-date. You know?"

"A *date*-date?"

"I *knew* we would enjoy dinner together. When I met you, there was just somethin' about you. I figured I just came on too strong and had scared you off, but I could make up for it . . . tonight. You'd see what I was really like."

"So to get me here . . . you lied to me?"

"Well, I wouldn't call it a lie. It was more like—"

"That's what *I* would call it," she insisted, "and I think any other woman would probably do the same."

"So I made a bad call?" He sighed and threw up his hands. "Look, just know that I had the best of intentions, here. I wasn't trying to do anything underhanded. I just wanted to . . . get to know you better. That's all."

Lauren pursed her lips again. She wasn't sure how she felt about this revelation. She was angry that he had lied to her and carried out this ridiculous charade the entire evening. But the other part of her was, in some strange way, very flattered. This guy had gone above and beyond to get her out on a date: creating a fictitious dinner party and hiring her as a caterer to do it. Plus, she *had* enjoyed having dinner with him. She had had a ball! Cris was funny and charismatic. Not to mention, incredibly easy on the eyes. He made her second-guess her decision to hold off dating anyone for a while.

"So are you going to walk out of here and never speak to me again?"

The room fell into silence. "No, I guess not," she finally uttered.

He instantly smiled.

"I understand why you did it. Sort of."

"To be honest, I was wondering if I was going to be able to pull it off. I'm not that good of an actor."

A hint of a smile finally crept to her lips. "You're better than you think. You definitely had me convinced. I thought you had really rude dinner guests who didn't bother to call to say they'd be late. And the way you were behaving, I just knew you weren't attracted to me."

"You really thought I wasn't attracted to you?"

"Oh, yeah! Every now and then, I would pick up on something, but I thought I was just reading you wrong."

"Really? So you didn't pick up that all night I've wanted to do this?"

Lauren didn't have a chance to respond before he cupped her face and lowered his mouth to hers. Her eyes widened in surprise as his warm lips pressed firmly against her own. She breathed in audibly, opening her mouth, and when she felt his tongue slip between her teeth, her eyes lowered. Her heart began to thud in her chest. She kissed him back tentatively, and before she knew it, her tongue was dancing with his. She let out a soft moan.

This was what she wanted. This was what she had been fantasizing about and trying to deny herself.

Cris released her face only to wrap his strong arms around her waist. She could feel herself being hoisted from the floor. Her feet dangled in the air and she wrapped her hands around his neck, holding on for dear life. She felt a warm stirring in the pit of her stomach that started to radiate across her entire body. It then concentrated between her legs and began to vibrate. She had never felt this way before, especially not with James, who made sex seem more like an obligation or a chore than an expression of passion and desire.

When she felt Cris's hands leave her waist and cup her bottom, a hardened mound pressed against her hip—an obvious sign of his arousal. Instinctively, she started to move against it, teasing it with her thigh, kneading it with her groin.

"Slow this down, Lauren," a voice said in her head. "Slow this down quick or you two are going to end up on top of that kitchen island behind you."

With a lot of effort, she wrenched her mouth away. When she opened her eyes, she saw that they were both breathing hard.

"I think we should stop," she whispered breathlessly.

Cris paused, like he was debating with himself, then nodded in agreement. He lowered her to the floor. She brushed her hair out of her eyes. He cleared his throat. They gazed at one another, now unsure what to say. She stared longingly at his lips and caught herself. She looked away.

If I don't get out of here soon, we're going to end up kissing again, she thought. *And I'm not prepared for what might happen after that.*

"So you said you didn't need me to clean up?" she asked, breaking the silence.

"Uh, yeah, I can take care of it."

"OK," she said quickly as she reached for her satchel. "Well, I guess I'll head out now."

"Now?"

"Yeah . . ." She gathered her knife kit. "I mean, if you don't need me to stay."

"Uh." He watched as she zipped around the kitchen grabbing her things. "I guess I don't."

"OK, well, see you around," she said with a wave. She almost ran to the kitchen exit.

"Lauren?" Cris called after her.

She stopped in her tracks and snapped her head around to face him.

"Yeah," she almost squeaked.

"Are you free next Sunday? I could come and pick you up at, say . . . two o'clock."

"Say 'no,' Lauren," a voice in her head urged. "Do you remember what it was like to kiss that guy? If you go out with him, it's over. No more focusing on you. No more 'Lauren improvement project.' You're going to fall for him and you're going to get sidetracked. Say 'no'!"

"O-o-OK," she heard herself stammer despite the warning, making Cris smile.

Chapter 12

Cris entered the farmer's market, whistling an upbeat tune. He was going on a date with Lauren that afternoon. Moving to Chesterton no longer felt like self-imposed exile. He wasn't in the NFL anymore, but at least he still had other things to look forward to: a new home, a new woman, and a new life.

He grabbed a wooden basket and decided to head to the fresh produce aisle. He wanted to pick up a few things for today's date. He couldn't compete with Lauren when it came to cooking, and he didn't plan to try, but he wanted to pack a picnic basket for the hot-air balloon ride he had planned for later. With a woman of discerning taste like Lauren's, he knew he had to pack high-end stuff. He wanted to buy some strawberries, grapes, figs, and artisanal cheeses that would go perfectly with a chilled bottle of Dom Perignon.

Cris smiled. He could see them now, sitting on a hilltop in rural Virginia, looking at the vibrant colors of the sunset over the horizon. In honor of the Fourth of

July weekend, he had even arranged for a private fireworks display when it grew dark. Maybe the night
would end with a repeat of the warm kiss they had
shared the last time he saw her.

*Maybe if you're lucky it'll go a little farther than
that, my friend*, he thought to himself.

But he wasn't going to rush things. She obviously
liked to take her time.

He knew his plans for today were teetering on over
the top, but he really wanted to go all out for her. She
seemed sweet but so withdrawn. He wanted to push her
out of her shell with a good time and a memorable
evening.

Cris glanced at the sign over the organically grown
strawberries before grabbing two cartons. He tossed
them into his basket. He did the same when he reached
the Emperor grapes and then continued to stroll. As he
drew near the glass display case filled with cheeses, he
leaned down to examine them more closely. Suddenly,
he felt a hard shove. He turned in surprise to find a
woman in a red wrap dress kneeling on the ground,
frantically gathering vegetables and fruits that had
tumbled from her basket to the hardwood floors when
she bumped into him.

"Oh!" she exclaimed with embarrassment as she
shoved her cell phone into what looked like a very expensive handbag. She reached for a rolling nectarine,
then looked up at Cris. "Why didn't I look where I was
going? I am so sorry! *So* sorry! Really, I am."

Cris quickly dropped to one knee to help her. She
looked up again at him before giving a loud sigh that
ruffled the bangs that had fallen into her face. "Thank
you *so* much!"

"No problem. Don't worry about it." He handed her a bag of apples that had tumbled near the cheese counter.

She was a beautiful woman, light-skinned with a trim figure. Her eyes were a warm hazel and framed with long, dark lashes, and her honey-brown locks cascaded over her slender shoulders and into one of her eyes. When they had gathered all of her spilled groceries and they had both slowly climbed to their feet, Cris got the nagging feeling that something about her seemed vaguely familiar. He just couldn't pin where and when he had met her before.

"I didn't knock anything out of your basket, did I?" she asked with a grin as she brushed her bangs out of her eyes. "I'm so scatterbrained sometimes. I was talking on my cell phone and not paying attention and *boom!* I run into you."

"No, I'm fine. I've taken worse hits."

"Worse hits?" She pointed her index finger at him. "Hey, don't I know you from somewhere? Aren't you . . . aren't you . . . a basketball . . . no! A *football* player?"

He shook his head. "Not anymore. I retired from the NFL last year."

"Because of your injury. Right! I thought I knew you!" She snapped her fingers. "You're Cris Weaver, right?"

"Yes, I am."

"I can't believe it! I ran into the wide receiver for the Dallas Cowboys." She leaned toward him and dropped her voice to a whisper. "You know, most of the people around here are Redskins fans, but personally, I've *always* preferred the Cowboys. Don't tell anyone I said that, though." She laughed affably and patted his shoulder.

"Don't worry, I won't."

Cris noticed that the V-neck of her dress had dropped several inches lower. It looked like her wrap dress had inadvertently come open as she knelt on the floor. She was revealing a great deal of cleavage. The top of her leopard-print bra was showing.

"Well," she said as she looked him up and down, "you might be retired, but you don't look like you've gained an ounce of fat since you were on the field. I guess you still work out, huh?"

"I try to."

"Oh, and it *shows*. It shows, honey!" She giggled. "So what brings you to Chesterton, Cris?"

"I guess I just needed a change of pace."

"A change of pace? I can understand that!" She patted his shoulder conspiratorially. This time her hand lingered on his arm. "Chesterton has its good side, but it's *nothing* like a big city like Dallas. Compared to Dallas, it's as slow as molasses." She looked him up and down again, gave a wink, and licked her ruby lips. She leaned in closer. "But we definitely have things here that you can't find in Texas."

I'm sure you do, Cris thought sardonically.

His old spider senses were tingling. This woman was nice but *too* nice. She was talking a lot and touching him even more, and he was starting to suspect that it wasn't because she was just an outgoing person who didn't have a good sense of personal space.

This woman with the perfect smile and abundant boobs was probably a groupie. He couldn't say that for sure, but something told him his suspicions were right.

"I should know," she continued, unaware of his growing doubts about her. "I work in historic preservation. In fact"—she began to rifle through her purse.

She pulled out her business card—"I can give you a tour of the town if you'd like. We were founded in 1698, so there are plenty of historic sites around here that even a few of the locals don't know about. We're renovating one of the colonial mansions. We're not opening to the public for another month or two, but I can get you in for a private tour. Give me a call if you're interested. I'd *love* to show you around," she gushed.

"Danger! Danger, Will Robinson!" a voice said in his head. But to be polite, Cris took the card from her. He casually scanned it with the intention of shoving the business card into the back pocket of his jeans to be forgotten amongst the spare change and lint balls, but he did a double take when he spotted the name.

"Cynthia *Gibbons?*"

"That's right!" She pointed down at a line of text. "And on there you'll find my office number and cell number, if you can't catch me at the office. Sometimes I'm off site. Like I said, give me a call and I can show you around." She lowered her voice seductively. "I can assure you that you'll definitely have a good time."

"Is your sister Lauren Gibbons?"

Cynthia's grin faltered. She cleared her throat before regaining her wide smile. "Why, yes, she's my baby sister! Do you know her?"

Now he realized why the groupie seemed so familiar. She didn't exactly look like Lauren, but she had similar mannerisms and facial expressions.

"Yeah, I do. In fact, we have a date set for this afternoon."

Cynthia's grin instantly disappeared. Her delicate brows knitted together. She brought a hand to her hip. *"You* have a date with Lauren?"

Her voice was tinged more with indignation than disbelief. You would think Cris was cheating on her from the way she reacted.

"Uh . . . yeah."

"What? That lyin' little bitch!" Cynthia let out an angry gust of air through her petite nostrils before stomping her foot on the hardwood floor. She narrowed her eyes at Cris while he stared at her in wide-eyed amazement.

"Give me that," she snapped before yanking her business card out of his hand. She shoved it back into her purse. "What a damn waste of time!" She closed the V-neck of her dress, covering her ample bosom. "I can't believe she didn't tell me! She knows the damn rules!"

Cynthia then abruptly turned away from him and tossed her grocery basket aside. It landed with a thump on a pile of bread rolls. She angrily strode down the produce aisle back to the front of the store, still muttering to herself, her long hair swinging behind her.

Cris had become mute with shock, but as he watched Cynthia stalk off, something in particular that she'd said stood out to him.

"Rules?" he repeated. "What rules?"

Jamal had said that Lauren came from a family of gold diggers. He claimed they were skilled women who had been running this game for generations. *"They're the Jedi Knights of gold digging, Cris!"* Jamal had exclaimed in his usual over-the-top way.

At the time, Cris hadn't taken Jamal very seriously, but after meeting Cynthia, and given what she'd just said, he was starting to wonder if maybe he had dismissed Jamal's warnings too quickly.

What had Cynthia meant by "she knows the rules"?

What rules? Were they rules that the Gibbons girls played by? Were they rules that they followed to ensnare men?

Cris slowly set his basket of strawberries and grapes on the cheese counter. Though he hated to admit it, his sense of unease was growing. He was starting to wonder if maybe Jamal had been right about Lauren all along. Maybe she wasn't sweet and withdrawn. Maybe she *was* a gold digger, but one with methods that were less obvious than her sister Cynthia's.

"Lauren knows how to use reverse psychology to make you think you *were the one who asked her out, but really she was after you the whole time,"* Jamal had insisted.

"Maybe he's right," Cris now muttered, only to shake his head a second later.

No, that can't be right.

Lauren was *real.* He had sensed it from the beginning. He felt it when he was around her. She couldn't have fooled him that easily. But he couldn't deny that evidence now pointed to the contrary.

Cris gritted his teeth as he left his basket and walked toward the market doors. His plans for later today would definitely have to change. No more hot-air balloon ride. No more champagne, chocolate-dipped strawberries, and expensive cheese. No more ten-thousand-dollar fireworks display. He would have to do something drastic to find out if the woman he could see himself falling for was really whom she appeared to be.

Chapter 13

Lauren anxiously scrutinized the line of dresses she had laid out on her fold-out couch, fighting the urge to bite her newly painted nails. Her phone rang again. She glanced at it but ultimately decided to ignore it. Her sisters had been calling off and on for the past few hours. Cynthia had even called twice. But each time, Lauren let it go to voice mail. She didn't want to be distracted by her family or their drama today. She wanted to concentrate all her efforts on preparing for her date.

Lauren picked up one of the dresses—a pink A-line with white straps that she hadn't worn in four years.

"I don't know. *Pink?* Is it too much?" She then tossed it onto the growing pile. "Or maybe this one." She held up a navy blue sheath and examined its baggy shape and long hemline. "No, too matronly. I don't want to look like an old lady."

Her eyes scanned the dresses again, but she felt no closer to making a decision than she had been when she'd first started choosing clothes an hour ago. Feeling defeated, Lauren sat on the edge of the bed, slumped forward, and dropped her head into her hands.

"Too bad I can't just go in my underwear," she whispered glumly as she sat in her bra and panties.

She hadn't felt this nervous in a long time, not since her first date thirteen years ago when she was an inexperienced teenage girl who was unsure of what to say or do, worried that she would mess up somehow. Since then she had learned to emotionally distance herself, treating each date more like it was a well-practiced theatrical performance. Depending on the man and what she wanted to get from him, sometimes the date called for her to play the shy virgin. Other times, she had to play the formidable temptress. Occasionally, she was the pleasant, patient listener who wanted to offer him nothing more than a shoulder to cry on.

The only concern she'd had in the past was hitting her mark, saying her lines, and making her date believe she was everything he wanted her to be.

But on this date with Cris, Lauren wouldn't be acting. She would have to be herself and that fact absolutely terrified her.

What if the more he learned about her, the less he liked her? That wasn't just negative talk; it was a real possibility. Most men went running when they found out about her past and the details about her family. They almost sprinted so fast they could break a world record. She couldn't blame them. But with Cris, the rejection would cut deeply.

Maybe I should just cancel it, she thought unhappily. She could tell him something came up at the last minute and it was impossible for her to go out this afternoon. That way she wouldn't have to worry about scaring him off and getting rejected. Canceling the date would remove both possibilities.

Seriously considering that option, Lauren raised her eyes and glanced at the clock on her wall. It was 1:42 P.M. That meant she had less than twenty minutes before Cris was supposed to arrive, and she was willing to bet that he was already on his way to her apartment.

If she canceled, she couldn't do it by phone. She would have to make up a lie and tell him in person. She didn't know if she was up to that. She had lied to many men in her life. She had no desire to do it again, especially with Cris. He deserved better.

"No, I've got to do this. I *can* do this."

She stood from her bed, turned around, and randomly selected a dress to wear.

"Hey," Lauren said with a nervous smile as she opened her basement apartment door fifteen minutes later. "You're early!"

Cris stood on her front stoop under the awning with his hands in his pockets. He looked casual—wearing faded denim jeans and a Polo shirt—but still alluringly handsome. His tattoos were on full display, adding a little edge to his clean-cut look.

"If you need more time, I can wait in the car." He pointed over his shoulder at the parking lot.

"Oh, no. No, I'm good." She stepped onto the stoop, stood next to him, and closed the front door behind her.

Lauren's hands shook slightly as she put her key in the lock. It took her a couple of attempts before she finally heard the deadbolt click. When she did, she cleared her throat and turned to face him.

"Ready!"

They walked toward his car.

Her heart was beating so fast she felt like she was running twenty miles an hour, but she told herself that even if she was a quivering mass of nerves on the inside, it didn't show that much on the outside. She had made sure of that.

After Lauren had finally dressed—donning an emerald green sundress and tan canvas sandals with straps that wrapped around her ankles—she had stood in front of her bedroom mirror and taken several deep, calming breaths. She had pushed down the voices of self-doubt. After all, she had had dinner with him before. It wasn't like this was their first date. And her past didn't matter. She was no longer the person she had been a year ago. She was an accomplished sous chef in one of the best restaurants in town. She was an independent, strong, and resourceful woman. She was just as worthy of a healthy romantic relationship as anyone else. With that little pep talk, her confidence felt less shaky. She was finally ready for their date.

She now trailed Cris, draping her sweater over her arm and fussing with the straps of her dress. When they reached the end of the parking lot and he opened the passenger door to a dented sedan covered in so much rust that the paint color was barely recognizable, she paused.

Lauren must have looked stunned because Cris instantly began to explain.

"Sorry," he said with an apologetic smile. He gestured toward the vehicle. "But my Jag's in the shop. So is the Mercedes. I had to find a last-minute replacement, so I borrowed this from a friend. I hope . . . I hope you don't mind the ride."

Lauren's shocked expression instantly disappeared. She grinned. *"Mind?* Why would I mind?"

"Well, I thought you might be embarrassed by it. It's in pretty bad condition. I could always try to get another—"

"Cris, look, I'll admit that it's not what I expected an ex-NFL player to drive, but it's fine—really. It's almost identical to my baby. I don't have much room to talk."

Cris gazed at her doubtfully, leaving her to wonder why he found it so hard to believe she didn't mind his car. It really wasn't that big of a deal.

"I guess we'd better get going, then." He gestured toward his car's interior, urging her to get inside.

When he climbed behind the wheel, she smiled. "So what's the plan for today?"

"It's a surprise. I'm not telling you until we get there."

"A surprise, huh?"

He nodded.

Lauren sat back in her seat with her hands in her lap, now curious. She could only imagine what the surprise could be.

Once, to surprise her for her birthday, James had chartered a helicopter and taken her on a flight around Virginia. He had finished it with a private, candlelight dinner in a stone gazebo at a small vineyard. As they ate, they were serenaded by a violinist. She had thought the evening was perfect until James had ruined it with some remark, a belittling comment that stuck in her head and refused to go away, even the next morning. But that was James; he just couldn't help himself. He *had* to make some dig to remind her he was in control, even when he was supposed to be showing her how much he adored her.

Lauren wondered now if Cris would try something similarly extravagant. He was just as much a man of money and means as James, if not more. What over-the-top date did he have planned?

As he drove, she tried to get a few clues from him, but he wouldn't budge. In fact, every time Lauren attempted to start a conversation, Cris would utter a few words before falling silent. He simply refused to talk. Finally, she gave up, hoping again that his odd behavior would cease once the date really began. Maybe he was just as nervous as she was.

After driving for twenty minutes, they took a road that led to the Chesterton fairgrounds, further piquing her curiosity.

What's going on here?

They drove another half mile and Lauren saw several cars parked along the shoulder, creating a pathway where men, women, babies in strollers, and excited children were trudging uphill. At the crest of the hill was the brightly colored and crazily decorated ticket gate to the town carnival. With the lowered car window, Lauren could easily hear the music from the merry-go-round and the jubilant screams of those riding the roller coaster and the Tilt-A-Whirl. She could smell the popcorn, hot dogs, and the faint whiff of cotton candy. She could see the top of the Ferris wheel and the parachute drop.

As the car began to decelerate and Cris parallel parked along the shoulder, Lauren gawked. "*This* is your surprise?"

Cris nodded, unbuckling his seatbelt. "I figured neither one of us had probably been to the carnival in years. It's definitely a change of pace." He paused and gazed at her. "Are you disappointed?"

Disappointed? Lauren thought with bafflement. She was too shocked to be disappointed. Of all the possibilities to consider, she never would have thought Cris had plans to take her to the carnival. Here she was envisioning helicopter rides and violinists. The idea that they'd spend their day on the Ferris wheel, licking flavored ice cones, and sampling cotton candy, seemed so childlike and without pretension that she couldn't help but smile. She was starting to like Cris more and more.

She unbuckled her seatbelt.

"Disappointed?" she repeated with a grin, opening her car door. "Of course not! Come on! I wanna ride the roller coaster!"

Chapter 14

"Oh, that was *so* much fun!" Lauren said as she walked through her apartment door hours later. Cris trailed behind her with a giant stuffed panda tucked under his arm, dragging oversized bags of cotton candy and popcorn.

They had spent most of the day at the carnival, riding roller coasters over and over again until they were almost nauseous. They played the coin toss, Whac-A-Mole, target shooting, and Skee-Ball, with Lauren outscoring Cris in most of them. He was a good loser, though, joking that his hand and eye coordination was a little off now that he had retired from the NFL.

"Guess I'm gettin' rusty," he had demured with a smile.

They ended their evening at a local diner, enjoying burgers, fries, and milkshakes while they shared funny stories. This time Cris asked most of the questions. He seemed eager to know more about her and her past. Lauren had to do a delicate dance around a few details. She wasn't quite ready to talk about her mother and her sisters and her time with James. She wanted to keep the date light and playful and sharing her family drama or revealing the darker chapters of her life would have impeded that.

It had been a nice dinner—a memorable one, in fact. The only glitch happened when Cris realized he had misplaced his wallet. He'd had it with him most of the day at the carnival, but he had probably lost it somewhere at the fairgrounds. Lauren instantly had insisted they go back and try to find it in the "lost and found" area. Maybe a Good Samaritan had turned it in, she had suggested. But Cris said it was no big deal. He had purposely left his credit cards at home and had only brought cash with him. The only thing the wallet contained was $60 and his outdated driver's license from Texas that had to be replaced with a Virginia license soon anyway.

Feeling bad for him, Lauren didn't bat an eye when he sheepishly asked if she could cover the tab for dinner.

"Of course," she had readily agreed, throwing a twenty-dollar bill on the table. After that, they left the restaurant holding hands. He drove her home, and during the whole car ride, Lauren marveled at how well the date had gone despite her nerves earlier that day.

See, you were worried for no reason, she had told herself. Now the only nerves she had were in anticipation of him kissing her again, which she desperately wanted.

"We really have to do that again." She closed the front door behind him as he stepped farther inside her apartment. She tugged the panda bear from his arm. "I can take that." She turned and set the bear on the end of the couch and pointed to her coffee table. "You can put the bags over there if you'd like, and please, have a seat. Welcome to my home."

Despite her offer to sit down, Cris stood awkwardly in the center of the room, looking as if he wasn't sure where exactly he was supposed to sit.

It was a tiny efficiency apartment with a quaint kitchen on one side of the room that had a basic four-burner stove, refrigerator, and microwave. The other side was currently occupied by a small armchair, coffee table, and large pull-out sofa, which also doubled as Lauren's bed. The only dresser in the room was of the simple particle board variety with a veneer made to look like it was made of birchwood. It contained less than a fourth of her clothes. The rest of her wardrobe from her old life was shoved into her coat closet and in one of the many closets at her mother's mansion. Perched on top of the dresser was an old television and VCR she had purchased as a set for thirty dollars at a yard sale. Her apartment walls were unadorned, with the exception of two small canvases her sister Dawn had painted.

Lauren knew her surroundings were humble, but she didn't realize quite *how* humble they were until she watched Cris gaze around him, a picture of bafflement. She saw her apartment for the first time through his eyes and felt a little embarrassed, maybe even defensive.

"I know it doesn't look the greatest, but I swear, the couch won't bite. No fleas or bedbugs here."

"No, I wasn't . . ." He paused, looking around him again. "I'm just . . . surprised . . . that's all."

"Surprised by what?"

He shook his head. "Never mind. Forget I said that."

Lauren was starting to feel the same way she had felt before he had arrived for their date: uneasy and nervous. She decided to push those thoughts aside, though. The evening had gone well, after all.

"Can I get you something to drink?" She walked to the kitchen. "Some water or tea, maybe? Sorry I don't have any coffee. I'm out right now."

"Tea is fine." He finally sat down on the couch.

Lauren busied herself in the kitchen, rummaging around the cabinets for an old box of Earl Grey tea while he continued to look around her apartment. Minutes later she set two cups and saucers on the coffee table and took a seat beside him.

"I feel like I've done most of the talking tonight," she said. "I hope I didn't monopolize the conversation."

"No, not at all. You know so much about me. I wanted to learn more about you. After all"—he paused and gazed at her intently—"there's still a lot I don't know about you."

"But you don't have to learn it all in one night, right? We have time." She reached for his hand and gave it a squeeze.

"I guess." He took his hand out of her grasp and reached for his teacup.

Disappointed, Lauren moved her hand back to her lap. She watched silently as he drank.

"You know, I can't say enough how much of a good time I had tonight, Cris. I haven't enjoyed myself that much in years. I thought the date was very . . . original."

He lowered his cup back to the table. "Original?"

"Yeah, I never would have guessed you'd do something like that. I thought it was . . . sweet."

"Sweet?"

She laughed nervously. "You're looking at me like I still have ketchup on my face." She paused, confused by his facial expression. He seemed angry. "Did I say something wrong?"

When he didn't answer her, her smile faded. "Cris, are you OK?"

"Lauren, are you being honest with me?"

"Honest about what?"

"About everything! I can't figure you out."

"Cris, I have no idea what you're talking about. What exactly are you trying to figure out about me?"

"If I lay all my cards on the table, will you lay out yours?"

What the hell does that mean? Why is he behaving like this?

"I'm serious now, Lauren. I don't want any lies."

That pricked her anger. "What lies? Cris, I suggest you tell me quickly what you're talking about because I—"

"The date we went on tonight wasn't the date I had planned, not the one I had planned a week ago anyway. I wasn't going to take you to the carnival and some greasy burger joint. I was going to take you on a hot-air balloon and we were going to have champagne and caviar and chocolate-covered strawberries. I even set up a fireworks display."

He continued to stare at her, waiting for her reaction.

"Well," Lauren said, now even more befuddled, "I . . . I guess that date would have been nice, too, but what does that have to—"

"My car isn't in the shop, either. I left it at home today and rented the car I used tonight."

"It's not in the shop?" She held up her hand. "Wait,

I'm really confused now. Why would you ask for that car if you already had—"

"I asked them to send over the worst rental they had on the lot, one that would make *anyone* embarrassed to be seen riding in it. And I didn't lose my wallet, either." He tugged his wallet out of his back pocket and tossed it onto the coffee table. "It was in my pocket the whole time. I just told you that so you'd pay for dinner."

Her mouth fell open in shock.

"I did all those things, Lauren, because I was testing you. I had to see if you were being honest with me or just pretending."

"Testing me? Why the hell were you testing me? You thought I was pretending to be *what?"*

"Pretending to be . . . well, pretending *not* to be . . . a gold digger. I wanted to see if you were really a gold digger."

Her eyes narrowed with fury.

"Look, when I first heard gossip about you, I didn't believe it. I said you didn't seem that way."

"You heard gossip about me?" She leaped from the couch. "What gossip? From whom?" She stomped her foot on the worn carpet. "Damn it, I wish the people in this town would get a life and mind their own goddamn business! I haven't done *anything* to anyone around here! Why would they—"

"I heard it from a friend who only meant well," Cris insisted, making her suck her teeth and angrily cross her arms over her chest. She started to pace around the small apartment. "I didn't believe him . . . until I met your sister Cynthia."

Lauren stopped at the mention of her sister's name. "You . . . you met Cynthia?"

"Yeah. She literally ran into me at the farmer's market this morning. You should tell her she's not very subtle. It's good to let a man know you're interested, but maybe she should tone it down a little."

Lauren uncrossed her arms.

He's right. When it comes to men, my sister has the subtlety of a Category 7 hurricane.

"She mentioned you. Before she walked away, she said 'Lauren knows the rules' or 'Lauren broke the rules' by talking to me. I can't remember exactly what she said, but I remember the rules part." He glared at her. "What did she mean by that?"

Lauren flopped back on the couch beside him, sending her skirt flying around her hips. She looked up, stared at her basement apartment ceiling, and closed her eyes.

Damn you, Cynthia! The one man in this town who doesn't know about all our family drama, and you had to ruin it! The one chance I had at starting fresh with someone!

"What rules was she talking about, Lauren?" he persisted.

I guess I've got to tell him now.

Lauren slowly opened her eyes. "The rules . . ." she began, pausing to clear her throat. "They're . . . they're what we play by to make sure no one steps on anyone's toes. It keeps us from fighting among ourselves." She hesitated. "For us, family always comes first, no matter what. It's also what you follow to maintain control and keep from getting . . . too attached."

"Too attached to what?"

"To men."

Cris gaped at her words, but quickly closed his mouth.

"OK, so tell me about them. What are the rules?"

"Why do you want to know this, Cris? I don't use them! It doesn't matter!"

"I said I would lay out my cards if you promised to lay out yours. So just . . . just tell me. What are the rules?"

Lauren lowered her eyes from the ceiling to look at him, feeling beyond embarrassed. In some way, she also felt like she was betraying her family. Cris would be the first man who had ever been told any of the Gibbons family's rules.

Grandma Althea definitely would roll over in her grave for this one.

"Well, some of them are . . . pretty basic," she began cautiously. "Don't go after a man that your sister has already called dibs on unless she throws him back. Then it's OK. There's another one about if you're going to live with a man who hasn't married you, make sure that you live with him long enough that it qualifies as a common-law marriage in the state where you live. When you do that, if he *does* leave you or if you leave him, you can still sue him for alimony according to state law.

"Then there's the one about always making sure that all leases for cars and apartments are in *both* of your names. If you chose the right guy, he won't default on anything that will damage his credit, so you know that your rent and your car payments will always be taken care of."

Cris was gaping again.

"Mama has a few rules about divorce. She's done it five times, so I guess she would know," Lauren muttered with a shrug. "She said you should only start working on your second stringer—"

"Second stringer? What the hell is that?"

"The next man you plan to marry," Lauren explained. "You should only start working on your second stringer the day after the divorce is finalized. If you do it too soon, it could compromise your settlement. Your ex could claim infidelity to the judge. But if you wait too long, the guy you had your eye on could get swept up by someone else."

Cris now looked shell-shocked.

"The rules change a little if you have children. If you have a girl, her training has to start early, usually when she's thirteen or fourteen. You try to—"

"*Stop!* Just stop!" Cris shouted as he held up his hands and stood from the couch. "I don't want to hear any more of this shit! *Training?* Are you serious? I mean . . . goddamn!" he exclaimed, now at a loss for words. "Jay was right! You guys *are* the Jedi Knights of gold digging!"

She gazed up at him, hurt by his reaction. "But you said . . . you said you wanted the truth. That's all I was—"

"Oh, yeah," he muttered with a nod and a cold laugh. "And you gave it to me! *Uncensored!* So is that all I am to you, huh? A potential alimony payment or a divorce settlement? Did you use all your years of *training* to work on me? Is that why you went out with me tonight?"

"No, Cris!" She shot up from the couch and walked around the coffee table to stand in front of him. "Those are the rules, but that doesn't mean I have to live by them! Yes, my mother and my sisters do things that I'm not proud of, but I swear that's not who *I* am!" She grabbed his hand. "I mean . . . not . . . not anymore. I've changed!"

"*Not anymore?* And when did you see the light,

Lauren? Fifteen minutes ago when we started this conversation?"

She pursed her lips. He was mocking her. Even though she had been honest with him and told him everything, he was mocking her.

Lauren let go of his hand and took a step back.

"Or was it three minutes ago when I called you on it?"

She turned away from him.

"Is that when you decided to change your ways? Is that when you had your epiphany?"

"No," she snapped, "it was eight months ago when my last boyfriend left me with a black eye, bloody nose, and busted lip."

Lauren walked back to the couch and sat down. She glowered down at her carpet, refusing to look up at Cris again.

"*A black eye?* No one would give you a black eye."

"I told you that I don't lie, Cris."

"But you're so . . . little," Cris said with disbelief. "You're barely a . . . Who . . . I mean . . . what man would hit you?"

"James Sayers," she sniffed. "He owns a law firm in town."

Cris's face clouded over. He nodded with recognition. "I've heard of him."

"*Everybody's* heard of him! He's Mr. Popular around here."

"And Mr. Popular hit you?"

"I told him he was too controlling," she mumbled, still staring at the carpet. "I told him that he acted like he owned me. I said I was leaving him and he *beat* me," she said before glaring up at Cris. Her eyes went glacial. "But he only did it once. I'm not that type of woman, Cris. I wouldn't let him beat me again. *No one* owns me, but me! And no amount of cash can buy me! I'm my own woman! Nobody can . . ." Her voice drifted off when she realized that she was shaking. She tightly linked her hands together and took a calming breath.

"Please tell me that you didn't let him get away with that. Did you call the police?"

"Of course I did! I drove straight to the sheriff's office and tried to file a report that night. I told some detective what had happened and the next thing I knew Sheriff McKinney himself shows up in the interview room. He asked me if I correctly remembered all the facts of that night. I told him yes. He asked me if I was sure I wanted to do this. I told him yes. He asked the detective to leave the room.

"That's when I knew something was up. It didn't feel right. When we were alone, the sheriff told me 'confidentially' that because there were no witnesses, it would be my word against James's. James could just as easily argue that *I* assaulted *him*. And lots of people in town aren't exactly fond of me or my family, as you well know. We're gold diggers . . . manipulators . . . schemers. No one would believe one of us, and even if they did, they'd probably say I was a whore who deserved what I got.

"But that didn't stop me either. I still wanted to press charges. So what if it was James's word against mine. I knew I was telling the truth! I knew I didn't deserve that! But then"—she closed her eyes—"But then the sheriff told me if I pressed charges, I'd better understand what was really at stake."

She glanced up at Cris. He looked appalled.

"He said someone powerful like James could make it hard for me and my family in Chesterton. We've been here longer, but a man like him—with his money and connections—pulls a lot more weight in town. That stopped me." She threw up her hands. "Look, I didn't give a damn about what James could do to me! What more could he do? I'm sitting there with a bloody nose and mouth! I'm in my nightgown and in a wool blanket the detective gave me. But my sisters and my mother and my niece still live here, Cris, and, well . . . I got the point. *Lesson learned!* Sheriff McKinney suggested I go, spend the night at my mother's, and sleep on it. I didn't come back the next day and I didn't press charges. So far it's worked out OK. James has left me and my family alone . . . most of the time."

"Most of the time?"

"We had one little incident a couple of weeks ago," she mumbled, remembering their last exchange in the grocery store parking lot. "But besides that, I haven't had any problems."

Cris shook his head. "I had no idea, Lauren."

"Of course not. That's one of the few stories the gossips around town don't know. But like I said, lesson learned. I changed my ways after that. So from now on, so that there's no confusion, so that no one misunderstands what they *can* and what they *can't* do to me, I don't accept money or gifts from men. The last check I've gotten from any man is the one you wrote me for catering your dinner party, and I didn't even want to accept that."

"I noticed." He shoved his hands into his jeans pockets.

"And you didn't have to hide your wallet tonight. I would have insisted we go Dutch anyway."

He gazed at the floor, now looking shamefaced.

She slapped her hands on her thighs and hoisted

herself to her feet. "Well, that's everything: My big, fat sob story. I laid all my cards on the table like you laid yours," she said with a false casualness, walking to her apartment door. "I'm a reformed gold digger from a family of gold diggers. I'm no virgin, but I haven't been around the block as much as you might have heard. The last relationship I had was an abusive one and tonight was the first real date I've been on since then. Now you know everything about me, about how screwed up my life is." She undid the chain and the lock on her door. "So I guess you'll be leaving now."

She didn't look at him as she swung the door open. Instead she stared down at the brass doorknob. It hurt to be rejected like this, as she had expected it would. And she was being rejected because of *what?* Town gossip? Mistakes she had made in the past?

But it's better that it happened now, before I got too attached to him, she lied to herself. *It's like ripping off a Band-Aid; better to do it quickly rather than slowly and painfully. Besides, I didn't want to fall in love anyway.*

Lauren was telling herself this, but it still didn't end the aching in her chest.

When Cris stood in the opened doorway, not saying a word, she sighed.

Why is he drawing this out? Why doesn't he just leave?

She stole a glance up at him just as he gently tugged her hand away from the brass knob and closed the door. He held her hand in his own, making her frown.

"You're not . . . you're not leaving?"

He shook his head and raised his other hand to gently caress her chin. Her frown deepened.

"But I thought . . . I thought you . . . you were . . ."

"I owe you an apology. I'm sorry for testing you like that. I didn't have the right to do that to you. I'm sorry for not trusting you, either."

Lauren had prepared herself for rejection, but she wasn't prepared for this. She was at a loss for words. Then suddenly, he did what she had been waiting all night for him to do. He leaned down and kissed her.

Cris pulled her toward him and she instantly relaxed in his strong arms, standing on the tips of her toes in her canvas sandals to meet his kiss. He was much, much bigger than she was, but he held her with a tenderness that made her forget his overwhelming size. He held her like she was a delicate figurine that had to be handled with care.

She closed her eyes, wrapped her arms around his neck, and opened her mouth to intensify the kiss, showing him that she wasn't as delicate as she might seem. Suddenly, his tenderness disappeared. He became more forceful and urgent. He met her tongue with his own, pressing her hard against him, making her moan against his lips.

Lauren's heart began to pound and a languid heat coasted over her, making her feel as if the temperature in the room had risen another twenty degrees. She started to feel that familiar tingle between her thighs that let her know that if they didn't stop soon, she could get herself into serious trouble. But she ignored that warning, letting him fist his hand in her hair and cup her bottom. She was acting on pure instinct, and instinctively, she didn't want the warm sensation to end.

She raised one of her legs, rubbing her thigh against his manhood yearningly, taunting him. His grip tightened even more and suddenly his hand went to the zipper of her sundress. He lowered it and then began to raise the skirt. It was then that reason, not instinct, kicked in for Lauren.

"You're going to end up stark naked if you don't end this," a voice in her head said as they kissed. "He's different, remember? You've changed your ways. You don't want to seduce him *this* quickly. *What will he think?"*

With great agony, she tugged her mouth away, catching him by surprise.

"Cris," she said breathlessly against his lips, "put me down."

"Why? What's wrong?"

"Just . . . just put me down."

He slowly lowered her back to the floor. She realized as she took several steps back from him that she wasn't the only one breathing hard.

She quickly raised the zipper of her dress and pushed her hair out of her face. He closed his eyes and took a long, calming breath. They stood in silence.

"Too fast?" he finally asked seconds later, opening his eyes.

She smiled and nodded sheepishly. "Even for a reformed gold digger."

"I'm sorry. I got carried away."

"No, it wasn't just you! I was just as willing as you were. Trust me! But . . . it just feels like . . . we need to—"

"Slow down a little," he said, finishing for her. "I get it. I got caught up in the moment."

"I did, too."

They looked longingly at one another for several seconds.

Her body still ached for him. The tingling between

her legs hadn't disappeared. Her nipples were so hard that they pressed urgently against the coarse cotton fabric of her sundress, begging to be let out and to let Cris's hands roam over them. But she ordered her body to pipe down.

"I should probably go," Cris said, reaching for the door handle.

She wasn't sure if she should be relieved or disappointed by his announcement.

"I'll see you soon, I hope?" She bit her lower lip anxiously.

He opened her front door and smiled. "How about next Sunday? I can pick you up at five o'clock."

"That works for me." He raised his hand to her face and slowly ran his finger along her jawline. He leaned down and kissed her again. This time it was a light, tender peck—a lot more restrained than the earlier kiss—but she felt the need inside her catch fire all over again. "I guess I'll see you then."

"OK," she said quietly with a smile.

When Lauren shut the door behind him, she fell hard against it, still smiling, holding her hand against her chest, willing her heart to stop racing. Suddenly, her phone rang. She slowly walked over to it, lost in a tranquil daze. The night had been more than she expected, filled with highs and lows, but it had ended on such a good note. She had poured her heart out to Cris—showed him all her scars—and he hadn't judged her. He had understood.

She pressed the ANSWER button on the phone and lifted her receiver to her ear. "Hello?" she answered dreamily.

When she heard the voice on the other end of the

line, her smile instantly disappeared. She narrowed her eyes into thin slits.

"Yeah, Cynthia," she said tightly. "Uh-huh . . . uh-huh . . . You don't say . . . Yeah, well, now that you mention it, Big Sis, I have a big damn bone to pick with you, too."

Chapter 15

"She broke *the rules!*" Cynthia shouted, pointing across the living room at Lauren.

Lauren crossed her arms over her chest and raised her eyes heavenward. Her eldest sister could be so melodramatic sometimes. She slumped back against the limestone mantel over the fireplace.

Dawn and Stephanie sat on the Queen Anne sofa facing both of them, making it obvious that they weren't choosing sides in this argument—at least not openly. Their mother perched on the end of her favorite settee, trying her best to act as mediator. She sipped daintily from a chilled glass of iced tea garnished with a mint leaf, placed it on a coaster on the end table beside her, and loudly cleared her throat.

"Cynthia, baby, I understand you're upset. But—"

" 'Upset' is putting it lightly, Mama!" Cynthia bellowed. "What's the point of having the damn rules if we aren't going to follow them? You gave her first dibs and she tossed him back! We were all there! We all heard her! She said she wasn't interested! He was fair game and she—"

"Maybe she just changed her mind," their mother ventured softly. "Maybe Lauren had a chance to look over his stats again and she decided he was worth the effort. I know *I* would have, in her position."

"I don't care about his stats," Lauren said, pushing away from the fireplace. "That isn't why I went on a date with him. When I agreed to go out with Cris—who has a name, by the way; I hate that we keep talking about him like he's some inanimate object."

At that, Stephanie covered her mouth and snickered.

"When I agreed to go out with Cris, I wasn't thinking about his money or that he's an ex-football player. He's a nice guy. He's very smart and sweet and—"

"Oh, bullshit!" Cynthia shouted. "Who the hell do you think you're kiddin'?"

"Cynthia," Yolanda said tightly, cutting her eyes at her daughter. "Watch your language in this house. I won't listen to another outburst like that!"

"Sorry, Mama." Cynthia shifted in her chair to face Lauren. "But you know damn well, Laurie, that the only thing that made you go on a date with Cris Weaver was the forty million dollars in his bank account!"

"That is not true!" Lauren shouted back.

"You act like you're so much better than the rest of us when you do the same damn thing we do! At least we're *honest* about it. Instead, you act like some prissy saint who's—"

"Just because I choose to no longer hunt men like they're wild game on the savanna doesn't mean I think I'm a saint! In fact, I'm far from it."

"You're damn right about that," Cynthia challenged.

"But I'm not going to pretend that what you do . . .

what you *all* do . . . is right," Lauren continued, ignoring her sister. "And I'm glad—hell, I'm damn near *elated*—that I stopped you from getting your claws into Cris! He doesn't deserve to be treated like an ATM. He's a good man, a good person! You'll just have to find your gravy boat somewhere else!"

Cynthia gritted her teeth and fumed. The other sisters stayed silent, happy to watch the argument from the sidelines for once.

Yolanda gazed up at Lauren. "You really *do* like him, don't you, honey?"

"Well . . . yeah. Yeah, I do."

It was hard to tell her mother and her sisters how she really felt about Cris. She doubted any of them had ever truly fallen in love before, or at least she had never seen any evidence of those emotions in them. The idea of loving a man for who he was—and not for his money or his power—was so foreign in her family.

And besides, Lauren couldn't say for sure if she *was* falling in love. She barely knew Cris. She was doubtful of her feelings, but they were so strong and so intense. It had to be more than lust.

"Like I said," Lauren began, clearing her throat, "he's a nice guy and—"

"I'm sorry, Mama!" Cynthia rose from her chair. "But I can't take any more of this bull . . ."

She stopped when Yolanda narrowed her eyes at her warningly.

"This *farce* . . . and I refuse to waste any more time listening. I have to get back to work."

"But you were the one who called the meeting!" Dawn argued, crossing her arms over her chest, causing the sleeves of her colorful slinky top to billow and the many bangles on her wrist to clink together. She had stayed quiet for most of Cynthia and Lauren's argument, but she wouldn't stay quiet now. "I canceled a gallery conference call for this and now you're just going to *leave?*"

Cynthia tossed her hair over her shoulder. "Lauren refuses to admit that she's wrong. I don't see the point of sitting around and listening to more of her lies." Cynthia then threw her handbag over her shoulder. "Good-bye, Mama . . . Stephanie . . . Dawn." She pointedly avoided saying good-bye to Lauren, put on her dark-tinted sunglasses, and walked out of the sitting room.

"Well, if Cynthia is leaving, I'm sure as hell not staying," Dawn said, rising from the sofa with hands on hips. She then abruptly turned and sashayed out of the room, a haze of color flying behind her.

Seconds later, Stephanie sighed, setting the glass she was holding onto the coffee table. "I should probably leave, too. I have a showing in an hour." She glanced down at her watch. "The house is going to be a tough sell at seven hundred five K, but I told my client I'd give it the ol' college try."

She then rose to her feet, awkwardly tugging down the hem of her short gray skirt and her tightly fitted suit jacket as she did so. She walked toward her mother and leaned down, giving an air kiss near both of the older woman's cheeks. She then glanced at Lauren, gave a sympathetic smile, and waved.

"See you at brunch on Saturday," she said quietly before striding out of the room in her patent-leather Louboutin pumps.

Yolanda pursed her lips. She then turned to look at Lauren.

"I wouldn't take what your sister said to heart, Laurie. That's just how she is."

Lauren walked toward her mother. "I've learned to ignore her. She's been that way since birth!" Lauren then flopped onto the sofa.

Her mother gave a small smile. "Cynthia takes the business of getting a man very seriously. We *all* do, Laurie."

"Look, I know how you feel about this, Mama, and I—"

"No, you don't," Yolanda said softly. "Not really."

Lauren watched as her mother stood from the settee and slowly walked to the other side of the room. She gazed out the window at the front yard with her hands clasped in front of her and her back facing Lauren. Standing there, she looked almost regal, like a queen gazing at her kingdom.

"Remember how I told you before that the biggest mistake you made with James was giving him too much power?"

"No, the biggest mistake I made with James was dating him in the first place."

"No, Laurie, in the right hands, James could have been molded into anything you wanted. That big ol' ego of his could have been used against him." She turned slightly and gazed coolly over her shoulder at her daughter. "But then again, it's never been in your nature to do the molding, has it? I've taught you what I could—all the tricks of the trade, as they say—but deep down, I could tell your heart was never in it, not like your sisters. You've never been very practical, Laurie. You've always been a hopeless romantic."

From anyone else, that would have been a compliment. But Lauren knew that was not what her mother intended, and she flinched at the sting of her words. Yolanda Gibbons *despised* romantics. She had banned her daughters from reading fairy tales when they were little and confiscated any romance novels she found in their rooms when they were teenagers. It wasn't the sex that bothered her so much as the sappy idealism: the swooning damsel in distress, the man coming to her rescue, and the both of them living together happily ever after.

"I won't have you reading this nonsense," she would say.

"There is nothing about the way I'm handling this that isn't practical, Mama," Lauren argued, shaking off those memories. "Cris and I are just getting to know each other and—"

"But you've already fallen for him," her mother countered, finally turning away from the window. She walked toward Lauren. "I can tell. Cynthia thinks it's an act, but I know better, honey. You understand that by falling for him, you're givin' him power over you, the *ultimate* control. I would think that after your bad experience with James, you would have learned your lesson by now."

"Cris is nothing like James."

"So you say." Her mother gave a cynical smile. "But give a man an inch and he'll take a mile. They always do."

"Well, maybe it's just the men *you've* dealt with."

Her mother's nostrils flared. Yolanda took a calming breath, then her polite smile returned.

"Your naïveté never ceases to amaze me, honey, but you're a grown woman, as you often tell me. I can't make you do what I want you to do. And there are only so many warnings I can give you. I know it's your decision." She stood in front of Lauren with her arms crossed over her chest. "But know this: The rules that I and your Grandmother Althea made weren't based on just any ol' whim. These were based on *real* experiences that we both had with life and men . . . the good, the bad, and the ugly. If you choose to ignore them, you do it at your own risk."

Her mother made it sound so dire, like falling in love was the same as leaping out of a plane without a parachute.

"Understood," Lauren answered succinctly as she stood and glared back at her mother, not wavering her gaze. "But respectfully, Mama, I'll take my chances."

She wasn't going to back down on this. She knew her mother, her sisters, and, yes, even Grandmother Althea, were wrong. All men weren't the same, and Cris and James were as vastly different as they come. Comparing them was like trying to compare a rock to a bird, or a tree to a waterfall. Just because they existed on the same terra firma didn't mean they were of like kind.

"Well, now that all your sisters have left, I guess you'll be going back to your restaurant."

"Yeah, I have to finish with prep work for the day. I told them I was stepping out for an hour or two to come here, but I should get back soon."

She watched as her mother leaned over and began to collect drinking glasses from the end tables.

"Why are you doing that?" Lauren asked.

Her mother glanced over her shoulder at her, looking confused. "Why am I doing what?"

"Why are you cleaning up? I don't think I've seen you pick up glasses after anyone my entire life," Lauren said with a snort. "Why don't you have Esmeralda or Rosa or one of the others do it?"

"Because I am perfectly capable of cleaning up after myself. Besides, Rosa is busy shining silverware in the kitchen. She hasn't done it in a month. The others"—her mother gave a casual shrug—"well, I just . . . gave them the day off."

Lauren followed her mother into the corridor. *"All* of them? Is it some kind of Catholic holiday I don't know about?"

"I wouldn't know, Lauren."

Lauren laughed. "Then why would—"

"I said I don't know!" her mother shouted, suddenly turning on her and making the iced tea slosh over the sides of the glasses onto her hands and the hardwood floor. "I *don't* know! So stop askin' me!"

Yolanda then turned and marched toward the end of the corridor.

There were many things that Yolanda Gibbons did to convey her displeasure: cutting her eyes, frowning, or giving a cold silence. But shouting certainly wasn't one of them. She said it was unladylike and undignified. So for her to do it now was definitely out of character.

"What the hell has gotten into her?" Lauren muttered to herself.

Chapter 16

"Where should I put these, Miss Gibbons?" the mousy-looking young woman asked.

Stephanie looked over her shoulder. She had been in the middle of sweeping the hardwood floors and doing some last-minute cleanup of her client's home when her new assistant, Carrie, came rushing into the dining room carrying a cardboard box filled with flyers that had just arrived from the printer. The flyers included professional photos of the house and all the important details related to today's showing. Stephanie liked to hand them out to visitors so that most of their questions could be answered simply by looking at the reference page.

Carrie teetered on her high heels anxiously, trying to balance the box in her hands. She blew a curly lock of chestnut-colored hair out of her eyes. It and several other curls had escaped out of her chignon. Her maze of freckles had disappeared completely now that her usually pale cheeks were bright red. The suit jacket she was wearing looked askew, as if it had been buttoned wrong.

Carrie had started the job a few months ago and was working out quite well, but she still looked frazzled whenever they had to do showings like these. Well, "frazzled" wasn't quite the word. She looked closer to absolutely terrified.

Stephanie smiled. "You can spread them out on the oak table in the foyer and put a stack of business cards next to them."

Carrie nodded before scrambling toward the dining room's arched entryway.

"Oh, and Carrie . . ."

The young woman skidded to a halt, almost stumbling on the afghan rug near the dining room table and falling face-first to the hardwood floor. She whipped around and faced Stephanie.

"Yes, Miss Gibbons?"

"Honey, chill out, OK? You look like you're about to pass out. It's just a showing. You know . . . people walking through a house eating crackers and asking silly questions. They're not going to bite you."

Carrie gave a nervous smile. "Yes, Miss Gibbons." She then scampered out of the room again.

Stephanie shook her head. *That girl really needs to chill out. She looks like she's going to explode.*

Speaking of impending explosions . . . Stephanie wondered if Cynthia had had her Hiroshima-worthy blast yet. Their eldest sister had been so furious at the family meeting today that Stephanie was sure steam was going to pour out of Cynthia's ears. Stephanie hadn't seen Cynthia yell that much since they were little girls and she and Dawn had stolen Cynthia's favorite Barbie and decided to hold it for ransom. Except now, Cynthia was pissed at Lauren because she believed Lauren had taken something else she *really* wanted. Their youngest sister had managed to seduce Cris Weaver right under Cynthia's pretty little nose.

Stephanie chuckled, sweeping the last of the dust bunnies into her plastic dustpan. She carried them and the broom back into her client's kitchen.

It was amusing to see Cynthia finally get her come-uppance. Stephanie hated that even when they were little girls, Cynthia had always believed she was entitled to first dibs on everything: toys and clothes, and later men and money. *Finally,* someone had put her in her place, though Stephanie was surprised that Lauren had been the one to do it. She also didn't get Lauren's whole claim about how she wasn't targeting Weaver for his wealth. She claimed to have actually fallen for the man.

Yeah, what the hell is that about, Stephanie thought as she dumped the dust and trash into a plastic trash can underneath the sink. She opened the door to the pantry and placed the broom and dustpan inside.

Was Lauren saying that to try to smooth things over with Cynthia or was she telling the truth? Stephanie certainly hoped her little sister was lying. She couldn't think of a prospect more alarming than falling in love with someone. That was definitely a family no-no. Stephanie had never fallen for a man in her life and hoped she never would.

"Miss Gibbons!" Carrie shouted, snapping Stephanie from her thoughts. *"Miss Gibbons!* A few cars are pulling into the driveway! They're here!"

Stephanie sighed and strolled out of the kitchen.

"That's all right, Carrie. We want them to come here. Remember? I told you: It's just a showing. Take a deep breath, honey."

And have a shot of tequila while you're at it.

Stephanie adjusted the lapels on her suit jacket and pasted on a smile. She walked through the dining room, sitting room, and into the foyer—giving one last cursory inspection to each of the spaces. The doorbell rang and Carrie looked frantic. The young woman was arranging, then rearranging the flyers on the oak table in stacks and then straight lines like she had a bad case of OCD. She looked on the verge of hyperventilating.

"They're fine, Carrie." Stephanie patted her assistant's shoulder. "Why don't you go into the kitchen and get a glass of water. I'll handle the first round of tours."

Carrie nodded, then scurried away. Her high heels clomped at a staccato pace across the hardwood floors as she fled to the kitchen. Thank God Carrie was a good assistant overall, because today that girl was definitely playing on Stephanie's last nerve.

Stephanie waited a beat and opened the front door.

"Hey, Jacob!" She greeted the real-estate agent who stood in front of her. "Glad you could make it."

"No problem. No problem," the lumbering man replied as he stepped into the foyer. He shook Stephanie's hand. "I told you my clients were eager to see some properties today. I figured we'd start here."

Stephanie peered over his broad shoulder. "Is that them?" she asked as the back car doors to a sea green Jaguar with dark-tinted windows flew open.

A boy and a girl, who both looked to be around nine years old, leaped out of the car and raced up the driveway toward the house, screaming at the top of their lungs. The boy was carrying a double-cannon water gun and started to shoot a blast of water at a blue jay that was docilely sunning in a birdbath near one of the azalea bushes. The girl twirled in a circle on the lawn, loudly singing off-key some vaguely familiar Disney tune. She was wearing a cubic zirconium crown and butterfly wings. She swung a glitter wand wildly in the air.

"Yes, it is," Jacob answered resignedly. "They've got quite the little caravan and"—he leaned toward her ear—"frankly, those twins are a handful. I wanted to spare my ears and my leather interior so I suggested my clients follow me instead of riding in my car. You won't believe how glad I am that they agreed to drive on their *own.*"

Stephanie laughed and glanced over Jacob's shoulder again.

The woman who exited the car was light-skinned and had her hair pulled back into a bun. She gazed around her, looking at the house and the surrounding neighborhood. She seemed blissfully unaware of the fact that her children were raising holy hell in the front yard, to the point that one of the neighbors had stopped mowing his grass and was peering over the white picket fence to see who was making all the racket.

While the woman smiled and sauntered up the walkway, her husband raced to the other end of the lawn.

"Terrence!" he barked. "Damn it, boy, leave that bird alone! And Melanie, stop dancing around and get back here!"

Stephanie looked at the man more closely. Her mouth fell open in shock.

Jacob sighed. "Stephanie, let me introduce to you Mr. and Mrs. Montgomery and their *lovely* children, Terrence and Melanie."

"Move," Hank said, giving his son a hard shove as they walked up the lawn toward the front door. He then looked up and locked eyes with Stephanie, who stood in the doorway. Hank's face shifted from surprise to alarm and then a masked reserve that almost made her laugh.

"Pleased . . . pleased to meet you," he choked.

Stephanie nodded, keeping her cool. "And you."

This wouldn't be the first time a man had lied to her about being married. In retrospect, the deacon had shown all the signs: going from hot to cold, abruptly ending their date, and then disappearing off the face of the earth for two weeks. But she had chalked it up to James scaring him off. Now it looked like she had been wrong. The deacon was leading two lives. She wondered if his wife knew he had a thing for whips and chains.

"Oh, this is a nice one, Hank," his wife said, patting one of the Corinthian columns as she mounted the brick steps. "Not as nice as our home back in Georgia, but close enough. Then again, *nothing* could be as nice as that house." She turned to Stephanie. "It was a renovated plantation . . . the *real* thing, not like the knockoffs you find so much around here."

Stephanie's smile tightened. She decided it was best not to respond to that one.

"Jacob, why don't you have your clients look around the house? See if they like the layout. I can answer any questions you have along the way."

Jacob nodded and ventured toward the living room. "Thanks, Steph. You can follow me, guys."

Hank's wife walked in first with her nose raised into the air. She gazed around her, frowning at the decor.

"A little cheap for my taste, but . . . it can be fixed."

Princess Melanie came in after her, pirouetting on the parquet floors. "Watch me be a ballerina, Mommy!"

She did a leap toward a podium by the door where a very expensive vase sat—one of the owner's favorites—making Stephanie's heart leap into her throat. The vase teetered wildly on its base, then miraculously righted itself. Stephanie gave a sigh of relief.

Next was Terrence.

"Wet T-shirt contest!" Terrence yelled before raising the barrel of his water gun. He sprayed at Stephanie, and she had just enough time to put her leather-bound folder in front of her breasts. If she had been a second slower, Terrence would have gotten his wish. She'd be standing there in a soaking wet silk shirt. Instead, the water bounced off her folder and trickled to the floor.

"Boy!" Hank yelled, slapping his son on the back of the head.

Terrence screeched with laughter before rushing behind his mother and sister, who had followed Jacob into the living room.

Stephanie sincerely hoped Terrence wasn't going to hose down the place. She may have to confiscate that water gun until the end of the tour.

Hank stepped through the door last. He lowered his eyes and grimaced.

"Nice family," she muttered sarcastically.

"I didn't know you were going to be here," he whispered.

"Obviously. If you had, I'm guessing you wouldn't have brought the wife and kids. The wife and kids you failed to mention anything about on *our date* two weeks ago, I might add!"

"Look, Steph, I—"

She held up her hand, stopping him before he had

the chance to make up another lie. "Save it, Hank. They're waiting for you. If you linger too long, Miss Georgia might get suspicious."

As if on cue, his wife started to shout for him. "Hank! Hank, where are you? Come and look at the kitchen!"

"I'll be right there, sweetheart!" He turned to Stephanie one last time. "Steph, I'm sorry I lied to you. But I wasn't sure you'd—"

"Hank!" his wife shouted.

"Just go," Stephanie said, waving him forward. Hank shuffled away with eyes downcast.

She closed the front door. "Men," she muttered.

How her sister Lauren had managed to fall in love with one was completely beyond her.

Chapter 17

"I'll tell you one thing," Jamal said as he dropped his putter into his golf bag and hopped onto the leather golf cart seat beside Cris. "You can definitely play some football, but you can't golf for shit!"

Cris laughed as he pressed down the gas pedal and the cart accelerated along the asphalt path.

The two men had spent most of the morning on Chesterton's pristine golf course, laboring over eighteen holes in the blazing hot sun. If there was one thing that managed to follow Cris from Texas, it was the daily swampy humidity during the summer that could make even walking a huge effort. His polo shirt was damp with sweat and clinging to his skin. His leather gloves felt soggy against his fingertips. He definitely looked forward to taking a shower and having a cool drink in the clubhouse later.

He wished he could blame his bad performance on the course in the searing August heat, but that wasn't the case. Even with his natural athletic ability, golf had never been his game. Despite Cris's handicap, Jamal still soundly beat him.

"I mean, you're *really* bad with a club, man," Jamal said with a smile as Cris steered the cart. They climbed another hill. "It was like playing my eighty-year-old nana."

"Rub it in just a little bit more, why don't you?"

"Oh, come on! I gotta rub it in! I beat the hell out of a Dallas Cowboy, a Heisman Trophy winner! I just thought because you had that whole sports and blasian thing going on, you'd be a lot better."

"*Blasian* thing? What the hell are you talking about?"

"You know, blasian: short for black Asian. Like Tiger Woods! Now *that's* a dude who can golf!"

Cris cracked up with laughter as they drew near the clubhouse. He pulled into one of the free spaces and they both hopped out onto the black asphalt that radiated a hazy outline of heat. They sought the shade of the clubhouse's blue-and-white-striped awning, then the air-conditioned foyer.

An hour after they arrived, both men emerged from the clubhouse showers and grabbed towels from the shower-room attendant before strolling into the locker room.

"So I meant to ask you . . . what's up with you and Lauren Gibbons?" Jamal inquired.

Cris raised his eyebrows. "What do you mean, what's up with us?"

"I mean, how's it going?"

"Good. Pretty damn good, in fact."

Cris and Lauren had been dating for more than a month now, and he hadn't been this happy in quite a while. Perhaps it was the thrill that came with a new relationship. Or maybe retirement allowed him to have a new perspective on life, to take joy in the simple things. Whatever it was, he really liked being around her. He looked forward to their easygoing dates and long conversations, and gazing at her beautiful face was a bonus.

Lauren had a unique combination of kindness, honesty, and sexiness that was hard to find nowadays. She was open with him and intimate—to a point. Emotionally, she held nothing back, but sexually, she was still keeping him at arm's length. To say that it was wearing on him was putting it lightly. He wasn't a guy who assumed a woman would have sex with him after three or four dates, but he *had* expected to have progressed beyond a kiss and light caresses by now. Unfortunately, anytime their clothes started to come off, Lauren would put on the brakes and he'd be left with a hard-on straining against the zipper of his jeans and a sense of frustration that would leave him tangled in knots all night. He didn't want to confront her about it, though. Considering the last relationship she had, he didn't want to come off as a bully. He just kept his desires in check and hoped things would evolve eventually . . . whenever she was ready.

"Has she robbed you blind yet?" Jamal asked with a good-natured grin, wrapping a towel around his waist.

Cris's smile faded. He glared reproachfully at his friend and opened his locker. He should have known this was coming.

"No, she hasn't robbed me blind . . . and she never will."

"Whatever you say, brothah." Jamal opened the locker beside Cris's and pulled out a duffel bag, then deodorant from the locker shelf. "I already gave you a warning. You know how I feel about it. If you want to—"

"Yes, you've told me ten thousand times how you

feel about it, Jamal. And I don't want to hear it any-more, OK?"

Jamal opened his mouth as if to speak again, to probably crack a joke. But Cris's stern gaze froze what-ever words were waiting to escape his lips. For once, Jamal held his tongue.

The two men fell silent, busying themselves with drying off and getting dressed. Cris had just finished tying the laces of his shoes when he heard loud male laughter, making both him and Jamal look up. Their eyes were drawn to the doorway leading from the showers, where two men strode into the locker room wearing towels around their waists and draped around their necks.

One was dark-skinned, short, and wiry with light tufts of hair on his chest. He looked to be in his early to late fifties. The other was much lighter in complexion, much taller, with graying hair and green eyes. The lines in his face showed he was probably the same age as his companion, but his body seemed a lot younger. He had the muscle tone of someone in his early thir-ties.

Cris had never seen either man before, but Jamal in-stantly smiled as if he recognized them.

"James! How ya doin', man?"

Both men at the other end of the locker room slowed their pace. When they saw Jamal, the light-skinned one mumbled something to the other before patting him genially on the back. His friend nodded and walked to the other side of the locker room, leav-ing him to join Jamal and Cris.

"Jamal, I didn't know they let the likes of you in here!" James joked, wiping his damp forehead with the edge of his towel. "When did you become a member?" He extended his hand.

Jamal shook it. His cocky smile broadened. "I've been a member for a couple of years now. I bribed a few people."

James chuckled.

"James, I want to introduce you to Cris Weaver. He's a longtime friend of mine. He just moved to Chesterton a few months ago."

"Oh, Mr. Weaver needs no introduction. I'm a big fan." James turned to Cris. "I watched you catch the pigskin for many years."

"Probably too many," Cris said humbly. "That's why I'm retired."

"Oh, you're still a young man in my book. I'm sure you have quite a few good years left in you." He extended his hand again. "It's a pleasure to meet you, Cris. You're probably partial to our friend Jamal over here. But if you ever need anything or any legal work on your behalf while in Chesterton, don't hesitate to contact the law offices of James Sayers, all right?"

Cris had been shaking James's hand, but froze when he heard his last name. His smile faded. His hold abruptly tightened to the point that James winced.

"You've . . . you've got quite a handshake there," James joked. His smile barely masked his discomfort.

"You're James Sayers?" Cris asked through clenched teeth, feeling his heart thud violently in his chest.

This was the man who had hit Lauren. *This* was the man who left a small, defenseless woman battered and broken. Cris had never felt such an intense, overpowering fury at someone in his life.

James nodded. "Yes, I am. Have you heard of me? Good things, I hope."

Jamal stared at his friend quizzically, sensing that something was wrong. Cris finally released James's hand.

"No, James. In fact, what I've heard about you isn't good at all. So you can save all the phony charming shit. I know *exactly* what you are."

James's brows knitted together in confusion.

Jamal quickly stepped forward and stood between the two men. "James, he doesn't mean that." He turned to Cris. "Come on, man, apologize. You didn't mean that. You barely know the man. You just met him. You can't—"

"I know enough! I know what Lauren told me! I know what he did to her!"

The buzz of voices and laughter in the locker room quickly died down to a low hush at Cris's outburst. Several curious gazes turned toward him.

"Lauren?" James asked. "You . . . you know Lauren?"

Cris saw something flicker in James's eyes then that let him know for sure that the stately-looking lawyer wasn't always as cool and pleasant as he pretended to be. A barely contained rage lingered in those irises, and it had only come to the forefront at the mention of Lauren's name. It burned intensely bright and then swiftly was snuffed out.

James slowly smiled. "Ah, I see we have a similar acquaintance. If we're talking about the same Lauren, take my advice: Anything she says should be taken with a grain of salt. The poor girl is a habitual liar, master manipulator, and an opportunist." He sighed deeply and shook his salt-and-pepper-speckled head. "Unfortunately, I found out the truth too late. By then I was out more than four hundred thousand dollars' worth of gifts, clothing, and vacations. I should have gotten receipts," he murmured, chuckling again.

"I've been trying to tell him," Jamal interjected. "I already gave him the lowdown about the Gibbons family. He won't listen!"

"It's understandable." James gazed at Cris. "You haven't lived here long. It's hard to believe a group of women could be so mercenary."

"Mercenary? Lauren isn't a mercenary! She's got too much pride for that. And stop grouping her in with her sisters! She's nothing like them! If you had—"

"Is that what she told you? She's more like her sisters than you know. In fact, I wouldn't be surprised if Lauren hadn't tracked you down the instant she found out you were moving to Chesterton." He tilted his head. "I kicked her out not too long before Thanksgiving. Did she tell you that, too? I would imagine she's in need of a new boyfriend—a new benefactor, shall we say. It seems you fit the bill, my friend."

"I'm not your goddamn friend," Cris said menacingly, making the flame of rage flicker in James's eyes again. "My friends are *real* men, and no real man would do what you did to her!"

Several eyes in the locker room widened in amazement.

"Cris!" Jamal shouted. "Have you lost your damn mind? You can't—"

"Jamal, Cris is obviously under a *dangerous* female influence. Try to be more understanding. We've all fallen prey to it at some point in our lives." James's voice sounded calm, but his strained polite smile said differently. "But I would advise you, Cris, to be careful. I wouldn't engage in any battles on Lauren's behalf. She's a good lay, but not *that* good. That gold-digging bitch really isn't worth it."

At those words, Cris suddenly wanted to leap forward and pound James senseless. He took a menacing step toward James and Jamal instantly pressed his hand against his chest, shoving him back.

It was Jamal and the other eyes in the locker room that stopped him. Besides, what would be his defense for beating James to a mangled pulp? No one knew about the abuse Lauren had suffered. As far as everyone in town would think, Cris was some deranged outsider who got violent with a respected member of the community for no apparent reason. Or worse, his anger was foolishly based on the word of a woman who almost no one in Chesterton trusted.

No, despite his anger, despite the urge to make James feel what Lauren felt that night many months ago, Cris would have to tread carefully with this one.

"Look, stay away from her," Cris said through clenched teeth, pointing at James. "Just stay the hell away from her! If I find out you even touched her again, I'll—"

"No need for threats." James's smile widened into a Cheshire cat grin. "I don't intend to seek out Miss Gibbons. Believe me. She's *all* yours."

He was lying. Cris could tell. This was a man who was accustomed to getting what he wanted. He wouldn't give up that easily.

"Well, Jamal," James said, "it was good seeing you again. I wish I could say it was a pleasure meeting you, too, Cris, but that would be disingenuous, now wouldn't it?"

Cris didn't respond. Instead he continued to glower

at James, still fighting the urge to smash his face into a million pieces.

James slowly walked away and the mood in the locker room gradually lifted. Everyone no longer seemed to gaze at them with pent-up breath, anticipating something volatile. The buzz of conversation gradually returned. A few men across the room laughed at a joke. But Cris still felt his heart pounding rapidly in his chest and his fists were still clenched. He took a deep breath and slowly felt the tension inside of him ease.

As James turned a corner and disappeared behind a row of lockers, Jamal reached out and grabbed Cris's arm. He whipped his friend around to face him.

"What the hell is wrong with you?" Jamal whispered.

"You don't know the full story, Jay. I know it seems like that came out of nowhere, but Lauren told me—"

"And you're going to take *her* word over his? See, this is why I didn't want you to hook up with that . . . that . . . scheming hooker! I knew this shit would happen!"

"Don't call her a hooker! I told you that you don't know all the details!"

"To hell with your details!" Jamal slammed his locker closed. He raised the strap of his duffel bag over his shoulder. "I have a reputation around here, Cris! I introduce you to my friends and business associates and *that's* how you treat them?"

"Jay, I know you're pissed. I know how it looks, but let's go to the bar and have a drink. I'll explain everything."

"I don't wanna have a goddamn drink! I don't want you to say shit to me!"

"Oh, come on, Jay!"

"Look, when you stop being pussy-whipped, give me a call, OK? Get your shit together! Until then, lose my number."

Cris watched in shock as Jamal marched off, pushing his way through a crowd of men who stood at the entrance of the locker room.

Chapter 18

Lauren paused from stirring her cake batter when she thought she heard a soft knock at her apartment door. She looked up from the glass bowl and glanced over her shoulder. She heard the knock again and lowered her spatula to her countertop before wiping her hands on the front of her apron.

"I wonder who that is," she muttered, glancing at the wall clock. It was fifteen minutes past ten.

She hoped it wasn't Cris. She had taken off a week from the restaurant and was enjoying her time with him, but their next date wasn't until tomorrow. She had planned to finish the gourmet strawberry shortcake that Paula had given her the recipe for and bring it to Cris's house. She hoped to surprise him with it, though he had said earlier that it was probably a good idea if she stopped making him so much food.

"I think I've gained about ten pounds since we started going out," he admitted with a laugh a few nights ago as he shoveled in another forkful of spaghetti that she had hand-pressed.

But she couldn't help it. It was her way of showing him how much she loved him. Because she *did* love him. She knew that now. She had believed for too many years that showing men affection could only be done with one's body. Now she knew that was a lie. You could do it with words, a look, or even . . .

"A cake," she now whispered to herself as she walked toward her apartment's front door. And it would be the best damn shortcake she would ever bake!

Of course, Lauren wanted desperately to share her body with Cris, too, but for now, she would hold off on doing that. She wanted him to know he was different from all the rest. She wasn't trying to manipulate him or trap him. She just wanted to love him, and she couldn't show him that if she reverted to her old ways.

Lauren pulled back the curtains over the two windowpanes in her front door. She stared in shock when she realized Cynthia's daughter, Clarissa, was standing on her front stoop, barely discernable in the awnings' shadows. She instantly unlocked the door and swung it open.

"Clarissa, honey, what are you doing here?" she asked, frowning again—this time with concern—as she gazed at her niece. "Is your mama OK? Is everything all right?"

Clarissa slowly raised her bowed head and timidly nodded. "Mama's fine, Aunt Lauren. She's on a date with some guy."

"So what's wrong?" She took a step forward and scanned the girl's face, instantly noticing Clarissa's puffy, reddened eyes. "You don't look good, honey. Have you been crying?"

Clarissa didn't answer. Instead she continued to stand near the stairs, shifting awkwardly from one foot to the other with one arm wrapped in front of her and the other hanging limply at her side. She anxiously gnawed her bottom lip. After what seemed like an eternity, she finally opened her mouth.

"I'm sorry, Aunt Lauren. I didn't . . . I mean, I didn't want to . . . but I didn't know where else to . . ." Her words faded as she lowered her gaze back to her feet.

"What's the matter, Ladybug?" Lauren whispered with a small smile. It was a question she had asked Clarissa many times when she was little, when the girl had seemed upset or sad.

Now in response, Clarissa burst into tears, catching Lauren off guard.

"Come inside." Lauren quickly stepped onto the concrete and wrapped her arm around Clarissa's trembling shoulders. She ushered her through the front door.

Though Clarissa was almost a foot taller than her aunt, it didn't take much effort to steer her toward the couch. The girl flopped onto one of the cushions as she continued to weep. Lauren sat down beside her.

"I can't do it! I *can't* do it, Aunt Lauren!" Clarissa dropped her face into her hands. "And Mama can't make me do it!"

"You can't do what, honey?" Lauren pulled Clarissa's hands from his face to hear her more clearly.

"Go . . . go out with him," Clarissa said between sobs and hiccups. "He's so *old,* Aunt Lauren! He's like . . . almost thirty!" She cringed and shook her head, whipping her long dark hair around her face. "It's so *gross!"*

Lauren raised an eyebrow. She wasn't aware that thirty years old was really that old and decrepit, but then again, she remembered this was coming from the mouth of a seventeen-year-old girl. Lauren remembered that when she was Clarissa's age, anyone older than twenty-one seemed practically ancient.

"Wait a minute," a voice inside Lauren's head suddenly shouted. "What's this stuff about Cynthia *making* her go out with this guy? What's that about?"

"Your mother wants you to have a date with this man?"

Clarissa wiped away her tears with the back of her hand. "Yeah, it's supposed to be Saturday night. He works for one of her boyfriends. He wants to take me out to dinner. But Aunt Lauren, I don't want to go! I told Mama I didn't, but she's making me go anyway. She said . . ." Clarissa sniffed. "She said that it's . . . about time . . . I-I got some practice."

Lauren should have known this was coming. Cynthia could only teach Clarissa so long before "sending her out into the field" to gain experience, and it looked like that time had finally arrived. But it was so obvious that Clarissa wasn't into this. She didn't want to be like her mother, grandmother, or great-grandmother. She didn't want to be a gold digger. Lauren could sympathize with Clarissa wholeheartedly. Maybe that's why, out of all her aunts, Clarissa had chosen to come to Lauren for help.

"Aunt Lauren, I swear, I will *run away* if she makes me go to dinner with that man! I'll get on a Greyhound bus and go far away from here and no one will ever see me again!"

"No, you won't."

"Why not?" the girl screeched, her voice now tinged with anger and panic. "I'd rather leave than have to do this!"

"Because I'd miss you, Ladybug." Lauren pushed

the hair out of her niece's eyes. "We'd *all* miss you. And you running off and living alone on the street isn't the way to handle this. It would only be worse for you out there."

Clarissa defiantly crossed her arms over her chest. "*How* could it be worse?"

Lauren leaned back against the couch cushion and gazed at her niece solemnly. "Because pretty young women like you have to do a lot more than eat dinner with thirty-year-old men to survive when you're out there on the street."

Clarissa's hard face softened.

"Because using your body to get food to eat and a place to live is the name of the game out there, and it makes girls older than their time. Some of them even turn to drugs and alcohol to forget what they've done, to get through the day."

Clarissa audibly swallowed.

Lauren placed her hand over her niece's. "You don't want to be like that, do you, Ladybug?"

"No," she finally whispered.

"I didn't think so."

"Then what *do* I do, Aunt Lauren? I can't run away and I can't go out on a date with that guy. I told you that. And Mama won't listen to me!"

"Let me handle it." Lauren smiled as she gave the girl's hand a reassuring squeeze.

"What do you mean?"

Lauren hesitated before she gave Clarissa her answer. She had avoided becoming involved in this even though she thought it was wrong the way that Cynthia was raising Clarissa to follow in her size-seven, gold-digging footsteps. After all, Clarissa was Lauren's niece, *not* her daughter, and as long as Cynthia wasn't putting Clarissa in harm's way, Lauren felt she had no right to interfere.

But Lauren's mindset on the whole issue had changed. Clarissa had come to her for help. The girl had obviously reached her breaking point, and someone needed to speak up for her. It looked like Lauren was going to have to be the one to do it.

Lauren slowly rose from the couch and reached for the cordless phone. She began to type in her sister's home number on the phone's buttons. "I'm going to call your mother and we'll—"

"*No!* No, Aunt Lauren, please don't do that!" Clarissa shouted as she jumped up from the couch. "She doesn't know I'm here! She doesn't even know I left my room! She grounded me when I talked back to her. I had to sneak out to get here!"

Lauren hung up the phone. "But honey, that's even more of a reason for me to call her. What if she's realized you're gone? She could be worried sick."

Clarissa, in a very unladylike manner that would have made her mother cringe, snorted in disgust. "She doesn't care about me. All she cares about is money and clothes and her stupid cars. She doesn't give a damn about me!"

"That's not true. Your mother *loves* you, honey."

Clarissa didn't look convinced.

"She just . . . she just has a bad way of showing it. But no one taught her . . . *any of us* . . . any better. She's doing the same thing that was done to her. She doesn't know any different, that's all."

Clarissa's pouty lips formed into a grim line.

"Let me talk to her." Lauren placed a hand on Clarissa's shoulder. "At least give *me* a chance."

"It won't work."

"But what do you have to lose if I try?"

For several seconds, Clarissa didn't respond. Then after some time, she threw up her hands.

"Fine," she mumbled before flopping back onto the couch. "Whatever! But I'm telling you, it's not going to make a difference. She won't listen."

Lauren started to dial Cynthia's number again, but paused before dialing the last digit. She gazed at her niece, who was nervously biting her recently manicured nails.

"I think you're wrong, Ladybug. I really do."

She listened as the phone began to ring on the other end.

"Where is she?" Cynthia asked through clenched teeth as Lauren opened her front door. Cynthia's hazel eyes, which were rimmed with runny mascara from crying, were now blazing with fury. "Where the hell *is* she?"

Lauren held up a hand, hoping to quell her eldest sister's temper.

Just as Lauren had suspected, Cynthia had realized after arriving home from her date at the symphony that Clarissa was not in her room. When Lauren called, Cynthia had answered the phone in tears and in panic, blathering about how she had checked every room in the house before finally concluding that Clarissa had, indeed, disappeared. Lauren quickly told Cynthia not to worry; Clarissa was safe at her apartment. Then the line abruptly clicked. Ten minutes later, Cynthia was charging down her front steps. She must have broken the speed limit and run quite a few red lights to make her way across town so quickly.

"Cindy, please calm down. She's already scared you're going to flip out on her. I didn't call you over here to—"

Cynthia didn't let her finish. Instead she barged past Lauren into the apartment, almost knocking her younger sister to the ground. She stomped in her four-inch heels into Lauren's living room.

Cynthia hadn't changed her clothes from her date. She was still dressed in a voluminous white evening gown. Diamond teardrop earrings dangled from her delicate lobes and diamond cuffs were around each wrist. Her lips were painted blood red and her hair was slicked back into a bun at the crown of her head.

She looks like the White Witch of Narnia, Lauren thought morosely.

Clarissa must have thought so, too, for she cowered on the couch under her mother's glare as if anticipating the moment when Cynthia would turn her into stone with the flick of a concealed wand.

"Horseback riding lessons," Cynthia began, her chest rising and falling with each shaky breath she took. "You've had them since you were eight years old. Credit cards . . . trips to Disney World, the Bahamas, and Europe . . . you said you wanted a BMW convertible when you get your driver's license next month. Did I tell you 'no'?"

"No," Clarissa whispered as she shook her bowed head.

"No, I didn't, did I?" Cynthia yelled hysterically. "You have everything any girl could ever want and this is the thanks I get? You go sneaking out the window in the middle of the night when I specifically forbade you to leave the house? You run away when I'm only trying to do what's best for you? That's the thanks I get? *Huh?* Answer me!"

Clarissa didn't respond. That seemed to anger her mother more.

"You're just selfish, Clarissa! You're a spoiled, selfish, little brat, and I'm tired of—"

Lauren stepped forward. "Cindy, that's enough. Stop yelling at her."

Like a coiled snake, Cynthia instantly snapped her head to look in her sister's direction. "Don't you tell me to stop! Don't you *dare* tell me to stop! I'm speaking to *my* daughter! This has nothing to do with you!"

"Yes, it does, because she's my niece as well as your daughter!" Lauren met her sister's glare with her own. "And I'm not going to stand here and let you call her names when I know she tried to talk to you about how she felt! You just didn't listen!"

Cynthia turned back around and scowled at Clarissa. "Wait for me in the car. I'm parked in the lot out front. I need to talk to your aunt in private."

Clarissa slowly raised her head. She gazed at her mother with tear-filled eyes. "B-but I . . . I thought—"

"Wait for me in the car!" Cynthia boomed, making Clarissa jump.

The girl quickly rose from the couch and dashed toward the front door. She and Lauren exchanged a meaningful look before she left.

I told you she wouldn't listen, Aunt Lauren, Clarissa's sad expression said as she quickly shut the door behind her. Lauren and Cynthia listened as she climbed the steps to the sidewalk above.

"Laurie, I'm only going to tell you this once, and I'm only giving you the courtesy because you're my sister." Cynthia pointed down at her, taking a menacing step toward her. "From now on, stay the hell out of my business, all right? She's my damn child and you have no right to—"

"She came to me for help! What should I have done? *Turned her away?*"

"She only came to you because you've probably been putting bullshit into her head!"

"What?"

"You heard me! You've probably been going behind my back all along and telling her that what I do is wrong and dirty, but from now on, you can keep your damn thoughts to yourself, little Miss Hypocrite! Stop trying to turn my daughter against me!"

"Cynthia, you are paranoid and delusional if you actually think I would do that!"

Her sister gave an icy smile. "You're just jealous! We all know you are. You made a bad choice, a *stupid* decision when you hooked up with James Sayers, and you're jealous of all of us for not falling into the same trap! You're miserable and you want to make everyone else miserable, too! But I won't let you do that to Clarissa! I won't let you—"

"Shut up! Just shut up! I didn't turn Clarissa against you! You're doing a perfectly good job of that yourself, you stupid bitch!"

Cynthia's mouth fell open. Her little sister had never spoken to her like that. Cynthia was usually the one who spit venom. Rarely did she get it spit back at her.

Lauren closed her eyes and took a calming breath, silently telling herself to count to ten. She couldn't reason with her sister if she got just as angry as her, and Cynthia needed a good dose of reasoning right now.

"I'm sorry. I didn't mean to . . . I'm sorry I called

you that. Look," Lauren began quietly, "I'm not going to lie to you. I don't think it's right to make a seventeen-year-old girl go out with a thirty-year-old man."

"He's twenty-seven," Cynthia said tightly.

"Whatever! He's still too old for her and I didn't have to tell her that. Clarissa came to that conclusion without my help."

"What's the big deal? I didn't tell her to have sex with him! They're just going out to dinner! Once she gets over her nervousness, she'll do fine. How else is she going to learn to use her techniques and how to—"

"She *told* you she doesn't want to do this and you're making her do it anyway. You're putting the rift between you two, not me!"

For the first time, Cynthia didn't shout her disagreement. Instead, she rolled her eyes.

"She's hurt and she's angry," Lauren continued. "This time when Clarissa ran away from home she came to me. But what happens the next time she runs away? What if she goes someplace where you can't find her? What if you never *see her again,* Cindy? Do you want that to happen?"

"Of course I don't."

"Then act like it!" Lauren took a step toward her sister. *"Please* don't make her do this."

They both stood in silence for what felt like an eternity.

"I went on my first date with a man when I was seventeen years old, Lauren."

Lauren nodded. "I know. So did I."

"I'm not asking her to do any more than what was asked of me. We all had to do it. That's how we learned. I'm only trying to help her!"

The love of her daughter was apparent in Cynthia's

voice and in her tired eyes. It was a warped love, but it was there all the same. Cynthia now looked less like a snow queen and more like a troubled, heartbroken mother.

"I don't know why she keeps fighting me."

"Because when she's pushed in a corner, she can be just as strong-willed as you are. Come on, Cindy. We didn't get a choice about what happened to us. We were *made* to follow that path. Let her make her own choice."

"She's just scared now," Cynthia argued softly. "We all were when we were that age, when we went out there the first time. She's overwhelmed. But she'll . . . she'll come around."

"Maybe. And if she does come around and tells you she wants to keep learning and training, so be it. Teach her. But if she doesn't come around, let it go. You have to let her make her own decision on something like this. You can't force it. It's not right."

"I don't know why I would bother listening to you . . ." She paused and Lauren's shoulders slumped.

So I guess I lost the battle then, Lauren thought.

". . . but I am going to listen to you *this* time. I'll let her make her own decision, but I still think it's a big mistake."

Lauren grinned.

"I'm only doing it because I love her," Cynthia said quickly, the hardness returning to her gaze and her voice. *"Not* because you told me to. Frankly, I couldn't give a damn what you think."

Lauren continued to smile, refusing to let her sister dampen her victory and budding good mood. "That's good enough for me!"

Her sister pursed her lips. For the first time, she slowly let her gaze scan around Lauren's apartment. She curled her lip in utter disgust.

"God, you live in a dump," she muttered, making Lauren laugh.

Some things never change, she thought, *my sister being one of them.*

Chapter 19

"So you two are OK now?" Stephanie asked as she stared down at her big toe with nail polish wand in hand.

She and Lauren were discussing the drama surrounding Clarissa running away to Lauren's house last night. Stephanie listened to Lauren tell the story while she painted her toenails bubblegum pink. As she wiggled her toenails and gazed at her feet, she contemplated the color. She wasn't too keen on the pink. Maybe it would be cute if she was thirteen years old. Not so hot at age thirty-three.

"Yeah, we're OK," Lauren said on the other end of the phone line. "You know how your sister is. Cindy is quick to get pissed off and—"

"Then act like nothing ever happened a minute later," Stephanie finished for her, putting her bottle of nail polish aside on the floor. She lay back on her chaise longue. "Yeah, I know."

"She just wants what's best for Clarissa. I get that. But Clarissa just isn't ready for all of this."

"Ready for all of what?" Stephanie asked with a frown as she reached for a style magazine that sat on the chaise cushion beside her.

"Ready for what all of us have been doing for the past thirty years, Steph. You know . . . trapping and seducing men and taking their money! She wants more out of life, and I support her decision. I told Cynthia that and I meant it. It's just not a good way to live!"

Stephanie fought the urge to roll her eyes. She hoped she wasn't going to have to endure another one of Lauren's sermons. Ever since Lauren had left James, she had been preaching her born-again gospel endlessly, like she was on a mission to save her sisters' gold-digging souls. Stephanie and Dawn didn't react quite as strongly to Lauren's admonishments about their lifestyles as Cynthia did, but all of them were getting wary of her routine. It was starting to get tedious.

Just then, the doorbell rang. Stephanie tossed aside her magazine, relieved to have an excuse to get off the phone before her sister started preaching.

"I mean, just think about it, Steph," Lauren rambled. "We've been taught all our lives that men are just—"

"You're going to have to hold that thought, Laurie. I have to call you back." She glanced over her shoulder at her bedroom doorway as her bell rang again. "Someone's at my door."

"Oh, OK," Lauren said. "Well, I'll . . . I'll talk to you later this week, huh?"

"Sure. Talk to you later. Bye," Stephanie sang before hanging up the phone. She put on her yellow silk robe and pattered in bare feet across the floor, walking on her heels, careful not to mess up her newly painted toenails. She pulled back one of the curtain panels and

scowled when she saw who was standing on her WEL-
COME mat.

Oh, Lord, she thought. *Not him again!*

She let the curtain close, unlocked her front door,
and swung it open. "What the hell do you want,
Hank?" she snapped, glaring at the philandering deacon.

She hadn't seen his lying ass since he brought his
family to the house showing a week ago. She had
stayed on her best behavior the entire time, pretending
as if she had never met him before in her life and only
making one tongue-in-cheek comment when his snooty
wife remarked that the home's backyard was a "little on
the small side."

"But it's the perfect size for Jack Russell terriers,"
Stephanie had responded.

"Jack Russell terriers?" his wife asked. "We don't
have Jack Russell terriers."

"Oh, you don't?" Stephanie had turned to look at
Hank, who instantly looked away, ignoring her pene-
trating gaze. "My apologies. Someone told me you
did."

Stephanie had assumed Hank had embarrassed himself enough and that would be the end of their short-
lived affair, but here he was, sniffing at her door again.
Some people were gluttons for punishment.

Some men are just too stupid.

"I bought you a gift," he said, holding a small shopping bag toward her.

The bag was Tiffany blue, and even in the dim
evening light, Stephanie could spot the unmistakable
TIFFANY & CO. emblem embossed on its side.

Oh, no, he didn't! How did this man know her

Achilles' heel? She had never in her life been able to turn down a gift from Mama Tiffany.

Stephanie cocked an eyebrow and yanked the bag out of his hand. She lowered her gaze and looked inside its depths. "What is it?"

He gave a tentative smile. "Open it and see."

She reached inside, pulled out a leather box, removed the cardboard belly band wrapped around it, and flipped the box open. A yellow-gold bangle bracelet sat in the center of the box. It was embedded with diamonds.

Nice, Stephanie thought. She put on the bracelet, held up her wrist in the air, and admired the jewelry in the light from the doorway lamp. *Very nice!*

"Can I come in?" he asked quietly, looking at her pleadingly. "Can we talk?"

Stephanie lowered her wrist and narrowed her eyes at him. She should probably tell him "no." Any man who showed up at a woman's house unannounced at eight o'clock at night didn't come just for conversation. The Honorable Deacon Montgomery probably had a lot more than talking on his kinky little mind. But he had just shown up at her house bearing what looked like a three- to five-thousand-dollar gift. (She planned to Google the bracelet later to confirm the exact price.) Stephanie had no plans to drop the panties, but she'd let him stay for a while. A bracelet like this had at least earned him that courtesy.

She waved him inside and Hank smiled eagerly before stepping over the threshold.

Neither of them noticed the car parked across the street *or* the woman sitting in the driver's seat wearing dark sunglasses who looked alarmingly like Hank's snooty wife. The woman sank lower in her car seat just as Stephanie shut the door behind Hank.

Stephanie led him into her daintily decorated living room and sat down on her off-white sofa. "What did you want to say?" she asked expectantly.

"I just . . . I just wanted a chance to explain myself."

"What is there to explain? You're married and you were trying to cheat on your wife. Seems pretty simple to me."

"But it's not!" he argued, pacing in front of her. "Look, I . . . I prayed on it and God . . . God wanted me to explain myself to you. He wants me to make amends."

She laughed. "Oh, He does, does He?"

Since when was God in the business of encouraging men to go out and cheat on their wives? *God does work in mysterious ways,* she thought. This was turning into one amusing night.

"God said to me . . . He said, 'Hank, you've got to explain yourself to this woman. You've got to tell her that you weren't trying to fool her. You just . . . you just couldn't tell her that you were married because you weren't sure how she would react. But you have needs . . . needs like any other man has. You were just trying to cater to those needs. That's all you were trying to do.' "

Hank stopped pacing and looked at her.

"My wife, Penny, she just . . . she just doesn't understand me, Stephanie. She won't do what I like . . . in the bedroom, you know. We do the same position once a month on Saturday evening like clockwork. She wears the same ol' pink lingerie set. We always have to wait until the kids are in bed and fast asleep. If I try to do anything a little different, she looks at me like I'm crazy. I tried to get her to do it . . . you know . . . doggie style once, and she said I must have had the devil in me!"

He started pacing again.

Stephanie sighed, propped her elbow on her knee, and dropped her chin into her hand.

This was the other downside of being a mistress. If it wasn't dealing with paranoid husbands and crazy wives, it meant listening to endless ramblings about boring stuff like this. What made these men think you wanted to be their shrink? Stephanie should probably get a Ph.D. in psychology for how many men she counseled through their depressing marriages.

"So after a while, I started to get tired of it, you know?" Hank continued, oblivious to her growing boredom. "So . . . so back in Georgia, I started to . . . I started to see other women. I didn't do anything wrong, at first. I just went on dates with them. I'd have dinner and maybe kiss one or two of them. It was innocent, completely innocent! Then . . . then the next thing I knew I was seeing *five* women at a time. I'd meet them at church or at the grocery store or at the post office. Now I was having sex *all* the time," he said gleefully, "and I was doing it any way and anywhere I wanted! I'm doing it doggie style in the shower and I'm . . . I'm getting my dick sucked in the backseat of cars . . . and sometimes . . . sometimes I'm even fucking two women at a time . . . and I loved it! I *loved* it!"

Stephanie wondered if he realized he was salivating.

"Then one of the women I met was into . . . into . . . you know . . . that bondage stuff. Her name was Leslie, but she wanted me to call her . . . to call her Mistress Candy. She used to wear a leather mask and these spiked high heels. She'd blindfold me, bend me over the bed, and whip me until I cried or I came, whichever happened first."

He stopped and slowly shook his head.

"And I knew . . . I knew after that, I couldn't go back. I couldn't go back to sex once a month on Saturday evening after the kids go to sleep. I couldn't go back to just missionary style and sex with all the lights off."

He fell into one of her armchairs.

"But then . . . but then Penny found out about what I was doing. She found a text message from one of my girlfriends. She wanted to take the kids and leave me, but I promised her I would be true to her. I would change. So we moved here to Virginia to start all over again. Stephanie, I haven't cheated on my wife in over a year. But we're back to the way things were before, and now I can't help myself. It's a . . . an itch I gotta scratch, and Penny won't help me scratch it!" He closed his eyes. "So I lied to my wife and I lied to you, too . . . and I'm sorry about that. But I don't have the devil in me. I don't! I'm just a man . . . just a man with needs."

Stephanie watched as he sat silently with his head bowed and in his hands. He looked so damn pitiful. She glanced again at the Tiffany gold bangle bracelet on her wrist, then at the hairbrush she had left sitting on her glass end table when she was brushing her hair earlier that day.

All right, she thought. *I'll be nice and throw him a bone.*

Hank was about to get an early Christmas present.

"Enough with the whining," she sneered, grabbing the silver hairbrush and rising to her feet.

He raised his eyes and looked at her, completely baffled. "Whining?"

She took off her robe and let it drop to the living room floor. He sat slack-jawed as she stood in front of him in her boy-cut panties and lace bra with her legs spread shoulder-width apart. She slapped the flat side of the brush against the palm of her hand, filling the living room with a loud *thwack.*

"Yes, *whining,* Hank. Because that's what it is. You expect me to feel sorry for you? You cheated on your wife. You *lied* to me!" She rapped the brush against his thigh, making him flinch, catching him by surprise. "You've been a very, *very* bad boy, Hank."

She could see a gleam return to his eyes. He loudly swallowed. "I . . . I have?"

Stephanie leaned toward his face so that their noses were mere inches apart. "Yes, you have, and what happens to boys who are bad . . . when they don't obey their mistress?"

"They get . . . they get punished?" he asked with a smile.

She nodded and stood back, gesturing with the hairbrush. "Exactly! So drop your pants and bend your ass over!"

She didn't have to tell him twice! He quickly rose to his feet, unbuckled his belt, and lowered the zipper of his pants. He let his Armani slacks fall to his ankles and then braced his hands on both arms of the chair. He bent over, revealing his boxer brief–covered behind.

Stephanie resisted the urge to burst into laughter. She knew she had to stay in character if this was going to work. She pulled back her arm and then swung, loudly smacking his ass.

"And the next time . . ." *Thwack!*

". . . you even think about . . ." *Thwack!*

". . . lying to me . . ." *Thwack!*

". . . you better damn well think again . . ." *Thwack!*

". . . because I will beat . . ." *Thwack!*

". . . the hell out of you . . ." *Thwack!*

". . . all over again!" *Thwack!*

When she heard him grunt and saw him shudder, then go slack, she knew she had accomplished her goal. Deacon Montgomery had finally gotten what he needed and she had gotten a nice bracelet out of it, too!

Stephanie watched as he took several breaths and slowly bent down and raised his pants back to his waist. He raised his zipper and turned to her. He was grinning from ear to ear.

"Thank you so much for that, Stephanie."

"You're welcome," she said grudgingly as she shrugged back into her robe. She then knotted the belt around her waist.

He took a step toward her, licking his lips. He reached for the belt of her robe and began to toy with it. "Can I . . . can I see you again?"

Stephanie tugged the belt out of his hand. "I'm afraid this was a one-time performance, Hank. Just think of it as a thank-you for my gift."

Hank nodded, looking a little crestfallen, and walked toward her front door. As he did, she noticed that he was walking funny. Maybe she had overdone it a little with the spanking, but, hey, he had seemed to enjoy himself. She wasn't sure how he was going to explain those red welts that were probably on his ass to his wife, but that wasn't really Stephanie's problem.

Hank opened the front door and turned one last time

to gaze at her. He gave a half smile. "Really, Stephanie, thank you for that. You don't know how much—"

"Don't mention it," she said, waving a hand at him dismissively.

He stepped through the door into the August night and closed her front door behind him. Stephanie locked her deadbolt and sighed. She had definitely done her good deed for the day.

She didn't know why Lauren and everyone else in this town knocked her lifestyle so much. Gold diggers like herself were performing a public service. Hell, she was a damn goodwill ambassador! Who *else* was going to spank cheating husbands until it put a smile back on their faces, until they were willing to go back home to their wives to give their unhappy marriages another try?

With that she walked back to her bedroom to repaint her toenails.

"I think I'll go with fire engine red," she said. "That's right. Red for Mistress Stephanie."

Chapter 20

Cris slowly trudged down the steps to his foyer when he heard his doorbell ring. Even though he had been looking forward to seeing Lauren all week, he suspected he wouldn't be much company. For the past several days, he had been in a dark mood and unable to shake it.

He hadn't talked to Jamal since their spat at the country club. He had picked up the phone to call his friend several times, only to hang up.

Jamal should be the one calling me, he thought angrily. *Jamal should be the one apologizing!*

After all, Cris had only been standing up for Lauren. If Jamal knew what James had done to her, he would have been rushing to her defense, too. Cris was certain of it. But Jamal had disappointed him. Instead of having his back, instead of taking his word first—without question, Jamal had turned on him and taken James's side instead.

"Which is just bullshit," Cris murmured as he walked across his marble floors to his French doors.

Compared to Cris, James was practically a stranger. James Sayers hadn't been Jamal's friend for more than fifteen years. That smug bastard hadn't played interference with Jamal's angry dates when Jamal forgot he had double booked, nor had he given Jamal the dire warning three years ago to check the neck of the hot club beauty who later turned out to be a transvestite! James hadn't driven Jamal home when he got so drunk he had puked on himself, subsequently messing up the newly vacuumed interior of Cris's Jeep Cherokee, and James damn sure wouldn't have Jamal's back in a fist-fight, as Cris had on more than one occasion!

James hadn't done and wouldn't do *any* of those things, which is why Cris was so pissed. He had been a loyal friend to Jamal for many years. All he asked for was the same loyalty in return.

Cris opened the front door and was greeted by Lauren's smile.

"Hey," she said cheerfully.

He rarely saw her out of her chef's clothes, but tonight she had on a white T-shirt, a short denim skirt that more than flattered her figure, and flat silver sandals. Her hair was down, cascading around her face and lightly brushing her shoulders. She was holding a cake box against her chest.

"Hey, beautiful," he replied softly, ushering her inside.

As her eyes scanned his face, her smile disappeared. "Are you all right?" He shut the door behind her and then took the box out of her hands.

He nodded, giving his best imitation of a smile. "Sure, I'm fine. Why wouldn't I be?"

He leaned down, linked an arm around her waist, and kissed her. Her lips were buttery soft and coconut sweet. He wanted to taste more, but she abruptly pulled her mouth away before he could.

"You're going to crush the cake," she muttered with a giggle, pointing down at the box. She studied him again. "Cris, you really don't look fine. In fact, you look mad as all hell."

"Why would I be mad?"

"That's a good question. I guess you'll tell me eventually."

"So are you finally going to tell me what's wrong?" she asked, plopping beside him, tucking a foot beneath her bottom.

Cris let out a tired sigh.

They were sitting on one of the leather couches in the great room and had just settled in to watch a movie on the plasma-screen television. Slices of the whipped-cream-and-strawberry-covered shortcake she had baked sat on the coffee table, waiting to be devoured. Cris wasn't in the mood to talk, to rehash what had happened between him and Jamal. He wanted to eat his damn cake and enjoy his woman's company. But it seemed Lauren wouldn't let the issue drop.

"I told you that it's nothing."

Lauren reached for the remote control beside him. She pressed a button and muted the television. "And I told you that you're full of it. I haven't known you for that long, Cris, but I think I've known you long enough to sense when you're acting differently." She raised a hand to his face and lightly rubbed his cheek. She gave a small smile. "You can talk to me."

"It's only going to piss you off, too."

"So what? I've got a thick skin."

He hesitated. "Fine, if you really want to know. . . . Look, I ran into your ex-boyfriend last week at the country club."

Lauren's lips instantly tightened. "I see." She closed her eyes. "So I'm guessing James said something to you."

"Of course he did. Assholes like that can never keep their mouths shut. There was a lot of shit-talking on his part, but I stood up for you."

Lauren opened her eyes and smiled. She squeezed his arm. "Thank you."

"You don't have to thank me. I wasn't going to let him talk about you like that, not while I was there anyway. He was only seconds away from getting his ass whupped, but . . . a friend of mine who's a member of the country club, who is sort of friends with James, didn't respond too well. He said I embarrassed him."

Lauren frowned.

"But you know what, to hell with him! Jamal and I have known each other long enough—nineteen years—that he should have had my back! If this ends our friendship, so be it."

"I didn't mean to cause a rift between you and your friend, Cris. Are you sure you two can't work this out?"

"What is there to work out? Men aren't like women, Lauren. We aren't fighting one day and best friends the next. That's not in our makeup. It's certainly not in mine. It's not in Jay's, either."

She tilted her head as she gazed up at him. "But if you've been close friends for *nineteen years,* Cris, that's more than just any friendship. He's kind of like a brother to you, isn't he? The crap you put up with from family isn't the same as what you would put up with from just any friend."

Cris considered her words. Perhaps that's why he was taking this so hard. He and Jamal had grown up very differently. They had vastly different personalities. But he thought he had a strong enough bond with Jamal that they were kind of like brothers.

"You know, I really hate my sisters sometimes. And I mean *hate*—with a passion. Cynthia was at my apartment a few days ago, barking orders at me. She's been bossing us around since we were little. Stephanie can act like such a selfish princess sometimes and that drives me crazy. Dawn is the smart one, but she can be just as cynical as Cynthia. Some days I think if I could get as far away from them as possible, I'd be *so* happy." She laughed. "But I love them, Cris, and they love me, too. For every bad side to them, there's a good side. Cynthia may be bossy, but she's also strong-willed and loyal to her family. Stephanie can be selfish, but she can also be sweet and kind when you need her. Dawn swears she knows everything, but I've seen her open her heart before. If I could put up with all their crap and still see what's good in them, in their core—you can definitely make up with Jamal. He doesn't sound half as messed up as they are."

"What if I don't want to make up with him. Maybe I think he should come to me first."

"Then men are more like women than you think."

She leaned over and kissed him. As their lips met, Cris felt a familiar stirring in the pit of his belly. Their eyelids lowered. He opened his lips and so did she. She linked her arms around his neck as their tongues delved into one another's mouths, as she pulled his bottom lip between her teeth. Before he knew it, their sweet kiss had morphed into something a lot hotter.

Cris grunted hungrily as he lifted her from the

couch and dragged her onto his lap. She adjusted, swinging one leg over the other side of him so that she was now straddling his waist. When he felt her pelvis grind into his hardened manhood, it was all he could do not to rip off her panties right then and there, part her legs, and enter the slick wetness in between her thighs. But Cris held back. He didn't want to rush this. He wanted to savor the moment: the smell of her, the feel of her against his fingertips, and the taste of her. He had to take his time.

He pushed up her T-shirt and tugged it over her head, revealing the red lace bra underneath. He quickly undid the clasps behind her back and pushed the bra aside, cupping one breast, squeezing it gently. He lowered his mouth to one of the nipples and she threw back her head and moaned.

He raised the hem of her denim skirt and felt her tense for the first time as his fingers began to explore past the elastic waistband of her silk underwear. He tested the moistness there, teasing her clit with his fingertips while sucking on her breasts. She breathed in sharply and her hands went from being wrapped around his shoulders to gripping the back of the couch. Her fingernails sank into the supple leather upholstery. He began to massage the wetness as he kissed her and her hips began to twist and buck, meeting his strokes. Oh, she was ready. He could tell. Now if only he could keep her going before she threw on the brakes again.

When Cris slipped two fingers inside her, Lauren breathed sharply, opening her eyes. She looked down at him with a heady gaze. The gyrations of her hips became swifter. Minutes later she started to moan against his lips and he took that as his cue. Using his fingers wasn't enough. He wanted to be inside her. He shifted

Lauren from his lap to the couch's cushions where she laid back. Just as he pulled down the zipper of his jeans and nestled between her thighs, he felt her push hard against his chest.

"Cris, stop," she murmured against his lips. "It's too soon."

Cris raised himself to his elbows and gazed down at her with panting breath. *"Huh?* You're not ready yet? Want me to go down on you?"

If it meant getting her in the mood, he'd happily "dive" right in.

She laughed. "I don't think my body could take that right now if you did," she answered, breathing hard. "No . . . it's too . . . soon. All of it! I can't . . . I can't do this."

He gazed at her in disbelief. *"What?"*

She pushed at his chest again. "Get up."

He did as she asked, begrudgingly. He sat up and went to the other side of the couch and watched as she pushed down her skirt and put her bra back on.

"Look, in the old days, I would do it," she said, reaching for her shirt. "I would have been all over you *weeks* ago, but I'm different now."

"How different?"

"Different enough that I know you can't use sex to get a man, to convince him to care about you."

"But you've *already* got me, Lauren!" he shouted, then paused, pushing down his frustration. "I care about you. You know that. You don't have to convince me of a damn thing!"

"Yes, I do. I have to convince you that you're different . . . and I can't do that if I give it up this soon." She sighed. "Look, I'm not trying to play mind games,

Cris. I'm done with that, but I think you'll respect me, you'll *understand* me more, if we wait a little longer."

He slowly shook his head. "Well, how much longer are we talking?"

She hesitated, then shrugged at him helplessly.

"Well, when you figure it out, tell me. I want to mark it on my damn calendar," he mumbled, adjusting the front of his pants.

Chapter 21

Three days later, Lauren stepped onto the cracked cement and into the warm August sun. She let the kitchen's steel door slam shut behind her as she strolled into the cooler shadows of the alleyway.

Phillip was the only other one out there. He was smoking a cigarette and lounging back against the alley's soot-covered brick wall. The lit cigarette now hung limply from the side of his mouth.

Lauren leaned against the wall beside him. She gazed up at him quizzically. "Should you be smoking?"

"Probably not."

"You're only going to make yourself sick again."

He glanced down at her. "So you're a sous chef *and* a nurse, huh?"

They had just finished the morning prep and were appreciating the couple of coveted hours before the lunch rush began. Lauren had told Cris yesterday that she would try to sneak to his house to spend some time together if she could. She badly wanted to. She had been so busy for the last couple of days that she hadn't seen him since that night when they had come dangerously close to having sex on his great room's couch.

"You say that like it's a bad thing," a voice in her head mocked.

Well, it is, she thought indignantly. Gold diggers were easy. Girlfriends were not, she resolved. If it meant her being celibate for a few more weeks, so be it.

"That thinking's a bit antiquated, isn't it?" the voice in her head replied.

Maybe, Lauren thought. But so far she had stuck to all the other rules of her new life, her new self. She couldn't just ignore this one because of her raging hormones.

"Walk with me, *chérie,*" Phillip said, breaking into the bubble of her thoughts. "It's too nice of a day to be standing back here with a bunch of stinky Dumpsters."

She followed him out of the alleyway onto Main Street. It was teeming with people this close to lunch hour and she and Phillip quickly blended into the crowd.

"So how do you like working here?" Phillip suddenly inquired as they walked along the sidewalk. "I haven't scared you too much with my crazy ways, have I?"

"Do you really have to ask? I *love* working here, Phillip. You know being a chef has always been my dream. I don't mind the long hours, the burns, and the cuts. It's totally worth it."

"I thought you would love it. The first day I met you, you had that hungry look. I know it when I see it. But in the beginning, I wondered if you could hack it. Out of all the people who applied for the line-cook job, you definitely were the most green."

"So . . . why did you hire me?" she asked cautiously.

Part of her was scared to hear what he was going to say, but the question was already out there.

Phillip blew a cloud of smoke from the side of his mouth. "Because I thought you were talented. I still do. A lot of people can learn how to cook, go to fancy schools, and mimic technique, but it takes true talent and skill to be a great chef, *chérie*. When you came to my house with that platter, I knew you had the potential in you. And . . ." He paused, tapping his cigarette so that the ashes fell onto the concrete. "I don't like people tellin' me what I should and shouldn't do. Phillip Rochon don't take orders like some errand boy."

"Huh? Who tried to give you orders?"

"That ex-boyfriend of yours."

Lauren stopped walking, wondering if she'd heard Phillip correctly. "My ex-boyfriend? You mean *James?*"

"The one and only." They started to walk again. "I guess he found out that you were tryin' to get the line-cook position at my restaurant. I don't know how he found out, but he did. He came strollin' in one day with his big talk." Phillip sneered. "He told me that it would be 'in my best interests' not to hire someone like you. He said you had a bad reputation around town, that you were an 'unsavory character.' He said you took money from him."

"I didn't take his money! He's a damn liar! He *gave* me that money! I was just stupid enough to . . . to . . ."

Her words drifted off. She glared at her feet with anger and humiliation. Her face felt like it was on fire.

James had actually gone to Phillip to slander her, to try to keep her from getting hired? The hate she now felt for her ex-boyfriend she couldn't put into words. She wished he would just leave her alone. Why did he keep lingering, haunting her like a malevolent phantasm? She finally took a deep, calming breath and tore her gaze from the sidewalk.

"Phillip, look, I'm . . . I'm sorry for that. If you want to know the truth, I did accept his money. But it's not like I stole it from him. He gave it to me freely because he"—her cheeks warmed again—"because he got something in return. I'm not proud of it, but—"

Phillip waved his hand. "You don't have to explain it to me," he assured mercifully. "That's your business. It ain't got anything to do with me, and I told him as much. I said what people do at home behind closed doors don't make a bit of difference in why I hire them to work in my kitchen. I don't hire junkies and I don't hire drunks, but everything else doesn't matter. I'm certainly no angel. That's for sure! I don't have room to judge."

Phillip took another drag from his cigarette. He blew out the smoke through his nostrils.

"Well, that's when your ex-boyfriend upped the ante. He said he could make it worth my while if I would just *forget* your resume, pretend like I never saw it. I let him show me the check. It was for fifteen thousand dollars. He went through the whole production of sliding it across the table. He thought he had got me then, but I shoved the check back at him and said I'm my own man. I have my own money. Nobody buys me and nobody sure as hell tells me what to do. And I didn't like how eager he was about the whole thing. I felt like if I took the check, I would be making a deal with the devil."

"He's not the devil," Lauren mumbled as they passed another Main Street storefront, "but he's probably as close as you can get to it here on Earth."

"Well, I'm glad he pissed me off enough to hire

you. I didn't do it just to spite him," Phillip quickly added, "but he certainly made me want to give you a chance. I hate smug sons of bitches like him."

"Thank you for being strong enough to stand up to him, Phillip."

"Oh, don't worry about it, *chérie*." He waved his hand again. "I hope your new man is a lot better than the last one, though."

"He's light years ahead of James, Phillip. There's no comparison between the two."

"Glad to hear it." He let his cigarette hang out the side of his mouth. "Because I don't need another man comin' along tryin' to bribe me. I wouldn't bother with pleasantries this time. I'd just kick him out on his ass."

She laughed.

They continued to walk down Main Street, both falling into a silent reverie as a cool breeze briefly abated the sweltering heat, allowing them to appreciate their surroundings.

Lauren had walked this street so many times in the past thirty years that she could close her eyes and still see it: the two-story brick fronts, the perfectly trimmed bushes, the oversized ceramic flowerpots filled with pansies and marigolds by the glass front doors, and the old-fashioned streetlamps. Feldman's Ice Cream Shop was still at the intersection of Main Street and Poplar Avenue with the "Flavor of the Day" advertised on the washable board in front. Across the street was Mimi's Coffee Shop and next door was Exquisite Florist. A block down was a bridal shop with the same three wig-less mannequins in the windows. Only the bridal dress fashions varied from year to year.

Lauren's eyes drifted to an antique store that had opened a few years ago. Old furniture wasn't really her thing, so she had never been inside the establishment, but it was nice to see something new on Main Street. She glanced at the window and then suddenly did a double take. She stopped and stared. Her eyes scanned the cherrywood Queen Anne secretary writing desk and chair in the center of the window display of wares and furniture. She thought she recognized the set. It looked eerily similar to a desk and chair set that her mother owned. It was almost uncanny. She wanted to take a closer look.

"Phillip, I'm going to take a little detour," she mumbled distractedly, making him frown.

"Everything all right?"

"Oh, everything's fine. I just want to check out something." She finally tore her gaze away from the window. "I'll catch you later, OK?"

"All right, *chérie.*"

She waited for a car to go through the intersection before crossing the street. As she drew closer to the store window, she realized it wasn't her imagination. The writing desk and chair were definitely her mother's. She could tell for sure by the pattern on the upholstered seat, the gold stitched roses and the red and navy blue stripes. But why would her mother's furniture be in a store window? Her eyes then shifted to an English grandfather clock at the other end of the window display. It also looked familiar: the mahogany case, the brass arch dial, and the rolling moon phases. She wasn't as sure about it, but it *could* be her mother's clock.

Lauren opened the antique store's front door. A bell rang overhead as she entered. She hesitated, frozen on the green WELCOME mat. The shop was dark and slightly dusty with a mothball and wood varnish smell that she always associated with old things. There was a heavy oak desk and an old-fashioned wooden cash register toward the front of the store, but no salesperson stood behind the desk. In fact, no one else seemed to be in the store but her.

"Hello," Lauren called out, her voice echoing in the silent room. "Hello?"

She stood awkwardly at the entrance, unsure whether to tap the brass bell by the cash register or turn and leave. Suddenly, an older white man with tufts of thinning white hair and thick glasses emerged from a room toward the back. He wore a white short-sleeved shirt and saggy brown corduroys held up by red suspenders. He came shuffling in with a stack of antique books with cracked bindings in his hands. Lauren stepped forward. She loudly cleared her throat.

"Umm, excuse me."

He almost dropped his books as he turned to her in surprise. He pushed his sagging spectacles up the tip of his nose and gave an awkward smile.

"Sorry, miss. I didn't know you were standing there." He placed the books on the oak desk. "How can I help you?"

"Well, I . . . I noticed the writing desk and chair in your window. I was trying to find out more about them?"

His smile widened. He walked toward her. "Are you a collector?"

"No, not really, but . . . my . . . my mother sort of is."

"Well, they are a wonderfully well-preserved writing desk and chair from the early 1900s," he explained, shuffling toward the window. He pointed at the chair. "The upholstery on the seat isn't original, though. That was added several decades later."

"Who sold it to you?"

His smile faded. He stiffened visibly and squinted at her uneasily from behind the lenses of his glasses. "Why do you want to know that?"

"Just curious. Like I said, my mother's a collector. She, uh, she likes the story behind the pieces as much as she likes buying the pieces themselves."

Lauren could tell she gave the right answer. The old man instantly relaxed his rigid shoulders. His awkward smile returned. "Well, unfortunately, there isn't much of a story behind this one. A woman sold them to me a few weeks ago, but she didn't have many details. She was quite lovely, but . . . she didn't seem to be one for conversation. She didn't seem very interested in haggling, either." He glanced back at the desk. "She said she was eager to get them off her hands, along with the grandfather clock in the window and the lovely French medallion-back sofa over there."

Lauren followed the gnarled finger that he pointed across the room. She instantly recognized the sofa in the shop's corner with its lush red velvet upholstery. The last time she saw it, it was sitting in her mother's living room.

"I just couldn't resist her offer." He raised his eyebrows expectantly. "Do you think your mother would be interested in any of those pieces?"

Why had her mother sold the furniture? Her mother *loved* those pieces. She coveted them more than she would a Cartier watch or a diamond necklace. All her antiques were treasured finds for her, one of a kinds.

It doesn't make any sense!

"If none of these fit your fancy," he said, mistaking Lauren's shake of the head for a no, "the woman said she'll bring me more pieces next week."

Lauren gazed at him in surprise. "What did you say?"

"If you come here next Tuesday, I can show the other pieces to you and your mother. Bring her along. I could give her a good deal."

Lauren nodded blankly, still stunned. She turned and walked toward the shop door.

Chapter 22

Lauren had told Phillip she was going to take a slight detour, but she had no idea how much of a detour it would be. She pulled to a stop in front of her mother's home, her delicate features now marred by a deep frown. She opened her car door and walked up the stone pathway, for the first time noticing that the landscaping along the front of the house looked a little shoddier than usual. Some of the bushes were badly in need of a trim. The dahlias had started to wilt and should have been pruned days ago. Crabgrass and dandelions were starting to peek between blades of grass on the once-perfect lawn.

Lauren rang the doorbell and waited patiently for one of her mother's many maids to answer. When she did not see a silhouette darken the windowpane along the front door, she rang again. Several seconds later, the door finally opened. Lauren gawked in surprise when she saw her mother standing in the doorway. Her mother *never* answered her own door.

What the hell is this about?

Though Yolanda Gibbons looked as flawless as usual, her glamorous clothes, hair, and makeup could not mask the fact that she looked resigned and weary.

"Mama?" Lauren asked, the confusion apparent in her voice. "Where's . . . where's Esmerelda?"

"She doesn't work for me anymore," Yolanda said quietly, stepping back from the door, ushering Lauren inside with an unfussy wave of the hand.

"Doesn't work for you?" She stepped into the entryway.

"Yes," Yolanda said casually, adjusting the cuffs of her blouse. "I had to let her go."

"Why? What happened?"

"I didn't know you had such an attachment to my employees, Laurie." She turned and started to walk down the hallway. "I could give you her home address if you'd like to send her flowers."

Lauren rolled her eyes at her mother's sarcasm. "Mama, what's going on?" She trailed behind her. She glanced into the open doorways as they walked down the corridor and saw that each room was glaringly empty. In fact, the whole mansion felt vacant. Their voices seemed to echo in the darkened rooms. "Where *is* everybody? You didn't just let go of Esmerelda. You got rid of all the other maids, too, didn't you?"

Her mother didn't answer her but instead continued with unhurried strides into the sitting room.

"And I went to the antique shop on Main Street today," Lauren continued, raising her voice so that Yolanda could no longer ignore her. "I saw your writing desk, grandfather clock, and sofa in there. The store owner said you promised him you would bring even more pieces next week. Is something wrong, Mama? Are . . . are you in some kind of trouble?"

Lauren watched as her mother slowly lowered herself onto her settee. "Nothing's wrong. I just needed to tighten my budget, that's all."

"I wouldn't call letting go of all the help and hocking your stuff at an antique store 'tightening your budget'!"

Yolanda's lips tightened. "Lauren, I shouldn't have to remind you, but I am a grown woman. I'm your mother. The last time I checked, I didn't have to explain myself to you or anyone else. Am I wrong?"

"Mama, I'm only trying to help! If you don't tell me what's—"

"And how exactly could you help me?" Yolanda shouted as she sprung from the settee, again catching Lauren by surprise. She raised her eyebrows mockingly. "Can you pay my mortgage, Laurie? Can you pay off my debts? You're in the same position I'm in, honey. You don't have anything! The only money you *had* was the money that James gave you and that's all gone! Maybe that's why he's come to me to collect. He can't get the money from you, so he thinks he can hold it over my head." Yolanda shook her head ruefully. "But the joke's on him. I don't *have* any more money to give!"

Lauren stilled. "James came to you asking for money?"

"Oh yes, and he was ever so helpful in providing me a final tally on paper of how much I owe." She sighed. "He threatened legal action if I don't pay him back according to his terms. He wanted to draw up a repayment contract. I told him to give me time to think about it."

Lauren lowered her eyes and stared at the Persian rug

beneath her feet. Every time she thought she couldn't hate James any more than she did, he did something that made her hatred for him ten times worse.

"I'm really sorry about that, Mama. I'm sorry that he would—"

"Don't apologize. As far as I'm concerned, James Sayers can get in line."

"Maybe . . ." Lauren swallowed. "Maybe Cynthia can help you with money, Mama, or . . . or Dawn can."

"They can't help." Her mother turned away from Lauren, crossing her arms over her chest. "They don't have enough."

"But why not at least ask?" Lauren suddenly remembered something. "What . . . what about the money Grandmother Althea left behind? Why can't you use that?"

"The money she left behind?" Yolanda gave a cynical laugh. She turned back around to face Lauren. "Oh, Laurie, whatever money your grandmother left was gone by the time her creditors got their grubby hands on it. I don't like to speak ill of the dead, but my dear mama, rest her soul, liked to spend money more than she liked to invest or save it. And I guess I'm more like my mama than I thought."

"So am I," Lauren muttered quietly.

So Lauren *and* her mother were both broke and in debt. How was that possible? Her mother had been married five times and had received at least a million dollars in divorce settlements. She had gotten money and gifts from her boyfriends for decades. Yet now she was selling off her furniture piece by piece to raise badly needed funds. Now she was alone in a seventeen-room mansion after firing her waitstaff and groundskeeper because she could no longer afford to pay their salaries. The whole thing seemed so ridiculous and so sad.

Lauren sank into the chair behind her. "So . . . what . . . what are you going to do now?"

"I don't know. If worse comes to worst, I might have to sell the house." She looked around the room forlornly, rubbing her shoulders. "But hopefully it won't come to that. After all, I've been researching new sources of funding."

"Sources? What sources?"

Yolanda's face suddenly brightened. "Oh, it's a good one, Laurie. I've heard that a *very* rich man in his midsixties—a widower—moved into an estate two towns over. They say he's very charming, though I haven't met him myself." She wrinkled her nose. "I heard he's not much to look at, but that's never mattered much to me. I just hope—"

"Wait," Lauren said, interrupting her mother. She held up a hand. "Wait! You mean you want to get a new man? *That's* your new source of funding?"

"Of course. What else would I be talking about?"

Lauren stared at her mother in disbelief. *She's actually serious.*

Even though Yolanda's life was now in complete disarray because of the poor decisions she had made in the past, her answer to all her problems was to do the same thing all over again.

"Mama, I don't . . . I don't think another sugar daddy is the answer to all your prayers."

Yolanda's smile disappeared.

"I just think . . ." Lauren tried to consider her words

carefully. "I just feel that getting involved with a man right now just for money—just to take care of your debts—will only make the situation worse."

"And as you told me, Laurie, I understand *you* feel that way, but I'll take my chances."

Lauren closed her eyes. "Mama, please hear me out. I—"

"Don't you have to get back to your restaurant?" her mother asked, scowling as she walked toward the doorway. "I don't want to keep you. I understand how busy you are."

Lauren could tell as she gazed at her mother's stern face that she was being shut out, that she would have a better chance of holding a conversation with a brick wall. Her mother was set in her ways. She believed in the holy book of gold digging. *Nothing* would shake her faith.

With a heavy heart, Lauren rose to her feet.

"You're right. I should go. Phillip's probably expecting me back soon."

Her mother gave a curt nod. "Thank you for the visit."

Lauren walked toward her mother. Just as she stepped into the corridor, she paused and turned to gaze at Yolanda.

"Look, I'm . . . I'm sorry I can't help you, Mama," Lauren muttered, hoping that her mother would get her true meaning, because Lauren was talking about more than money. The kind of help her mother needed couldn't be done with just a checkbook. "You know I would if I could. We may have our differences, but . . . you know I would do almost anything for you guys, right?"

Yolanda's scowl instantly disappeared. "I know,

sweetheart. But it will be all right." She pushed back
her shoulders. "I am Yolanda Gibbons, honey. If anyone can find a way out of this, I certainly can."

Lauren hesitated, forced a smile, and nodded. She
slowly walked down the corridor to the front door,
hoping that her mother was right.

Chapter 23

Jamal typed a few keys on his keyboard before gazing at an open case file on his desk. He was flipping a few pages when his phone rang. He glanced at the caller ID and saw that it was the front desk calling him.

"Yeah?" he asked distractedly, raising the receiver to his ear, still staring down at the text on the page. It was a muddled deposition. He would definitely have to take lots of notes.

"Mr. Simmons, you have a gentleman at the front desk who says he'd like to speak to you," the receptionist droned into the phone. "He says he doesn't have an appointment."

"Did he tell you his name?"

The receptionist paused. The phone line went silent. She returned seconds later with a loud sigh. "He said his name is *Mr. Uptight*. I don't know if he's joking or what."

Jamal slowly shook his head, knowing instantly who it was.

"Should I tell him he needs to make an appointment?" the receptionist asked.

"No. No, tell him I'll be down in a sec."

Cris stood anxiously by the black lacquer receptionist desk, leaning against it as he waited for Jamal.

"He said he'll be downstairs soon," the older white woman drawled, adjusting her headset on her gray hair helmet. She then pointed to the leather couch on the other side of the carpeted waiting room. "You can have a seat."

"I'm fine standing. Thanks," he muttered, making her narrow her eyes at him. She loudly huffed, then haughtily faced her computer flat screen.

Cris didn't care if he was annoying her. He had too much nervous energy to sit on a couch right now. He had taken Lauren's advice to heart and decided to try to talk to Jamal. She was right. He and Jamal had been friends since college. A friendship that had lasted that long was worth salvaging. Lauren had made the suggestion to send Jamal a note if he couldn't work up the will to call him. But Cris thought against it. That was a "woman" thing to do. No, if he was going to make up with his longtime friend, he would do it *his* way.

A few minutes passed before the elevator doors opened. Jamal stepped out into the waiting room, looking tired and irritated.

"What's up, Cris?"

"Hey." Cris pushed himself away from the receptionist desk. "Have you had lunch yet? Want to grab something to eat?"

Jamal shook his head. "I'm really busy, man. I've

got this big case coming up in court in a few days and I was—"

"Come on, take a break," Cris insisted, nudging his friend's shoulder. "It might do you some good. Just an hour. Eat some buffalo wings, have a beer." He paused. "Plus, we should . . . we should talk."

Jamal gazed at Cris for several seconds, his face solemn as he considered his friend's words. For a moment, Cris wondered if his longtime friend was going to refuse him. He watched Jamal with bated breath until Jamal finally said, "OK, I guess I can step out for lunch, but *you're* paying."

The two men kept the conversation light as they walked down Main Street to a sports bar three blocks away from Jamal's law offices. They talked about the baseball season, the weather predictions that said this week's temperatures would reach at least one hundred degrees, and the new Mazda Jamal was thinking about buying. As they stepped inside, they were instantly met by the sound of an Angels vs. Orioles game playing on the flat-screen television over the bar and the sound of bawdy conversation and laughter. The room was filled with plenty of men and a few women. A light haze of smoke hung in the air along with the heavy smell of greasy, fried food.

The hostess sat them at a highboy table with a red-and-white-checkered tablecloth. It was near the front of the bar room, adjacent to the floor-to-ceiling windows where both men could people watch as they talked. Soon after a waiter took their order—two beers, fire engine hot Buffalo wings for Jamal, and an Angus burger and waffle fries for Cris—they fell into an awkward silence, waiting for the other to speak first. They had exhausted all casual conversation. It was time to get to the nitty-gritty, the reason why they both were here.

Cris loudly cleared his throat. "So . . . uh . . . I wanted to explain to you . . . you know . . . what happened at the country club."

Jamal's facial expression instantly became sullen. He leaned back on his barstool as he ate from the sports bar's complimentary nacho basket at the center of the table. "You don't have to explain," he said between chews. "*Lauren Gibbons* happened. She screwed with your head and you acted accordingly, making an ass out of yourself."

"I didn't make an ass out of myself! I had to stand up for Lauren, especially in front of that asshole!" He took a calming breath. "Look, Jay, you've got it all wrong about her. She's really a—"

"—scheming, heartless gold digger," Jamal said drolly. "Yeah, I know. Everyone in town knows. You're just too damn blind to see it, brothah."

"Look, I'll admit her past isn't the prettiest. I'll admit she's done some dirty things! She's taken advantage of men. She's used them for their money. But she was taught to be that way. She's trying to change!"

"So she says. But it's probably just some game she's running. She's a great con artist, Cris. Like you said, she was taught to be that way."

Cris clenched his jaw. He closed his eyes and thought for a second, trying to figure out a way to reach his friend, trying to break down that mental wall Jamal had erected around himself. He opened his eyes again.

"Do you remember sophomore year in college?" Cris suddenly asked. "You remember Portia Stanley?"

Jamal put down his nacho and perked up. "Hell, yeah, I remember her! She was gorgeous and she had those great . . ." He cupped his hands over his chest and grinned, mimicking her bountiful breasts that still stood out in his memory, almost two decades later.

"She used to drop by our dorm room all the time," Cris continued. "She'd always just *happen* to show up at the student union when we were having lunch. She went to all my games."

"Yeah, she was crazy about you, man!"

"No, she wasn't," Cris said bluntly, making his friend frown again. "She didn't give a shit about me. I could have been *anybody.* Any star player on the football team would have sufficed. That's why I never asked her out. She was a groupie . . . and I saw her from a mile away. My dad taught me to be on the lookout for that type of woman just as early as Lauren's mom started teaching her to be a gold digger. My spider senses have *never* failed me, Jay. They aren't failing me now, either."

The waiter returned with their beers and their orders. Jamal sat silently for several seconds, not touching his food. Cris could see his resolve starting to wane.

"You *really* think she's changed, Cris?"

"I'd bet my life on it," Cris answered firmly.

"But why? Why the big turnaround? Those women have been the same damn way for the past fifty years!"

"I think a lot of things played a role in it. She's been questioning her whole lifestyle for years, even if she was too scared to ask those questions out loud. But she blames James. He was the big push she needed. He beat her up badly. She had to run away from him and ended up running away from that life, too."

"Now that's what *definitely* makes me think she's full of it! I don't believe that shit for one second! James is a good guy. I've known him for the past seven years. He would never, *ever* do that! He would never hit a woman!"

"She said she knew no one would believe her," Cris said, sampling his fries. "It was her word against his and no one would take the word of a Gibbons over James Sayers." He paused. "I guess she was right."

Jamal angrily shoved aside his plate of Buffalo wings. "OK, fine, I'll play along then. She's changed. James is the biggest asshole in the world. But even if it's all true, even if she isn't a gold digger anymore because James beat the crap out of her, why are you even bothering with her? You hate drama! You always have, and this girl is knee-deep in it. Either way, it's not worth it! She's got too much damn baggage, Cris!"

"I know, but trust me . . . it's worth it. *She's* worth it!"

"Oh, she is?" Jamal asked sarcastically. "And that reason would be?"

"Well, because . . . because . . ." Cris thought for a second. "Because . . . she makes me feel emotions I haven't felt in a long time. I mean . . . I love her, Jay."

"You love her?" Jamal stared at Cris, completely stunned. "How the hell can you love her? You've only known her for less than two months!"

"I didn't know there was a time line requirement for this sort of thing."

"You know what I mean! It's just . . . well . . . kind of sudden. You're a dude who takes things slowly. Saying you're in love with her already, seems . . . kind of fast."

"What can I tell you? People change. Lauren's changed. I guess I have, too. She changed me."

Jamal let out a low whistle. "Seriously, Cris, I don't understand the voodoo that this girl does to you. But I guess I don't have to understand it." He tilted his head and smiled. "She must be *really* good in bed."

"I wouldn't know." Cris took a sip from his beer. "We haven't had sex yet."

Jamal's eyes widened comically. *"What?* Oh, hell, no! If you're going to put up with all this drama, you better get in those panties, posthaste! You should be knocking it out every night! I know *I* would."

"Of course you would, Jay."

Jamal finally started to eat his Buffalo wings, spiting particles of food as he spoke. "Hey, did I ever tell you about the chick in Miami that I met five years ago?" He licked the red tangy sauce off his fingers. "I mean, that girl always had some shit going on. She had a crazy-ass mother, a stalker ex-boyfriend, and this killer yappy Chihuahua who wore a diamond collar. But, man, let me tell you! She could do things to my dick that could make a brothah sing! I mean, she could . . ."

Cris grinned as he bit into his burger while Jamal spoke. It seemed like things with his friend were back to normal.

Chapter 24

"I still don't see why you need to buy a new dress," Lauren said as she slouched into the suede club chair in the posh dressing room. She gazed with boredom at her sister Stephanie. "I *know* you. You probably still have dresses at home with the tags on them. Why can't you wear one of those?"

Her sister twirled on the carpeted platform, admiring herself and her plum silk gown in the three-way mirror. She gave a wink and a smile at her reflection, making Lauren roll her eyes.

"Because wearing an old dress is something I just don't do! Besides, it's a special occasion. We've got to look our best or Cynthia won't let us hear the end of it."

Grudgingly, Lauren nodded in agreement.

The Historic Preservation Association was holding a major party in less than two weeks in honor of the recent renovations of one of the historic mansions outside of Chesterton, a project that Cynthia had spearheaded. All the Gibbons girls had agreed to attend the event to show their support. Lauren planned to ask Cris to go with her. But unlike her sister Stephanie, Lauren did *not* plan to buy a new dress for the occasion.

Not only could she not afford to buy a dress, but dress shopping wasn't at the forefront of her mind right now. She was still shaken by the news of her mother's debts, and frustrated that she couldn't offer her mother much financial help. She couldn't even get James to back off of Yolanda. She knew what his terms were to get him to do that, and there was no way she was going back to him. No way in hell!

Cynthia, Dawn, and Stephanie had all agreed to pool their funds to provide a safety net for Yolanda for a while, at least until Mr. Widower-Two-Towns-Over turned out to be the meal ticket their mother believed him to be. But they all agreed that there was no way they could afford to pay for the mansion if the situation became much worse. They would have to put up for sale their childhood home.

Lauren was angry and frustrated. She wished she wasn't so broke and so powerless. There was no way she would ever go back to her old life, those gold-digging ways, but there were times like these that definitely tested her resolve. What she wouldn't give for a magic money wand to make all the bad things like bill collectors and men like James go away.

"Would you like more champagne, ma'am?" one of the salesgirls asked as she held a silver tray near Lauren's elbow, snapping her from her thoughts.

"No, thanks." Lauren adjusted in her chair. She halfheartedly held up her half-full glass. "I'm still good."

The salesgirl nodded politely. She then walked across the dressing room and disappeared behind a sliding glass door that led back to the store floor.

"So what do you think, Laurie?" Stephanie smoothed the dress bodice with the palms of her hands. "Isn't it gorgeous?"

Lauren tilted her head and squinted at her sister. "It's nice."

"Nice?" Stephanie challenged as she stared at herself again. "It's more than 'nice.' A thousand dollars gets you nice. Six thousand gets you *gorg*eous."

"How much a dress costs doesn't change how it looks, Steph."

"But knowing how much it costs changes how you *wear* it, which makes it look better!"

Lauren figured there was no point in arguing with her sister. If Stephanie was bent on the idea that an expensive dress looked better than a cheaper one, Lauren knew that there was nothing she could do to dissuade her. She took a sip from her half-full champagne glass as her sister continued to preen in front of the mirror.

"You can try on your clothes back here, ladies," said the salesgirl. Her muffled voice came from the other side of the dressing room wall. Suddenly, the sliding glass door opened again, revealing three black women in Capri pants and colorful blouses who looked to be in their early forties.

"This is one of our more private dressing rooms," the salesgirl informed proudly as she crossed the room with a stack of clothes slung over her arm.

Lauren gave a casual glance toward the three women as they entered. They were laughing and talking to one another, giggling over some joke. Lauren couldn't recollect their names, but one or two looked familiar. She had probably seen them back in town at the grocery store or somewhere else on Main Street.

She smiled politely at them in greeting before turning back around to look at her sister, who was still standing on the platform.

Stephanie turned and faced the women as they entered. She grinned. "Well, isn't it a small world? Hello, Mrs. Montgomery! How are you?"

The light-skinned woman in the center of the three, who had blond highlights, stopped talking the instant Stephanie spoke. Lauren assumed she was Mrs. Montgomery.

The two others who stood on both sides of Mrs. Montgomery continued to chatter and giggle until she elbowed one of them and focused her gaze on Stephanie with laserlike intensity. The portly, dark-skinned one beside her followed the woman's stare. She loudly whispered something into Mrs. Montgomery's ear, who then nodded. The two other women took in an audible breath and then frowned with disapproval. Now all three women were glaring at Stephanie.

Lauren lowered her champagne glass from her lips. *Just what the hell is going on?*

"I haven't . . . I haven't seen you since the open house . . . you know, on Westlake Drive," Stephanie said nervously. "How have you been?"

Mrs. Montgomery didn't respond. Instead she continued to glower at Stephanie, shooting daggers at her with her eyes.

The tension that Lauren had felt only vaguely now grew in the dressing room by tenfold.

"I'm going to put your clothes here, ladies," the salesgirl said as she hung several dresses and blouses on individual hooks. She seemed oblivious to the growing strain in the room. "I'll return in a few minutes with your champagne and hors d'oeuvres. Let me know if you need anything, OK?"

She smiled as she walked back across the dressing room, opened the glass doors, stepped through, and silently shut them behind her. Her high heels echoed across the hardwood floor on the other side of the dressing room wall as she walked back toward the store floor.

Lauren had heard the expression "the room was so quiet you could have heard a pin drop." That expression came to mind at this moment as her sister stood stiffly like a mannequin in front of the three-way mirror and the three women continued to huddle on the other side of the dressing room, staring Stephanie down. Only Lauren broke her casual pose. She leaned forward in her chair, prepared for anything.

"Can you believe this?" the portly, dark-skinned woman finally uttered with a curl in her lip.

"Sorry, ladies," the tall one with the glasses said. "My girlfriend told me this was a nice place. But I didn't know they let just any type of *trash* in here! If I did, I wouldn't have come."

At that, Stephanie snapped out of her trance. She quickly gathered the voluminous fabric of her skirt into her hands and stepped off the platform.

"Well, it was nice seeing you again, Mrs. Montgomery," Stephanie said with a false airiness. She turned to Lauren. "On second thought, I won't buy the gown after all." Stephanie walked back to her dressing room stall. "You ready to go, Laurie?"

"Ready when you are," Lauren said as she sprang out of her chair.

"Oh, look at her run!" Mrs. Montgomery chided with a biting laugh. "I wonder if she runs as fast when she's chasing after other people's *husbands!*"

"So how were you planning to pay for that dress?" the portly one shouted after Stephanie. "Let me guess. With somebody's husband's credit card!"

"Did you like the bracelet? I saw Hank bought it for you from Tiffany's!"

Lauren followed her sister into the beige stall. She shut the door behind them. "Steph, what the hell is going on?"

"Nothing! Nothing!" Stephanie whispered shrilly in return as she pointed over her shoulder. "Just help me with this zipper so I can get the hell out of this dress and we can get the hell out of here!"

"Did you sleep with one of their husbands?"

"No!" Stephanie's face twisted with desperation. "Look, I'll explain it to you later. Just help me out of this damn dress!"

Lauren began to lower the zipper down Stephanie's back.

"Just to let you know . . . I wasn't surprised when I found out about you and Hank," Mrs. Montgomery said on the other side of the stall door. "My Hank's never been able to keep his hands to himself, especially when low-class hookers like you throw themselves at him! But I guess you just couldn't help yourself, could you? I heard all about you, Stephanie Gibbons, *and* your slutty ways! I heard what you're all about!"

"You know what they say about the Gibbons girls," one of her friends shouted. "If there's a man with money around, a Gibbons girl can't be far behind!"

Her words were followed by an "uh-huh" and sharp laughter.

"Open your wallet and they'll open their legs!"

"You're just a bunch of whores! *All* of you!" Mrs.

Montgomery shouted as she slapped her open palm against the door.

Lauren froze. Her heart began to thud wildly in her chest. Her hands began to shake. She turned and glared at the closed stall door.

Stephanie stared at her little sister. "No, Laurie. No! Don't go out there!"

Lauren undid the door lock.

"Laurie, what are you *doing?* Don't go out there! They're gonna beat the hell out of us!"

Lauren slowly opened the door to meet Mrs. Montgomery's glare. She tilted her head and leaned against the door frame. She then defiantly crossed her arms over her chest. "What did you just say?"

Though Lauren stood only five-foot-one-half-inch tall, there was enough fury on her face to make her seem two feet taller. The woman's angry gaze faltered. She took a hesitant step back from the stall doorway.

"I . . . I wasn't talking to you. I was talking to *her,*" she said as she pointed over Lauren's shoulder to Stephanie, who was holding the gown's bodice to her chest.

"No, you were talking to me. You called my family, and by extension *me*, a whore," Lauren said with eerie calmness. "I just wanted to make sure I heard you clearly. You did call us whores, didn't you?"

The woman took several steps back. She bumped into her friends, who were standing behind her. The dark-skinned one loudly sucked her teeth.

"You *are* whores," she spat. "Everyone in town knows it! A bunch of *broke* hoes, as a matter of fact. I heard that even that *mama of yours* has started to sell off her furniture because no man was willing to pay for her old ass anymore!"

That was it. That was the trigger!

Minutes later, if anyone asked Lauren what had happened at that point, she couldn't honestly remember. It was like she had blacked out. She only came to reality minutes later when the salesgirl was tugging her backward by the shoulders and she realized she was sitting astride the dark-skinned woman, who was screaming and covering her face with her arms. The one with the wire-framed glasses, which were now askew on her face, was sitting on the dressing room floor with her legs crossed. She wept quietly as she held her reddened cheek in her hand. Stephanie was in her bra and panties, grunting and rolling around on the floor with Mrs. Montgomery. Stephanie seemed to be winning her fight.

"You can't do this!" the blond salesgirl yelled. "This isn't that type of store! Vanessa, call mall security! Call the police!"

Lauren blinked as she slowly came to. She saw the full carnage that surrounded her. Chairs were overturned. The champagne glasses and tray of hors d'oeuvres had crashed to the floor, and canapés and chocolate-covered strawberries were now enmeshed in the gray plush carpet.

"Get her off of me!" the dark-skinned woman screamed. "She's crazy! She's trying to kill me!"

Lauren looked over at her sister, who gave Mrs. Montgomery one final shove before triumphantly staggering to her feet.

"I think we should go now, Steph," Lauren said with huffing breath.

Stephanie nodded.

"What? Who's going to pay for this?" the salesgirl shouted as Stephanie stepped into the stall and grabbed

her sundress and her purse. "Who's going to pay to clean up this mess? You ripped a six-thousand-dollar dress!"

"The dress wasn't that cute anyway," Stephanie muttered as they opened the sliding glass door and stepped out of the dressing room.

They reentered the shop floor and were greeted by stares from the several women who stood stark still. Realizing they were still half-naked, Stephanie hastily tugged her dress over her head and shoved her arms through the straps while Lauren adjusted her blouse, which had been ripped open. They walked down the center aisle of the shop, ignoring the gazes of amazement that followed them.

They quickly made their way through the mall, taking a different path than they originally planned when they noticed a mall security officer racing toward the second level, where the dress store was located. They still garnered stares from each person they passed as they drew near the outdoor parking lot.

We must look insane, Lauren thought as she tried desperately to fix her hair.

As the adrenaline from their dressing-room boxing match disappeared, shame gradually washed over her. Lauren couldn't believe she had done that. She had beaten a woman she barely knew, slapped another, and nearly got arrested—because of what? To defend the honor of her family, the *same* family that on many occasions she had called whores herself? In fact, secretly she had called them a lot worse!

What was I thinking?

Stephanie laughed as they drew near their cars. "Oh, I can't wait to tell Cynthia and Dawn about this one! You should have seen yourself in there, Laurie! That woman had to have you by about seventy pounds and you still whooped her ass! I handled mine, too!" She clapped her hands. "Talk about the Gibbons girls, huh? Do that and you get *beat down!"*

Lauren narrowed her eyes at her sister. "Did you have sex with that woman's husband, Stephanie? That Hank guy she was talking about? And don't lie to me!"

Stephanie sat on the hood of her BMW. She casually reached into her purse, flipped open a gold compact, and examined her reflection. "Damn it, that bitch scratched my cheek," she mumbled. "And I was going to do another house tour tomorrow. I'm going to look like a hot mess!"

Lauren took her sister's refusal to answer her question as a "yes."

"I do not believe this! You *did* have sex with him!"

Stephanie slid off the hood. "No, I didn't."

"Yeah, right! Why the hell should I believe you?"

"It's the truth! We didn't have sex!" She wrinkled her nose. "I just . . . I just spanked him a little."

"What?"

"Girl, don't look at me like that! It was what he needed!" she argued, flipping her compact closed with a *click.* "Believe me! I was helping him out! That guy is working through some serious issues, and it's not like his wife was gonna spank him! Come on, you saw her! That chick's so tight-assed you could stick a coal up her butt and make a diamond. She should be *thanking* me!"

Lauren gritted her teeth. "I stood up for you. I stood up for *all* of you! I almost got put in handcuffs to defend a family of women who steal other people's husbands and aren't even ashamed about it!"

"I wasn't trying to steal her husband! I told you! I

just spanked him. That's all! I got a gold diamond bracelet out of it! I thought it was a fair exchange. Besides, it was more like . . . it was more like . . . I borrowed him for a bit. You know how it is."

"You *use* men!" Lauren pointed up at her sister. "You hunt them down! You take their money! And you use them until they get tired of you or until they don't have any more money to steal! You sell yourselves to the highest bidder!" she yelled as tears began to fill her eyes. "You're all just a bunch of . . . of . . . gold-diggin', ass-spankin' whores! And I'm tired of it! I'm tired of getting dragged into your crazy bullshit!"

"Our crazy bullshit?" Stephanie shouted. "What about the bullshit you dragged *us* into with James? Huh? What about that?"

"I didn't drag you! You guys were just as happy to use him like I was, and now we're all paying the price for it! You're not going to make me feel guilty about this, Steph! I'm tired of all of you making me feel guilty! I'm tired of *all of you!"*

Stephanie looked deeply wounded by her sister's words. "But . . . we're sisters. We always have each other's back. You have mine. I have yours. That's what Mama taught us!"

"Well, maybe she taught us wrong!"

Stephanie watched as Lauren climbed into her car.

"Where are you going?" she asked as Lauren turned on the ignition and threw the car into reverse, tires screeching in her wake.

"Lauren! Lauren!" she yelled as the car drove out of the parking lot.

Chapter 25

"Lauren? Lauren?" Cris called from the other side of her front door. He knocked again. "Baby, if you're in there, open up."

"I'm coming," Lauren answered tiredly as she shuffled across her living room in her bedroom slippers, tank top, and drawstring shorts. She had already addressed the few scratches on her face with hydrogen peroxide and strategically placed Band-Aids, but she was still nursing the swollen knuckles of her right hand with a sandwich bag filled with ice cubes. Nothing could be done for the few bruises that were starting to sprout all over her body, probably the result of the wild tumble she took to the ground during the dressing-room brawl.

She slowly opened the door to find Cris leaning against the frame, gazing down at her.

"Hey."

"Eh, Rocky. Did you get a knockout in the eleventh round or the ninth?"

"Very funny." She turned around and walked back

into the living room. He followed her after shutting the door behind him.

"You all right?"

She slumped back onto the couch, still holding the ice pack to her knuckles. "My self-respect is in worse shape than I look, if that's what you mean."

He sat down beside her. "What happened?"

"Don't you already know? I mean . . . I would have thought the story had traveled at lightning speed by now."

"The town version has," he said as he studied her with his dark eyes and rubbed his hands together. "But I wanted to hear *your* version of what happened."

She grumbled loudly. "Just the same ol', same ol'." She raised the ice pack to look down at her knuckles and flexed her sore hand.

She wouldn't be handling any knives anytime soon. It would probably be a good idea to tell Phillip she wasn't coming in tomorrow.

"Stupid Lauren gets wrapped up in family drama, and Stupid Lauren makes an ass of herself. This time I just ended up assaulting a few people in the process."

"So you *did* start the fight, then?"

"Well, yeah, kind of . . . I guess."

He slowly shook his head. "Damn it, Lauren . . ."

"Look, Cris, I know what I did was dumb! I don't need any lectures. It was completely out of character for me. That's not the type of person I am."

"So why were you that type of person today?"

"Because that chick pressed the wrong button! She shouldn't have talked shit about me, my mom, or my sisters even if . . . even if most of it is true."

"But Lauren, baby," he said quietly, "you can't punch everyone who talks shit about your family. This isn't a school yard. You could get arrested. You could end up in jail and—"

"I know that." She clenched her jaw so hard it hurt. "I told you I don't need a lecture, especially from you. You don't know what it's like!"

"What *what's* like?"

"Everyone in town respects you! You're Cris Weaver, the big-time NFL wide receiver! You don't know what it's like to have everyone think the *worst* of you, to have people whispering things about you as soon as you walk into a room. Hell, before you even *get* into a room!" She tore her gaze from his. Her eyes drifted to the carpet. "I've tried so hard to prove to everyone around here that I've changed. I don't want to steal anyone's husband. I'm not trying to take anyone's money. I bust my ass in that restaurant every day because I want to feel worthy of their respect, Cris. It's like I'm saying 'Look, everybody!' " she shouted with tears welling in her eyes. " 'Lauren Gibbons did it all by herself! She didn't need any man to give it to her! No one pulled any strings! I did it *all* by myself!' " She angrily tossed her ice pack aside. It landed on the scuffed coffee table and slid across its wooden surface before tumbling to the floor. "But they won't accept that. They keep throwing the past and my family in my face! They won't let it go!"

Cris watched her quietly weep.

"Lauren," he began softly as he placed a warm hand on her shoulder, "why are you trying to prove anything to those people? Who cares what they think? Besides, if you hate the people in this damn town so much, why don't you leave? Why do you stay here?"

Lauren wiped her tears away with the back of her hand. "I used to think it was because I couldn't stand to be away from my mom or my sisters. I could kill them sometimes for the things they do, but I still love them. They're all I've ever known. But now . . . Now I'm not so sure that's the reason. I think it's something else." She finally tore her gaze from the carpet and looked up at him. "I think . . . I think I'm scared, Cris."

His frown deepened. "Scared of what?"

Tears began to fall onto her cheeks again. She licked her lips, nervous at the fact that she would finally express her deep, dark fear aloud.

"I'm . . ." She hesitated. "I'm scared that everyone else in the world will see me the same way that everyone sees me in Chesterton. I'm scared that the chef's coat and the smile won't hide it." She pointed at her chest. "They'll look at me and they'll see me for what I really am."

Cris raised his eyebrows expectantly, waiting for her to finish.

"A whore. They'll know I'm a whore, Cris. Then I won't be able to lie to myself anymore. I'll know I'm not fooling anyone."

Cris fixed her with a measured gaze. "You really think that's what people would see?"

"I don't know." She exhaled and grabbed the ice pack from the floor. "Like I said, I'm too scared to find out."

She wiped the last of her tears away and sniffed for the last time. She noticed after a few seconds that Cris was still staring at her. She gazed back at him.

"What?"

"Do you want to know what I see when I look at you?"

She gave a tired smile. "I'm afraid to ask."

"You shouldn't be. Because I see someone who didn't

have the best upbringing, who was taught a lot of wrong things, but managed to overcome them and try to make things right. I see a woman who had a man belittle her and beat her, but she didn't let him break her."

When her gaze started to wander to the floor, he grabbed her chin and shifted her head so they gazed into each other's eyes.

"I see a woman who has more strength in her than I've seen in *anyone*. And I see a woman who has been trying so hard to prove she's changed her ways that she's kept me at arm's length. She won't let me in."

Lauren was instantly hurt by his words.

"That is *not true!* I haven't tried to keep you at arm's length. I've told you everything . . . everything . . . there is to know about me! I've done everything to show you that I care about you, that I . . . that I love you, Cris."

"Everything short of sharing your bed with me."

She closed her eyes, unable to argue with that. Yes, she hadn't slept with him, but it wasn't to put distance between them. He had to know that. If there was anyone she desperately wanted to feel a connection with— mind, heart, *and* body—it was Cris.

"But we could easily change that. Let me stay the night."

She bit down hard on her lower lip, trying desperately to think of an excuse why he shouldn't stay, but she could not. *He* wanted this. *She* wanted this. But something still held her back.

"You're . . . very important to me, Cris," she said softly, finally opening her eyes, trying to put her tangled thoughts into words. "I've screwed up a lot of things in my life. I just . . . I just don't . . . want to . . . mess this up, too."

"So don't."

"But it's not that simple!"

"Yes, it is."

He then cupped her face and lowered his lips to hers. A warm tingle flowed from his lips to all points in her body. She wanted to pull away from him but couldn't work up the will to, not when he made her feel like this.

He shifted his hand from her chin to the back of her neck and carefully tilted back her head as their kiss deepened.

She could taste her own salty tears and she could taste him. Their breathing grew heavy, almost synchronizing. When she felt herself being pressed back against the couch cushions, she didn't try to sit up. She let Cris lead the way.

The soreness from earlier disappeared, along with the feeling of helplessness. She felt warm, content, and secure in his arms. But the warmth was growing more and more intense, into a searing heat with each caress and each kiss. Her hesitation was quickly dissolving under his touch.

He tugged her tank top over her head and tossed it to the carpeted floor. She wasn't wearing a bra underneath, so he instantly cradled one of her breasts in the palm of his hand, teasing the dark nipple, making it gooseflesh. His other hand slowly descended past the elastic waistband of her shorts and parted her legs as his nimble fingers began to fondle her clit, coaxing forth a supple wetness between her thighs. She moaned. She bucked. She twisted beneath his touch.

His eyes darkened with pleasure as he watched her writhe. He pulled his hands away and Lauren took that as her cue. She eagerly pushed her shorts and underwear over her hips and down her legs, figuring now was the moment that he would enter her.

With James it had always been that way—a few minutes of foreplay before he had her bent over the side of the bed.

But Cris—once again showing how much he was unlike her ex—did the opposite. He left her there panting, practically squirming with sexual need as he stood and slowly undressed, unbuttoning his shirt and lowering the zipper of his jeans, as he hungrily gazed down at her. And she hungrily gazed up at him, letting her eyes rake over his body: his muscles, his glowing brown skin, the tattoos on his shoulder and back. Standing there, he looked eerily like some Polynesian god who had just descended to earth, ready to take his maiden.

When he pulled off his underwear, she saw the *very* visible evidence that he was just as aroused and eager as she was, but he was taking his time. When he finally finished undressing, she grabbed his hand and eagerly tugged him back down to her. Despite her small size, she pulled him with enough might that he fell against her and the couch, making them both smile.

When Cris eased between her thighs again, she knew without question that she wouldn't be able to hold back this time around. Despite her worries and misgivings, she wanted him. She wanted him so badly, she swore that she would explode if she couldn't have him tonight.

They kissed languidly, enjoying the sensation, having their fill of one another. Her fingers traced the landscape of his back and shoulders as his mouth lowered and he nibbled at her breasts. He kissed her again and she gripped his manhood, feeling it tense in her grasp, listening to him groan at her touch. He pushed her legs wider and she felt his fingers slide inside her then. She closed her eyes. As his fingers moved, gliding in and out, she shivered and bucked, whimpering against his lips.

The entire time, his manhood pressed against her urgently, leaving a moist trail along her thighs, but Cris continued to hold back. He shifted her upward so that her head draped over the edge of the couch, making her feel lightheaded, almost dizzy. She couldn't see what he was doing now. But she felt him kiss her breasts again, then her stomach. He hooked her calves over his shoulders and lowered his mouth between her legs. She shouted out then in surprise, unable to hold back when she felt him kiss her, stroke her. He licked her clit and sucked it. He was pushing her to the brink, and just when she felt as if she had finally hit her crest, he stopped and she whimpered. He climbed back on top of her and she could tell from the look in his eyes, on his face, that he was being pushed to the brink himself.

He paused and reached for his jeans, which were discarded on the floor. She watched as he began to sift through his pockets and pulled out a condom wrapper from his wallet. Within seconds, he had the condom on and was kissing her again. But by now, Lauren was starting to grow impatient with their foreplay. She would end the torture if he wouldn't.

Lauren pressed her hands against his chest and shoved him onto his back with strength she didn't know she had. She steadied herself and lowered her hips, guiding him inside her. She breathed in sharply at the sensation and he moaned. As her hips began to move and she braced her hands against his chest, they commenced the slow, languid rhythm of lovemaking. After several minutes, his grip around her hips tightened. She saw him grit his teeth and furrow his brows. She knew he was close to coming.

Lauren still hadn't quite reached her pleasure peak, but again, she was used to it. She had never successfully reached orgasm with any of her lovers. At least with Cris, she could take joy in being this close to him, in finally sharing something with him that she had yearned to share for so long.

But again, he proved himself different. Instead of giving a satisfied grunt and going slack, he abruptly shifted, pushing her onto her back, taking the reins. The pace of their lovemaking suddenly increased. She felt her legs being spread apart wider and wider as he dove deeper and deeper, harder and harder, all the while kissing her, telling her how much he loved her. That's when she started to feel it.

It started at her center, a knot that seemed to tighten more and more with each passing second. Then the vibrations started and her heart began to thrum like a bass string in her chest. All she could hear were their moans and the blood pounding in her ears. She dug her fingernails into his shoulders and gritted her teeth, fighting to catch her bearings, shocked by what was happening to her body. Then suddenly all thoughts disappeared. She felt the waves crest over her and she cried out just as Cris started to shout when he could hold back no longer.

And then it ended. With blissful exhaustion, she slumped back against the couch and he collapsed on top of her. His body lay limp and she closed her eyes, content with the feel of him on top of her, enveloping her in his warmth. She didn't want the moment to end.

Minutes later, Cris sat up and smiled as he gazed down at her.

"Hmm, look at that," he mumbled. "We're still here. We made love and the world didn't implode."

"Barely." She grinned. "I wasn't sure if *I* was going to implode for a second there."

"Same here, baby. You know, I bet we could even do it again and the world would still be here. Maybe even a *third* time."

"A third time?" she asked, holding back her giggle. "A gambling man, are we?"

"When the odds are in my favor, I am." He ran a finger along her jawline. "Are you a gambling woman, Miss Gibbons?"

She tilted her head and smiled up at him coyly. "Sometimes . . . under the right circumstances."

"Well, I don't think you'll get any circumstances better than this."

Then he kissed her, ending their playful banter and starting their lovemaking all over again.

Chapter 26

Cris awoke the next morning before Lauren on her fold-out couch, momentarily forgetting where he was. The previous night felt more like a steamy dream than reality. But he instantly regained his bearings and realized that it hadn't been a dream when he felt Lauren at his side, sleeping soundly. He shifted slightly, careful not to wake her, and gazed down at her as she slept.

Lauren had finally let down her last barrier last night and they had expressed physically the emotions that had left him fighting need and frustration for months. He knew how much of a battle it had been for her to finally let go, but he hoped she realized she didn't have to be afraid anymore. He knew she wasn't a gold digger. He trusted her completely. Now if only she would just trust his judgment and trust *herself,* they would both be better off.

He slowly rose from the bed and walked across the living room to her bathroom. He rinsed his mouth out with mouthwash and took a quick shower, though it was a challenge. Lauren was a petite woman, so getting in and out of her tiny shower stall that was only half a foot away from her toilet and pedestal sink probably wasn't that big of a deal for her. But at six foot two with a muscular frame, Cris had to carefully negotiate the space, careful mindful not to splash water everywhere. He was starting to feel claustrophobic by the time he toweled off and opened the bathroom door.

Though he was sure he had awakened her with all the noise he had made, he was happy to see she was still slumbering blissfully. He smiled as he gazed at her, and a thought suddenly popped into his head. She had surprised him with so many meals in the past few weeks: sumptuous dinners and delectable desserts. Perhaps it was about time that he cooked a meal for her. It would be the perfect way to kick off their first morning-after together.

He slid into his boxers and walked across the room to her kitchenette to make her breakfast. He opened the fridge and rifled through the shelves before finding a carton of eggs and a loaf of whole wheat bread. The breakfast would be far from the five-star breakfasts she could make him, but he figured she would appreciate the effort. He'd have a plate waiting for her by the time she woke up.

Cris lowered the bread slices into her toaster and saw a frying pan on one of the open shelves. He began to quietly open kitchen drawers in search of a spatula, though one drawer wouldn't open on the first tug. He tugged a little harder. As he did, the drawer suddenly popped open and a series of envelopes spilled onto the kitchen floor.

"Shit," he muttered.

Cris glanced over his shoulder to see if his mishap had woken her up. Lauren mumbled in her sleep and turned onto her belly, but she didn't awake. He relaxed and began to collect the envelopes back into a neat pile but paused when one caught his eye.

"Second notice?" he whispered, scanning the large red letters. He scanned another bill. "Final notice?"

He started to flip through the stack, examining each page. Lauren was behind on payments on several credit cards, an unsecured loan, even her phone bill. When he saw the amounts she owed, his stomach plummeted.

"What the hell . . ."

"Put them back," a voice in his head suddenly warned. "Put them back and pretend like you never saw them. She put them there because she probably didn't want anyone to find them."

No, he argued silently. *She put them there because she didn't want to* face *them. That's a huge damn difference!*

He couldn't believe that she was in such a dire situation financially and she hadn't said anything, she hadn't asked for help. Why would she do that?

Shame, Cris thought. He was sure of it. Like her family, like her past, she was ashamed of her debt and trying to move on from it. But shoving it to the back of a drawer wasn't moving on. This was just sheer stupidity.

Cris gathered the rest of the bills and walked over to the sofa. He gently shook her shoulders. Lauren smacked her lips and murmured in her sleep. He shook her again. She slowly opened her eyes and gazed up at him. She gave a lazy smile as she turned over in bed.

"Mmm, good morning," she said and then stretched and yawned contentedly. She glanced at the kitchenette and saw the pan sitting on the burner. The smell of toast was in the air.

"What are you cooking?" she asked as she slowly raised herself to her elbows. She modestly held the cotton sheet to her chest and wiped her eyes. "Need any help?"

Cris didn't answer her. Instead he tossed the pile of bills onto the empty pillow beside her, making her frown.

"What's this?" she asked.

"You tell me."

Lauren shifted to a sitting position and picked up one of the envelopes. She squinted at the text. "Where . . . where did you get these?"

"From one of your drawers in the kitchen . . . where you left them."

"Why were you going through my drawers?" she asked, seemingly with dismay and then with disbelief. She dropped the envelope to the mattress and glowered at him. "While I was sleeping you were digging through my things?"

"I wasn't 'digging.' I was just—"

"You *were!* You were digging through my things and snooping on me. Don't lie, Cris! I can't believe this!" She slammed her balled fist down on the mattress. "I let a man spend the night for the first time in I don't know *how long*, and he's already going through my things! It's so typical! It's like being with James all over again! I told you that I don't like to be—"

"I was looking for a spatula for the damn eggs and I couldn't find one! So I started opening drawers and I found those bills instead!" He pointed down at the forgotten stack of opened envelopes, angry at her reaction. "Besides, don't turn this around on me! What the hell are you doing shoving fifty thousand dollars' worth of bills in the back of your kitchen drawer? Why haven't you paid them?"

She turned away from him, refusing to meet his gaze.

Seeing the look of humiliation on her face, Cris could feel his anger wane. He took a step closer to her. "Are you . . . are you in some kind of trouble, Lauren?"

"That's none of your business," she snarled as she wrapped her bedsheets tightly around her body.

"None of my business?"

"Yes!" she shouted as she climbed off the bed. "None of your business, Cris! Look, just because we had sex doesn't mean I have to answer to you! You're not my keeper! *OK?* I can take care of it myself! It's my problem! Not yours!"

Cris's concerned frown settled into a stony scowl.

"Well, if you're so capable, then why haven't you taken care of it already?"

"Because I don't have the money, obviously," she muttered in return, gathering the bills back into a stack and walking across the living area to her small kitchen. The back of her bedsheets dragged behind her like a broken mermaid tail. She stumbled slightly before kicking some of the fabric aside.

The phone began to ring as Lauren opened the kitchen drawer. "Just let it—"

" 'Just let it go to voice mail.' I know! That's what you *always* say! Is it a bill collector, Lauren? Is that who keeps calling? Are *they* the reason why you never answer your phone?"

She ignored him and tossed the bills back into their drawer. She then slammed the drawer shut.

"How bad is it?" he asked as the ringing of the phone finally died. "And be honest with me. How much do you owe?"

"I told you that it's none of your business!"

"Damn it, Lauren, I *care* about you! That makes it my business! How much money do you owe?"

Her back was to him so he couldn't see her face, but he could tell she was embarrassed and hurt by his discovery. He watched as she leaned against the counter with her head down. She stood there so long in silence that he was about to ask her the question again, but he didn't have to. She finally gave her answer.

"Eighty-four thousand dollars."

His eyes widened.

"Give or take a few hundred," she said, turning around to face him.

He gazed at her, absolutely stunned.

"Don't look at me like that! I know I was stupid. I know it was a mistake, but I just got used to James paying for everything! Then . . . then he stopped paying and—"

"Left you holding the bag," Cris said, finishing for her.

Lauren slowly nodded. "That . . . among other things."

"What other things?"

He could see her hesitating again, like she was debating whether she should tell him the rest. This part had to be particularly bad based on the pained expression on her face.

What the hell is she going to drop on me now?

"James loaned my mother money . . . and some of my sisters," she said softly. "Now he wants all the money back unless . . . unless I go back to him. He said that's the only way he'll forgive their debts."

"Damn it, Lauren, why didn't . . ." Cris stopped himself. He shoved down his anger. "Why didn't you tell me any of this before?" he asked more calmly seconds later.

"What was I supposed to say? 'Sure, I'll sleep with you, and by the way I owe almost ninety thousand in credit-card bills. My ex-boyfriend is blackmailing me, too. I hope you don't mind.' "

"You know I would have helped you! I still can help . . . if you'll let me."

Her lips tightened. She crossed her arms over her chest and stubbornly shook her head. "No, I've told you before and I meant it: I don't want any of your money! That's what got me into all this trouble in the first place. I won't rely on a guy again! I can take care of myself! I'm capable. I *can* do it!"

"Do it with what, Lauren? You don't have eighty-four thousand! It's only going to get worse. Either you'll have to file for bankruptcy or you'll end up owing even more money!"

"That's not your problem!"

"Lauren, I'm not James. I'm not going to turn on you and hold my money over your head later. Please . . . let me help you!"

Tears welled in her eyes. "I said 'no,' damn it! No! No! *No!*"

"*Why not?* Tell me why!"

"Because you may not be James, but you are *still* a man! Don't you get it? I can't depend on you!"

Cris was struck speechless. It felt as if she had just

sliced into his chest, ripping open his heart. It took a few seconds for him to recover from that one.

"That's right, I'm a man," he said quietly. "But I'm also in love with you, and I thought you were in love with me, too. I thought we *trusted* each other! You say you're different from your sisters, but you're more like them than you think, Lauren. The same distrust they have for men, you have, too. The same walls they put up, you put up, too. No one gets let into that precious little female circle of yours. You won't accept money from me, not just because you don't need it or you're too proud to take it, but because you don't trust me." He raised his eyebrows. "And why don't you trust me? *Because I'm a man!*"

At that, she bowed her head and closed her eyes. "I think you should leave."

He gazed at her, not saying a word. She was hurt, but he felt the ache ten times worse. He realized that the woman he had fallen in love with believed she couldn't depend on him, that it would show weakness if she did. He was offering her help and she was turning him away.

Jamal had cautioned him in the beginning about Lauren. *"I'm warning you, man! That way lies suffering and pain!"* Jamal had been right, except Cris didn't feel the pain in his wallet but in his heart.

"Fine. Have it your way." He reached for his shirt, which had been tossed over the arm of the only chair in her living room. He quickly shoved his arms into the sleeves, not bothering to button it closed. He put on his pants, shoved his feet into his shoes, grabbed his socks, wallet, and car keys, and headed for the front door.

He didn't want to look at her. He didn't want to see

if she was sad or angry or remorseful or indignant. He
just wanted to get out of there.

He opened her apartment door.

"Cris!" he thought he heard her call after him as he
shut her door behind him and stepped outside. He didn't
turn back.

Chapter 27

Lauren stood at the burner, gazing listlessly at the sizzling pan in front of her, lost in thought.

She had woken up this morning like a zombie, taking a shower, throwing on a T-shirt and jeans, getting into her car, and driving to the restaurant for morning prep. But the whole time, Cris's image lingered in the back of her mind, and that image was of him walking out her front door. The finality of it broke her heart.

Why did he have to dig through her things? He was the last person in the world that she wanted to know about her debts. She knew that Cris had only been trying to help, but she was proud of her independence. She was proud of how she looked when she saw her reflection in his eyes: smart, sexy, and self-reliant. But once he found her stack of bills, that image disappeared. For the first time, she saw pity in his eyes. It only left her ashamed and angry. *That* was why she had kicked him out.

She wished she could replay that moment. Do it all over again. Maybe then she could . . .

"*Chérie*, watch out!"

Lauren jumped back in surprise just as the ball of fire leaped from the saucepan, sending flames as high as two feet. The blue and orange flames missed her face by mere inches, but she hadn't been quick enough to keep the towel she was holding around the handle from catching fire. She jumped again in alarm and screamed as the burning towel tumbled from the kitchen burner to the tiled floor.

"I'll get the fire extinguisher!" one of the line cooks yelled. Two others rushed toward her, trying to stomp the fire out with their tennis shoe–clad feet.

"Get away from there!" Phillip shouted, charging forward with tongs in hand.

The meaty man shoved the two younger cooks aside, catching them by surprise with his brute strength. He quickly picked the burning towel off the floor with the tongs before tossing it into one of the stainless-steel kitchen sinks. He turned on one of the faucets and the fire went out in seconds, doused by a blast of cold water. A gray curl of smoke rose from the sink.

All the cooks were awestruck, amazed at his quick thinking. Meanwhile, Phillip mumbled angrily to himself, then turned off the faucet.

"The only thing y'all would have succeeded in doing is burnin' your damn legs!" Phillip shouted at the two line cooks who still gazed at him, open-mouthed. He then turned to Lauren, glaring at her. "Girl, what were you tryin' to do? What the hell were you thinkin'?"

Her cheeks flushed with heat. She opened her mouth, then closed it. "I'm sorry, Phillip. It was just a mistake. I didn't mean to make the heat that high. I must have added too much oil. I don't know what—"

"I put you in charge! I picked you to run my kitchen . . . not to burn it down to the damn ground!"

Lauren gazed at Phillip, now ashamed. She should have known better. She should have reacted better. She could have caused a serious fire.

She looked around the kitchen at the other cooks, who stared at her with a mix of shock and puzzlement. Nathan, the floor manager, had rushed into the kitchen when he heard the commotion. He now crossed his arms over his chest and smiled at her triumphantly.

"I'm . . . I'm sorry," she whispered. Tears welled in her eyes. She walked around Phillip to the big steel door that led to the alleyway. The other cooks cleared the path for her. She kept her head down the whole way.

When Lauren reached outside, she fell back against the alleyway's brick wall and took several long breaths. The tears spilled over her cheeks freely now, making her feel stupid and emotional in a silly female sort of way. Worse, she wasn't crying because she had almost turned her face into a melting candle or had embarrassed herself in front of the rest of the kitchen staff. She was crying because no matter what she did, it seemed that her past would always drag her down. She was crying because she missed Cris, but her pride wouldn't allow her to call him and ask him to come back. She was crying because it felt good to cry.

Just then she heard the steel door open again. Lauren hurriedly wiped her eyes with the back of her hand as Phillip stepped into the alleyway and walked toward her.

"You all right, *chérie*?"

She sniffed and forced a smile. "I'm fine. I'm sorry for falling apart in there. It won't happen again, chef."

He wiped his hands on his apron before putting them on his hips. "You don't seem to be yourself today. You sure you're all right?"

"Really, I'm OK. I . . . I just had a rough start. I've got myself together now."

He gazed at her for several seconds, then sighed. "All right, *chérie*. I'm gonna need you to keep it together. I ain't feelin' my best today."

Lauren took a closer look at him, and for the first time realized that his brow was covered with sweat and his skin was grayish and clammy. His breathing was a little labored, too. He didn't look well.

Lauren instantly rushed toward him. "What's wrong, Phil?"

"Nothin' you need to worry about," Phillip said with a dismissive wave of the hand. "Just a little headache. But I'm gonna need your help. So please . . . hold it together. I need my second-in-command to help steer the ship."

She nodded again and opened her mouth to ask him if he was going to see a doctor soon, but Phillip turned his back on her and disappeared inside. She gazed at the closed steel door. Phillip was in bad shape and he was still giving it his all in there. Meanwhile, here she was wallowing in self-pity.

"Hold it together, Lauren," she whispered to herself. "You've got to hold it together."

By the time the lunch rush began, Lauren had gotten her groove back. She pushed all thoughts of Cris, her mother, and her sisters far from her mind and concentrated only on cooking, plating, and making sure the kitchen ran with a seamless efficiency. She was ever conscious of Phillip's presence in the room and his watchful, worried eyes. She wanted to show him that he could still trust her. Of all people, he was the last person she wanted to disappoint.

She added the last details to a plate of braised beef short ribs with a side of Yukon potatoes and collard greens. She placed it on the stainless-steel shelf and shouted the order before turning her attention to another dish.

"*Chérie*, come over here," Phillip ordered from the other side of the kitchen. She scurried toward him.

He dipped a spoon into a pot of French onion soup and handed it to her. "Try this. Enrique here"—he jabbed his thumb over his shoulder at the sheepish-looking line cook behind him—"butchered my recipe somehow. I've added a few shakes of salt, but it still ain't got what I'm lookin' for. Maybe you got an idea how to fix it."

Lauren stepped forward. She sipped from the spoon and frowned, licking her lips. She thought for a bit. "I wouldn't add any more salt. It's *too* salty now. No, I say add a little more beef broth, maybe some pepper. See if that helps."

Enrique nodded.

"I guess my taste buds are a little off today," Phillip said.

"It all starts to taste the same when you've sampled enough dishes in a matter of hours," she assured with a smile, turning around to head back. "Well, I better finish that plate of blackened catfish. It has to be out before—"

She stopped midsentence when she heard the clatter of pans and steel behind her. She turned to find Phillip on bended knee, grabbing at his chest, surrounded by pans, soup ladles, and forks. Some of the hair in his slicked-back ponytail had come undone and now hung limply in his face.

"Phillip?" Lauren rushed forward and fell to her knees. She wrapped her arms around him. *"Phillip? What's wrong? Tell me what's wrong!"*

"I think . . . I think I'm havin' a goddamn heart attack." He almost sounded surprised.

A second later, he closed his eyes and collapsed. She nearly fell with him as he crumpled to the floor.

Lauren began to shout. She screamed for someone to call 911.

Chapter 28

Stephanie retrieved a ceramic platter from one of the overhead kitchen cabinets and placed it on the granite island. She opened a Tupperware container of freshly baked chocolate-chip cookies and began to arrange them on the plate.

It had been a rough week. She was still reeling from the PR fallout that came after her fight at the dress salon. Two of her clients had called her yesterday to tell her they would rather go with another real-estate agent to represent their properties. Another half dozen had threatened to fire her, but had only reconsidered after some pleading on her part. She finally convinced them that her personal life had no affect on her ability to sell or to help them buy a home.

All of this was in addition to the fact that she and Lauren still hadn't spoken since their post-fight blowup. Dawn and Cynthia said they hadn't heard anything from Lauren, either, for the past couple of days. She seemed to be freezing all of them out. Stephanie was now starting to wonder if Lauren had really meant what she said and wasn't just speaking out of anger in the mall parking lot that day. Was she really tired of all of them? Did she really see them all as just a burden? That statement had hurt Stephanie particularly badly.

They had never been accepted by the people in Chesterton. Even if men in the community were willing to date them, Stephanie knew she and her sisters still sat on the fringes of all the social circles in town. All the Gibbons girls had to rely on were each other. If they didn't have one another, they were no longer a family of social outcasts. They were just . . . alone.

The thought of having to face all the taunts, put-downs, and whispers without her sisters by her side absolutely terrified Stephanie.

"Miss Gibbons, I think . . ." Carrie walked into the kitchen. "I think I'm ready to handle a house tour today."

Stephanie looked up in surprise from the platter of cookies she was arranging, pushing her morose thoughts aside for the time being. "Are you sure?"

Carrie hesitated, then nodded. "Yes. Yes, I'm sure. I want to get my real-estate license next year and . . . and if I'm serious about being an agent, I need to learn how to do this."

Stephanie smiled. "Well, I'm very proud of you for taking the initiative, Carrie. I know this part of the job isn't one of your favorites."

"It isn't . . . but it has to be done, right? I'll only get better if I get some practice."

The doorbell rang and both women gazed at one another.

"Well, it looks like you're about to get some practice right now."

"Looks like it," Carrie said, smiling nervously.

The doorbell rang again.

"It's your house tour. Go ahead and answer."

Carrie nodded again before adjusting her suit jacket, pushing back her shoulders, and heading toward the foyer.

Stephanie beamed. So her mousy assistant was finally starting to venture out of her hidey-hole. Rather than shadow Carrie during the tour, Stephanie decided to stay in the kitchen for now. At least she could hear what was going on in the foyer from here. She'd only intervene if it sounded like Carrie was having problems or the young woman's nerves were starting to get the better of her.

Stephanie returned her attention to the arrangement on the platter, sorting her last stack of cookies. She heard Carrie open the front door. "Hello! Welcome to the—"

"Stephanie! *Stephanie!*" someone yelled a second later.

When Stephanie heard the familiar voice calling her name, she cringed.

Oh, please tell me this man is not here!

"Sir, you can't just come barging in like this!" a panicked Carrie shouted. "We're conducting showings today! Sir!"

"Stephanie, where are you?"

Stephanie lowered her head and thumped it against the granite counter.

Hank Montgomery had been blowing up her phone for the past couple of days, leaving bipolar phone messages. One moment he'd be ranting about how she had ruined his marriage, that his wife refused to speak to him, and that now he was in danger of being kicked out of his church. The next day he'd leave a message saying that all he could do was think about her and how she had "freed" him. He had even shown up one night at her house, yelling for her to come out and speak with him. She told him that she would call the police if he didn't get off her damn lawn.

If Stephanie had known that one spanking would get her into this much trouble, she would have just taken the Tiffany bracelet and shut the door in his face. She should have just let him go home to boring missionary sex with his snooty wife.

Married men, she thought with a slow shake of the head. *They always come with the most drama.*

"Stephanie!" He ran into the kitchen and stopped when he saw her.

Hank, who was usually immaculately dressed, didn't look too good today. He was wearing a wrinkled linen shirt and pants. The shirt wasn't properly buttoned. He had dark circles under his eyes like he hadn't slept for days. In his arms was an enormous bouquet of pale pink roses and white Asiatic lilies.

"I found you," he said, smiling ear to ear.

"I'm so sorry, Miss Gibbons!" Carrie cried. "He just . . . he just *barged* in! I—"

Stephanie held up her hand. "It's OK, Carrie. I'll handle it. You can go back out there and get ready for the house tours."

Carrie paused. She glanced warily at Hank.

"Are you sure, Miss Gibbons?"

Stephanie nodded.

Carrie hesitated again before finally walking out of the kitchen.

"I had to come here." Hank rushed toward her, making her take several steps back. "I had to see you,

Stephanie. I had to get this off my chest, but you won't talk to me. You won't return my phone calls!"

"For a good reason." She scowled up at him. "You've lost your goddamn mind!"

"I haven't lost my mind! I'm in love with you!"

She sighed in exasperation.

"Penny wants to leave me again. But I . . . I don't care. I want us to be together. You complete me, Stephanie. You can give me what I need!"

"Hank, I told you that was just a one-time performance. I'm not the dominatrix of your dreams, sweetheart. That isn't my thing. I just did it as a thank-you. I don't whip men on a daily basis."

"But you *freed* me!"

"I didn't 'free' you! Stop saying that! I spanked you with a hairbrush! That's all!" She grabbed his arm and ushered him toward the kitchen's entrance. "There. I heard what you had to say. You got it off your chest. Now you can leave."

"But I'm in love with you!" he shouted, yanking his arm out of her grasp. "Doesn't that mean anything to you?"

"Hank!" Hank's wife's shrill voice echoed in the foyer.

You have got to be kidding me!

"What is it with you people?" Carrie yelled. "This is a place of business!"

"Hank!" His wife walked into the kitchen. When she saw Hank and Stephanie together, she narrowed her eyes into thin slits.

Mrs. Montgomery was in worse shape than her husband. Not only did she still have a bruise on her cheek from the fight at the dress store, but she also had bags under her eyes and looked like she had gotten dressed in the dark.

"I heard that your car was here! I can't believe you would go running after this bitch again, you lying piece of shit!"

Oh, this was going to get ugly. Stephanie wagered she could take on Mrs. Montgomery again if she had to, but she certainly didn't want to get in a fistfight in one of her clients' homes. Her professional reputation was tarnished enough. She glanced at Carrie, who stood in the kitchen entryway looking dazed and bemused. Stephanie mouthed, "Call the police."

Carrie snapped out of her malaise and nodded. She ran back into the foyer.

"You said you didn't want to be married to me anymore!" Hank shouted back at his wife. "What do you care if I see her again?"

Mrs. Montgomery's eyes began to water. Her bottom lip quivered. "I gave you thirteen years of my life, Hank! I gave you loyalty and . . . and love and—"

"You nagged me and acted like you were my mama, not my wife! You never did what I wanted in bed! You wouldn't do anything I asked for!"

"*Sex!* That's all you ever think about!" his wife sneered. "I swear you are addicted to it, Hank! You need to pray on that! You should go to the reverend and—"

"The reverend can't tell me a goddamn thing! He's got three girlfriends of his own!"

His wife sputtered. "How *dare* you talk about the reverend that way! Just because you're a sinner doesn't mean everybody is! You need to pray that God takes the devil out of you, Hank!"

"It's not the devil! A man wanting to get his dick

sucked every once in a while doesn't mean he's been taken over by demons!"

Stephanie leaned against the fridge and stood silent as they argued.

The married couple's quarrel carried on for another fifteen minutes before the cops finally showed up. Stephanie watched in relief as Mr. and Mrs. Montgomery were escorted from the premises by a bored-looking patrol cop.

Soon after the police car pulled off, a BMW pulled into the driveway.

"Oh, thank God they left before our next tour," Carrie said as she stood beside Stephanie in the doorway, adjusting her hair. "Do you want me to take this one?"

A man and a woman climbed out of the BMW and strolled up the walkway, smiling as they gazed at the house.

Stephanie chuckled. "We can *both* do this one."

After that little fiasco with the Montgomerys, Stephanie needed the distraction.

She watched as the couple approached, holding hands. They looked like they were in their mid- to late thirties. The plump woman was wearing a bright orange sundress and wide-brimmed straw hat. She pushed up the hat's floppy brim and stepped forward first, climbing the brick steps.

"Oh, this house is just lovely!" she gushed. "It's perfect for us, Dante!"

Her dark-skinned companion smiled and nudged her shoulder. "Don't act so overeager, baby. We haven't even seen the inside yet."

She giggled and stepped through the doorway. "I guess that's why we're married. You keep me from getting too crazy."

"Hi, my name is Stephanie Gibbons," Stephanie said, shaking the woman's hand. "I'm the real-estate agent for today's property. Pleased to meet you." She glanced toward her assistant. "Carrie, will you hand her a flyer, please?" She then looked back at the woman. "This has all the pertinent information about the house, but if you have any additional questions, I or my assistant, Carrie, will be happy to answer them."

"Thank you!" The woman pushed back her hat and raised her gaze to the foyer's ceiling. "Oh, Dante, look at that chandelier!"

Her husband, Dante, stepped through the doorway next while his wife stood a few feet away, hurling a flurry of questions at Carrie.

"Pleased to meet you," Stephanie said, smiling politely and offering her hand for a shake.

He slowly looked her up and down, hungrily licked his lips, and grinned. "Pleased to meet you, too." He then shook her hand and winked.

Uh-oh, Stephanie thought, tugging her hand out of his grasp like he had bitten her.

This was a bad case of déjà vu. She wasn't doing this again!

She anxiously cleared her throat. "Carrie, why don't you give this lovely couple a tour?"

"You . . . you want me to do it . . . *by myself?"*

"Sure! Why not? I'll just be straightening up . . . somewhere."

Stephanie dashed out of the room. When she reached the kitchen, she saw the bouquet Hank had left behind, sitting on the counter. She stomped toward the bouquet, grabbed it, opened the cabinet underneath the sink, and dumped it into the wastebin, closing the lid on her *last* affair with a married man.

Chapter 29

Cris slouched back in his lounger, flipped a page in his book, and absently reached for his beer on a nearby end table. He took a sip and set the bottle down again, let his eyes scan over the words on the novel's pages, and tried to become engrossed in the story, but he wasn't succeeding. He then glanced at the clock on the great room wall. When he saw what time it was, he angrily clenched his jaw.

It was nearly ten o'clock. Almost another full day had gone by, and he still hadn't heard anything from Lauren.

Cris had waited patiently the entire week for Lauren to call him or come to his home. Well, "waited" wasn't quite the right word. It wasn't like he was staring at the phone, willing it to ring. He had his pride after all. He had gone about his normal daily routine, waking up at eight a.m. and working out in the gym, doing conference calls with his business associates, supervising the upkeep of his property, and meeting up with Jamal for a beer after hours. But all the while, in the back of his mind, he wondered when—and *hoped*—that Lauren would reach out to him.

He even would have accepted an e-mail from her, but she had made no attempt to contact him, to tell him she overreacted the morning she kicked him out of her apartment. She hadn't come to him to say she wanted his help, either.

Stubborn, he thought, slowly shaking his head in frustration. *She's so goddamn stubborn.*

Sharing hours with her, sharing a bed together, hadn't made a bit of difference. It was as if the months they had spent together hadn't happened. And he had been willing to look beyond her tangled and warped past. He had stood up for her to Jamal and had to restrain himself from beating the hell out of her ex-boyfriend. So many had called her a whore and he had staunchly stood by her side. He had been ready to love her completely, to trust her, but she hadn't been willing to do the same.

The realization still broke his heart.

Just then, his doorbell rang. Cris raised his gaze from his book and glanced toward the great room's entrance. The doorbell rang again and he shut his book.

Was it Lauren?

It could be, though at this point he wasn't sure how he would feel if he found her standing on his doorstep. He was still hurt, not to mention angry as all hell at her.

The doorbell chimed a third time.

"So you won't hear her out?" a voice in his head asked. "You wanted her to come to you to apologize, and now you won't even answer the door?"

With a heavy breath, he pushed himself to his feet. He slowly walked out of the great room, down a corridor to the front door. He paused before turning the steel knob and pulling the door open. When he saw who was standing in the shadow of the entrance light, he stared in surprise.

"Alex?"

The brunette beauty gave a bashful smile and then batted her long, dark eyelashes. "Hi, Cris."

"What . . . what are you doing here?"

He peered over her shoulder at the black Lincoln Town Car sitting idle in his driveway. A driver sat at the wheel, gazing with boredom out the windshield at the manicured lawn.

Alex, who was decked out in a formfitting, expensive-looking red business suit, shrugged her slender shoulders. "There's a conference near Dulles where our PR firm is showcasing. I knew you weren't that far out of town, so I decided to pay you a visit. I figured it would be better than being stuck at some stuffy old airport hotel." Her smile widened. "So are you willing to give a lady some shelter?"

Cris leaned against the doorframe.

If Alex had arrived more than a week ago, he would have told her she had made a big mistake by showing up here unannounced. He had moved on and was already in a new relationship with a woman he loved very much. Having Alex at his home would have only complicated things for him. But that was a week ago. Now that he and Lauren had broken up and it seemed pretty unlikely that they would get back together, those complications weren't there anymore.

"You should have called, Alex."

"And if I had called, what would you have said? Huh? I thought the element of surprise would work in my favor."

"What if I was on a date? What if I had a woman here?"

"Oh, come on, Cris! I *know* you. You're a gentleman to a fault. Even if you had some groupie here, you'd toss her out rather than turn me away. I wasn't worried."

"I wouldn't be too sure about that."

"Cris, if you want to argue with me, we could just as easily do it inside." She took a step toward him, reached out and touched his shoulders. "Come on. Let me stay . . . just for a few days, *mi amor*. For old times' sake."

He knew what she was doing. It was as obvious as the Chanel No. 5 perfume she wore. She was trying to weasel her way back into his life. He wouldn't be surprised if the story about the conference was a total lie, and Alex had simply gotten tired of waiting on him to take her back and made up a story to come to Virginia, to show up on his doorstep. That was completely Alex's style. Yet he couldn't bring himself to tell her no. Maybe it was his lingering anger at Lauren or Alex's seductive smile, but he found himself rolling his eyes as he waved her inside. Besides, the house had plenty of rooms. It wasn't like they would be sharing the same bed, and frankly, if his heartbreak lasted long enough, he may not be that against the whole idea of sharing a bed with Alex again.

Alex instantly grinned and turned to look at the driver.

"You can bring them in, Felipe!" she shouted, cupping her hands around her mouth like a megaphone. She then winked at Cris before striding confidently through the front door. As she stepped into the foyer, she put her hands on her hips and grinned. "Nice place, Cris."

Cris watched as the driver popped open the trunk and opened the driver's-side door. Seconds later he started unloading suitcase after suitcase, setting her suitcases on the driveway. When he was done, more than half a dozen sat around the car's back bumper. He grunted as he carried a few to the door and dropped them in front of Cris like he was releasing boulders.

"Can you take these inside?" the driver asked. He then motioned over his shoulder with a jab of his thumb. "There's a couple more in the backseat that I gotta get."

"Great," Cris murmured sarcastically as he lifted one bag and tossed the strap of another onto his shoulder. He walked back inside. "What the hell have I gotten myself into?"

Chapter 30

Lauren wiped the remaining tears away from her puffy eyes as she gazed at the roadway. The streets were mostly deserted this early in the morning and dimly lit by streetlamps that were losing their brightness with the rising sun. She sniffed and swallowed loudly, squinting at the signs on the side of the road, hoping not to miss her turn. Though the route was familiar to her, she knew in her shaky state she could easily get lost.

At least Phillip was no longer in the intensive care unit. The doctors had had to do emergency surgery soon after he was admitted—a triple bypass—and though the surgery had been successful, the doctors said it had been "touch and go" for a while as they worked on him.

After Phillip came out of surgery, Lauren hadn't known whom to call. Phillip had no real family to speak of. His beloved grandmother had died more than a decade ago. His other relatives he hadn't seen in years. When she finally rounded up a few phone numbers and made some calls, most of his friends and colleagues in other parts of the country seemed too busy with their own lives to make the trek to Chesterton to rush to his aid.

Worried about him, knowing that he was in the hospital all alone, she was distracted most of the time at the restaurant. She messed up orders and regularly forgot the important plating details that she knew Phillip considered sacred. More than once she had wanted to throw up her hands and just head to the hospital, but she talked herself out of it and stayed. Phillip would have had a heart attack all over again if he knew his kitchen wasn't being run properly.

Between the lunch and dinner service, she would rush to his bedside, usually keeping vigil alone with the exception of a few loyal line cooks who showed up for a few hours in the hospital room. She realized, sitting at his bedside, that Phillip was the closest thing she probably would ever have to a father figure. He had offered her guidance and taken her seriously when others had not. She felt like she owed him this. She *had* to stay at his side.

Lauren had never been much of a churchgoer or a person who prayed, but she prayed fiercely, asking God to make Phillip better. For four days, she waited patiently for him to open his eyes.

And when he finally woke up at around five a.m. that morning, she wanted to shout and weep with joy. She called for the nurse, who came into the hospital room and checked his vitals. Lauren was ushered out of the room when a doctor more thoroughly examined Phillip later. Phillip was still too medicated to be coherent, but he was awake and on the mend. Lauren rushed into the linoleum-tiled hallway, instantly wanting to share her elation with someone.

Her first instinct hadn't been to call her mother or even her sisters. She instantly started to dial Cris's number on one of the pay phones. She wanted him to come to the hospital so she could cry on his shoulder with relief. But just before dialing the last digit, she stopped herself, remembering what she had said to him the last time she saw him. She had kicked him out of her apartment and her life. There was no way he would come to the hospital to be with her.

At that thought, she hung up the phone and slumped into one of the leather-cushioned chairs in the hospital hallway, feeling tears prick her eyes again.

I've treated him so badly, she thought with regret. But she loved Cris. When it came to men, he was the closest thing to perfect that she could imagine. And despite all her faults, he loved her, too. She was sure of it. It scared her enough that she had almost lost Phillip, her mentor. Now she had pushed the one man she truly loved away.

She had to talk to Cris. She *had* to get him back.

That's when she decided to leave the hospital, feeling comfortable to do so now that Phillip was awake and in good hands. She didn't want to talk to Cris over the phone. She wanted to see him in person.

Lauren decelerated as she took the winding, paved road that led to Cris's property and finally his home. Her hands on the steering wheel were trembling with nervousness. She licked her parched lips and grimaced, not knowing what to expect, dreading the worst.

She and Cris hadn't seen each other in almost a week. She had no idea how he would react with her arriving out of the blue, ringing his doorbell. She hoped he would at least give her a small window to explain herself. She hoped that he would listen.

As she neared his house and his columned portico came into view, she took a slow breath. A minute later, she parked in his driveway and took her keys out of the ignition. She closed her eyes and sat quietly for several seconds, trying to calm herself. Finally, she opened the driver's-side door and slowly climbed out of her car. The morning air was cool and crisp and the world around her was eerily quiet, so quiet that she could hear the rapid pounding of her heart in her ears, and her shallow breaths.

She glanced at her reflection in one of the car windows, only confirming what she suspected all along: She looked horrible. She hadn't had a good night's sleep in days. She wasn't wearing any makeup and her clothes were wrinkled. She hadn't even had the chance to comb her hair, but she had to see Cris. She didn't want to delay this any longer.

Lauren climbed the three steps to Cris's French doors. She rang the doorbell and patiently waited for Cris to answer. Her eyes were downcast. Her lips moved silently as she practiced what she was going to say. When one of the French doors finally opened, she charged full steam ahead, not wanting to lose her nerve.

"Cris, I know you may not want to see me, but I have to tell you that . . ."

Her words faded when she realized that it wasn't Cris standing at the front door.

The glamorous woman leaned casually against the

door frame with a chilled glass of orange juice in one hand and a folded newspaper in the other. Her glossy, raven black hair cascaded in waves around her shoulders. Her belted white silk robe was slightly parted, revealing the sky-blue negligee underneath.

Lauren's mouth fell open in shock.

"Yes? May I help you?" the woman asked, cocking a finely arched eyebrow.

Why was this woman here at Cris's home, and more important, why was she in her nightgown?

Lauren quickly recovered. "I . . . uh . . . I came to . . . to speak to Cris." She licked her lips. "Is . . . is he here?"

"As a matter of fact, he is." The woman took a languid sip from her glass. She scanned her eyes over Lauren. Her gaze lingered on Lauren's wrinkled clothes and her disheveled hair. "And may I ask who you are?"

Lauren felt the all-too-familiar prickle of anger seep within her veins. "My name is Lauren. May I ask who *you* are?" she snapped.

The woman broadly smiled. "Alejandra Delgado. I'm Cris's girlfriend."

Lauren felt as if someone had punched her in the gut. "Gir-*girlfriend?*"

Cris had mentioned his *ex*-girlfriend Alex once or twice, but he hadn't said anything about her making the trek out to Virginia. He hadn't mentioned them getting back together, either.

"Yes, his girlfriend." Alex gazed at Lauren's crestfallen face. "Aww, are you one of his fans? I hate to disappoint you, honey. So many women think he's single. Maybe I could cheer you up by getting you his autograph. I'll—"

"I didn't come for his autograph! I . . . I came to talk to him. I wanted to . . ." Her words faded.

"You wanted to what?"

I'm too late, Lauren thought dismally. *I came too late.*

Lauren backed away from the front door. Her legs felt rubbery, unsteady beneath her. She turned, almost stumbling as she did so. She shakily walked to her car.

"If you leave an address, I can have him mail you an autograph," Alex called after her, still smiling. "Just tell me who he should sign it to."

"I don't want his damn autograph!" Lauren shouted back, jumping into her car.

She pulled off seconds later with tires squealing. She didn't look in the rearview mirror so she couldn't see Alex smile cunningly while standing in the doorway.

Lauren mumbled to herself as she drove. She wasn't sure if she should be angry at Cris for getting back with his ex and not telling her, or angry at herself for pushing him back into his ex's arms. Either way, she knew it was officially over between them. He had obviously moved on.

Chapter 31

"Who was that?" Cris asked tiredly with a yawn, walking down the staircase into the dimly lit foyer.

He had heard the doorbell ring minutes earlier, thinking it was odd to get a visitor at this early hour. For one fleeting moment, he had hoped it was Lauren, but then talked himself out of that wish.

Why would she come here now at this hour? Just let her go.

Nevertheless, he was on his way to answer the bell when he realized Alex had already gotten there before him and opened the door.

Alex turned, shut the front door behind her, and smiled. "Some strange woman." She tucked her newspaper underneath her arm and drank from her glass. "Either a groupie or a stalker or both. I swear those women never give up. I hope you have a good alarm system."

Cris frowned. It was a bit presumptuous of Alex to answer the door in her robe and nightgown like she was the lady of the house, but he decided to let it slide.

She would only be here another day or two—thankfully. There was no reason to start an argument with her over something as petty as her attire.

"Did you get her name?" He stepped off the last riser. "Did she say what she wanted?"

Alex hesitated. She pursed her lips, then turned the dead bolt lock. "No, she didn't. I told you she was strange. You're lucky I answered and not you. You could have had a real nutball on your hands, but I guess finding me here scared her off."

"Well . . . thanks." He headed toward his kitchen. "I was just going to grab some breakfast if you—"

"Oh, don't worry about that, *mi amor*. I've got it covered."

Alex brushed past him, her hips swaying as she sashayed into his kitchen. The high heels of her satin slippers clicked over the marble foyer tile. Cris followed her.

Only weeks ago, Lauren had been cooking dinners in that gourmet kitchen. Now it was Alex rummaging through his industrial-size refrigerator and opening and closing oak cabinets. Again, Cris felt uneasy seeing her there, looking so comfortable. She wasn't his woman anymore, yet she kept acting as if she were.

"How about I make you your favorite, huevos rancheros?" She removed a carton of eggs from one of the refrigerator shelves. "Would you like that?"

"You really don't have to do that, Alex. I can make myself a quick breakfast. Besides, I don't have any tortillas."

"Don't worry," she said with a wink as she opened his pantry. "I bought tortillas at the grocery store yesterday." She then set the bag of tortillas on his kitchen island. "Just sit back and I'll have breakfast ready in the next thirty minutes or so."

When had she had time to go to the grocery store?

As Alex set a pan on one of the oven burners, he walked to his pantry closet and opened the double doors. He gazed at the pantry shelves.

Not being much of a cook, Cris usually purchased only food staples like bread, deli meats, a few canned soups, and some fruit. Now the shelves were stocked with items he never would have purchased himself: gourmet sauces, virgin olive oil, artisan breads, and several pastas. He opened his refrigerator and noticed a similar change.

Cris narrowed his eyes as he gazed at Alex, who was humming merrily as she began to grate tomatoes and onions for breakfast.

"Isn't it just like the old days, Cris?" she said, smiling whimsically.

"Yeah. Eerily so."

That evening, Cris was playing pool by himself in his game room. He leaned over the pool table, lining up a corner pocket shot. Suddenly, he felt warm air blow on his right ear, making him jump in surprise.

"Boo!" Alex said with a giggle.

Cris tossed aside his cue stick. He grumbled with irritation. "Damn it, *don't* sneak up on me like that!"

"Oh, did I ruin your game, *mi amor*?" She wrapped her arms around his waist, pressing her breasts against his back. "I'm sorry."

"No." He firmly tugged her hands away. "You just . . . you just caught me by surprise. That's all. I was about to call it a day anyway."

He then turned around to face her.

Alex was wearing *very* short drawstring shorts and a white tank top with no bra. She knew it was one of his favorite "sexy" outfits she wore. In fact, he had always found it sexier on her than if she had worn a bustier and thong. Unfortunately, despite knowing what he knew about Alex, he couldn't say he was immune to her outfit's power even now. He could feel the familiar stirring as he gazed at her. His eyes glanced hungrily at the dark nipples that were visible through the flimsy tank top fabric.

"Be strong, man," he could hear Jamal's voice urge in his head. *"Be strong!"*

Cris quickly averted his eyes.

"No other plans for this evening?" she said with a seductive smile.

"Not really."

He picked up the pool cue and walked across the game room. He placed the cue stick in one of the empty spots on the wall rack.

"I'll probably veg out in front of the TV and fall asleep in an hour or two."

"Boooring!" Alex hoisted herself onto the pool table. "Fall asleep? Are you kidding me? The night's still young, baby!"

He watched as she reached for one of the billiard balls and casually tossed it into the air before catching it in her hand. Alex spread her legs and swung her dangling feet over the carpeted floor. She raised an eyebrow and smirked her glossy lips. "Would you like to hear my suggestion of what we could do?"

He shook his head, quickly guessing what that suggestion would be. "Not really."

She chuckled, spreading her legs even wider. "Oh,

Cris . . . Cris . . . Cris. *Mi amor,* what am I going to do with you?"

The temperature in the room seemed to rise about ten degrees. Cris sighed, sensing it would be in his best interest to get out of there quickly before he did something he would regret later.

"Good night, Alex." He walked toward the game room doorway. "You're free to use the room as long as you like. Just turn the lights off when you're done."

As he passed the pool table, she reached out and grabbed his wrist. He could have easily yanked his hand away, but he didn't. Instead, he allowed himself to be pulled toward her. Alex slowly placed one of his hands on her breast. He cupped it and she smiled. She then guided his other hand between her thighs.

"Just like old times," she whispered huskily, wrapping an arm around his neck. She then fiercely tugged his mouth down to hers.

They kissed eagerly, losing themselves in the heady sensation. She tugged his bottom lip between her teeth as she raked her fingers over his broad back. He shoved his fingers into her hair and cupped her bottom.

I should stop this, Cris silently told himself. *I should stop this right now.*

Logic said that he should, but his hormones said different—and his hormones were winning out.

She abruptly shoved him away from her. She grinned as she tugged her tank top over her head, revealing her bare breasts. What little resolve he had melted away at that point. She tugged down the zipper of his jeans and rubbed his arousal. They kissed again and she hopped from the table. She dropped to her knees and shoved down his pants, then his boxers. She languidly began to stroke him.

"Baby, I'm going to make you regret ever leaving me," she murmured just before taking him into her mouth.

Cris's eyes flashed open. That was the bucket of ice cold water he needed. He shoved at her shoulders and she tore her mouth away and stared up at him, surprised. He glared down at her.

"Ever leaving you?" He raised his boxers and jeans back to his waist. "What do you mean *I* left *you?*"

She smiled, slowly climbing back to her feet. "Cris, it's just an expression, baby! You know . . . sexy talk."

"That wasn't fucking sexy talk! You meant exactly what you said. You said I'd regret ever leaving you, when that isn't true! I asked you to come with me, Alex! You told me you had your career and family back in Texas. You refused to come with me. *You* left *me!*"

She sighed and rolled her eyes. "Cris, I'm about to give you the blow job of your life and you really wanna argue with me?" She looped her arms around his neck. "Let's not talk about this now, baby."

"Why? Because it's the truth?" He wrenched her arms from around him and shook his head. "You dumped me, Alex. I can't understand how you can forget that fact!"

"OK, fine! Fine! I dumped you! But what did you expect?"

"For you to come with me! For you to stand by me!"

"Look, Cris, when we met, you were a star player on the Dallas Cowboys. You had sponsorship deals! You were on cereal boxes, for Christ's sake! You were big time and going places! I followed you around game after game, neglecting my own career to support you! Then suddenly you decide out of the blue to retire *without* discussing it with me! You just expect me to follow you to the middle of Nowhere, Virginia, and I'm just supposed to be OK with that?" She crossed her arms over her bare breasts. "No, I don't think so! I didn't hook up with Cris Weaver to become Mrs. Joe Nobody in Virginia!"

"*Mrs. Joe Nobody?*" he repeated with disbelief.

So all these years, Alex *had* been a groupie. He should have sensed it. She had always loved the star-studded parties, all the attention. She had loved using his name to get into places, to get what she wanted. Now he understood the truth.

"So why did you even come back? Why the hell did you come here?"

She pursed her lips again. "Because being with a *rich* Joe Nobody is better than being with no one at all. I could go after another football player or a baller, but I wouldn't know what I was getting. A lot of them are whores, knuckle-dragging assholes who will run after anything in a skirt. At least I wouldn't have to worry about that with you."

He didn't get any comfort in her backhanded compliment.

"I'm going to give you until tomorrow morning to pack up your shit and get the hell out of my house. OK? And you'd be smart not to darken my goddamn doorstep again."

He stepped away from her and strode toward the game room's entryway, wanting to kick himself for being so stupid.

"Oh, come on, Cris! This isn't about me leaving you!" she yelled after him as she reached for her tank top. She tugged the garment back over her head. "If it wasn't for that Lauren woman, you would take me back! Don't deny it!"

Cris stopped in his tracks. He turned and gazed at Alex in shock. "What did you say?"

"Lauren . . . or whatever the hell her name is," Alex spat as she dressed. "The woman who looked like she needed a shower and a hair stylist. She showed up on your doorstep this morning."

"What?" Cris glared at her. "You said you didn't know who she was!"

"Well, I lied," Alex answered succinctly with a cold smile. "I guess she's the new chick you've moved on to, but I'll tell you something, Cris. She is nothing . . . *nothing* . . . compared to me, baby! You took a step down when you went to that."

"Get the hell out," Cris said angrily. "I take back what I said about you leaving tomorrow morning! I want you to get the hell out of my house tonight! Stay at a goddamn hotel for all I care!"

"Fine!" she shouted as she walked out of the game room. "There's nothing to fucking do around here anyway! Enjoy your life in the middle of nowhere!"

Cris listened to Alex stomp down the hallway and then slam one of the mansion's doors behind her. When silence fell upon him, he slowly shook his head. He leaned against the pool table and closed his eyes, feeling his heart thudding wildly in his chest. After some time, the pace slowed.

"Lauren," he muttered aloud.

So Lauren *had* come after all and she "looked like she needed a shower and a hair stylist." That didn't sound good. That didn't sound good at all. He wondered what had happened to her in the past few days to leave her in such a state. He wondered if that was the reason why she hadn't called him.

Chapter 32

Lauren gazed into her bathroom mirror. Under the glare of the halogen bulbs, she half-heartedly applied her makeup. She closed her blush compact, stared at her reflection, and sighed.

She was preparing to go to tonight's Historic Preservation Association fund-raiser, as she had promised her sister Cynthia more than a month ago that she would. She was still annoyed at her family and resentful of all their drama, but she had given up being angry at them. They were the only family she had, after all—despite how screwed up they all were.

Cris was right in at least one regard: nothing broke the Gibbons's "precious little female circle." No matter what, they always stuck together.

A sharp ache expanded in her chest every time she thought about Cris, but she assumed it would become fainter over time, to the point where she couldn't discern the ache at all. For now she would just have to live with it. To be honest, even hearing his voice hurt a little.

That was part of the reason why she hadn't answered the phone when he'd called yesterday. She saw his name and number on her caller ID and let it go to voice mail. Besides, she wasn't sure what to say to him now that he had moved on to someone else. She was nowhere near the point where she could wish him happiness, so she decided to go with the old adage, "If you can't say something nice, don't say anything at all." When she saw he had left a voice message, she promptly deleted it.

Still gazing in the mirror, Lauren ran her hands over the front of her sapphire blue chiffon floor-length gown, trailing her fingers along the sweetheart neckline and then the sequined embellishment at the waist. Soft curls fell around her cheeks. Diamond teardrop earrings skimmed her shoulders. She looked beautiful and alluring, but she didn't feel that way. She felt sad and hollow.

"Just get through it," she muttered to herself. "Get through it like you always do."

She then turned off the bathroom light, readying herself for the long and painfully boring night.

A half hour later, Lauren pulled her car in front of the limestone steps of Glenn Dale, an antebellum mansion on one of the many historic plantations outside of Chesterton. She handed her keys to the smiling valet and stepped onto a red carpet that led up the steps to the entrance.

Subtle, Cynthia, she thought with a small smile, fighting the urge to roll her eyes.

She was instantly met by the sound of a twelve-piece orchestra, which played a lively Vivaldi tune inside, and the buzz of partygoers that gathered near the mansion's doors. She slowly climbed the steps, steeling her shoulders, ignoring the gazes and whispers that followed her as she walked into the shadows of the loggia, then the orange glow of the front hall.

In search of her sisters, Lauren walked into the crowded parlor, where she was immediately offered a glass of champagne by one of the waiters. She thanked him and accepted the drink, then looked around.

Cynthia and her staff had done a good job of renovating the mansion, restoring it to the original hodgepodge of neo-Palladian clean lines and Renaissance revival embellishments. Every historic detail was there, from the gold candlesticks on the mantel to the William-and-Mary-style desk in the corner. Lauren scanned the room, her small smile reemerging as she admired her sister's handiwork. But her smile faded when her eyes settled on a familiar face in the throng of people. She felt the sharp pain again.

Cris stood on the other side of the parlor, engrossed in conversation with a few businessmen from town who looked vaguely familiar. For some reason, she had assumed he wouldn't be here tonight.

"Fat chance of that," a voice in her head mocked. "He's a helluva lot more popular in Chesterton than you are. If *you* got an invite, he certainly did."

He wore a tuxedo that fit him so well it had to be tailor made. The tux and his debonair manner changed him from a simply handsome man to a strikingly gorgeous one.

As if he sensed her staring at him, Cris raised his almond-shaped eyes and gazed back at her. She watched as he mumbled something to one of his companions. He then placed his glass of white wine on a nearby end table and walked across the parlor, seemingly toward her.

Lauren's breath caught in her throat. She didn't want to talk to Cris—definitely not now. She'd probably angrily ask him how he could get back with his girlfriend. She would shout accusations, curse him out, maybe even burst into tears, making yet another scene that would leave her mortified later. Her gaze quickly darted around the room, looking for a way to make a hasty exit as Cris drew closer. She spotted the entrance to the neighboring dining room, raised the hem of her gown, and walked quickly toward it.

"Lauren!" He called after her. "Lauren!"

She ignored him and instead eased her way through the crowd. The dining room also was filled to capacity with couples, so that everyone stood shoulder to shoulder. It was like jostling for space in a conga line. She could barely hear Cris calling her name now. The murmur of the crowd and the symphony music echoed off the coffered ceilings and the forest green walls.

As Lauren pushed deeper and deeper into the throng, she glanced over her shoulder to see if she had lost him. Cris was peering around him, still searching for her. Someone tapped him on the shoulder and he turned. The partygoer smiled and shook his hand before introducing him to a woman and another man. Cris was once again dragged into a conversation, making the tenseness in Lauren's shoulders unravel.

That was close, she thought. But she knew she couldn't do this forever. She couldn't keep avoiding him. Eventually, she would have to talk to him again.

But thankfully, tonight would not be the night.

Chapter 33

"I'm leaving after Cynthia finishes her speech," Lauren whispered before gulping down the last of her champagne. She had been at the party for more than an hour and had managed to avoid Cris for most of the night. She spent the majority of her time standing alone, trying to fend off the advances of the men in the room who hadn't been in Chesterton long enough to know about her reputation. The rest of the time she hung around her sisters.

Dawn turned her focus from the lectern at the center of the front hall, where people were starting to gather, to Lauren who now stood beside her.

Dawn was wearing a floor-length taffeta ensemble in canary yellow. An elegant diamond choker adorned her long neck.

"What do you mean you're leaving? You're not going to stay for the actual dinner?"

"No. My head would explode if I had to sit at a dinner table with half of these people. I'll stay for Cindy's speech, but after that, I'm going home."

"Laurie," Dawn said tensely, "Cindy asked us to come here because she needs our support. She already feels like she's walking in hostile territory. She wanted some friendly faces in the crowd tonight."

"Look, I took off of work to be here. You know how crazy things are at the restaurant since Phillip had his heart attack. What more does she want from me? I said I would stay for—"

"Cindy says it's like the whole town has turned against her—against *all* of us—because of the little stunt you and Stephanie pulled at the dress shop a few weeks ago. And quite frankly . . . I feel it, too. I don't get invites to any of the parties anymore. My calls are hardly if ever returned. It's like I'm persona non grata around here."

Lauren pointed at her chest. "And you're blaming me for that?"

"Well, who else should I blame?"

Lauren's mouth tightened with outrage.

"Look, the *least* you could do is stay for the entire event or until Cindy says that it's OK for us to leave." She sucked her teeth. "Stop acting selfish for once. This isn't about you! Try to think of someone else besides yourself."

"Selfish? *Selfish?*" Lauren repeated with disbelief, glaring up at her sister. She pointed her finger up at Dawn. "Let me tell you something! OK? I didn't pull some 'little stunt' two weeks ago. I stupidly stood up for *our* family . . . something that I now regret!"

"Keep your voice down," Dawn hissed as people began to turn and look toward them. Dawn forced a smile and waved at one of the couples who now stared at them openly.

"Hello! Great to see you again!" she called to them.

They waved back and regarded her warily before turning back around to face the orchestra.

"And as so far as the town turning against you, everyone in this town *always* has been against you, Dawn!" Lauren continued, undeterred by her sister's angry glare. "Don't you get it? They may smile in your face, but they don't like you! They don't like *any* of us! They've never wanted us here!"

"Keep your voice down!" Dawn repeated in a sharp whisper, yanking the glass out of her sister's hand. "And lay off the champagne while you're at it. You've obviously had too much to drink."

"I'm not drunk! I'm just telling the truth. They don't want us here because they think we're whores!"

Now more of the conversations in the room fell silent. Ears pricked and eyes widened. Smiles began to curve on random lips. Dawn now gazed at her little sister, dumbfounded and well aware of their growing audience.

"They think we're whores who are out to steal their boyfriends and their husbands. They think that all we care about are money, clothes, and cars. They think we're cheap!" Lauren closed her eyes. "And I'm tired of it. I'm tired of all of them. I'm tired of this whole goddamn town!"

Lauren could feel tears streaming down her cheeks now. She wiped at them furiously with the back of her hands and sniffed. "I-I have to g-get out of here."

"Lauren," Dawn called as Lauren began to shove her way through the crowd of partygoers to the French doors on the other side of the room. They led to a brick terrace. Her sister followed her and grabbed her shoulder. "Damn it, Lauren, don't do this now! I know you're upset. I get it! But Cindy is about to make her speech!

Pull it together and come on! I'm not going to chase after you."

Lauren shoved off Dawn's hand and continued her angry strides. This time, her sister didn't follow.

"Lauren, wait up!" she heard Cris shout from behind her.

She picked up the pace, almost stumbling over the hem of her dress.

People turned to stare at her as she crossed the room, alarmed by her rudeness, but she ignored them all. She walked through the French doors and ran down the flight of steps to the gardens below. When she reached the lower level, she gripped the railing, and closed her eyes. The tears still fell but not as heavily now. She opened her reddened eyes and gazed into the dark garden in front of her. The smell of gardenias filled the warm September night air. She could still hear the orchestra music playing upstairs.

"Pull yourself together, chérie," she could hear Phillip urging her.

She was a big weepy mess and all because the people in town didn't like her? No, that wasn't the reason. She was falling apart because of Cris.

Lauren couldn't stand it, knowing that Cris was with someone else. She had stubbornly pushed him away and into the arms of his ex and now she would have to live with her decision. She hadn't cared about what people thought when she was with him. But having Cris in this town and seeing him with his girlfriend at parties and on Main Street and at the farmer's market and everywhere she turned would be unbearable. It felt like thousands of eyes were on her, waiting for her reaction. And what would they see on her face? Longing? Disappointment? Heartbreak?

"I can't do it," she murmured sadly. "I just can't do it."

"Can't do what?"

Lauren instantly dropped her palms from her face and turned to find James standing a few feet behind her, halfway underneath the shadowy overhang of the terrace.

"Can't do what, beautiful?" Laughter tinged his voice as he circled her and drew near to the banister.

Lauren sniffed and took a hesitant step back. "How . . . how long have you been standing there?"

"Oh," he uttered slowly, tilting his head and reaching out to run his finger along her jawline. She flinched at his touch. "Long enough." He chuckled before extending a white handkerchief to her. "Are those tears over Mr. Wonderful upstairs? Did he finally toss you aside?" He smirked.

Lauren ignored the handkerchief James offered her. "Cynthia's probably starting her speech soon. I should get back—"

"You know, you owe me a thank-you," James began casually. "One of the women you had that little fight with a few weeks ago wanted to file charges against you and your sister. The sheriff let me know about it and I had a little talk with her husband. He's not a bad guy. He's an old golfing buddy of mine with a bit of a gambling habit. He owes me a great deal of money. I reminded him about that and voilà, she decides she doesn't want to press charges anymore. Isn't that a fortunate coincidence?"

Lauren had wondered why the fight hadn't come back to haunt her. She should have known that James had pulled some strings behind the scenes.

"Thank you," she said tightly, feeling the words corrode on her tongue.

"See what I can do for you, Lauren? With a snap of my fingers, I can make all your problems go away. All you need to show is . . ." He trailed his fingertip along her collarbone before letting it dip between her breasts. When she shrank back, he smiled. ". . . a little appreciation."

Lauren tried to walk around James to head back toward the stairwell. He stepped in front of her, blocking her path. Lauren's eyes instantly leaped to his face. She didn't like what she saw in those green eyes.

"What are you trying to do? Run back to him? I told you he doesn't want you. Not anymore. Did you honestly think a man like that would take a woman like you seriously? He knows your type, Lauren."

Lauren narrowed her eyes. This is how it always was with James. He could go from syrupy sweet to a poisonous bite in less than a minute. His fangs were definitely out now.

"Just get away from me!" She attempted to walk around him again. This time he grabbed her arm and tugged her against him. Lauren winced.

"When you were with me, you were *exactly* what you should have been. You didn't have to pretend with me, because I *know* what you are. You know what they would have called you in the olden days, Lauren? A concubine. You'd live in your master's house, eat his food, have his children, and in exchange, he'd expect you to shut up and keep him happy. But they don't have fancy words like that anymore. You know what they'd call you now? A hooker on retainer." He grinned despite the strain of keeping ahold of her as she twisted and turned in his arms. "How do you like that? Our line of work isn't that different. We both work for an hourly rate and we state our fees up front. All we need to do is keep the client happy."

"Damn it, let go of me!" she shouted, but the orchestra reached a crescendo and Lauren knew that none of the partygoers could hear her. Besides, some of them wouldn't come to her rescue even if they *had* heard her. They would see what's happening now as her just deserts. But where the hell were Dawn and Stephanie? Where were her sisters when she needed them?

"Look," James said as he shoved her into the shadows beneath the terrace, "I've been very patient with you. I've let this drag for almost a year, but I am tired of playing games! You've had your fun. You've made your point, and now it's time for you to come back home!"

"I am *not* going back! I'm not your damn concubine! I told you, it's ov—"

He silenced her words by wrapping his hands around her neck. Lauren felt herself being lifted and savagely shoved back farther into the shadows and up against the moss-covered brick wall under the terrace. His grip tightened.

Oh, my God! He's lost it. He's finally lost it!

With her air supply cut off, she began to flail desperately. Lauren reached around in the darkness for anything possible she could use to defend herself, but grabbed only thin air and flecks of brick that crumbled from the wall as she scratched the damp, aged surface. She kicked, wriggled, and punched her balled fists against his neck and shoulders but to no avail. Just as she could feel herself blacking out, James finally released his hold from around her neck. Lauren took in quick gasps of air, preparing to scream again, but then she felt a hand clamp over her mouth as if he sensed what she planned to do next. With his other hand, he grabbed at the voluminous fabric of her skirt, shoving it upward. Lauren squealed in horror against the palm of his hand. She realized what he was about to do.

Oh, God, no! Don't let this happen! Don't let him rape me down here! Please don't let him do it!

She screamed again as the hem of her skirt reached her waist.

"Lauren," Cris suddenly called. "Lauren! Lauren, are you out here?" He turned and squinted against the darkness into the shadows where James and Lauren were tussling. "Lauren, are you in there?"

When Cris came into view, Lauren took her chance. She bit down hard on the fleshy part of James's palm, making him yell and release his grip. When he did, she shoved as hard as she could, sending him off balance and falling back against the facing wall. She slid to the ground, gathered her skirts, and bolted to the garden railing where Cris was standing. She then fell into Cris's arms, catching him by surprise.

"What the hell?" Cris exclaimed, frowning down at her. He scanned her red eyes and disheveled hair and gown. "What's going on?"

Meanwhile, James was quickly recovering.

"You little bitch," James muttered as he flexed his bitten hand. "I'm really going to beat the shit out of you for . . ."

His words drifted off when he stepped from under the terrace and realized Cris was holding her.

Lauren's chest heaved up and down as she fought to catch her breath. She pointed at James.

"He . . ." She brought a hand to her chest, trying desperately to steady her breathing. "He . . . tried . . . to . . . rape me."

James quickly pasted on a smile. "Nonsense!" He adjusted the lapels of his tuxedo and his bow tie. He took a calming breath. "Don't listen to her, Cris! We were just catching up and got a . . . a little carried away, if you know what I mean." He laughed. "You came down here and caught us by surprise. She's just a little embarrassed, that's all." He turned to Lauren. "Rape? Why would you say a thing like that, baby? Don't lie to the man."

"I wouldn't lie about something like that! You tried to rape me!"

James's smile tightened. "Lauren, honey, keep your voice down. Someone might hear you. What are people going to think?"

"I don't care what they think! Let them hear me!"

"Would you listen to her? She's hysterical. It doesn't make any sense. Why would I try to do something like that here at a party with *all* these people? It doesn't make any sense," he repeated softly. "Come on, baby, you know we were only having some fun. Come back over here and—"

"Look at his hand, Cris!" She pointed at James again. Tears ran down her cheeks. "He's bleeding. I had to bite him to get him off of me! I swear to you I'm not lying!"

Cris tightened his protective hold around her shoulders. He gazed down at her. "I know you're not. I wouldn't doubt you, Lauren."

"Then you're a bigger fool than I thought if you take her word over mine! You know what she is! Half the men in town have—"

"Maybe you should just shut the hell up while you're still ahead!" Cris shouted. "Part of me wants to call the police and tell them what you did to her, but the rest of me just wants to beat the shit out of you right here and now!"

Lauren's pulse raced with newfound alarm. She quickly shook her head as the orchestra started another overture, drowning them out again. "No. No, don't do that, Cris."

James grinned. "You'd be smart to listen to her. I've got friends in high places around here. No one's going to arrest me, certainly not based on the word of a town whore," he said, casually pointing to Lauren. "You're new to Chesterton and don't know any better. I understand. But I'd hate to see you run out of town so soon. So . . ." he said as he took several steps forward. He buttoned his dinner jacket and pointed toward the stairwell. "Why don't you just run back upstairs and let me handle my—"

James didn't get the chance to finish before Cris punched him, knocking the older man back several feet. It had happened so fast that Lauren barely noticed when Cris removed his arms from around her, stepped forward, and took the swing.

"I've got friends in high places, too, you piece of shit," Cris said, glaring down at James, who was still on the ground, wiping the corner of his bloody mouth with the back of his hand. "And I've got just as much cash to throw around. You may scare most of the people in this goddamned town with your big money and big talk, but I'm not afraid of you! You hear me?"

James started to rise to his feet, but before he did, Lauren also had something to say.

"And if you *do* come after him or me or my family

again," she warned quietly, taking a step forward, "I won't keep silent this time. I'm going to the police. I'm going to file charges. Even if not a single person in Chesterton believes me, I'm still going to do it." She leaned over her ex, no longer intimidated by his menacing gaze. "And you'll have to explain to all your clients—*especially* the ones who don't live around here—why you were charged with assault and attempted rape. Even if I don't get you thrown in jail, I'll make sure I embarrass the hell out of you. I'll make sure people always wonder if you did it. I'll make sure your name and mine are linked together forever in their minds."

She could see the rage again in his eyes and the hate, but a dawning of awareness was also there. He wanted to shout at her. He wanted to punch her. But for once, he held himself back. Finally, he realized that he had something to lose and that he was equally matched. They had gotten through to him.

James rose to his feet, brushing the dirt and mossy grime off the seat of his pants. He adjusted his dinner jacket and cleared his throat. The orchestra music had finally died down and Lauren could hear Cynthia's voice over the loudspeaker followed by polite applause.

"So that's how it's going to be?" James asked, the anger thinly veiled in his voice. "After all we had, Lauren? After all I've done for—"

"Again," Cris murmured, "quit while you're ahead." He waved toward the stairs. "Just get the hell out of here."

James flinched. He wasn't used to being talked to that way. But he kept silent and slowly trudged to the garden's stairs, eyeing them as he did.

Lauren watched as he climbed each step, until he reached the top and she saw his back disappear past the arch leading into the front hall.

He'd have a hard time explaining the busted lip and bloody hand to the other partygoers, but it could be a lot worse. It'd be harder to explain being escorted out in handcuffs.

"Are you all right?" Cris asked from over her shoulder, snatching her from her thoughts.

Lauren turned, gave a pained smile, and slowly nodded. "I'm fine. A little roughed up." She reached for her slightly bruised neck. "But I've . . . I've had a lot worse."

"You shouldn't have used calling the cops on him as a bargaining chip," Cris said. "That bastard deserves to go to jail for what he did to you tonight and what he did to you before that, *regardless* if he called the cops on me or made my life a living hell."

"If it keeps a choke collar on him, that's all that matters to me," she said softly, lowering her eyes. "I didn't want him to go after you, too." She paused. "I'm . . . I'm sorry I dragged you into this, Cris. It's not what I wanted."

"You didn't drag me into this. I came after you because I *wanted* to, and thank God I did or things could have gotten a lot worse for you down here." He tilted his head and looked at her searchingly. "I've been chasing you around all night, Lauren. Didn't you realize that?"

"Yes, but . . . I don't know why. I thought you didn't want anything to do with me."

"Why would you think that? Because you kicked me out of your apartment?"

"Well, yeah, and . . ." She let her gaze drift to the garden behind him, unable to meet his eyes. "I came to your house and your girlfriend said—"

"My girlfriend? Alex told you she was my girlfriend?"

Lauren hesitated, then nodded.

Cris gave a lofty roll of the eyes. "Yeah, well, that lying, scheming bitch hasn't been my girlfriend in months. The last time we were a couple was back in Texas. I just dumbly allowed her to stay at my house for a few days while she was in town. That's all. I kicked her out a couple of days ago."

"Kicked her out?"

"Yeah—her and her thirteen suitcases."

Lauren fought back a smile. "So you two didn't get back together? You're not a couple?"

"No, we're not a couple."

Lauren let those words settle into her. She had resolved that she would have to move on because Cris had moved on to someone else. But that obviously hadn't been the case. The possibilities for them were endless again.

"Cris, I—"

He held up a finger, silencing her. "Wait. I see something."

Lauren watched as Cris walked past her into the shadows of the terrace where she had been fighting for her life minutes earlier. He emerged seconds later, holding her diamond pendant necklace in his hand.

Lauren's fingers instantly leaped to her throat again. She had been so shaken up that she hadn't realized her necklace was gone.

He smiled as he gave it a quick wipe on the front of his jacket. "I believe this is yours."

She reached for the necklace, but he shook his head and motioned for her to turn around. As he placed the jewelry around her neck, she breathed in one unsteady breath, feeling his warm fingers linger on her back and then her shoulder blades. When she turned back around, he raised a hand to her cheek, then let it fall to his side.

"I don't know about you, but I'm ready to call it a night."

She chuckled. "I was ready to leave an hour ago."

"If you feel too shaky to drive, I can take you to your place. It wouldn't be a problem."

She gazed into his eyes. "I'd much rather go home with you."

And she meant it. She wanted to go back to his house and share his bed. She wanted to share the next few hours until morning with him and many hours after that until they all added up to a lifetime.

He wrapped an arm around her shoulder and guided her toward the stairs. They left the party together and that night made love until the wee hours of morning before falling asleep in each other's arms.

Chapter 34

"How're the strawberries?" Cris asked as he leaned back against the plaid wool blanket on one elbow. He peered at Lauren over the wicker picnic basket nestled between them.

He had asked her the question while she was mid-bite. Lauren giggled as juice from the luscious strawberry trickled from the side of her mouth to her chin. She wiped at the drops with the back of her hand. "Delicious," she mumbled between chews.

"Damn, you've got it all over your mouth. Let me take care of that for you." He then leaned toward her and licked the juice off the corner of her lip. They tumbled back onto the blanket and she laughed and shrieked as he continued to lick and nibble at her before finally rewarding her with a soul-stirring kiss.

It was a cool fall October afternoon—so cool, in fact, that Lauren had thrown another wool blanket over her jeans-clad legs to ward off the chill. From this vantage point—a hilltop just on the outskirts of Chesterton—they could see the fall foliage, the lush hues of red, orange, yellow, and green.

Of course, this view didn't compare to the one they had enjoyed earlier. They had finally taken the long-delayed hot-air balloon ride and Lauren had gazed in awe at the blue, cloudless skyline and the countryside. She and Cris stood silently with their arms wrapped around each other as they floated over Chesterton, appreciating the scenery around them. She was grateful for the moment, for being with him. She had lots of things to be grateful for now.

Cris finally tore his mouth away from hers. He slowly pushed himself up and rose to his feet. He stretched and turned to her, smiling.

"Feel like going for a walk?" he asked, holding out his hand to her.

She wiped her sticky fingers on one of the gingham napkins and nodded. "Sure." She took his hand.

Cris dragged her to her feet and she groaned at the slight soreness in her legs from sitting in the same position for so long. They packed what was left of their meal into the picnic basket and held hands again. She let him lead the way as they trudged to another hill, the fall leaves crunching beneath their feet as they went.

Thanks to Cris and her own courage, so far James had stayed true to his promise to leave her and her family alone. For weeks, she had waited for him to slither his way back into her life like the snake that he was, or to start harassing her mother and her sisters again, but the threat of telling the whole town, his business partners, and the press about what he had done to her seemed to keep him at bay. She knew it wasn't her threat alone that had done it, though. James was a man who not only wielded power, but respected others who wielded it. He was intimidated enough by Cris now that he didn't want to spar with him. That was a smart decision on his part. One of the few he had made in the past year.

Lauren's family was still as crazy as ever. Her industrious mother had landed a date with the rich widower two towns over. Yolanda was sure she could persuade him to marry her within the next six months and all her money troubles would be solved. Lauren wasn't as convinced, but she didn't tell her mother that.

Cynthia, Dawn, and Stephanie were still in hot pursuit of new sugar daddies. All of them had asked if maybe Cris had some NFL friends that Lauren could introduce them to. She had to disappoint them by telling them no.

"I'm sorry. But I wouldn't subject my worst enemy to your sisters, Lauren," Cris had said with a lofty roll of his eyes when she told him about her sisters' inquiries. "And I damn sure wouldn't introduce them to any of my friends!"

Though Cynthia still was a gold digger through and through, mercifully she had kept her promise to suspend Clarissa's gold-digging "training" for a while. So Lauren's niece had managed to start her freshmen year at Temple University without the added pressure of having to move to campus, find all her classes, and cram for her exams *while* learning the many ways to ensnare a man. Lauren hoped Clarissa was enjoying her freedom . . . for however long it lasted.

Phillip was also out of the hospital and done with his recovery. He had been taking it easy for weeks, delegating most of the responsibility for the restaurant's kitchen to Lauren in his absence. He had broken the news to her a few days ago that he would stay on as owner of Le Bayou Bleu, but he would no longer be the head chef of the restaurant.

"The doc said I gotta take it easy, *chérie*," he had grumbled. "He said if I don't want my ticker to wear out on me again, I'm gonna have to put up my knives and spatula. Get off my feet."

Lauren had been sad to hear that she would no longer be elbow to elbow with her dear friend and mentor in the kitchen again. Knowing the restaurant's reputation, Phillip would probably be replaced with some snooty chef from a five-star restaurant in New York City, someone who would never get their hands dirty working the line or lower himself by having drinks with the dishwashers and busboys.

"I hope whoever takes over can fill your shoes, Phillip," she had mumbled, teary-eyed. "There's no chef who could come close to you."

"Humph, and don't I know it! Phillip Rochon is one of a kind, *chérie*, but . . ." He had smiled. "I guess you'll have to do. I certainly taught you enough. You can handle it."

Lauren had blinked in surprise. "What?"

"I want you to take over as head chef of my restaurant. I told you. I don't trust my baby to anyone! If I leave her to you, I leave it in good hands."

Lauren had been so taken aback by his words, she had gazed at him dumbfounded for several seconds. Finally, she had broken out of her stupor long enough to leap up and give him a bear hug.

"Watch out now! You're gonna kill me before I have a chance to sign the damn paperwork!"

Lauren and Cris continued to climb the next hill with him lugging the picnic basket. Her tennis shoes sank into the damp grass and the hem of her jeans was soaking wet. Perspiration was on her brow. Her breathing became labored. He was really making her work for this view!

She was only seconds away from telling him that she couldn't walk any farther before Cris set down the basket and turned to her.

"Now look at that," he said, pointing off into the distance.

She followed his finger and smiled.

She could see Chesterton more easily from here. She gazed at the cars slowly driving along Main Street, the various steeples of United Methodist, St. Ignatius, and the Baptist church at the end of Broadleaf, and the savings and loan's clock tower. From here, the town was beautiful, even if she knew up close it could be very different sometimes. But for better or for worse, it was her home.

"I want to give you something." Cris suddenly reached into his jacket.

Lauren was staring off into the distance, distracted by the tranquil view, smiling to herself. When she turned and saw Cris tugging a folded white envelope from his jacket's inner pocket, she frowned.

"I want you to take this." He handed it to her. "No arguments. In fact, don't say anything. Just accept it."

"Cris, what is this?"

But even before he answered and tried to press the envelope into the palm of her hand, she knew what it was.

"It's a check. About ninety-five thousand or so. I put

a little extra in to cover any fees or penalties you might have to pay. But that should cover all your outstanding bills, I think."

Lauren gazed down at the envelope, feeling her stomach clench into knots. It had been such a nice moment. Now she was being brought back to reality. "Cris, I can't ta—"

"*Yes,* you can. After all we've been through, yes, you can. I need you to trust me and let me help you."

But he had already come to her rescue. He had already helped her—in more ways than one. She didn't want his money, too.

"You'll pay me back. I know you will."

She tiredly closed her eyes. "Cris, baby, you and I both know damn well I won't be able to pay back this money. It's too much! That's more than I make in a—"

"There's more than one way to pay someone back, Lauren. You just have to hear all the terms."

She suddenly opened her eyes, taken aback. "What . . . what terms?"

Cris gave a knowing smile and wrapped his arms around her waist, drawing her toward him.

Lauren eyed him uneasily. "What terms, Cris?"

"First, I want you to take the money to pay off your debts," he said, leaning down, teasing her lips. "Then I want you to move out of your apartment. Next, I want you to move in with me. I want you to stay with me. I want you to be *mine,* Lauren."

If any other woman had heard those words, she'd be ecstatic, but instantly Lauren's heart sank. So those were his terms? To get the money, she would have to move in with him, she would have to be his? This arrangement sounded very familiar. In fact, she remembered having a similar agreement with James more than two years ago.

"So you escaped one sugar daddy only to run into the arms of another," a voice in her head mocked.

Why did she keep coming back to this? What was it about her that made men think they had to take *care* of her?

Why keep fighting it, she thought sadly, silently accepting her fate. She wanted to be with Cris. She loved him and needed him, but not in the way he thought. Her mother had been right at least about one thing: Loving Cris this strongly gave him the ultimate power over her. He wielded so much power, in fact, that now she was willing to give up a goal that she had focused on for almost a year: obtaining her independence and self-resolve. It hurt that being with him meant she would have to go back to her old ways, but . . .

So be it. She was a Gibbons girl, after all. She had denied it for quite a while, but being a kept woman who pleased her man was practically in her DNA.

Lauren stiffly nodded. "Fine, Cris. If those are your terms, I accept them. I'll . . . I'll be yours."

He cocked an eyebrow. Now *he* was the one frowning. "Well, don't sound so excited."

"I'm sorry!" She shoved back from him. "But I'm not going to pretend everything's gravy about this! I understand how this goes. Believe me. I've been through this before. Whatever you want, I'll do it!" She suddenly glared up at him, tears welling in her eyes. "But I'm not doing it for the money! OK? I said it and I meant it: I don't want your goddamned money! I'm doing it because I want to be with *you.* I'll be yours if that's what you want."

"No, you don't understand, Lauren. You're talking

about this like I'm making a damn business proposition, like I'm trying to buy you! I don't want you to just be mine! Hell, I want to be yours, too!"

She gazed up at him, confused.

"I'm asking you to marry me, baby." He reached into another jacket pocket and pulled out a small velvet box. He then pulled back the lid.

Lauren blinked in surprise, gazing at the solitary diamond ring he held in front of her.

"You're . . . you're asking me to marry you?"

"Well . . . yeah."

This time when she blinked back tears, it wasn't out of anger. "I'm sorry. I'm so sorry, Cris." She wiped at her tear-stained cheeks. "I just thought—"

"Yeah . . ." He removed the ring from the box. "I know what you thought. But that wasn't what I was offering. I'll try not to be insulted."

He placed the ring on her finger and she gazed down at it. She slowly shook her head in amazement. Suddenly, her happy tears morphed into laughter.

Cris gazed at her in bemusement. "OK, this was not the reaction I expected. Why are you laughing?"

Lauren held her stomach as she laughed even harder. "Oh, Cynthia is definitely going to lose her shit over this one! She swore this was my goal all along . . . to try to snag you before any of them could. She's going to be so pissed!"

Cris smiled before tugging her back toward him. He then wrapped his arms around her again. He locked his hands around her waist so she couldn't get away from him even if she'd tried.

"Well, I'm less concerned with what Cynthia has to say about this than what *you* have to say. I just asked you to marry me and I haven't heard you say 'yes.' "

Lauren grinned as she stood on the tips of her toes and wrapped her arms around his neck. "Yes. Yes!"

They kissed and Lauren was suddenly taken back to the first moment they'd touched lips. She had been so nervous back then, trying so hard to keep from falling for him.

A lot of good that did me.

Lauren pulled back her head and gave a wry grin. "I hope you realize what you're getting into. When you marry a Gibbons girl, you get a lot of baggage and a lot of drama." Her expression suddenly became somber. "I won't let my family come between us, Cris, but I won't let them go, either. They're all crazy. They drive *me* crazy! But I love my mother. I love my sisters and I won't—"

"Lauren, I'm not asking you to give up your family. I know you love them. I just want to make sure that 'this' "—he pointed to himself and then to her—"always comes first."

She nodded emphatically. "Always, Cris." And she meant it.

"So . . . how much drama are we talking about exactly?"

At that, Lauren laughed. She laughed so hard her stomach hurt.

Don't miss the next book in the Gibbons
Gold Digger series,

Another Woman's Man

On sale in May 2014!

Chapter 1

(Unwritten) Rule No. 5 of the Gibbons Family Handbook:
Family always comes first—while men come somewhere between shoes and handbags.

"He's amazing!"

"I know! Isn't he brilliant?"

"The show is wonderful! Just wonderful!"

If they only knew, Dawn Gibbons thought as she glanced around the crowded gallery.

She looked at the people strolling throughout the exhibition space, at the couples who stared at the canvases on the exposed brick walls and nodded their heads in appreciation, and she wanted to give herself a toast. She hadn't thought she would be able to pull this off, considering the limited amount of time she had to organize this exhibition, considering how much arm twisting she had to do to get tonight's featured artist to just pick up a paint brush and *paint something!* But she had done it. Despite all the obstacles she had faced, tonight had been a resounding success. Dawn didn't toast herself, but she downed what was left of her Moët & Chandon and smiled.

"Great work, darling!" said Percy, the gallery's owner, in his British accent as he sailed toward her.

He was wearing a leather jacket and faded jeans today—an outfit that was much too young for a man his age. His thinning gray hair was pulled back with a rubber band, leaving a knobby stub of hair at the end. The three top buttons of his silk shirt were open, revealing the wiry hairs on his pale chest. He wrapped a lanky arm around Dawn's waist and gave her an affectionate squeeze.

"Thanks, Percy." She wrinkled her nose at the overpowering smell of his cologne and nodded. "It did turn out well, didn't it?"

"We should go somewhere after the show and celebrate, darling," he whispered warmly as he leaned toward her ear. The smell of his cologne became five times stronger. The heat of his breath on her cheek almost singed her. "Maybe you'll finally let me take you out to dinner." His hand descended from her waist to her ass. He pet it gently—like he would a purring kitten—and winked one of his blue eyes at her. "What do you say?"

"Oh, you don't have to do that." She slowly removed Percy's hand from her bottom. "But thank you for the offer."

Percy was one of the few rich men in Dawn's social circle that she hadn't dated, and quite frankly, she didn't have any plans to ever date him. He was her boss! Her art and her work as gallery director were more important to her. Unfortunately, Percy wasn't accustomed to women turning him down, which probably made him even more eager to get her to dinner and finally get into her pants. She was a challenge to him now, the Mt. Everest that he still had yet to climb. But she desperately wished he would take his mountain boots and pick, and climb somewhere else.

"I should go around the room and mingle." Dawn patted his arm soothingly, hoping to soften the blow of her rejection. "You know, make sure everyone is enjoying themselves and— more importantly—buying the artwork."

"Yes. Yes, of course, darling." His smile tightened, barely masking his disappointment. "Mingle! Mingle! Don't let me keep you."

She turned and walked away, handing off her empty glass to one of the waiters who strolled around the room with Lucite trays covered with hors d' oeuvres and champagne glasses.

Her sister Lauren's restaurant Le Bayou Bleu was catering the event with Southern-style, high-end cuisine that all the patrons couldn't seem to get enough of. In fact, she heard whispers from the staff that they were dangerously close to running out of food.

Lauren couldn't be here tonight herself to supervise. She was still on maternity leave and was at home with her infant son, Crisanto Jr., but Dawn's other two sisters had shown their support by coming to the event. Her very pregnant sister, Stephanie, had waddled through an hour ago. She had purchased one of the smaller pieces on display before leaving the gallery with a mouthful of shrimp. Dawn's eldest sister Cynthia had left fifteen minutes later. She said she had a date with a very wealthy construction company owner and had to run home to change clothes.

"He's handsome, charming, and he pulled in seven

figures last year, girl. You never know," Cynthia had re-marked. "He could be *the* one!"

By "*the* one" Dawn assumed Cynthia really meant number three, since this would be Cynthia's *third* husband if she managed to get this one down the aisle. Though—truth be told—Dawn had little room to talk herself. She had been married twice before also, con-tinuing the long tradition of women in her family who married often and divorced just as frequently. But un-like Cynthia, Dawn had little interest in finding a third husband.

Dawn had been doing some soul searching and self examination lately with all the changes that were going on around her. Two of her sisters had fallen in love. One had recently had a baby and the other had one on the way. Dawn felt like she had reached a point in her life when obtaining a rich husband wasn't as important to her anymore. Besides, rich men were a lot like tem-peramental artists whose work she featured at her gallery. They both required coddling and their egos had to be constantly fed. She didn't have time to cater to both right now.

Dawn continued her path across the gallery, adjust-ing the cowl neck of her maroon top and the hem of asymmetrical wool skirt as she went.

"Congratulations, dearest," said Madison McGuire, a small-town girl who made good by marrying one of the most powerful lobbyists in Washington, DC. Now the wealthy D.C. socialite patronized the local art scene.

"Thank you for coming, Maddie!" Dawn said, lean-ing forward and lightly kissing the air beside Connie's rouged cheek.

"Oh, I wouldn't miss it for the world!" Maddie exclaimed. She took a sip from the champagne glass. "The exhibit is fascinating . . . and of course, I have to do my research!"

"*Research?* You know, a little birdie told me that you're thinking about buying the Sawyer Gallery, but I wasn't sure if that was just a rumor."

Maddie laughed. "Oh, it's not a rumor. I can assure you of that! Martin Sawyer is ready to move on to a new venture and I told him I'd happily take the gallery off his hands. We signed the paperwork a month ago. I plan to hold our grand opening sometime in the spring." She leaned toward Dawn and whispered, "Do you think you would be interested in changing venues? I'd love to have you at the helm of my gallery."

Dawn glanced across the room at Percy who was idly groping some bouncy young blond as he stood among a circle of friends.

Maddie's offer was certainly tempting. Unlike with Percy, Dawn wouldn't have to worry about Maddie patting her ass and trying to seduce her on a weekly basis. Plus, Dawn had always admired Maddie. If there was nothing a Gibbons girl loved more, it was a fellow woman who used her wiles and her wits to climb the socioeconomic ladder, a woman who knew how to "get her hustle on" but to do it with grace and style.

But Dawn liked the control Percy gave her over the gallery. She loved her staff. She was comfortable here.

Dawn sighed. "I don't think I would, Maddie, but thank you for the offer."

Maddie glanced in Percy's direction. He and the blond were now making kissy faces at each other, making Dawn cringe.

"Are you *sure*?" Maddie asked again. "I heard Percy can be quite the handful."

You have no idea, Dawn thought. She hesitated then nodded. "I'm sure."

"Oh, well. It was worth a try." Maddie waved her hand. "Always good to see you, Dawn."

"You too," Dawn replied continuing to make her way across the cavernous space. She stopped now and then to talk to and kiss the cheeks of a few patrons, but she soon noticed two men that she hadn't seen before. They were standing near one of the floor-to-ceiling canvases on the far side of the gallery. They drew her attention because their staid business attire made them stand out like sore thumbs from the rest of the flamboyantly dressed art crowd.

The shorter of the two men stood in front of one of the paintings, gazing at it admiringly. The elderly gentleman was dark-skinned and very distinguished looking with his navy blazer, tan slacks, white dress shirt and penny loafers. He leaned his weight against a bamboo cane as he bent forward to read the plaque near the painting.

Beside him was a man who was almost a foot taller and was several decades younger. He was less engrossed by the artwork than his companion. Instead, he stared in amazement at the people in the gallery as if he were watching circus performers. His honey-colored skin and short dark hair was in striking contrast to his pale gray eyes that she could see distinctly even at this distance. He was handsome, though a little too straitlaced for her taste.

Accountant?, she thought as she scanned his perfect black suit, sensible blue tie, and starched white shirt. *No, he's probably an actuary, I bet. Any person who dresses that boring has to be in insurance.*

She slowly walked toward them. Boring or not, they

could be prospective buyers—wealthy suburbanites with a lot of cash to spend who wanted to impress their friends with the discovery of a hot new artist.

"Hello," Dawn said. She extended her hand. "My name is Dawn Gibbons. Is this your first time at our gallery?"

She offered her hand to the older gentleman first. He hesitated before taking it.

"Hello," he said softly, finally shaking her hand. His wrinkled face filled with warmth. "It's a . . . a pleasure to finally meet you, Dawn. I . . . I had debated on coming here tonight. I couldn't work up the nerve at first until my friend, Xavier, here," he nodded toward the younger man who stood silently at his side, "agreed to come with me. But I really wanted to . . . Oh, listen to me ramble. I should introduce myself first." He cleared his throat. "My . . . My name is Herbert Allen."

"Pleased to meet you, Mr. Allen." She nodded in greeting. "Thank you for coming to our gallery." She pointed toward the painting. "So tell me . . . Are you interested in this piece?"

He paused and gazed at her quizzically. "You've . . . you've never heard of me before?"

Dawn's smile faded. She shook her head. "No, I'm sorry. I . . . I haven't."

He looked crestfallen.

Now put on the spot, Dawn quickly flipped through her mental rolodex, trying to recall the name, Herbert Allen, but she came up with a blank. She hoped he wasn't someone important. Percy would be royally PO'd if he found out she had offended one of his friends.

Suddenly, something came to mind. She snapped her fingers. "Oh, I remember now! I'm so sorry. Tonight has been so crazy and I've been so frazzled!" She laughed and patted his shoulder, turning back on the charm. "Herbert Allen. Yes, I remember. We met at the spring benefit last year, didn't we?"

He and the younger man exchanged a look. He then slowly shook his head. "No, we didn't meet at a spring benefit. In fact, we've never met before. I had . . . I had hoped your mother had mentioned me, at least." He shrugged. "But I guess not."

Dawn frowned. "My mother?"

He took a deep breath and gazed into her eyes. "I'm your father, Dawn."

"What?" Her gaze shifted between the two men. "I'm sorry. Is . . . is this some kind of a joke?"

"No, it's not a joke. I really am your father."

He took a step toward her and she took a hesitant step back, trying desperately to process what she was hearing.

"Dawn, I wanted to have a chance to—"

"Wait. Wait! Stop! Back up!" she shouted, holding up her hands. Her heart thudded like a snare drum in her chest. "What are you talking about? What do you mean you're my father? I . . ." She took a deep breath, fighting to regain her calm. "I haven't seen or heard from my father in thirty seven years and you. . . you just show up out of the blue like this! You just blurt this out!"

His eyes lowered to the hardwood floor. "I know and I'm sorry. I didn't want to do it this way, but I don't have—"

"No!" She furiously shook her head. "No, I'm not . . . I'm not doing this."

Dawn turned around and walked away from him. She angrily strode toward the gallery's revolving glass doors, ignoring the curious stares that followed her as

she passed. She felt like she had been ambushed. Was
he really her father? If so, why did he chose tonight of
all nights to announce himself? Why hadn't he picked
up a phone and called? Couldn't he have sent a letter?
This was ridiculous! She was practically trembling
with anger and confusion. She had to get out of there.

"Darling, where are you going?" Percy called after
her, but she ignored him.

Dawn stepped into the gallery's foyer. It was decorated for the holiday season with garland, holly and
twinkling Christmas lights, but she certainly wasn't in
the holiday mood right now. Just before she reached
the doors, she felt a strong hand clamp around her
wrist. She whipped her head around and looked up.
When she did, she was staring into the gray eyes of the
wannabe actuary. His warm touch and gaze instantly
made her tingle, catching her by surprise. It was a feeling she didn't want right now. She yanked her wrist out
of his grasp.

"Can you hear him out?" he asked. "It took a lot of
courage for him to come here tonight!"

"*Courage?*" She glared up at him. "Is that what you
call it? Why didn't he find that same damn courage ten
or twenty years ago? Where the hell has he been all this
time? Why is he doing this here? Why *now*?"

His stern face softened and once again she was
struck by how handsome he was.

"Look, Herb knows that he hasn't been the best father to you. Believe me. But your mother didn't exactly
make it easy for him these past years."

Dawn narrowed her eyes at the mention of her mother.
She crossed her arms over her chest. *"Excuse me?"*

"Look, all that it'll take is ten minutes of your time.
He came all this way. Just . . . Just let him explain him-

self. Please? He has a lot that he would like to get off his chest and he doesn't have much time left to do it."

"What? What do you mean?"

"Your father is sick, Dawn. He has cancer . . . and the prognosis isn't good."

Dawn's arms dropped to her sides. She stared at him in disbelief.

God, this was a lot to take in! Here she was in the middle of an exhibition and her apparent long-lost father had suddenly popped up out of nowhere, and now she had the added shock of finding out he was dying from cancer. What was she going to find out next? That a spaceship had landed outside the gallery? Dawn closed her eyes and raised her hands to her now throbbing temples. She desperately wished her sisters were here. She could use one of their shoulders to lean on right now.

"Will you give him a chance?" Wannabe Actuary asked quietly. "Hear what he has to say?"

Dawn opened her eyes. She was still furious, but part of her worried that she would regret this moment if she walked out the gallery and didn't come back.

"Fine."

She then walked back across the gallery with Wannabe Actuary trailing behind her.

As she crossed the room, she examined the older man more closely. He had skin the same shade as her own and large dark eyes she could have easily inherited. Those dark eyes now gazed at her worriedly.

Her mother had never talked about her father, or any of her sisters' fathers for that matter.

"As long as he takes care of his financial obligations to you, what difference does it make whether you see him?" Yolanda Gibbons would ask when her daughters were younger and they openly wondered why they had not received as much as a birthday card or telephone call from any their fathers. "*We're* important," Yolanda would insist. "Not a man who knows absolutely nothing about you."

Though Dawn had longed for her father in her younger years, she had gradually accepted her mother's opinion on the issue as she got older. If Dawn's father really had cared, he would have tried to contact her. He would have moved heaven and earth to let her know he wanted her and loved her. Now as she watched the man claiming to be her father take uncertain steps toward her, she knew there was no real explanation he could offer for his absence all these years. But she would listen. She would give him his ten minutes then send him on his way.

"Thank you for coming back," he said gently. He leaned most of his weight on his cane. "I apologize for how I did this. I didn't want to tell you this over the phone, and I didn't know how to—"

"Not here," she said firmly, cutting him off. "We can talk in my office."

She walked around him and led him toward a corridor filled with a series of rooms at the back of the gallery. She paused at her office door and turned. "In here," she said, motioning toward the doorway.

He glanced up at the younger man.

"I'll take it from here, Xavier," he said. "Thank you."

Xavier looked at Herbert, then at Dawn. Their eyes met. She cocked her eyebrow in challenge. Was he going to insist he come along?

After some time, Xavier finally nodded. "Okay, I'll . . . I'll wait here."

Herbert continued down the corridor.

"But call me if you need me!" Xavier shouted out to him.

Herbert nodded and waved him away. "Don't worry. I'll be fine."

"Is he your bodyguard or something?" she whispered when Herbert stood next to her.

She still eyed the actuary guardedly. He equally scrutinized her from the other end of the hall.

"Close," Herbert said with a soft chuckle. "He's my lawyer . . . well, corporate counsel for my company."

Lawyer, huh?

Well, she guessed he wasn't an actuary after all.

Dawn ushered Herbert into her small eight by eight-foot office and shut the door behind him. She had kept the space simple in its decor with an industrial design desk and leather chairs. A book shelf was on the right wall. The only adornment in the office was the several paintings by the gallery's many artists and a few works of hers.

"Have a seat," she said, gesturing to one of the chairs opposite her desk.

She sat down in her rollaway desk chair and watched as he carefully lowered himself into his. When he sat down, he let out a barely stifled groan.

He does look sick, she thought as she looked at his slightly ashen face.

"Dawn," he began, "I understand that you're angry with me, but I didn't want to put this off another day. I've been putting off coming to see you for weeks now."

"Why?"

He lowered his eyes. "Because I know it's something I should have done years ago and I feel like such a . . . such a bastard for taking so long to do it, sweetheart."

Sweetheart . . . It was odd hearing a stranger call her that.

He hesitated. "When you were a little girl, I had thought about seeing you. But your mother and I did not part amicably, to be honest. I allowed my feelings toward your mother to taint whatever possibility we had of developing a relationship. I was . . . I was wrong for doing that."

Dawn didn't say anything in response. What was there to say?

"I didn't find out about you until after you were born," he continued. "My lawyer at the time got a letter from your mother stating that she had a baby and that she was seeking child support. I was . . ." He paused again. "I was very shocked . . . and angry. You see, Yolanda and I hadn't dated for very long."

"Long enough to make a baby though," Dawn interjected, leaning back in her chair.

"That is true." He nodded in agreement. "I'm not denying that. But again, we had dated only briefly. We were together for only a month or so and then I was transferred to my company's satellite office in Europe. I never got the chance to really know her. Then my lawyer found out a bit more about her . . . her background. The marriages . . . how she dated wealthy men almost exclusively . . . When I found out, I felt . . . manipulated . . . *duped*, in a way. Like she had used my affections and—"

"*Trapped you*?" Dawn finished for him. She rolled her eyes. "Look, if you're here to talk shit about my mom, we can end this conversation right now." She began to rise from her chair. "Thank you, Mr. Allen, for your visit, but—"

"No, no! That's not what I intended. I just . . ." He took a deep breath. "I just wanted you to know why I did what I did. There's no excuse for it, but that was my thinking at the time. Please, Dawn. Please sit down."

Her nostrils flared. She slowly lowered herself to her seat, crossed her legs, and adjusted the hem of her skirt.

"Sweetheart, I didn't come here to insult your mother or to make you angry. I came here to try to make amends. I'm not well. I have . . . I have prostate cancer . . . and despite my doctors' best efforts, it's . . . it's spread."

"I'm sorry to hear that," she said quietly and she meant it.

He cleared his throat. "When you're faced with an illness, you start to reexamine your life and the mistakes you've made. Not building a relationship with you was one of my biggest mistakes, and I. . . I would like to rectify that if I can."

"How?" she asked.

"I'd like to get to know you, Dawn. . . to spend time with you, if you will allow it. Maybe we can have dinner together or spend a day or two together. Whatever you would like to do, I'm willing to do it."

Dawn closed her eyes again. She didn't want to be cruel, but this was too much, *way* too much. She hadn't even known this man existed until fifteen minutes ago. Now he wanted to build a relationship. She opened her eyes.

"Maybe. But can I . . . can I take some time to think about this?"

He gazed at her for a long time then finally nodded. "Sure, I understand."

But he didn't look like he understood. He looked disappointed.

Dawn rose from her chair and he followed suit. She walked him to her office door. When she opened the door, he turned and looked at her.

"Even . . . even if we don't see one another again, Dawn, it was a pleasure to finally meet you," he said, offering her his hand.

She shook it. "It was a pleasure to meet you too, Mr. Allen."

He gave a small smile. "Please, you don't have to call me dad, but at least call me Herb."

"It was a pleasure to meet you, Herb."

He opened his jacket and handed her a business card. "If you do wish to meet again, here is my number. I do hope . . . I do hope to hear from you, Dawn. I sincerely do."

"Thank you," she said, taking his card.

She watched as he stepped into the corridor. He was still gazing at her as she shut the door behind him. When the lock clicked, she fell against the wooden slab and let out a pent-up breath she didn't know she had been holding all this time.

Don't miss the second book in the Gibbons Gold
Digger series,

The Player & the Game

On sale now!

Chapter 1

**(Unwritten) Rule No. 3 of the Gibbons Family
Handbook:** Never give a man your heart—and
definitely never give him your money.

Busy, busy, busy, Stephanie Gibbons thought as she
hurried toward her silver BMW that was parallel
parked in the reserved space near her office. Her stilettos clicked on the sidewalk as she walked. Her short,
pleated skirt swayed around her hips and supple, brown
legs with each stride.

She shouldn't have gone to the nail salon before
lunch, but her French manicure had been badly in need
of a touch-up. Unfortunately, that slight detour had
thrown off the entire day's schedule and now she was
running ten minutes late for the open house.

The spring day was unseasonably warm, but it was
tempered by a light breeze that blew steadily, making
the newly grown leaves flutter on the numerous maples
lining Main Street in downtown Chesterton, her home-

town. The breeze now lifted Stephanie's hair from her shoulders and raised her already dangerously short skirt even higher.

She adjusted the realtor name tag near her suit jacket lapel, casually ran her fingers through her long tresses, and reached into her purse. She pulled out her cell phone and quickly dialed her assistant's number. Thankfully, the young woman picked up on the second ring.

"Carrie, honey, I'm running late . . . Yes, I know . . . Are you already at the open house?" Stephanie asked distractedly as she dug for her keys in her purse's depths. "Are any buyers there yet? . . . OK, OK, don't freak out. . . . Yes, just take over for now. Put out a plate of cookies and set the music on low. I'll be there in fifteen minutes . . . I know . . . I have every confidence in you. See you soon."

She hung up.

With car keys finally retrieved, Stephanie pressed the remote button to open her car doors. The car beeped. The headlights flashed. She jogged to the driver's-side door and opened it. As she started to climb inside the vehicle, she had the distinct feeling of being watched.

Stephanie paused to look up, only to find a man standing twenty feet away from her. He casually leaned against the brick front of one of the many shops on Main Street. He was partially hidden by the shadows of an overhead awning.

He looked like one of many jobless men you would find wandering the streets midday, hanging out in front of stores because they had little else to do and nowhere else to go. Except this bored vagrant was a lot more attractive than the ones she was used to seeing. He also was distinct from the other vagrants in town because

she had seen him several times today and earlier this week.

Stephanie had spotted him when she walked into the nail salon and again as she left, absently waving her nails as they dried. He had been sitting in the driver's seat of a tired-looking Ford Explorer in the lot across the street from the salon. Though he hadn't said anything to her or even looked up at her as she walked back to her car, she had the feeling he had been waiting for her.

She had seen him also on Wednesday, strolling along the sidewalk while she had been on her date with her new boyfriend, Isaac. The man had walked past the restaurant's storefront window where she and Isaac had been sitting and enjoying their candlelit dinner. When Stephanie looked up from her menu and glanced out the window, her eyes locked with the stroller's. The mystery man abruptly broke their mutual gaze and kept walking. He disappeared at the end of the block.

The mystery man had a face that was hard to forget—sensual, hooded dark eyes, a full mouth, and a rock-hard chin. He stood at about six feet with a muscular build. Today, he was wearing a plain white T-shirt and wrinkled jeans. Though his short hair was neatly trimmed, he had thick beard stubble on his chin and dark-skinned cheeks.

"Are you following me?" Stephanie called to him, her open house now forgotten.

He blinked in surprise. "What?" He pointed at his chest. "You mean me?"

"Yes, I mean you!" She placed a hand on her hip. "Are you following me? Why do I keep seeing you around?"

He chuckled softly. "Why would I be following you? Lady, I'm just standing here."

He wasn't just standing there. She sensed it.

"Well, this is a small town. Loitering is illegal in Chesterton. You could get arrested!"

"It's illegal to stand in front of a building?" Laughter was in his voice. He slowly shook his head. "We're still in America, right? Last time I checked, I was well within my rights to stand here, honey. Besides, I'm not panhandling. I'm just enjoying the warm sunshine." His face broke into a charming, dimpled smile that would have made most women's knees weak. "Is that a crime?"

Stephanie narrowed her eyes at him warily.

She didn't like him or his condescending tone. He was attractive, but something emanated from him that made her . . . uncomfortable. It made her heartbeat quicken and her palms sweat. She wasn't used to reacting to men this way. Usually her emotions were firmly in control around them, but they weren't around this guy. She didn't like him one bit.

"If . . . if I catch you standing here when I get back, I'll . . . I'll call the cops," she said weakly.

At that, he raised an eyebrow. "You do that," he challenged, casually licking his lips and shoving his hands into his jean pockets. Defiantly, he slumped against the brick building again.

Stephanie took a deep breath, willing her heart to slow its rapid pace. She climbed into her car and shut the driver's-side door behind her with a slam. She shifted the car into drive and pulled off, watching him in her rearview mirror until she reached the end of block. He was still standing in front of the building, still leaning under the shadows of the awning, still

looking smug as she drove to the end of Main Street and made a right.

Finally, she lost sight of him.

"Shit," Keith Hendricks muttered through clenched teeth as he pushed himself away from the brick building once he saw the taillights of Stephanie Gibbons's BMW disappear.

"Shit," he uttered again as he strode across the street to his SUV, pausing to let a Volkswagen Beetle drive by.

Though he had played it cool in front of her, he had started to sweat the instant Stephanie's eyes had shifted toward him.

He was getting sloppy. He had decided to get out of his car and walk near her office to try to get a better vantage point, to see if her boyfriend, Isaac, was going to meet her here today. But Keith hadn't counted on her noticing him standing there. More importantly, she had noticed *and* recognized him from the other occasions that he thought he had been discreetly tailing her and Isaac. It had been a mistake, a rookie mistake that wasn't worthy of the four years he had spent as a private investigator.

"You messin' up, boy," he said to himself as he opened his car door, climbed inside, and plopped on the leather seat. He shut the door behind him and inserted his key into the ignition.

But he had to admit he was out of practice. This was his first real case in months.

He had been eager to accept this one, to sink his teeth into something meaty. He had been tired of the busy work that had filled his days for the past few months. Stokowski and Hendricks Private Investigators had been going through a bit of a dry spell lately. With the exception of this con artist case, they had been doing nothing but process serving for months, delivering summonses and subpoenas. When Keith left the ATF to start the PI business with retired cop and family friend Mike Stokowski four years ago, process serving wasn't exactly the exciting work he had had in mind. He had hoped things would pick up soon. Now they finally were, but this case had been complicated.

He had finally located Reggie Butler also known as Tony Walker *now* known as Isaac Beardan. The con artist and Casanova had left a trail of heartbreak and several empty bank accounts along the Eastern Seaboard. Each time Isaac moved on to his next con, he changed his name, his look slightly, and his story. It made him a hard guy to find.

One of the most recent victims from which Isaac had stolen thirty thousand dollars worth of jewelry had hired Stokowski and Hendricks PI to track him down. Keith had traced the smooth-talking bastard here, to the small town of Chesterton. Keith still wasn't sure though if Isaac worked alone on his cons. He didn't know what role his girlfriend, Stephanie Gibbons, played in it—if any. Hell, maybe Isaac had selected her as his next victim.

"Don't worry about her," a voice in Keith's head urged as he pulled onto the roadway. "You finished your part of the case. You found him. You've got photos . . . documentation. The police can track him down now and press charges. That's all that matters."

But was that all that mattered? Should he warn the new girlfriend about Isaac?

An image of her suddenly came to mind: her pretty cinnamon-hued face; the limber legs like a seasoned dancer that were on full display underneath her flowing, pleated skirt; and her full red glossy lips. He remembered the stubborn glare she had given him too, trying her best to intimidate him, but failing miserably.

"If you tell her the truth, she'll tell Isaac," a voice in his head warned. "It'll put him on the run again. The authorities will never be able to track him down."

Keith frowned as he started the drive back to his hotel. It was true. Isaac would know he had been found and only move on to the next place and start a new con. No, Keith couldn't tell her the truth about Isaac. He had worked too hard on the case to throw it all away now.

"Maybe she'll figure out he's full of shit by herself," Keith murmured as he gazed out the car's windshield.

But he knew that wasn't likely. Isaac was well practiced at this game. He was a champion player. Keith doubted Stephanie Gibbons would be any different than any of the other saps Isaac had swindled.

GREAT BOOKS, GREAT SAVINGS!

When You Visit Our Website:
www.kensingtonbooks.com
You Can Save Money Off The Retail Price
Of Any Book You Purchase!

- **All Your Favorite Kensington Authors**
- **New Releases & Timeless Classics**
- **Overnight Shipping Available**
- **eBooks Available For Many Titles**
- **All Major Credit Cards Accepted**

Visit Us Today To Start Saving!
www.kensingtonbooks.com

All Orders Are Subject To Availability.
Shipping and Handling Charges Apply.
Offers and Prices Subject To Change Without Notice.